GAME

Books by Anders de la Motte

Game
Buzz
Bubble

GAME

BOOK 1 OF THE GAME TRILOGY

ANDERS DE LA MOTTE

POCKET BOOKS
New York   London   Toronto   Sydney   New Delhi

Pocket Books
A Division of Simon & Schuster, Inc.
1230 Avenue of the Americas
New York, NY 10020

This book is a work of fiction. Any references to historical events, real people, or real places are used fictitiously. Other names, characters, places, and events are products of the author's imagination, and any resemblance to actual events or places or persons, living or dead, is entirely coincidental.

First Pocket Books paperback edition August 2014

POCKET and colophon are registered trademarks of Simon & Schuster, Inc.

For information about special discounts for bulk purchases, please contact Simon & Schuster Special Sales at 1-866-506-1949 or business@simonandschuster.com.

The Simon & Schuster Speakers Bureau can bring authors to your live event. For more information or to book an event, contact the Simon & Schuster Speakers Bureau at 1-866-248-3049 or visit our website at www.simonspeakers.com.

Manufactured in the United States of America

10 9 8 7 6 5 4 3 2 1

ISBN 978-1-4767-9445-7
ISBN 978-1-4767-1290-1 (ebook)

To Anette

ACKNOWLEDGMENTS

MY WARMEST THANKS to all the Ants out there, without whose advice and achievements the *Game* could never have become a reality.

Blinking is supposed to be the fastest movement the human body is physically capable of.

Even so, it hardly compares to the brain's electrical synapses.

Not now! was the thought that flashed through his head when the light hit him.

And, from his point of view, he was absolutely right. There ought to be more time, plenty of time—that was what he had been promised. After all, he had followed the instructions to the letter, had done exactly what he had been told to do.

So this shouldn't be happening.

Not now!

Absolutely not!

His surprise was entirely understandable, not to say logical. And it was also the last sensory impression of his life.

A millisecond later the explosion turned him into a charred jigsaw puzzle that would take the police forensics team more than a week to put together. Piece by piece, like a macabre family game, until he was more or less back in his original shape.

But by then the Game was long since over.

Game (Geim)

A competitive activity involving skill, chance, or endurance on the part of two or more persons who play according to a set of rules, usually for their own amusement or for that of spectators.

An amusement or pastime

A state of being willing to do something

Evasive, trifling, or manipulative behavior

An animal hunted for food or sport

A calculated strategy or approach; a scheme

A distraction or diversion

Having or showing skill or courage

An activity for recreation

—www.wiktionary.org

www.dictionary.com

www.urbandictionary.com

Winning isn't everything, it's the only thing!

—*Vince Lombardi*

1 | WANNA PLAY A GAME?

THE TEXT FLASHED up on the screen for the umpteenth time, and for the umpteenth time HP clicked it away in irritation. No, he didn't want to play any bloody game; all he wanted to do was figure out how the cell phone in his hand worked, and whether it was possible to do anything as simple as make a phone call with it?

The commuter train from Märsta, early July, heading toward the city.

Almost thirty degrees, his top sticking to his back, his mouth already dry. Predictably, he was out of cigarettes, and the only consolation was the breeze generated by the speed of the train, forcing its way through the pathetic little ventilation window above his head.

He sniffed his T-shirt a couple of times, then checked his breath. The results were pretty much as expected. A road game, hangover, and the smell of something rotting in his mouth. Yee-haa! An almost perfect Sunday morning, if it weren't for the fact that it was actually Thursday morning and he should have been at work two hours ago. So much for that period of probation.

But so what?!

It was only a crap McJob anyway, a bunch of assholes with a fully paid-up jerk in charge.

It's important to be one of the team, Pettersson. Yeah, right! Like he was going to hum "Kumbayah" and play team-building games with a load of losers. The only reason he was there was so he could make a new claim for unemployment benefit afterward.

Suck my ass, mofos!

He had noticed it shortly after the train left Rosersberg. A small, silver-colored object on the seat on the other side of the aisle. Someone had been sitting there a minute ago but had got off and the train was already moving again. So there was no point waving and shouting about it now, if he was seriously considering Doing the Right Thing.

As if . . . !

Anyway, everyone had a responsibility to look after their own damn stuff, didn't they?

So he glanced quickly around instead, looking for security cameras with a practiced eye, and once he'd concluded that the carriage was too old to have any, he changed seats so he could examine his find at leisure.

A cell phone, just as he had thought, and his morning suddenly got a bit better.

One of those ones with a touch screen on the front instead of an old-fashioned keypad.

Sweet!

It was odd, but he couldn't find the manufacturer's name anywhere, but maybe the phone was so exclusive that there was no need for one? Unless the engraved lettering on the back was actually a brand name?

It said *"128,"* in light-gray lettering slightly less than a centimeter high.

He couldn't remember ever hearing of a phone company with that name.

But what the hell . . .

It must be worth five hundred kronor or so from the Greek who dealt in stolen cells. The alternative was spending a couple of hundred disabling the IMEI code so the owner wouldn't be able to stop the thing working, then he could keep it for himself.

But that was hardly an option . . .

Last night had blown a definitive hole in his already overstretched finances. He'd had nothing in his account for ages, and he'd already used up all his other lifelines. But with a bit of hustling here and there he'd soon be back on his feet . . .

You could never keep someone like him down for long; the cell was living proof of that. He held the phone up to examine it more closely.

It was small and neat, hardly bigger than the palm of his hand, and the shell was made of brushed steel. A small hole in the back indicated that it was equipped with a camera, and at the top was a clumsy black clip, presumably so you could fasten it to your clothes. The clip was in marked contrast to the otherwise minimalist design, and he was about to see if he couldn't take it off when the screen suddenly came to life.

Wanna play a Game?

it asked, showing two icons for Yes and No.

HP started in surprise. In his comatose, hungover state he hadn't even checked if the phone was switched on.

Careless!

He touched his finger to the No icon, then tried to work out how to get the menu to appear. If he was lucky, he'd be able to use the phone for a few days until the owner managed to block it.

But instead of a normal Start menu, the phone just kept repeating the question, and now, as with growing irritation he clicked it away, goodness knew how many times later, he was on the verge of giving up.

Fucking shit phone!

He swallowed a couple of times in an attempt to stop himself throwing up. Fucking hangover; he ought to know better than to mix his drinks, and he was so desperate for a cigarette that he felt like he was going to explode. And as for that girl, Christ, she was a dog, but what could you expect if you went out on the pull in the burbs?

He'd made up some excuse about a hockey match he'd promised a friend he'd show up for and had made a quick exit when the morning sunlight mercilessly revealed the shortcomings of the previous evening's catch. To judge by the bitch's feeble protestations, the feeling had been pretty mutual. *"Run, Forrest, run!"*

But he wasn't really in any hurry to get back to Maria Trappgränd. A stop to see the Greek, some easy money that ought be enough for a hangover pizza and then a few beers at Kvarnen.

There was always space for that in the diary.

If he was lucky, there'd be enough left over for a bit of weed, because the cell was no standard design like the ones he sometimes happened to "chance" upon. Five hundred to a thousand kronor pure profit, all in all not a bad day, in spite of the hangover and the tropical heat.

The screen flashed again and his finger had almost gone automatically to the No icon before he noticed that this message was different.

Wanna play a Game, **Henrik Pettersson**?
Yes
No

HP stiffened in his seat.

What the fuck . . . ?

He glanced around quickly a few times. Was someone messing with him?

There were maybe ten, twelve other passengers spread out around the carriage, and apart from a mother with two hyperactive kids, almost all of them seemed to be in the same sluggish morning coma as him. Not one of them so much as glanced in his direction.

He checked the screen again. The same text. How the hell could the phone know his name?

He looked around but was left none the wiser. Then he clicked the button for No.

A new message flashed up immediately, this time in Swedish.

Are you really sure
you don't want to play a Game, HP?

He almost flew out of his seat. What in the name of holy fuck was going on here?

He shut his eyes tight, took a couple of deep breaths, and regained control of his galloping hangover anxiety.

Just keep calm, he thought. You're a smart lad. And this isn't the fucking twilight zone.

Either this is *Candid Camera* or else one of your mates is mucking about with you. Probably the latter . . .

Mange was top of the list of suspects. An old friend from school, good with technical stuff, owned a computer shop, got furious about anyone disparaging his newfound Arab god, and he had a really sick sense of humor.

Yep, no doubt about it. This was one of Mange's sick jokes!

Relief spread through his body.

So, Mangelito.

It had been ages; HP had actually thought that getting married and his new religion had turned Mange soft, but the little bastard must have been biding his time for this masterstroke.

Now he just had to work out how it all fitted together, and then find a way to turn the joke back on Mange.

It was damn well thought out so far, he had to give the little floor kisser credit for that.

HP looked around once again.

Nine people in total in the carriage, twelve if he counted the young kids.

Three teenage girls, an alcoholic, two stereotypical Swedish men about the same age as him, somewhere around thirty. An old boy with a stick, a pretty decent girl of twenty-five or so with a ponytail and wearing running gear (it must have been the hangover that stopped him noticing her earlier), and finally the woman with the kids.

Whichever one of them Mange the Muslim had managed to recruit, they had to have some sort of electronic gizmo to be able to send the messages. Sadly, that didn't exactly make the list much shorter. Five of them were clicking on some sort of electronic gadget, and, if you counted the earplugs the alcoholic was wearing, at a push you could stretch the list of suspects to six.

His weary brain came to the conclusion that it was more

the rule than the exception to mess about with a cell on the train, not just to send texts but to kill a few minutes with one of those stupid cell-phone games.

So, Einstein—not really much wiser!

His head was throbbing from the unexpected exertion, and his mouth was still bone-dry. Strangely enough, though, he did feel slightly more alert.

So what happened now?

How was he going to get his own back?

He decided to go along with the prank for a while, so first he pressed the No icon, then, when the question was repeated, the icon for Yes.

Oh yes, he'd play along with it for a while and pretend to be taken in, and the more he thought about it, the more he realized that this was actually pretty cool. A good way of passing time on a boring train journey.

"Fucking Mange." He grinned, before a new message appeared on the screen.

Welcome to the Game, HP!

Thanks! he thought, leaning back.

This was actually going to be interesting.

Even before the wheels of the heavy vehicle had stopped, Rebecca Normén was out on the pavement. The heat that hit her was so intense that she wanted to get back into the cool of the car at once.

Three weeks of high summer in Sweden had made the streets so hot that the tarmac had started to stick to your shoes, and the bulletproof vest she was wearing under her shirt and jacket was hardly making things any better.

After quickly surveying the scene and deciding there was no danger, she opened the door and let out her charge, who had been waiting obediently in the backseat.

The guard on the door of the main government offices at Rosenbad was for once awake enough to open the door immediately, and a few moments later Sweden's minister for integration was safely inside the thick walls of the government building.

Rebecca had time for a quick coffee in the canteen and then a trip to the toilet before returning to her driver to check they were ready for the next move.

She looked at the time. Fourteen more minutes to wait, then a short walk along the quayside to the foreign ministry for a meeting with the minister, who, unlike her own charge, had a full team of bodyguards. At least two, usually more. A whole team, the way it should be.

"Personal protection coordinator" was her job title, presumably because "one-man bodyguard unit" didn't sound particularly reassuring. The minister for integration was deemed a suitably demanding job for someone with less than a year's experience as a bodyguard, at least in the opinion of her boss. Medium-to-low threat level, according to the latest analysis. Besides—and this may have been more significant—none of her older colleagues wanted the job of personal protection coordinator . . .

As she emerged from the main entrance she caught her driver quickly tossing his cigarette in the gutter next to the car.

Unprofessional, she thought with irritation, but what else did she expect?

Unlike her, he wasn't a proper bodyguard but a less skilled version intended to save the state money. A chauffeur with a bit of extra training and a badly fitting bulletproof vest, employed by the transport unit of the Cabinet Office rather than the Security Police. Twenty years older than her and with obvious problems taking orders from someone younger, let alone a woman.

"Ten minutes," she said curtly. "Stay here with the car until we get there."

"Wouldn't it be better if I drove to the foreign ministry now? It's usually a hell of job finding anywhere to park there."

His objection was predictable. The driver, Bengt, his name was, had decided on principle to have some sort of opinion about everything she said. There was a hint of "Listen, young lady . . ." in every sentence he uttered.

As if age and gender automatically made him an expert at protecting people.

Clearly his one week of training hadn't taught him that backward was safe, but that forward was unknown territory and therefore higher risk. Idiot!

"You'll wait here until I tell you to drive over!" she snapped, without bothering to explain her decision. "Any questions?"

"No, boss," he replied, without making much effort to hide his irritation.

Why on earth was it so hard to get certain types of men to accept a woman as their boss?

Either they tried to get the better of you and take control, like Bengt here, or worse, made insinuations and comments about your sex life, or lack of one.

Offering you their services, whether or not they happened to be married . . . And if you were stupid enough to complain to your own boss you were soon out in the cold. She'd seen plenty of examples of that.

She never dated colleagues out of principle. Mixing your work and private life soon got way too complicated. Put simply: don't shit on your own doorstep.

The fact was that she never actually dated anyone. Maybe dating itself was too complicated?

She shrugged to shake off the unwelcome thought. Right now her job was her priority.

Everything else could wait.

No sooner had they gone 'round the corner of the government offices than she realized something was wrong. A minute ago, when she had checked out their route in advance, there had been three people leaning over the railing by the waters of Norrström. Two of them holding fishing rods, and the third dressed in fishing gear too, even if she couldn't see a fishing rod. None of them had seemed to pose any great threat.

But when Rebecca and her charge, along with the minister's constantly chattering assistant, approached the place where the three men were standing, she noticed a change in their body language. She automatically slid her right hand inside her jacket, putting her thumb on the barrel of her pistol, and her fingers on the telescopic baton and police radio attached to her belt. She just had time to put a warning hand on her charge's right shoulder when it happened.

Two of the men spun around and took a couple of quick steps toward them. One of them unfolded some sort of poster that he held in front of him, while the second raised his hand to throw something.

"Sweden protects killers! Sweden protects killers!" the men screamed as they rushed toward the minister.

Rebecca reacted instantly. She pressed the alarm button on her radio and in one sweeping gesture she pulled the baton out of her belt, extended it to its full length, and brought it down through the middle of the intrusive poster. She felt the baton hit something hard and saw the attackers take a step back, momentarily off balance.

"Back to the car," she shouted at the minister for integration, as she pulled the woman behind her back. With the baton raised over her shoulder she backed away quickly toward the car, her hand still gripping the minister's upper arm.

"Victor five, we're under attack, repeat, we're under attack, get the car ready!" she yelled into the little microphone in her collar: it had started transmitting automatically when she pressed the alarm.

It would be at least three minutes until reinforcements arrived, probably nearer to five, she calculated rapidly. She could only hope that Bengt hadn't dozed off behind the wheel so they could make a quick getaway.

Just as they got back to the corner of the building their attackers made a new attempt to reach Rebecca and her charge. Something came flying through the air and she hit out at it automatically with her baton.

Rock, bottle, hand grenade? she managed to think before tepid liquid rained down on her face and upper body. *Dear God, please don't let it be gasoline!*

Finally, they were around the corner again and she looked quickly behind her for Bengt, hoping that he remembered enough of his minimal training to have opened the car doors for them.

But the turning circle where the car had been parked was empty.

"Fuck!" she hissed but was drowned out by the assistant's screams.

"Blood!" he cried, almost in falsetto. "Christ, I'm bleeding!"

Rebecca twisted her head again and suddenly realized she was having trouble seeing. A red fog was descending over her eyes and she rubbed the hand holding the baton across her nose.

No car, no Bengt, and their attackers right behind them. What to do?

Make a decision, Normén, make a decision now! her brain shrieked at her.

Backward known and secure, forward unknown and dangerous. But what to do if your escape route had suddenly been cut off? They didn't teach you that on the bodyguard course. Improvisation had never exactly been her strong point. She was close to panic.

"Over here!" she heard a voice shout.

The guard had opened the door wide and had taken up a position halfway between it and her. He'd drawn his baton and was staring at the corner where their attackers ought to have appeared by now.

With a couple of quick strides Rebecca half-pulled and half-shoved the minister for integration through the door that they had left just a few minutes before. She could still hear the assistant's hysterical sobbing behind her but paid him no attention, concentrating on getting her charge to safety.

It wasn't until several minutes later, after reinforcements had arrived and the situation had calmed down, that she realized that the whole of her upper body was covered in blood.

2 | TRIAL

Dear HP
This is a trial game worth 100 points.
Try it out, and if you like the experience,
decide if you want to continue playing.
This is your task:
At the next station a man
in a light coat will get on the train.
The man will be carrying a red umbrella.
For 100 points, you must take the umbrella
before the train reaches Stockholm Central.
If you succeed I will unlock the phone and it will be yours
to use as long as you participate in the Game.
Do you understand?
Yes
No

This was actually fucking cool. HP grinned to himself as he clicked on Yes. Real *Mission: Impossible* stuff—all that was missing was the dry voice and the telephone going up in smoke.

"This message will self-destruct in ten seconds . . ."

He still hadn't managed to work out which one of the other passengers was working for Mange, but it didn't really matter. He thought he had a pretty good idea of what it was all about now. Either he was expected to chicken out and would have to put up with weeks of crap about what a coward he was, or else—and this was more likely, now he came to think about it—there'd be some trick with the umbrella. It would be glued down, or would spray water, or give him an electric shock when he tried to grab it, and one or other of the passengers would film it so he could enjoy his humiliation on You-Tube for months to come. It really was a beautiful setup, and now it was too late to back out.

> Excellent!
> When you get the signal to start playing, fix the phone
> to your clothes with the camera facing out, so
> we can see how you get on with your task.
> Do you understand?

Yep, he understood. Fix the phone to his front, camera outward.

YouTube, here I come!

HP grinned again. God, Mange was an ingenious bastard. This set a whole new standard. As he clicked on Yes once more, he realized to his surprise that his hangover was almost gone.

> Good, HP!
> You can start your task.
> Good luck!

The screen went dark.

Okay, better follow the rules for a bit longer, he thought, and attached the phone to his belt, with the camera facing out, as per the instructions.

As the train pulled slowly into Sollentuna Station he could feel his heart start to beat faster.

The man with the light coat got on at the far end of the carriage and it took a few moments before HP saw him. An ordinary-looking Swede, about forty, one meter eighty or so, same as him. Dark-framed glasses, hair combed back, a summer suit and coat, he noted as the train set off from the platform. That had to be hot?

The man's lower half was hidden, so HP couldn't see if he really was carrying an umbrella. There was only one way to find out.

He stood up and started moving slowly through the carriage toward the man. For some reason he had started to sweat, his T-shirt was sticking to his chest, and his palms itched, but this time it was more than just the hangover.

As he passed the teenage girls one of them suddenly burst out laughing and the sound made him jump. *Pull yourself together, this is only a game, an elaborate prank, nothing to get excited about.* Stealing a crummy umbrella was hardly that much of a challenge for him. He'd nicked considerably better things than that.

Now he could see that the man was carrying a black-and-white paper bag, one of those designer ones with a rope handle and a big logo to show the world that he could afford to shop in the smartest shops. A cylindrical object stuck up from one side of the bag. The umbrella!

HP felt his pulse start to race. He had to admit that this was actually pretty exciting. Stealing something while the whole thing was being filmed . . .

Okay, so the man in the coat was in on the whole thing, but even so. There was something appealing about the whole situation that he couldn't quite explain. But he really didn't want to make a fool of himself.

"Next stop Karlberg. Karlberg, next stop," the speaker in the roof announced, and he felt the train start to slow down. He took a few more cautious steps toward the man, who hadn't so much as glanced up at him.

Then the train jolted several times and stopped at the platform. The doors opened, letting in a smell of warm tarmac and hot brakes. HP took another step forward. *Here we go!*

"Pigs' blood," Superintendent Runeberg said from behind his desk, leaning back in his chair.

Although several hours had passed since the events outside Rosenbad, and even though the office was air-conditioned, Rebecca was still sweating. Her hair was wet from the shower, and in the absence of anything better she had put on her gym kit, the only clean clothes she had in her locker.

"They threw pigs' blood at you and Lessmark," her boss went on. He was a thickset man in his midforties, with a steely gaze, spiky blond hair, and a suntan that went all the way up to his scalp.

A perfect example of a bodyguard. Good-looking too, if you like the overpumped type, she thought.

But those days were far behind her now.

Strangely, considering what had happened, she felt pretty good, with the possible exception of a bit of adrenaline-fueled trembling that she was doing her best to hide. She had done her job and her charge was okay; that was the main thing. She could think through the details later.

"According to Forensics, one of the men threw a balloon

filled with pigs' blood at the minister for integration, but you burst it with your baton and most of the contents ended up on you. The minister escaped with a few drops on her jacket and a serious bruise on her arm from where you were holding her."

He paused but before she could work out if she was expected to say something, he went on:

"One of the evening papers seems to have pictures already, which would explain why the third man wasn't involved in the actual attack. Presumably he was busy taking pictures. The free market and the free press in beautiful harmony. The minister sends her thanks and best wishes, by the way. I doubt the same could be said of the perpetrators," Runeberg said.

Rebecca gave a short nod in response.

"According to eyewitnesses, the men escaped on foot, running across Gustave Adolf Square and in through the back entrance to the Gallery shopping mall. Our uniformed colleagues in the regular force stopped the subway, but before they managed to get hold of someone in charge and the order was actually given, at least four different subway trains left Stockholm Central, and one from Kungsträdgården nearby, so if they were stupid enough not to just melt into the crowds around Sergel's Square there were plenty of opportunities for them to get away on the subway."

Runeberg shrugged in resignation.

"One advantage of doing this sort of thing in broad daylight in the middle of the city is that it's a lot easier than most people think to get away," he concluded.

"While you were cleaning yourself up I had a quick chat with your driver, Mr. Göransson. He claims that you told him to go ahead of you to the foreign ministry and wait there, which was why you had no escape route," Runeberg went on in a businesslike voice. Rebecca jerked in her chair.

Not only had Bengt disobeyed her orders and put her and her charge in danger, now the fat little bastard was lying to save his own skin. Trying to blame her for everything, what fucking nerve! If he'd done his job and the car had been where it should have been, she would have been fine; she could have managed perfectly well without backup.

She opened her mouth to protest, but her boss raised a hand to stop her.

"Take it easy, Normén. You don't have to say anything, I know the bastard's lying. In the ten months that you've been with us, no one's been more by-the-book than you. You don't do anything without considering it from every angle, and your colleagues have nothing but praise for your efforts. The other day one of them said you were one hundred ten percent professional, and I wouldn't disagree with that assessment. You're a pretty good bodyguard, Normén. For a rookie, anyway . . ." He grinned. "Besides, Göransson is a hopeless liar. He was sweating like a pig and was almost in tears at the end of our little talk. So, since approximately an hour ago, his services have been at the disposal of the job market. I don't give a shit what the union says. I threw him out of the back door myself," Runeberg concluded with a smile, nodding happily at Rebecca to confirm that he had done precisely what he said.

Little boys, she sighed inwardly before realizing that he had actually praised her work, so she opted to lower her eyes respectfully to underline her status as grateful subordinate. As usual in this sort of system, you had to make the best of things and not make a fuss.

The fact that the guard on the door had had to help still annoyed her, but Runeberg had just called her a good bodyguard, which wasn't bad for a *rookie* with less than a year's experience.

Not bad at all!

HP counted to ten in his head and glanced at the platform one last time before stepping up to the man in the coat. The man looked up at him in surprise from the newspaper he had just pulled out of his pocket.

"Tell Mange he's still a carpet-licking bastard!" HP shouted into the man's ear, as he snatched the umbrella from the paper bag and, just as the doors were beginning to close, he leaped out onto the platform. He landed so hard that he almost lost his balance and had to take a couple of lurching steps to stop himself falling flat on his face.

Fuck me! he thought as he sprinted toward the steps at the far end of the platform. It wasn't quite the stylish exit he had planned, but what the hell. He had the umbrella, the task was accomplished, and none of the nightmare scenarios he'd been imagining had come true. The umbrella had been no problem, no explosions, no cascade of water, and no grinning TV presenters telling him he'd just been caught on *You've Been Framed, Candid Camera,* or some similarly classy program.

Apart from the stumble as he left the train, everything had gone according to plan and he could relax and enjoy the adrenaline coursing through his body and driving out the last remnants of his hangover.

Not bad at all! And the guy didn't half-look surprised when he'd told him to say hello to Mange.

Panting hard, he took the flight of steps in five long strides, and his momentum carried him through the station and out onto Rörstrands Street. By the time he had jogged to St. Eriksplan he was soaked in sweat, even if he wasn't particularly out of breath.

He'd always been good at running, ever since school. He wasn't much good at most other things, but he had a decent turn of speed.

The barriers at the subway station were unmanned, so he hopped over the turnstile to get in. He didn't give it a second thought. He'd never paid for commuter trains or the subway, not even when he could afford to. It was a matter of principle. Power to the people!

It wasn't until he was sitting down in the carriage that he realized he still had the phone attached to his belt. He pulled it off and looked at the screen.

> Congratulations, HP!
> You have successfully completed your trial task
> and your game account has been credited with 100 points.
> The telephone is now unlocked and under the **Game** icon
> you will find more information about how to continue playing.
> We recommend that you read the section
> concerning the Rules of the Game, and think carefully
> about whether you want to continue playing.
> If you would prefer not to, our paths will go separate ways
> and we ask you to leave the phone in the letter box at
> Bellmansgatan 7.
> Best wishes,
> *The Game Master*

. . .

"I was thinking about moving you up," Runeberg said.

"Alpha needs new recruits before Sweden takes over the EU presidency. You haven't really been on the job long enough, but after today's events Vahtola and I agree that you're ready. You start on Monday, assuming that Dr. Anderberg has no objections on mental health grounds. Any questions?"

She simply shook her head.

"Well done, Normén, if you carry on like this you'll do well here," he concluded, pushing his chair back from the desk.

"Your debriefing with Anderberg is in ten minutes. Once that's out of the way you can finish for the week. That's all. Right, I'm off to the gym."

He stood up to indicate that the conversation was over, and Rebecca followed suit. Her head was spinning and she couldn't help letting slip an unprofessional smile.

The Alpha group, the reinforcement team, the elite of the Personal Protection Unit. From Monday she would be one of them. No more beginners' jobs, just serious, qualified bodyguards' work.

Well done, Normén—clever girl!

When she knocked on the psychologist's door nine minutes and fifty seconds later, she was still trying to suppress the annoying impulse to smile.

3 | ARE YOU REALLY SURE YOU WANT TO ENTER?

WHEN THE BELL on the door of the stuffy little shop started playing the opening notes of the theme to *Star Wars*, Magnus Sandström—or Farook Al-Hassan, as he now called himself—gave no indication of having heard it. He just carried on reading the crumpled copy of *Metro* spread out on the counter in front of him, scarcely bothering to glance up at the visitor.

"Salaam alaikum, brother HP," he muttered from the corner of his mouth.

"Hi, Mange." HP grinned as he sauntered toward the counter. "Anything interesting in the paper today? Let me guess: the recession's getting worse, Hammarby lost again, and some nuts blew something up somewhere, probably in Baghdad, Bombay, or maybe Timbuktu?"

"Portugal," Mange sighed, looking up reluctantly.

"Huh?"

"The nuts blew something up in Lisbon—an empty luxury yacht, to be precise. No one knows why. But you got two out of three. Hammarby are damn useless these days."

He folded the paper and straightened up, with a sullen look on his face.

23

"And you know perfectly well that I want to be called Farook now," he added flatly.

"Of course I know, Mangey boy! If you insist on turning yourself into a second-class carpet seller, that's your decision."

He nodded demonstratively at Farook's Middle Eastern trousers, silk waistcoat, and long shirt.

"Just don't expect me to buy into that bullshit. You were Mange when we started school, when we used to smoke your mom's cigarettes behind the Co-op, and when you lost your virginity to that fat Finnish girl in a tent at Hultsfred. So that's who you are to me, regardless of whatever you, your wife, or your latest god think, okay?"

Mange/Farook sighed again. There was no point arguing with HP when he was in this mood, he knew that from experience. Better to change the subject completely, that usually worked. HP was fairly easily distracted.

"And to what does my humble little shop owe the honor of this visit, young Padawan?" he said instead, holding out his hands to indicate the cramped space.

The shop consisted of some thirty square meters of worn cork matting, plus a couple more hidden behind a shabby bead curtain behind the counter. Practically every available surface, as well as several that weren't—on the floor, along the walls, and even up on the ceiling—was packed full of things, mainly computers and electronic components and accessories. Cases, hard drives, cables, print cartridges, and various USB gadgets jostled with printed signs for various games and all sorts of discontinued products. A worn-out air-conditioning unit above the door was fighting a noisy losing battle against both the summer heat outside and the warmth generated by the countless machines within the shop.

At the back of the shop two computers were whirring, ostensibly for demonstration purposes, but in practice used as an Internet café, as indicated by the neat lettering of the printed sign hanging askew above the grimy coffeemaker. The machine bore another sign offering free coffee to paying customers, but there was a distinct absence of these right now.

As usual, the lighting was subdued, mostly provided by the various screens spread around the shop. Together with the feeble fluorescent strip light above the counter, these made up the only opposition to the sheets of paper taped across the barred window that effectively blocked out all sunlight.

HP pulled the cell phone out of his inside pocket. With a triumphant gesture he slapped it on the counter in front of Mange.

Game over, mothafucker!

But instead of giving up and admitting everything, Mange merely adjusted his dark-framed glasses and leaned forward with interest.

"A new cell . . . pretty cool design. Haven't seen one like that before. Found or bought?" he summarized as he looked up again.

"You tell me, Mange." HP grinned, but without quite achieving the degree of triumph he was hoping for in either the comment or the smile.

The confidence he had felt when he slapped the phone on the counter had vanished. This wasn't turning out the way he'd expected. Mange had never been able to keep a straight face, even when it didn't really matter. When they were younger, Mange had let HP and the others down more than once, and he had been expecting him either to confess at once, or to make a pathetic and embarrassing attempt at denial. But neither had happened, and his hastily improvised Plan B, which involved staring angrily at Mangelito, met with the same meager response.

Not a hint, not a blink or a twitch of the eye—none of the things that usually happened to a little geek when he was out of his depth. And his voice passed the test too . . .

"Huh . . . what you talking about, brother?"

HP tilted his head and made a last, halfhearted attempt.

"So you're telling me you don't know anything about the little practical joke someone played on me on the train from Märsta half an hour or so ago?"

"Nope, not a clue, scout's honor," Mange said, raising two fingers to where his hairline had once been.

"Do you feel like initiating me into the mysteries of the Märsta train over a cup of Java?" he asked, taking another look at the cell, evidently keen to get to know it better.

"Sure," HP muttered.

So what the fuck was really going on?

"Well, if you don't have any questions, we're done here."

Rebecca shook her head and was off the sofa before the psychologist had time to stand up. She knew that debriefing was important and that it was just standard procedure after an incident like the one she had been involved in earlier, but that didn't mean she had to like it.

She didn't like talking in confidence to strangers; she'd had more than enough of that growing up. Even though she couldn't have been more than six or seven years old when it started, it hadn't taken her long to work out the "right" answers. Wide-open eyes, a childlike smile, just enough confidentiality for the lies to sound sincere. It had worked well then, and it was surprisingly easy to use the same technique, with only modest adjustments, in the adult world.

"Thanks, Dr. Anderberg, I'm a bit shaken, but basically I'm fine," and a few more similar standard-issue clichés. The same shaky smile and shy eye contact, that usually worked. But today it felt unusually difficult. Her words rang slightly false, and the performance wasn't as convincing as usual. She was having trouble keeping track of her thoughts and focusing.

The composed feeling she had had in Runeberg's office had suddenly vanished without a trace.

Her thoughts kept racing away and she was having trouble keeping her focus. The sounds were still echoing in her head. As soon as she let them loose her pulse started to race and she saw it happen all over again. The shouts from the men attacking them, the alarm, the blood-filled balloon bursting. Then Lessmark's scream . . . In retrospect, the panic-stricken falsetto had become distorted in her head. Younger, more shrill. Like something she'd heard before. Her mouth felt tight and she swallowed drily a couple of times in an effort to lubricate it. *Concentrate, Normén!*

She had glanced furtively at Anderberg a few times, trying to sneak a look at his notes, but if the psychologist had noticed anything he'd concealed it well. He'd stuck to the standard questions, running through the usual script, and making a couple of dutiful attempts to probe a bit deeper, but mercifully quickly he gave up his attempts at incisive analysis and accepted the concise answers she gave him. Her performance seemed to hold in spite of its shortcomings; it was good enough, once again. And now the conversation was over at last.

They shook hands, and it wasn't until she was halfway across the courtyard of Police Headquarters, heading toward the garage, that she realized that her T-shirt was soaked with sweat.

Anderberg stood at his window and watched her go. He took a deep breath, held it for a few seconds, then let out a deep sigh.

"Police Inspector Rebecca Normén, thirty-four, thirteen years' service," he said quietly to himself. Her career path had been fairly conventional. A few years in patrol cars after graduation from Police Academy, picking up drunks and shoplifters, breaking up fights. Then a stint in Crime via the custody-section duty desk. Then the usual—watching, investigating, and pulling in wife beaters, burglars, and muggers until she had enough experience for the Security Police and the body-guard unit. Good references, but not exceptional. None of the overeffusive statements that were fairly common in the service when you wanted to get shot of a difficult colleague.

She could probably have applied to the Personal Protection Unit a couple of years earlier. After the foreign minister was murdered the group had been expanded considerably, and female applicants had been particularly hard to find—and were therefore particularly welcome.

But Rebecca Normén had taken her time. It looked like she had wanted to put in the years and gain experience in the regular force before leaving reality behind for the secret world of the Security Police. He himself had given her a "highly suitable," the second highest of the four grades used in recruitment.

"Focused and ambitious, possibly slightly reserved," was how he had summarized her in his notes on that occasion, and nothing he had seen in today's conversation had given him any real reason to change that judgment.

And she could also be considered fairly attractive, he added slightly guiltily to himself, well aware of how unprofessional the comment was. As if to make up for this slip, he qualified the thought by adding *if you like the tall, sporty type,* which he didn't.

Rebecca Normén had dark eyes, defined cheekbones, and a slightly too pointed nose, which, in his opinion, made her face more interesting than conventionally beautiful. Her sharp features were emphasized by the fact that she always pulled her hair back in a tight little ponytail down her neck.

But Inspector Normén wasn't the type to draw attention to her appearance. Little or no makeup, nails cut short, and strictly practical clothing—with the possible exception of today, although he guessed this was because of the incident a few hours earlier.

Even though she had made obvious efforts to be obliging, her manner was reserved, almost defensive, offering no opening for confidential conversation. To judge from her personnel file, Rebecca kept a low profile in her unit, did her job, and studiously avoided the morass of workplace romances that was otherwise so common in the force. More than half of her male colleagues probably thought she was lesbian, and the ones who knew better had the sense not to cross the line between private life and work that Normén obviously guarded so zealously.

He doubted whether any other officer had ever got particularly close to her. A smart move if you wanted to get on in the force, and Rebecca Normén was definitely both smart and ambitious. The fact that she didn't want to share her personal thoughts and secrets with a psychologist hardly made her unique in the force, rather the opposite.

In spite of this there was something about her that unsettled him. A vague feeling that he couldn't quite put his finger on. As if there was something there, something she was hiding behind the rigidly maintained façade and was desperate not to reveal.

He hadn't made any notes about this at her recruitment, so either it was just more obvious now, or else he was simply more attentive than he had been last year. But he got the impression that he had picked up a small, almost imperceptible fracture in her otherwise so polished and professional exterior.

He couldn't quite shake the feeling that it was all just a façade, some sort of game where the packaging didn't quite match the contents. On the other hand, he could be wrong. Psychology was hardly an exact science, after all.

He fetched a mug of coffee and sat down at his computer. When it came down to it, Rebecca Normén had demonstrated that she was more than capable of handling every aspect of a critical situation, so what else was there to say?

Right now she was the bosses' favorite, and it would take more than a few vague suspicions on his part to get them to change their minds. If he couldn't back up his feeling with facts, he would just have to let it go. After all, this concerned another person's career, and he of all people ought to know that gut instincts were way down the priority list within the police service.

Everyone has their secrets, so why should Rebecca Normén be any different? he thought as he settled to write his report.

· · ·

Welcome to the Game, HP!
On this page you will be informed about the
basic rules and regulations for participants.
I recommend that you read them carefully and think things
over before deciding whether or not you wish to continue.
Do you understand?
Yes
No

Yep, he understood all right, rules, blah blah blah, but—
more important—more information.

Just what he needed!

As soon as he got home to his little two-room flat on the
steeply stepped alleyway of Maria Trappgränd, he threw all
the windows wide open in a vain attempt to stir up the stale
air inside. The bitter coffee from the computer shop was still
bubbling in his stomach and it dawned on him that he hadn't
actually eaten anything since the burger he gulped down when
he was drunk the previous night. And he was desperate for
a cigarette. A crumpled, half-full packet of Marlboros that
he found under the sofa after a bit of a search solved the latter problem, and he took a couple of deep drags and relaxed.
Sweet!

With the cigarette hanging from the corner of his mouth
he mounted a raid on the fridge, but without any great expectations. Apart from a couple of cans of beer it offered thin
pickings, but the ice-covered freezer compartment actually
managed to produce a frost-damaged Gorby pie. He zapped
the little delicacy in the microwave and settled down at the
kitchen table, fiddling with the cell and trying not to burn his
mouth on the melted cheese.

It was all pretty straightforward. Even though the touch screen was fairly large, there were only five icons. Phone, calendar, email, Internet, and the one he was after—"The Game."

He clicked Yes and a new text appeared instantly.

> Welcome to a new dimension of gaming, a world
> where reality is a game and the Game reality.
> Welcome to the most intense gaming experience in the
> world!
> Welcome to **the Game**!

He couldn't help smiling at the bombastic tone, then ran his finger across the screen to scroll down to the next piece of text.

> **Definitions**
> Participants in **the Game** are known as **Players** and
> are handpicked after a careful selection process.
> Every **Player** is given various **Assignments** by the **Game
> Master** who is the person who directs **the Game**.
> The **Assignments**, if carried out correctly, result in
> a number of **Points**, as well as a matching quantity
> of American dollars, which will be paid into an account
> to which the **Player** has free access.
> All **Assignments** are documented by the **Players**
> themselves with the help of the handheld unit, and in
> specific instances also by **Functionaries** or other **Players**.
> All visual material is the exclusive property of **the Game**
> and will be presented at regular intervals in edited form
> together with the league table on the **High-Score Page**.

At the end of each round of **the Game** a **Winner**
will be declared, and they will receive a **Reward**.

HP frowned. If this was a joke, then it was a damn convincing one.

So had he been selected to take part in whatever it was
called . . . a live game or something? It was all a bit too close
to those ridiculous historical reenactments, really, people on
Gotland dancing about in homemade chain-mail costumes.
Or kids dressing up as vampires with plastic fangs and capes.
How the hell had he got involved in something like that?

The page had two links. He clicked the first, marked **Rules
of the Game**:

Rules of the Game
To guarantee a satisfactory experience for all parties,
there must be a set of **Rules**, as in all games.
These Rules are absolute and must not under any
circumstances be broken.
Rule 1: Never talk to anyone outside the **Game Community**
about **the Game**.
Rule 2: The **Game Master** directs **the Game**, allocates
assignments, rewards, and—if necessary—punishments.
The **Game Master**'s authority is absolute, all
decisions must be obeyed and there is no right of appeal.

Consequences
Breaching or disobeying the **Rules of the Game** will result
in immediate **Disqualification and Expulsion**.

HP sighed and pulled out another Marlboro, lit it, and took a deep drag. So far he was no wiser than he was when he started. He was clearly being invited to take part in some sort of weird game that seemed to take place out in the real world. But why him?

Not that he didn't like gaming; he had Counter-Strike and World of Warcraft on his computer, and obviously Guitar Hero on his PlayStation. But they didn't make you run around town like a fucking Duracell bunny. But on the other hand, there was that bit about money and rewards . . .

Getting paid to play games, he could definitely live with that. Professional gaming was actually something he'd looked at before. But how the hell could they know that?

He clicked the second link. Just like the heading said, it contained something that looked like a high-score table. In the left-hand margin was a series of numbers, which at a guess represented different players. At the top was someone called "58," who had evidently managed to scrape together more than five thousand points by completing seven tasks. If every point was the equivalent of one American dollar, as the earlier page suggested, then number fifty-eight had earned something like forty thousand Swedish kronor, presumably tax free, just by playing a game. Not bad, not bad at all in fact! His interest was definitely piqued.

So what did he have to do to get his share of the dosh? He scrolled down through the list of high scores, right to the bottom, where, surrounded by a number of other players on one hundred points, he found number 128. The same number as on the back of his phone. He clicked the little icon of a reel of film alongside the number. A new window opened up, showing a shaky film sequence, and he heard his own voice crackle through the phone's little speaker:

"Tell Mange . . . still a carpet-lick . . . bastard!"

The picture bounced up and down. Train doors, tarmac, then a shaky sequence of some steps and a bit of Rörstrandsgatan. Then the whole sequence over again, but this time filmed from the side with considerably better focus and less shaking, and once again he saw himself steal the umbrella and jump out of the carriage. From the angle of the shot, it had been recorded either by the attractive young woman in training gear, or one of the thirty-somethings. Christ, the look of surprise on the man's face when he took the umbrella was priceless! He clicked to repeat the film and watched it again.

First, his own recording, then the one taken anonymously. It was almost like reliving it, but with all the details more defined. The look of surprise on the young girls' faces, the drunk jumping when HP started shouting, the look of shock on the man in the coat, which seemed to suggest that he had no idea what was going on. This was massive, totally massive!

HP had nicked stuff before, it wasn't that . . . It was actually bloody cool to be able to watch it again, even if he didn't look quite as slick as he'd imagined. It was like getting a repeat of the adrenaline rush, just with more time to enjoy the finer nuances.

After a while he tried a button marked Mix and to his delight discovered he could watch the two clips alongside each other, his own on the left and the other one to the right, perfectly synchronized, the whole event seen from two different angles.

When he had watched the film for the fifth time he realized that his heart was thudding with excitement.

4 | SAFE OR ALL IN?

SHE NEEDED NEW clothes. Even though the blood would probably come out if they were dry-cleaned, she had thrown her jacket and trousers in the nearest bin as soon as she got them back from Forensics.

Runeberg had understood.

"Make sure you get a receipt and we'll sort it out, Normén," he had said, so she had just spent the past hour or so in the outfitters in Östermalm that supplied their uniforms. Getting measured and trying things on, marks in white chalk and pins. It felt like a luxury to be able to buy clothes like this, and on work time as well.

The sales assistant knew what she was doing. One size larger than normal gave enough space for the bulletproof vest and the equipment carried on their belts. Just shorten the arms a bit and take in the shoulders.

The uniform had to sit well without getting in the way. It wasn't supposed to look like a hand-me-down.

Runeberg may have told her to take the rest of the day off, but according to the roster, she was supposed to be working that afternoon. She didn't have any other plans, so it made sense to get everything out of the way now.

Runeberg was okay. If you could just look past his macho attitude he was a decent boss, possibly even one of the best she'd had. And decent bosses didn't exactly grow on trees in the force. Length of service and connections were often more important than competence.

Even so, she liked being a police officer; she really liked it. The feeling of doing something important, meaningful. Doing something for society.

But "Protect, help, see that justice is done" was only one aspect of what attracted her to working in the police. Another important aspect was the feeling of being chosen. Someone who had been handpicked more than once in the course of her career, who had passed countless tests and exams and had shown that she was made of the right stuff.

As a woman within the force it wasn't enough to pass the entrance exam. You also had to prove that you weren't a UW—a uniformed witness who was no use at all when things kicked off. You had to prove you could deal with critical situations on your own.

That was why the business with the security guard at Rosenbad still annoyed her. Without the car she had been stuck, felt almost paralyzed, and if their attackers had chosen to carry on they would have been in a tricky situation. She couldn't quite shake the insidious thought that it was the guard on the door who had saved the day rather than her. That she didn't really deserve her place in the Alpha group.

Maybe it sounded like something from the Stone Age, but the police force was to a great extent still run according to male rules. Regardless of anything that equal-rights legislation might have to say about the percentage of women in the force, ninety-five percent of all criminals were men. And if a woman wanted to join in properly and not tuck herself away on some cozy office chair the moment the opportunity arose, you had to show that you had what it took. That you weren't bothered about getting filthy and beaten up. She had no problem whatsoever with that, though it had been hard learning to take control of the situation and hit back. But a number of years on patrol had certainly helped.

She had read somewhere that the body replaces practically all of its cells over a seven-year period. Even if that sounded made up, the thought appealed to her, that she was literally a new person after everything that happened. That she was a different, much better person than she had been then.

The identity she had assumed with the job played a large part in that change.

She was proud of her job, and the rectangular police badge that she took everywhere with her, no matter where she was. Its metal shape had even left an impression on the outside of the pocket of her jeans, just like the little tubs of chewing tobacco did with ice-hockey boys. She couldn't really explain the feeling she got when she held it out and introduced herself as "Normén, Police." She couldn't imagine life without it. So why didn't she feel completely happy?

Are you really sure you want to Play, HP?

Hell yeah, he was sure. Absolutely certain! The entire thing was a complete no-brainer. Getting paid for running around the city and mucking about—who the fuck wouldn't want to be part of something like that?

And then there was the whole thing about being filmed.

He couldn't really explain why, but seeing himself on film like that was . . . exciting, in the absence of a better word. Not exciting in a sex way, no, this was a completely different feeling. Or was it?

But it wasn't really the thing about watching himself do cool stuff from loads of different angles that appealed most. Even if he still liked the idea, the initial intensity of the buzz he got when he relived the theft had had time to fade a bit now. Sure, he wasn't about to deny that it still made his pulse go up when he watched it over again, but it was no longer top of the list.

No, what appealed to him even more was the discovery that there were other people out there who could see what he was doing, watching his clips, and even rating his performance.

He hadn't really figured out what was going on the first time he was on the site, but after a couple of days messing about and checking out the various functions he had a better grasp of what it was all about.

To start with, the Game wasn't live in the way he had thought at first; it was more like an alternative reality game. A sort of mixture of computer game and reality where the two worlds merged together, according to the definition on Wikipedia, and so far that description seemed to fit pretty well.

But apart from the participants there were a load of other people watching. An audience who, if he understood correctly, even paid to be allowed to watch!

It was pretty logical, really, because why else would you set up something so advanced if you weren't going to make some money from it? Where else would they get all the dollars that were paid out in prize money and paid for at least 128 pretty advanced cell phones with built-in webcams?

Whatever, these viewers could watch, rate, and comment on what the participants were doing. He'd already got a couple of comments himself: "*Cool man!*," "*Like the shouting!*," and "*Nice start, adding you to my favorites*" had all been added to the little comment section attached to each player's high-score ranking. His viewers had given him an average of three stars out of five. Total strangers who had clicked on him, watched, and liked what they saw. Giving him cred for what he'd done. It was just so fucking cool!

The comments he had got were gnat's piss compared to what people had written about number fifty-eight, who was still at the top of the list. "*58 For The Win!*," "*You rule*," and "*58 rocks!!!*," as well as a shitload of smileys and other stuff that meant that Fifty-Eight's comments section was actually several pages long. Five stars out of five, top marks, in other words. Cred and love from an entire cyberworld, what a fucking kick that must be!

But HP didn't actually know what Mr. Five-Eight had done to deserve all the praise. As a player he could only see his own clips. A shame, but maybe there would be a way around that later on . . . There was one exception, though. At the top of the page, just above the leaderboard, was a link to what was called "Mission of the Week," where they evidently posted a successful task for everyone to see.

This week the clip was of Player Twenty-Seven, who was currently in fourth place. HP had watched it at least twenty times by now. The clip showed a bloke in a balaclava smashing the windshield of what looked like an American police car, then emptying a foam fire extinguisher into the vehicle. The whole thing was filmed on the cell fixed to the guy's chest, but also by another cameraman standing farther away. What made the mission extra cool was it took place in broad daylight, in the middle of an unidentified big city with a load of stuffy pedestrians around the car. The clip had also been professionally edited and had its own sound track, Public Enemy's "Fight the Power."

> Got to give us what we want
> Gotta give us what we need . . .
> We got to fight the powers that be!

The icing on the cake was when the cops got back from the doughnut shop or wherever they'd been and discovered their ride had been wrecked. All of it carefully documented by the cameraman, who even managed to catch some of the swearing before he had to break off and run for his life.

Praise was raining down on Twenty-Seven's comments section and HP could only agree with it. It was totally fucking cool, and pretty damn ballsy too! Maybe a bit too adventurous for him, but what the hell? On the other hand, it had to be less risky to fuck with the cops in Sweden than in the States. Over there you could easily get your head blown off if you were unlucky, and that sort of thing didn't happen much here at home, at least not very often.

"Do you feel lucky, punk? Well, do you?" *Bang, bang!*

He finished his Dirty Harry imitation in front of the steamed-up bathroom mirror, holstered his finger, then dutifully ran a comb a couple of times through his long hair and inspected the results with satisfaction as he blinked at his reflection.

"Looking good, Louis!"

"Feeling good, Billy Ray!"

A quick check of his pockets. Cash—check, cigs—check, keys—check. He picked up the cell on his way out. It was time to play. Game on!

She had grabbed a coffee in the Sture Gallery, then cruised quickly past all the twenty-year-olds with Daddy's credit card crowding around the boutiques along Library Street, then turned to head along Hamngatan toward the main subway station at T-Central. Even though it was the height of the holiday season, the Friday rush-hour traffic was almost at a standstill and the exhaust fumes were mixing with the summer smells of tarmac, cigarette smoke, and food.

It was almost evening but she still had a couple of hours of her shift left. She had been planning to go to the gym, but she didn't really feel like it now. Even if the incident on the quayside was more than twenty-four hours ago her body still felt sluggish. Almost as if the adrenaline rush had left her with a hangover. But if these were the aftereffects that Anderberg had warned her about, she could certainly put up with them.

She decided to head off toward the block housing Police Headquarters anyway. Her occupational injury form would be waiting in her pigeonhole and it made sense to get that out of the way before she started with the Alpha group. So, the blue subway line to the courthouse.

She headed diagonally across Sergels Square toward the entrance to the subway station.

In spite of all manner of schemes from the police and social services, she noted that the dealers were still standing dutifully around their marketplace by the doors. Not even the latest renovation had scared them away and these days their presence didn't seem to surprise anyone, not even the tourists.

It was as if the poor bastards had become a fixed element of the urban scene. Whatever, it was nice to get into the cool of the station concourse.

She showed her police badge at the turnstile and took the escalator down toward the blue line.

The escalator up toward T-Central. He latched onto a mother with young children and snuck through the open gate for strollers, just as he had done on his way in. Then quickly across the station concourse and out through the doors to Sergel's Square.

Even though it was evening the heat hit him like a wall. A couple of junkies were slumped drowsily under the shelter of the roof; it looked like they'd had thin pickings that day. Presumably the dealers went on holiday as well? HP thought he recognized one of them and nodded curtly as he went past, but the look in the man's eyes was so glassy that he probably couldn't see farther than the end of his nose. Smack was a load of fucking shit, no doubt about that. He was more than happy with Miss Mary Jane. It was an absolute joke that the law made no distinction. No one had ever overdosed on dope as far as he was aware.

He walked across the uncovered part of the square, then went down the slope to the subway shopping level, and a few minutes later he was standing in front of the doors with the golden handles.

A quick check of his watch; 18:43. He was two minutes early.

He wasn't used to wearing a watch.

GAME   45

When he'd received his instructions and realized that he'd
need a watch, he'd spent at least half an hour hunting through
his boxes. Eventually he had managed to dig out a shabby old
Casio that had to be at least ten years old, but somehow it
was still working. He had called the speaking clock and to his
surprise the number still worked: "At the third stroke it will be
eighteen forty-five precisely . . ."

The flashing LED light on the cell interrupted his thoughts.
He opened the new message expectantly.

> Welcome to your second assignment, HP!
> Today's mission, if you choose to accept it,
> is worth 400 points.
> Do you want to continue?

He clicked Yes at once.

Four hundred points, almost three thousand kronor, and
a serious jump from the swamp at the bottom of the list of
hundred-pointers.

> Excellent!
> Take the lift up to the bookshop.
> Don't forget to carry the phone with the camera facing
> out.
> Press the button below when you're in position.

An icon marked Ready appeared at the bottom of the screen.
HP realized that the palms of his hands were already
clammy with excitement. This was seriously fucking cool!

He was a secret agent, a man on a mission. *Pettersson,
Henrik Pettersson.*

He opened the doors, went down the escalator, cruised through the mere mortals looking at espresso machines and ridiculously overpriced chocolate, turned the corner to the lobby, where the lifts were, and pressed the Up button. A couple of minutes later he got out on floor 3, turning his face away from the security camera out of habit and gliding in among the bookcases.

He clicked on Ready.

The reply came at once.

Follow the White Rabbit!

At first he just stared uncomprehendingly at the screen, then after a couple of seconds he understood.

Of course! A bit cheesy, maybe, but still pretty cool! Whoever it was who designed the assignments, at least they seemed to have a sense of humor . . .

Grinning, he started searching the bookcases, running his fingers along the books until he found the one he was looking for. *Alice's Adventures in Wonderland*, the reference bible for all film buffs. He pulled out the book and leafed through the pages, and when he made his discovery he noticed to his surprise that he was so excited that he almost dropped the white plastic card on the floor. "Floor 5, 18:55" was written on it in ink, but otherwise the card was blank.

HP frowned. He knew the department store inside out; it was unbeatable for distracted tourists, or if you just wanted to kill a couple of hours people-watching. He was one hundred percent sure there were only four floors. A quick glance at the Casio told him he had three minutes to solve the mystery.

The staircase was opposite the lifts, and once again he kept clear of the eye in the sky, just in case. Marble and brass, smart as anything. *Trip trap, trip trap.* "Clever billy goat Gruff, trip-trapping over the troll's bridge . . ." He giggled.

Yes, he was right. The fourth floor was the top one, at least for mere mortals.

The sign made that very clear. But behind a locked door the stairs carried on at least one more floor up.

He fumbled with the plastic card, pressed it against the card reader beside the door, and heard a bleep. But the door remained locked. Then he saw the little sticker.

"Card plus code," it said, and his mood fell like a stone.

What fucking code?

After a couple of moments' thought he tried tapping "1855" into the keypad, but it protested instantly with an angry double bleep. He glanced anxiously around but everything was okay. The floor seemed completely deserted.

So what now?

He released the cell from his belt, but the screen was blank. No help from the phone, then.

Unless . . . It had to be worth a try.

He pressed the card to the reader once more and tapped in the number 128, then added a zero after a moment's hesitation.

A simple single bleep, then the lock clicked.

With his heart pounding he opened the door and carried on up to the fifth floor.

A metal door and another card reader confronted him there.

A quick glance over his shoulder, a bleep from the reader, and then he was in. His senses were on high alert; he could taste the adrenaline in his mouth. All that was missing were some dramatic strings, otherwise it was perfect!

Up here there was a narrow corridor with a sloping ceiling, flickering lights, and a series of more metal doors along one side. Much less stylish than on the floors below. So what happened now?

Just as he finished the thought the cell started flashing again—almost as if it were reading his mind. Kind of spooky!

He pulled the cell free from his belt and was about to read the message when a voice made him jump and he dropped the phone on the concrete floor.

Ladies and gentlemen, the shop will be closing in five minutes. Thank you for your custom. We are open again at ten o'clock tomorrow morning. The food hall will remain open until eight o'clock.

Christ, it startled him! He must have been standing right under one of the loudspeakers. Almost time to change his underwear.

Muttering, he picked up the cell and checked the message.

Third door on the left.

The white rabbit worked for the third time and suddenly he was standing in a bare concrete room full of humming boxes, cable runs, and other equipment. There was a smell of electricity and warm metal.

Far wall, black box,
press Ready when you're in position.

There were loads of boxes, but as luck would have it there was only one black one. An old thing made of Bakelite that stuck out badly among all the other anonymous gray metal boxes. Two plastic-covered buttons on the front, one blue, one red.

He pressed Ready.

> Well done, HP!
> For tonight's assignment you get to choose between the buttons.
> When the countdown reaches zero I want you to press one of them.
>
> If you choose the blue, everything will carry on as usual, you will get your money and further tasks of the more basic sort.
> A steady, secure income, spiced with just enough excitement.
> But if you choose the red button the clock will stop on your old life and you will enter an entirely new experience, the like of which you have never even dared to dream of.
> The risks are greater here, but so too are the rewards, of course. Only a very small number of people are qualified for this level. The question is: Have you got what it takes?
>
> The choice is yours, neither of the options is wrong, and regardless of which choice you make, you will have passed this evening's assignment.
> Do you understand?

He clicked Yes.

> Excellent, HP!
> Think carefully and then make your decision.
> You have twenty-five seconds as of now.
> Good luck!
> *The Game Master*

The message vanished and was replaced by a countdown.

24
23
22

This was utterly fucking supercool! Talk about his cup of tea! So which should he choose, the blue pill or the red one?

Evidently they were both right, but it looked like only one of them would have any sort of real effect?

12
11
10

He could feel his heartbeat in his temples.
Play it safe or go all in?

6
5

Obviously there was only one answer.

Adventure without risk was fucking Disneyland! Time to find out exactly how deep this rabbit hole really goes!

2
1

He pressed the red button.

The box clicked, then there was a faint rumble. The lights in the ceiling flickered.

HP held his breath.

When she had finished her report she took a stroll around the Crime unit to see if any of her former colleagues was on duty. Seeing as the Personal Protection Unit was only a secondment, she still had her basic post. But the corridor was empty, which wasn't so surprising seeing as it was almost seven o'clock in the evening. The few poor bastards who weren't off on holiday would at least have had the sense to finish work on time.

After her interview with Anderberg she had been driven home in a patrol car, so her bicycle was still down in the garage of the police station. The quickest way down was through the lift in the custody section, so she took the stairs down to "the beige kilometre," as some bright spark had christened the long corridor.

Down there everything was in full swing, as usual on a Friday evening. All the holding cells were already full, and a couple of tired detectives were dashing between the numerous rooms where several patrols were giving their reports. One particularly troublesome drunk, escorted by two sturdy uniformed officers, took up most of the available space in front of the duty officer's glass cubicle.

Friday nights, all the drinking and fighting, had doubtless been useful experience, but she didn't exactly miss it . . .

One of the uniformed officers nodded in acknowledgment as she passed and she returned the greeting. On the way out to the lift she could hear his police radio crackle to life:

Control to all units!
Patrol cars to Hamngatan and the NK department store . . .

Nothing happened. Not that he knew exactly what he'd been expecting, but still? Surely there should have been some sort of response? After the dramatic buildup, surely some flashing warning lights or wailing sirens was the least he could expect? People running along the corridor, maybe some angry banging on the door?

But this . . . ? A whole load of nothing.

Disappointed, big-time!!!

He waited another minute or so, then left the room dejectedly and slouched down the stairs. It wasn't until he crossed the street and made it as far as the trees in the King's Garden that he slowly began to get it.

". . . just stopped," one bloke was saying in surprise to another, pointing up at the building that HP had just come out of.

"Isn't it usually lit up as well?" he heard a couple of passersby say.

Then he saw people holding up their cells, and soon there was a mass of people taking pictures. So he looked up in the same direction as them to see what had caught their interest, and suddenly his disappointment was blown away and replaced by an entirely new, indescribable feeling that he had never come anywhere close to before.

His heart was doing backward double somersaults inside his chest. His feet almost left the ground and he felt his jeans tighten over his crotch.

This was so totally fucking brilliant! Talk about mission accomplished!

High up above the copper roof, the huge, illuminated NK clock, which had rotated above the city for fifty years almost without interruption, had suddenly stopped.

The hands of the dark clock face were pointing at seven o'clock precisely. And he realized that the Game Master had been right. A new age had just begun!

5 | PLAYING THE GAME

SOMETIMES, USUALLY WHEN she was dreaming, she could still see his face in front of her, the way it looked the very last time their eyes met. First the fury, then surprise, and finally the terror in his eyes when he realized what was happening—that he was about to die.

She always relived the moment as a film running in increasingly slow motion. The way he hung there, almost weightless between heaven and earth, between life and death, while his arms moved slowly in circles, flailing, initially to regain his balance, then to grab at salvation. But for a short while physics seemed to have made an exception and allowed him to balance on the edge even though he ought to have fallen already. As if the laws of gravity had left him there long enough for Rebecca to have time to see the terror and accusation in his eyes. She on the floor, just a meter or so from his feet, close enough to be able to reach, to stretch out a hand to rescue him.

Like so many times before the whole sequence of events slowed down until everything was entirely still, almost like someone had pressed a pause button. And for a single intense moment it was actually there, for real, the chance for her to reach out her hand and try to undo what had been done. Save him. If she wanted to.

But even though she tried to convince herself that she loved him, that she regretted it and certainly didn't wish him any harm, it didn't help. Because deep down inside her, in a place that reason couldn't reach, she still wanted—even though more than thirteen years had passed since that night—nothing more than for him to fall. That his face should be smashed beyond recognition, that his arms and legs be broken like matchsticks, and his hands, the soft hands that she had loved and feared more than anything else in the whole world, crushed to bloody fragments against the solid ground far below.

And at the moment when the hatred once again broke free inside her, someone pressed Play and her wishes came true.

Often that was when she woke up, at the moment when he disappeared from sight, and she avoided having to hear the sound of his body hitting the ground five floors below.

But not always.

Not today.

The muffled, soft sound was still echoing in her ears as she gulped down a quick breakfast by the kitchen sink. It was almost drowned out by the sound of traffic as she cycled fast along Rålambsvägen, but was still echoing weakly at the back of her mind as she made the mountain bike jump the curb on Drottningholmsvägen, and still hadn't vanished completely by the time she pulled up breathless beside the guard's box by the cellar entrance at Fridhemsplan.

She stopped at the barrier, showed her police badge to the guard inside, who waved her past absentmindedly, evidently more interested in the cell phone he was fiddling with instead of concentrating on his job.

Yet another incompetent idiot, she thought angrily before she rolled down through the tunnel beneath the Kronoberg complex, its cool darkness effectively shutting off the outside world and all of its sounds.

"Come on, put a bit of effort in, for God's sake! This isn't a housewives' exercise class!"

Sweat was pouring from the six bodyguards. Five men, one woman. Down on the floor, ten push-ups, quickly up on your feet again, ready, kick, punch, punch. Then down again. Twenty sit-ups and back up into position again. Ten reps in total, then switch with your partner. A firm grip around the waist, kick, punch, punch.

Her sparring partner was strong and his blows almost penetrated the padded shield in Rebecca's arms.

Bang, bang, bang.

Three more, then change again.

The self-defense instructor was living up to his name today. Peter Pain hadn't got his nickname simply because he was British.

The first training class for the rookies in the Alpha group. Evidently Vahtola had requested a serious session to challenge the newcomers to her group. Rebecca could see their boss watching them from the glass passageway above the self-defense room.

Approximately forty-five minutes had passed and the tempo had been relentless so far. Even though they were all in good shape, more than one of them was starting to flag now.

"Okay, stop, gather 'round."

Peter Pain beckoned them all over. There was a collective sigh of relief and Rebecca noticed to her delight that several of her male colleagues had to rest their hands on their knees to catch their breath. She was tired, but not as tired as the biggest of the men.

That's the advantage of having a bit less muscle, boys; it takes less oxygen to keep it going. She smirked silently before Pain's new orders interrupted her.

"Restraint and release, groups of three, two holding, one trying to get loose. Questions? Okay, get going, and I want to see some speed! Go, go, go!"

She ended up with two big men who she knew slightly already. Stefan and Dejan, the former a muscle-bound guy about one meter ninety tall, the latter only a bit smaller.

"I'll start," Dejan said and gestured to Rebecca to grab him from behind while Stefan took up position to lock Dejan's arms from the front.

"Ungh . . . !" Dejan twisted loose easily with some sort of advanced martial-arts technique as he let out a loud roar.

"Nice, Savic, but drop the Karate Kid bullshit!" their instructor said from the side of the mat.

Rebecca glanced up at the glass passageway. Vahtola was still watching, and it looked like the head of the unit was focusing particularly on her trio.

"Ungh!!!" Dejan was free again, this time even more easily.

Shit, she'd lost her concentration and Pain wasn't the sort to let it pass.

"Get a grip, Normén! If you want to belong to the elite you need to step it up!"

The third attempt, and now she knew pretty much how his tactics worked. Dejan took a quick step to the side before twisting free, so what would happen if she kneed him at the back of his knee in the middle of the step?

The answer proved to be that he fell backward into her arms, and that she and Stefan could easily spin him around and lay him out on the mat.

"Good, Normén, that's how it's supposed to look!" Pain clapped his hands and Rebecca couldn't help throwing a smug glance up at the glass passageway. Vahtola's expression hadn't changed.

"Let's switch!" Dejan said tersely. He was red in the face and clearly not happy about being bundled over in front of their new boss.

"I'll take the back."

Before Rebecca had time to react, he'd taken up a position behind her and got her in some sort of headlock. Both arms around her neck, his right arm over her throat locked onto the other arm, his left hand clasping the back of her neck.

It felt like she was in a vise.

She quickly tried to get at the arm across her throat, but Wikström, standing in front of her, caught her wrists and held her arms tight. She struggled and jerked, trying to get free, but Dejan evidently wasn't about to let that happen.

It was payback time, and instead of loosening his grip to give her a chance, he tightened his grasp. Her feet were almost off the ground now.

"Come on, Normén," he snarled in her ear. "Show us what you can do!"

Rebecca could feel her eyes starting to flutter. His grip was so tight that both her airway and blood supply were being cut off. She tried to get free again, this time more frenetically, but Wikström didn't appear to have noticed that everything was on the point of spiraling out of control, and was still holding her wrists tight.

Her field of vision was shrinking and she could feel herself on the verge of panic. She was stuck, she couldn't breathe, couldn't move. Immobile and in another person's power, someone who wished her harm. Exposed. Helpless. And all of a sudden she was no longer in a gym in Kronoberg but in a flat in one of the southern suburbs and the man holding her was no longer a colleague whose pride had been wounded.

"I'm going to kill you, you little bitch," he snarled in her ear, and she could tell from the tone of voice, the one that terrified her so, that he meant every word. This time she would die for sure!

The panic she usually kept such a firm grip on welled up and filled her head, pumping adrenaline into her fading muscles and taking command of her body. And suddenly she felt a new burst of life.

She let herself fall toward the floor like a sack, and when the grip on her neck relaxed a couple of millimeters she launched up with both feet and thrust backward and upward with such force that they almost toppled over.

Rebecca felt the back of her head hit something hard, felt something break, and when she raised her feet and kicked out in front to strike a different target, the force of the kick altered their center of gravity and they collapsed onto the mat.

For a moment everything went black, then her sight gradually came back.

She was sitting on the floor with her back against the flattened Dejan, with his legs on either side of her. A few meters in front of her Stefan was curled up, clutching his stomach. In a flash she was up on her feet, turning toward Dejan, who was still lying down. His hands were over his face, but to judge by the trickles running between his fingers, that wasn't enough to stem the flow of blood.

"What the fuck, you crazy or what, Normén?" he squeaked as he stared at her, sounding simultaneously suspicious and accusing.

She didn't quite know what to say.

"I . . ." she began uncertainly, but Peter Pain interrupted her.

"Damn fine work, Normén, that's the way to bring them down! Savic, you were asking for that so you'd better take yourself off to the nurse to get yourself patched up. Wikström, do you need to go too?"

Stefan waved his hands dismissively as he got heavily to his feet.

"Just lost my breath, nice hit, Normén." He nodded toward her.

Rebecca blushed, feeling simultaneously guilty and pleased. Maybe Dejan's nose was a bit unfortunate, but on the other hand he had been asking for it with his stupid macho posturing.

She'd done her job, managed to get free on her own, and she hadn't been some helpless victim.

Not like then.

Absolutely not like then!

She was different now, stronger, better, braver. A completely different person.

When she eventually dared to glance up at Vahtola, she saw a faint smile on the other woman's face.

Birkagatan 32, be there at 18:00.

It wasn't exactly a difficult instruction, but this time he had at least prepared himself better. In spite of the heat he had

62   ANDERS DE LA MOTTE

dug out an old army jacket that someone, he couldn't remember who, had left in his flat after a party ages ago. The jacket had loads of pockets, which he had stuffed with various useful things, and it had straps on the front that would be perfect for holding the phone.

The clip of number twenty-seven had eventually made him realize where the camera ought to be to get the best pictures. No more rubbish bouncing at waist height like on the train or at NK, from now on nothing but headshots.

The viewers, or fans, as he was calling them more and more often, had been impressed with the NK stunt.

Even if he didn't know who they were, he felt increasingly sure that they were his kind of people, solid guys who he'd be happy to share a chilled beer with if the opportunity arose.

He'd actually tried to find a way to get into the community. He'd tried to find an entrance portal where you could sign up as a member and then play, watch, and maybe even chat to the fans. Find out a bit more about who they were and why they liked him in particular.

But he'd failed. The search terms he had used didn't come up with any links that worked, so membership seemed to be by invitation only. Which was a bit of crap, because seeing other players' clips would have been fucking cool, not to mention the direct contact with the fans, but there wasn't a lot he could do about it.

The Game was more impartial this way—he reluctantly accepted that.

After his second task he had strolled intentionally slowly along the quayside of Skeppsbron, walking backward at least half the way so he could enjoy his handiwork as long as possible. Once he'd got home to Maria Trappgränd the Game had already put up a professional montage. First, his own shaky footage from the inside interspersed with external shots of the clock. Then a split screen with the countdown in the middle. His hand and the buttons on one side, the rotating clock on the other. Three, two, one, click, and time stopped above the center of Stockholm.

Five hundred lovely points, a personal message of congratulations from the Game Master, and a load of new comments, as well as clambering a few notches up the high-score list.

To say it was cool didn't even come close! He'd been forced to jerk off not once but twice before he could get to sleep.

Up out of the subway at St. Eriksplan, into Tomtebogatan, and then right at the corner. As he approached the address he could feel his pulse rate go up. He decided to cross over Birkagatan to be able to observe his target in peace and quiet from a doorway almost opposite, and to have a well-deserved cigarette.

There wasn't anything odd about the address.

A perfectly ordinary residential building built sometime in the early twentieth century or so, at a guess. Four rows of windows, plus the skylights on the roof gave five floors in total. From the look of it, the ground floor seemed to be mostly shops and offices, and presumably the top floor was some sort of luxurious loft apartment.

So what now?

He pulled the phone from the strap on the left shoulder, where, after much deliberation, he had decided to attach it, and swept it across the building, zooming in on the front doorway, then out to give the big picture again. When he was finished he noticed the little red light start to flash.

Behind the telephone box next to the Co-op

was all it said, and HP frowned unhappily as a minute or so later he fished out a plastic bag that had been stuffed behind the gray telecom engineers' box on the other side of the street.

Had he come all the way out to Birkastan to pick up a lousy package?

What sort of shit assignment was this?

But before he had time to look in the bag the light flashed again and when he had read through the third message of the evening he felt his heart starting to race with excitement.

This was more like it!

He checked that the camera was working, then fastened the phone in its place.

Then he tapped in the door code he had just been given and heard the lock click.

Lights, camera, action! he thought excitedly as he opened the door and slid in.

The first target spun around like a flash!

Off to the right, her brain registered as her instincts did the rest. She pushed her jacket open with her right hand, pulled her pistol from the holster, and as soon as the barrel was free she aimed it in front of her.

She brought her left hand up to meet the gun, put her hand over the casing as she continued to raise her pistol hand, which made the mechanism feed a bullet into the chamber. The moment her right arm was fully extended, with her left hand now supporting the three fingers on the barrel, she fired off two quick shots at the center of the target.

The entire movement hadn't taken much more than a second.

Rebecca backed away slowly, still with the Sig Sauer ready to fire, her eyes sweeping in both directions above the barrel. When she had retreated ten meters from her mark, the next target suddenly popped up, this time way off to the left.

She quickly spun around and without even thinking she fired off another two shots halfway through the movement.

Bang, bang!

Another five-meter retreat, then the final target appeared, low and in the center, not much bigger than a head. Half a second later this target too had two neat nine-millimeter holes acceptably close to the center.

"Stop, cease fire, cartridge out!"

"Cease fire, cartridge out!" she repeated back to the firing instructor, took her finger off the trigger, pulled out the magazine, and then released the seventh bullet, which was already in the chamber.

Once that was all done she put the gun back in her holster, then took off her earplugs and protective glasses to await the judgment.

"Nice shooting, Normén; you need slightly better tempo on the first series and less of a pull on the second, but generally, like I said, nice shooting!" the instructor told her.

Rebecca nodded appreciatively at the critique; she had fumbled slightly with her jacket, lost a fraction of a second, and then tried to make up the time on the second series.

Squeeze the shot off, don't pull! she told herself as she taped stickers over the holes in the second target, ten centimeters or so higher than she had intended.

She had had trouble with her shooting when she started at

Police Academy. The weapon and, above all, the bangs frightened her, and to begin with she had shut her eyes before she fired. Fortunately the academy ran an extra class for anyone not used to guns, and after a few evenings of intensive practice her fear had changed into something entirely different. Once she had got over her distaste and mastered the basic technique, the pistol made her feel safe. As if no one in the world could get at her as long as she had the Sig in her hand. The size and strength of any opponent suddenly didn't matter at all for someone holding a firearm.

And if both parties were armed, you had to shoot first and shoot best. So she had practiced, properly down in the firing range in the basement, but just as much at home with the authentic replica of her service pistol that she had bought in a model shop.

Draw, bolt action, fire.

Draw, bolt action, fire.

Fifty times each morning, and the same again each evening.

Squeeze the trigger, don't pull. Over and over again, until it was deeply engrained and there was no one in her class or even her year who was quicker than her. She had worn out two replica pistols so far, but it had been worth it!

Even in her current unit she was among the fastest, and when their shooting instructor checked the day's results for both accuracy and speed, she came second, beaten only by a guy from the Western District.

Shortly afterward she called her answering machine to leave a message reminding her to increase her training that same evening.

. . .

The staircase was wide, made of gray marble, reasonably worn after a century or so of use. The banister was polished teak and a small, more recent lift for two people at most had been squeezed into the center of the stairwell.

He checked out the stairwell carefully before setting off upstairs. He was heading for the second floor. The building evidently had another wing built out into the rear courtyard, seeing as there were doors off in that direction after every half flight. Single doors to the flats facing the courtyard, double doors to those facing the street, he noted before he reached the third floor.

Four doors, all of them with neat brass signs and one of them, the second from the left, with the right name combination. So far, so good. By this time his heart was pounding in his chest, and not exclusively because of the stairs.

He looked around the stairwell and landing once more before he got going.

First he pulled an old blue woolly hat over his head—he'd already cut holes in it for his eyes and mouth, just like number twenty-seven. Then he pulled out the things that had been in the bag. The first, a little rubber wedge, he pushed under the door that was his target, kicking it to make sure it was properly inserted. Then he took a deep breath and pressed the doorbell. At the moment the door handle was pushed down from inside he pulled out the can of red spray paint that had been in the bag along with the rubber wedge, and set to work.

It took a few seconds for the man in the flat to realize what was happening, and HP had got almost halfway through the text before the man started trying to open the door seriously.

Suddenly the aimless jerking of the handle stopped and a moment later the whole door shook, as if the man inside had

given it a real shove. HP noticed to his horror that the wedge
had slid out a bit on the slippery stone floor, and that there
was now a centimeter-wide gap between the double doors. He
caught a glimpse of a furious red face and heard the man inside yelling at him, but it was too late to stop now. Instead he
gave the wedge a hard kick, which he hoped would make it
hold for a few more seconds, long enough for him to complete
his task.

"I'll get you, you bastard, I'm going to get you, you cow-
ardly little fucker!" the man inside roared as he kept shoving
at the door.

The gap was growing wider and HP felt himself starting
to panic. But he couldn't stop now, he only had a couple of letters left. Nobody loves a fucking quitter, certainly not the fans.

Suddenly he heard a door to his right open and when he
turned his head he saw a girl of about twenty peer out. As
soon as their eyes met she pulled the door closed again in horror, and he heard the safety chain rattle behind it.

Fuck, he'd almost forgotten that he'd got the balaclava over
his head!

There was another shove to the door and this time HP
could see the wedge sliding back on the stone floor. All the guy
in there had to do was pull the door back and it would be free.
He could just see a muscular tattooed arm and a shaved head
through the gap between the doors and had a sudden flash
of inspiration. He raised the spray can and fired off a blast
of paint at the furious face and was rewarded with a roar in
response as the door closed again.

Direct hit!

With two quick gestures he completed his work of art and
had just turned toward the stairs when all hell broke loose

behind him. Without looking back he threw himself down the stairs.

He took the first flight in two strides and when he reached the landing halfway down he heard the man up above take up the chase with a roar. Two more strides, first floor, two more to the next landing, then just one more flight of steps left to freedom. He could hear thuds and heavy breathing behind him, though not close enough to stop him getting away. But when he turned the corner to the last flight down to the exit he saw that his escape route was blocked. A woman was just squeezing a bulky baby carriage through the front door and there was no way he could slip past. The gorilla behind him seemed to have worked out what was going on because he let out a triumphant yell somewhere just behind HP.

"I've got you now, you fuck!"

Panic welled up inside him, but instead of running straight ahead and getting caught like a rat by the baby carriage, HP spun around past the lift and carried on toward the back door out into the courtyard.

He raced out into the walled yard without slowing down, and took aim at the carpet-beating frame off to one side. The gorilla was gaining on him; he was literally at his heels, so close that he could hear his labored breathing.

HP leaped up onto the frame and from there jumped up toward the top of the wall high above. He managed to grab the edge with both hands, and kicked wildly with his legs against the wall to get his upper body up to the top.

It worked!

He struggled hard to get to the strip of tin crowning the wall and managed to swing one leg over. But just as he was about to pull up the other one he felt someone grab hold of his trouser leg and he was left sitting astride the wall, clinging on for dear life.

From the corner of his eye he could see his pursuer and could feel the man trying to get a better grip around his ankle.

Panicking, HP started to kick his left leg wildly in an effort to get free. Suddenly his foot hit something solid and he heard a grunt, and without warning the grip on his ankle let go. It came as such a shock that HP lost his balance and tumbled helplessly into the flower bed on the other side of the wall.

He landed with his face down and got a mouthful of soil.

When he got up a couple of seconds later and began to stagger toward a gateway that he guessed must lead out onto St. Eriks Street, he could still hear the gorilla roaring on the other side of the wall.

Once he was out on the street he decided against the closest subway station and sprinted off instead along Karlbergsvägen toward Odenplan. When he reached the entrance four minutes later and reduced his speed, he realized that his whole body was shaking.

Congratulations, HP!

the screen said once he had sat down in a subway car and got control of his trembling hands.

You have successfully completed
your third assignment, worth 700 points.
I have also decided to award you 100 extra points

for an accomplished performance. Your film clip
is expected to be ready in 23 minutes.
Greetings from
the Game Master

So in other words he would just have time to get home to watch everything repeated, and wallow in the love of the fans. Fuck, this was seriously cool!

When the door of the flat closed behind Rebecca she was almost too tired to go through her new routine. For a moment she toyed with the idea of not actually bothering this time, that everything was good enough as it was. But then her anxiety took over and she spent almost three minutes locking, unlocking, and then relocking all of the four locks that were attached to the door.

When she was finally happy, sufficiently convinced that everything worked and that the flat was secure, she threw her soaking-wet gym clothes into the little washing machine, staggered into the living room, and collapsed on the sofa.

"Hello!" she said in the direction of the bedroom, but no one answered.

It had been a long time since there had been anyone there.

Yet she couldn't help saying something, anything, so as not to feel so alone.

"Hello . . ." a voice suddenly answered, and her heart skipped a beat before she heard it continue and realized that she was listening to her own voice.

". . . you've called Rebecca. I'm not home right now, but leave a message and I'll get back to you."

She threw herself at the phone and just picked up the receiver before the answering machine bleeped, but whoever it was who had called had already hung up.

Hell! She'd put the phone on Mute while she was doing yoga the previous evening and must have forgotten to reset it.

Oh well, they'd call back if it was important.

The odds were fairly short that it would be a call from work about some overtime, something which for once she didn't feel inclined to do.

The intense training of the past few days had left her worn-out and tonight she just wanted to sleep. She might do a short session in the gym tomorrow, but she was planning to spend the rest of her day off catching up on a bit of well-deserved rest.

She went through her messages. The following were all reminders from herself:

"Rebecca, remember to book a time in the laundry room and pay the Nespresso bill, it's due on the twenty-fifth."

"Step up the training regime with the Sig, Normén."

"This evening there's that documentary about serial killers that you ought to watch. Discovery, eight o'clock."

She gave a wry smile at her own orders as she deleted the messages. It was odd how strange her own voice sounded when she heard a recording of it. Almost like another person on the tape. A distant relative with a few common features, but more stern and cold. But then the sound quality wasn't very good. She actually thought it was rather a silly habit to use the machine like this. Maybe it was time to get a new cell? Then she could type up her reminders instead of carrying on with all these endless calls. A suitable project for the next time she had a few days off.

She picked up the phone and reset the ringtone, and fought a sudden impulse to call Henke. She actually missed him, more than she cared to admit. But that would have to be tomorrow now, or sometime over the next few days, she promised herself before she put the phone down and switched on the television.

A few minutes later she was lost in a deep, dreamless sleep.

The clip exceeded all expectations! It looked as if someone had set up a camera on the landing, because he couldn't see a single movement that suggested a human hand behind the images that had been posted alongside his own under his profile. Even though the events had only taken place an hour or so before, everything actually seemed even more dramatic than he remembered it.

The door shaken by the gorilla's shoves, the terrified girl poking her face out, and not least his own masked figure tagging the entire door. He looked at least as cool as Twenty-Seven had done when he sorted out that cop car!

And the text on the door looked pretty damn good:

REMEMBER RULE NUMBER ONE!

That was a message the grass inside was guaranteed never to forget. A little reminder from the Game Master about what the rules were, basically. Silence is golden . . .

Damn it all to hell, the guy must have been a bodybuilder or something, because he looked pretty fucking solid when he came storming out onto the landing.

The sequence from the yard was almost as good. Because he'd only been half-lying on top of the wall, the camera had been pointing in the right direction and he could get a better idea of the effects of his kicking.

You could make out a powerful lower arm and parts of a furious face sliding in and out of the shot, then his own size-forty-three Nike landing in the middle of the gorilla's face before everything became a mess of sky and soil when he fell down the other side of the wall.

At a guess, the orc on the other side had been too pumped up on steroids to get over it.

Too bad, sucker!

Time to cut back on the anabolics.

He grinned broadly and pressed Repeat one more time.

The fans liked it when you fried rats. The comments had already started to appear and his average rating had crept closer to four stars. With a bit of effort he'd have passed the boundary to "good" by the morning.

And why not? After all, he was pretty much born for this. A hitman in the service of the Game Master!

The jacket had been a stroke of genius; the new clip was a hell of a lot better than the previous ones. You could even watch the run down Karlbergsvägen without feeling seasick, and he made a note to remember to pull off the balaclava sooner next time. It wasn't until a couple of old women had screamed in terror somewhere near Hälsingegatan that he had remembered that he still had his face covered.

He'd make sure he did better next time.

Because there was definitely going to be a next time!

6 | ALL THE KING'S HORSES...

From: Talent Acquisition
To: Game Master
Subject: Candidate Evaluation 128

Name: Henrik Pettersson
Alias: HP
Age: 31
Height: 179 cm
Weight: 72 kg
Build: Slight
Hair: Medium blond
Eyes: Blue (see attached passport photograph)
Status: Unmarried
Family: One sibling (a sister with whom he has only sporadic
   contact)
      Both parents deceased
Profession: Various, currently unemployed
Address: Maria Trappgränd 7, Södermalm, Stockholm, a two-
   room flat that he inherited from his mother
Number of completed assignments: 5
Total points: 2200
Current ranking: 23

Current level: 3

Method of recruitment: Recommendation

Education: 9 years of basic Swedish schooling, mixed grades

Started but did not complete 3-year course in economics in Swedish high school

Has twice started but never completed adult education courses

Other qualifications: None

Leisure interests: The candidate spends most of his time watching television and films, mainly American TV series, action films, comedies, and erotica. He often plays Counter-Strike without belonging to any particular group or clan. Less regular player of World of Warcraft, where his avatars are usually Rogues belonging to the Horde.

Internet habits: thefragarena.com, various file-sharing sites for downloading films and music, the Block (a Swedish trading site often used to dispose of stolen goods), YouTube, as well as various pornographic sites. A frequent user of MSN. Has recently opened a Hotmail account under the name Badboy.128

Medical history: One broken arm and two broken ribs in relatively quick succession during the 80s. The case was passed on to social services on suspicion of child abuse. Appendix removed 1992. Latest medical examination 2007 (conducted during probation) showed no abnormalities apart from THC in his blood (the active substance in cannabis-related drugs such as hash and marijuana). No history of allergies, heart problems, impaired immune system, or intolerance to any medication.

Social service records: After the referral from the health service (see above) the children were placed in care for the duration

of the investigation. This decision was revoked a short
while later and the case was dropped. Further instances of
suspected child abuse followed, but the only result was a
number of visits by social workers. One entry in the register
refers to a police report, but this could not be identified.

Father deceased 1995 (stroke), mother 1997
(cancer). The records also mention the candidate's use
of narcotics (hash and marijuana), as well as truancy and
disruptive behavior at school. There is also a care plan
established after a district court judgment (see below).

Criminal record and police register: The candidate's first
conviction occurred shortly after his seventeenth birthday,
and concerned numerous instances of minor narcotics
offenses and one instance of vehicle theft: he was given
a probationary sentence under the supervision of social
services.

Shortly after his eighteenth birthday he was convicted
of aggravated manslaughter and sentenced to ten months
in a secure young-offenders' institution. Later entries in
police surveillance logs indicate minor narcotics offenses,
suspected trafficking in stolen goods, and minor larceny.

His most recent conviction was almost two years ago,
for one case of dealing in stolen goods, one instance of
aggravated unlawful driving, and one instance of minor
narcotics offenses. As a result he received a probationary
sentence and a fine.

Other official records: The candidate has five notifications
for nonpayment registered with the enforcement service,
principally for unpaid household bills for his electricity
and telephone, as well as unpaid standing charges for the
building he lives in. It is worth noting that every case has

been resolved before the bailiffs were called because his
sister settled the debt.

Personal characteristics: All sources describe the candidate
in similar terms. He is intelligent, quick-thinking, and
imaginative, but is also described as lazy, unreliable, and
self-centered. He usually prefers simple solutions to long-
term engagement, has obvious problems with authority,
and has few serious friendships or family relationships.

Assignments: Apart from the trial assignment (scenario
12a), the candidate has successfully carried out four
assignments (up to difficulty level C3).

He regularly watches his own film clips, checks the
comments often, and is quick to respond positively to
invitations of new assignments.

So far the candidate has shown no signs of doubt or
anxiety about possible consequences, either on his own
account or such as the assignments might generate.

Recommendation: Candidate 128 demonstrates almost all
of the qualities required by a successful Player. He is
impulsive, intelligent, and dynamic, while exhibiting little or
no empathy for others.

The candidate appears to regard himself as an
unfortunate victim or outsider. Someone who for reasons
unknown is always being unfairly treated or is simply
unlucky. He therefore believes that he has the right to do
what is best for himself in all circumstances, usually at
the cost of others or of society, without, for that reason,
having to take any responsibility for his actions.

The candidate has no family to speak of, has problems
with long-term relationships and intimacy, as well as with
trusting or being trusted by others.

Even if money plays a part in his motivation, his main incentive is recognition and attention (so-called cred) from his peers. For someone who loathes authority, 128 allows himself to be led surprisingly easily, but only under the condition that he can perceive all choices and decisions as his own, and that everything is happening on his terms.

In light of this, the undersigned recommends that the candidate is raised to level two and that further evaluation take place after an assignment of level D1 difficulty.

Sincerely,

Donovan

Talent Acquisition

HP was fucking like he was in a trance.

He was Rocco Siffredi, Paul Thomas, and obviously the legendary Ron "The Hedgehog" Jeremy, all rolled into one. This evening he was the Emperor of Fucking, and he twisted and turned his willing but still somewhat surprised partner in order to explore all imaginable variations of copulation.

The third shag within two hours or so, way beyond his usual average. They had already worked their way through a quick ride on the sofa, then a standing missionary fuck on the kitchen table with her long legs resting on his shoulders, and he was currently busy frenetically penetrating the lady in question from behind with such force that the entire bed seemed on the point of collapse.

His hands had a firm grasp of her broad hips. Breasts and ass bouncing in time with her moans of pleasure, as he speared her harder and harder with his rock-hard porn-star cock.

"A bit more, a bit more, I'm almost there," she whimpered breathlessly. But he didn't give a damn. Because he was the King of Fucking, the Prince of Penetration, the Ayatollah of Fuck 'n' Rolla! But, more important than that, he was also Mr. Clip of the Week, first runner-up and number one hundred and twenty-fucking-eight! The coolest dude in the Game, and the thought of that made him considerably harder than his partner and her undoubted feminine charms could ever have done.

With a couple of final powerful thrusts he concluded his masterpiece, and at the moment he pulled out and sent a cascade of slushy love joy over her sweaty back there was only one thought in his mind: he should have had the camera on!

She lay next to him in the darkness and glanced over at his sleeping silhouette. Maybe not the smartest guy in the world, exactly, but at least he was damn good in bed, and this evening he had seemed unusually inspired.

They had known each other for about six months, after meeting in a bar somewhere in the city center, and because she had been feeling particularly lonely and in need of physical intimacy she had, against all of her usual principles, gone back to his flat with him that same evening. The sex had been good right from the start and after that it had been difficult to stop.

There was something about him that appealed to her, that got her going. Not that he was especially handsome or exaggeratedly sexy; he was probably somewhere in the middle on both scales. Maybe it was simply the fact that he wasn't a police officer but just a completely normal guy who lived in the completely normal world that appealed to her most. Either way, they met up every now and then, usually when *she* was in the mood. She wasn't after a relationship and he had never protested against the arrangement that had developed. But she still couldn't quite shake the feeling that she was exploiting him. Rebecca suspected, or possibly hoped, that he already had a proper relationship, but she had chosen not to ask and he hadn't felt obliged to tell her anything more about himself. Whatever it was they shared, it wasn't about feelings but physical attraction, and that didn't really call for any details, or at least that was what she liked to think.

Oh well, it probably didn't matter. They were fuck buddies, to be blunt about it, even if she wasn't fond of that particular term. She stroked his back guiltily and heard him mutter something in his sleep.

The Game Master had promised him an entirely new world, and so far he wasn't exactly disappointed! He could watch the clips any number of times, and by now he probably already had.

Assignment number four had been pretty neat. He had removed the wheel nuts from a Ferrari belonging to a sleazy lawyer while the guy was sitting ten meters away having an after-work drink with his hotshot friends at Sturehof's pavement café. The car was of course parked in the parking bay for deliveries beside the concrete mushroom in the middle of Sture Square, so that everyone could see his flashy fucking penis extension, but in spite of that no one had noticed a thing.

The tools were waiting for him, neatly wrapped up in a plastic bag, inside the cistern of one of the toilets in the Sture Gallery, and once HP had got going it had taken him less than three minutes to remove the nuts on the wheels facing the street.

Even though it was Friday evening and there were loads of people around, no one reacted to what he was doing, not even the cop who strolled past just half a meter behind his back. It was actually bloody weird that people cared so little about what other people were doing, at least until Mr. Sleazy Lawyer tried to do a wheel-spinning U-turn to head back up King's Street.

Both wheels flew off more or less instantly and suddenly the stupid bastard got considerably more attention than he had been expecting. Apart from the hundred or so who stood there laughing and pointing in an outpouring of Schadenfreude, HP counted at least five others apart from him who were filming the beautiful car as it sat there straddling Sture Street. The shiny and presumably absurdly expensive disc brakes were properly embedded in the tarmac, and according to the report in the *Daily News* the following day it had taken almost an hour for the recovery truck to get the vehicle cleared out of the way.

But by then HP was long gone. He hated Sture Square, more than ever at weekends, and didn't want to spend any more time there than was absolutely necessary.

The last he had seen of the car's owner was the man standing there crying like a little girl, leaning on the boot of his ruined darling car, but HP hadn't felt the slightest bit of sympathy for his victim. Mr. Sleazy must have deserved the treatment, you could tell just by looking at his stuck-up face, his slicked-black hair all greasy with Rogaine, and his flashy suit. With a car like that, you were practically asking for trouble, and that's precisely what HP had provided.

HP had never liked lawyers anyway. The only time he had ever been stupid enough to employ a law twister, it hadn't exactly helped him. The bastard had been completely incompetent, hadn't done his homework, kept calling him Håkan, and stank of drink masked by mints in court. HP should have known better than to accept the first name suggested by the court, but he had only just turned eighteen and even if he knew all the signs of heavy drinking backward, it would take a bit longer before he had the same sort of grasp of the legal system.

Everything had been a complete fucking mess that time.

Ten months in a secure young-offenders' institution had been the result.

Public defender, my ass! More like "public defiler," or possibly "proper defrauder," to judge by Mr. Sleazy's ridiculously expensive ride. So now at least he got the chance to deliver a bit of payback to the ambulance chasers, and it felt pretty damn good!

Suck my cock, you stuck-up Sture Square wankers!

As per his instructions, he had the wheel nuts couriered anonymously to the law firm the following week, and for the first time it dawned on him that everything, the whole deal with the Game, was a hell of a lot bigger than he had imagined.

Because what was really the point of sending the wheel nuts back to Mr. Sleazy? It was almost like doing the guy a favor, and probably saved him a few thousand kronor off the repair bill. Why not ditch them in the waters of New Bridge Bay and have done with it?

The only answer he could think of was that someone wanted to see the look on the guy's face when he got the package. And that was when he finally understood. That there were actually other people like him out there, not just in the USA, but here in Sweden, and probably in other countries as well.

He had already worked out that the gorilla on Birkagatan was involved somehow, and that the stupid fucker hadn't kept his mouth shut and had blabbed about the Game. That was obviously what the text he had sprayed on the door had been about. And it probably wasn't Lewis Carroll himself who had left the pass card in the book or worked out how to switch off the clock on the NK roof . . .

But the bigger picture still hadn't really sunk in before he figured out that someone had been selected to conclude the assignment with the lawyer. That someone would stand there filming as the GQ-reading little jerk opened the parcel and went red when he discovered his own missing wheel nuts. Someone just like HP, with an assignment to carry out and a camera to document it with, and the same probably applied to whoever it was who managed to come up with a Ferrari wheel wrench and hide it in a toilet cistern in the Sture Gallery. So at least three little assignments and the same number of participants just to piece together the whole and give Mr. Sleazy a weekend he'd never forget.

The whole thing was fucking refined; he had to take his hat off to whoever it was who organized all this.

The assignment had given him 1,000 points, and the next morning he had found a foreign credit card on his doorstep. This time he guessed the pin code correctly first time.

In total the account turned out to contain $2,300, which matched the number of points he had on the list. He just had to stick the card into the nearest ATM and withdraw what he wanted.

It had been more than enough for the *Sopranos* box set he had been dying to get his hands on and a family pack of best Moroccan from his friendly neighborhood dealer. Then he had settled back on the sofa, puffed the magic dragon, and blown the heads off some rookies in Counter-Strike. Then home-delivery pizza and a bit of male bonding with the boys in the Jersey mafia. Life was pretty sweet!

But in spite of all this, it was the fifth assignment that was the really cool one. The one that transformed him into Mr. Clip of the Week, first runner-up, and, a few hours later, the Omnipotent Pope of Pussy-Crashing.

As well as a permanent hard-on, task number five left him with 2,500 nice new dollars in his account, but to his own surprise the money was becoming more and more like an agreeable by-product. Considerably more important than the cash was all the love he was getting in his comments section: "128 FTW!," "all d kings horses couldn't stop u ;-)," or "W00T one-twoeight!!1!," to list just a few. He had an average rating of 4.8 stars and he had received a personal message of congratulations from the Game Master himself.

Not bad for a rookie!

He was flavor of the month!

He was in the zone!

He was on his way to the top!

She woke up early, slid out of bed, and, without waking him, silently gathered up her clothes and put them on. She didn't really like staying the night, but she had been so exhausted by the recent days' training and by the previous evening's activities that she had fallen asleep for once.

Ever since that first evening, they had met in his flat, which suited her fine. She liked him, absolutely, but it didn't feel right to let him inside her flat. It would be sending out the wrong signals, giving him false hope. Much easier to meet like this, get it over and done with, then go home. Blame having to get up early, the way she always did.

He was actually a decent guy. A bit scruffy maybe, his flat could do with freshening up, and it wouldn't hurt him to get his hair cut more often.

But fundamentally a good man, considerably better than she deserved.

She just shouldn't have fallen asleep.

She really shouldn't have fallen asleep.

He moved in his sleep and for a few panic-stricken moments she thought he was going to wake up. What would she say if he did? How could she explain that she was about to sneak out like a thief in the night, without even saying goodbye? Or, even worse, what would happen if he tried to pull her back into bed for a morning cuddle? Snuggle up together and exchange secrets?

She felt her pulse racing.

Calm down now, for God's sake, Normén!

Then he settled down and she could tell from his breathing that he was sleeping soundly.

Thanks goodness!

Time to go. Had she got everything?

She did a quick check of her jeans pockets.

Keys—yep, police badge—yep, cell phone—missing . . .

She looked quickly around the dimly lit bedroom, eager to get going. There it was, on the middle of the desk. Relieved, she picked it up and saw that his cell was sitting next to it. A smart design, all thin and brushed steel, no bigger than the palm of her hand, with nothing but a touch screen. A little flashing red light was the only indication that it was switched on. She couldn't remember ever seeing one of that model before, or this one in particular, come to that. He must have only just got it. Probably cost a fortune, she thought as she carefully closed the front door behind her.

When HP opened the baggage locker at the Central Station, at first he didn't realize what he was staring at. The green, cylindrical object reminded him most of an aerosol can and for a moment he almost felt disappointed. Was there another rat who needed a reminder of rule number one? He'd been expecting something better.

He stuffed the object into the bag he'd brought with him, and because the subway was full of people he wasn't able to take a closer look at it until he'd shut the door of his flat behind him. He felt like he'd been taken for a ride; the assignment had started so promisingly with the key to the locker taped under a table in a branch of Wayne's Coffee on the steep part of Goth Street. It was classic spy-film stuff, sitting there among all the unsuspecting latte slurpers, the anxiety of feeling under the table, and the excitement when his fingers touched something hard.

He already had an idea of what the key was for before the cell told him where to find the lock it fitted.

So why all this James Bond cloak-and-dagger shit, just for a can of spray paint?

But now that he'd had the chance to inspect his find, everything suddenly got more exciting. He guessed almost at once that it wasn't an aerosol. It was actually a bit ridiculous that he'd ever been thinking along those lines. You only had to see the handle halfway along one side and the pin at the top to realize that this was far more dangerous than a can of paint. And instantly his pulse started to race with anticipation.

"M84 Stun Grenade," it said in military lettering, and a quick check on Wikipedia was enough to confirm what something like that was used for. The grenade, which was also called Flash and Bang, was a so-called non-lethal weapon. For anyone who didn't understand faggy military-speak or play Counter-Strike, it was a weapon whose primary use wasn't killing people.

Unlike ordinary hand grenades, the M84 didn't fire out shrapnel that mutilated and killed those around it, but instead caused a hell of a big bang as well as a flash of light that made the sun look like a 15-watt lightbulb. The point of the grenade was to knock out your enemy by making him blind and deaf and making him crap himself long enough for you to pick him up alive. Most antiterrorism and police forces in the civilized world seemed to have M84s in their arsenal, and the descriptions of the grenade's effectiveness were overwhelming: "very powerful," "extremely useful," or "highly efficient" were just a few of the positive reports that various users had given the M84, and now HP suddenly had one of his own.

A real one!

The only question was: What did the Game Master want him to do with it?

From: Game Control
To: Game Master
Subject: Extracts from police report 0201-K246459-10
    (candidate 128, assignment 1006-09)

On the above date, patrol car 1054 with Police Inspector Janson and Police Constable Modéer was ordered to the junction of Kungsträdgårdsgatan and Arsenalsgatan as a result of an as yet unclassified incident involving the Horse Guards. A number of patrols and ambulances were despatched simultaneously to the same location and Police Inspector Janson was appointed as acting head of the police operation.

At the location the patrol met Lieutenant Arne Wolff from the Svea Life Guards' dragoon battalion, who told them the following:

Together with twelve fellow officers and a total of forty conscripts, Wolff was ordered to form a mounted escort for a cortège from the Royal Stables to the Royal Palace, on the occasion of the state visit from Greece.

The cortège contained the president of Greece and his wife, as well as Their Majesties the king and queen.

Wolff reports that they left the Royal Stables in the following formation:

First went two mounted police officers who were primarily responsible for dealing with any traffic issues. Then came the head of the escort and his adjutant and the color guard (2 + 4 men), then the first troop of the escort (2 + 20 men), of which Wolff was acting commander from a position at their rear.

Behind Lieutenant Wolff followed the first carriage of the cortège, containing the president and His Majesty the king, then the second carriage with the president's wife and Her Majesty the queen. Behind the royal carriages came two further mounted police officers and then the second escort troop, this too consisting of two officers and twenty soldiers.

Usually the route would follow New Bridge Square,
Hamngatan, Regeringsgatan, reaching North Bridge via
Gustav Adolf Square, then Skeppsbron to the Palace. But
because the bridge is closed for repairs an alternative
route was chosen, via Kungsträdgårdsgatan and crossing
the water by Strömbron instead.

When HP had finally received his instructions, he understood at once that this assignment was considerably more difficult than any he had carried out before. There was actually a
risk of him getting caught, and if he did he would have considerably more trouble with the judicial system than for switch-
ing off a clock, spray-painting a door, or removing a few wheel
nuts. This here was some serious shit, and he didn't exactly
have an unblemished criminal record to fall back on. He'd end
up behind bars for this if anything went wrong . . .

Really, he should have turned it down, but he could already
feel his excitement bubbling inside him. This would provide
damned good pictures. World-class stuff, maybe clip-of-the-
week material! He'd never heard of anyone doing anything like
it, so he'd be the first. And he couldn't just back out of a challenge like that.

An offer you can't refuse . . .

It would be important to plan the operation carefully.
Complete the assignment, get good pictures, and find some
way of getting away without anyone working out who he was.
He thought he had a pretty good idea of how it could work, he
just needed to get a few things together.

When the first escort troop was level with Wahrendorff
Street, Wolff noted from his position in the procession that

an object was rolled out toward them from somewhere
in the crowd of onlookers along the left-hand pavement.
The object in question appeared to be some sort of metal
cylinder, somewhat reminiscent of a can of spray paint,
and it stopped in the middle of the front part of the troop,
whereupon a number of horses jerked and caused some
anxiety in the ranks.

The Goat's moped was a stroke of genius. HP had bor-
rowed it before and his amiable neighbor and court supplier
had never been interested in what he wanted it for.

"Just take it, no problem, here's the key," was as usual the
response he got, and half an hour later he nicked a decent
black helmet with a dark visor from a motorbike parked in the
square down at Medborgarplatsen.

He'd checked the route of the cortège on the net, then he
went down to do a recce and came to the conclusion that the
end of Wahrendorff Street was the best place to carry out the
assignment.

The whole cortège would have made it into Kungsträdgårdsgatan by then, and with a bit of luck both the king
and Her Mayonnaise the queen would get to enjoy a proper
funfair ride when his new M84 friend went off. Then he could
head back up Wahrendorff, be at New Bridge Square before
you knew it, then up Birger Jarlsgatan and hard left into the
Klara Tunnel, and from there he'd have plenty of options.

He'd be back on safe territory on Södermalm before the
suspect's details had even got out, and by then he'd have ditched
the black helmet in the water, and would have taken off his
jacket and just be wearing a white T-shirt and the Goat's basic
red moped helmet.

No chance of anyone connecting him to the description of the suspect, and even if they did, so what?

How much evidence would they have?

> Suddenly there was a powerful explosion and a flash of blinding light that together caused total chaos in the cortège. Most of the horses in the first troop, including Wolff's, bolted at once, either along Kungsträdgårdsgatan or directly into Kungsträdgården itself.
>
> Wolff describes himself as a very capable rider, but the flash of light and explosion left him so stunned that he, along with the majority of the dragoons, was thrown off his horse at once and left lying on the pavement by Kungsträdgården.
>
> When he came to his senses a few moments later he observed that the horses pulling the carriage of His Majesty the king had reared up and were about to bolt. Instinctively he grabbed hold of the snaffle of one of the horses to help the driver calm them. This however did not succeed at first, and the carriage raced some twenty meters down Kungsträdgårdsgatan with Wolff hanging from the harness.

Jesus what a fucking massive great explosion! Even though he'd thrown loads of flashbangs in Counter-Strike and read about the effects on the net and even seen YouTube clips of the M84 in action, none of that came close to doing the little fucker full justice.

Up with the switch, out with the pin, and then just roll it in among the horses. Okay, a bit harder IRL than online, but not that bad. Even though he had earplugs, sunglasses, and the visor pulled down, the blast and the flash of light still took his breath away. It was a bit like pressing pause on television, and the image freezes while the program and the sound roll on behind it.

He had to blink hard several times to shake the effect from his retinas and get his eyes back to real time. And what he saw exceeded all his expectations! The street was a fucking war zone! Beaten-up riders everywhere, horses bolting, rearing up, and generally going crazy. One horse went through the glass of one of the outdoor cafés, a couple of others mowed down one of the newly planted trees in the avenue in Kungsträdgården and carried on blindly into the park through a cluster of parked bicycles. People taking a Saturday stroll through the park had to leap out of the way of the panicked creatures to avoid getting run down or having their heads kicked in. People screaming, horses whinnying, kids crying, and in the middle of all that one of the royal carriages came racing down the street with some guy hanging off the side of one of the horses. It was like a Hollywood film, only better.

Much, much better!

HP couldn't stop staring at the destruction, and it must have taken a good thirty seconds before he remembered that he had caused it and that it was probably high time he left.

> After several minutes of chaos among wounded dragoons, horses, and onlookers, it was ascertained that the royal and presidential couples were all uninjured, albeit shaken, and that there didn't appear to have been any attack aimed at them specifically.
>
> See separate witness statement from Wolff for further details.

When patrol 1054 arrived on the scene a dozen
horses were still running loose in the area. At least
fifteen members of the escorting troop and another
seven onlookers were deemed by the paramedics to
have injuries requiring immediate medical treatment, so
Kungsträdgårdsgatan was blocked off in both directions
and an evacuation operation with extra resources was put
into action.

Superintendent Nilsson assumed the role of head
of the police operation at 12:04. On the advice of the
Security Police, vehicles were called from the Royal
Stables and these, under escort from patrol cars 1920
and 1917, as well as members of the Personal Protection
Unit, took care of the onward transport of the royal party
to Stockholm Palace.

The pictures were brilliant! As well as his own, which were
now almost razor sharp and hardly moved at all, thanks largely
to the new strap he had fashioned from an old rucksack, the
Game Master had placed no fewer than two other cameramen
in Kungsträdgården.

How the hell they knew exactly where HP was going to
strike he had no idea, but by this point he had ceased to be surprised at the reach of the Game. Maybe someone had followed
him when he did his recce, or perhaps the cell had a built-in
GPS tracker? Whatever, the results exceeded all expectations
and just a few hours later he was Mr. Clip of the Week, Mr. A
Number One, and the Ayatollah of Fuck 'n' Rolla.

Television and the papers would be busy for at least a
week and he laughed himself almost harelipped at all the
so-called experts who pontificated about the perpetrator and

the motives behind what had quickly become known as "the Kungsträdgården incident."

According to one of the evening tabloids he was a right-wing extremist, according to the other he was a left-wing activist, all depending on the ideological position of the paper in question.

The television channels, on the other hand, were more into the international terrorism angle. The most commercial station that had employed the most expensive expert even dared to identify a new Swedish network with "connections to Al Qaeda."

The only thing all those smart-aleck know-alls with their millions of high-school grades had in common was that they were all wrong!

Totally and utterly damn wrong, in fact!

There was no conspiracy, no terror network, no political agenda. There was just him.

The single shooter. A man with a mission.

Henrik "HP" Pettersson, the man, the myth, the legend, and he had beaten all of them! Among all the thousands of other deadbeats, the Game had selected him specifically. They had seen his potential, evaluated his talents, and set him on track.

And as thanks he had stepped up and struck a totally fucking massive home run!

Just thinking about it made him rock hard again!

7 | FAIR GAME

You murdering little whore!
Someone like you shouldn't be allowed in the police!

THE NOTE WAS waiting for her when she opened her locker and for a moment she was almost surprised. But then reality caught up with her. A little white Post-it note with the police force logo in the top-right corner, just like the others, and fixed to the edge of the little shelf toward the top of the locker.

She touched it, stroking her fingertips over it, and silently repeated the words that had been written in red ink. Round, almost childish lettering, yet the message was anything but innocent. Really she ought to pull it off, crumple it up, and get rid of it. But she knew that if she did, it would only be replaced with a new one. And why not, really? The note was basically right.

A *"murdering little whore,"* that's what Dag's sister had called her at the funeral. Deathly pale, with her arm around her sobbing mother, Nilla had pointed and shouted those very words so loudly that no one could have missed a single syllable.

"It's all your fault, you murdering little whore. You killed him, you and your damn brother!

"How the hell have you got the nerve to show yourself here?"

The church had fallen utterly silent. Even the priest seemed to be staring at her as she stood there alone in the middle of the aisle, among all the seated black-clad figures.

And she knew that Nilla was right.

She didn't belong there; she had nothing in common with the people who were mourning Dag's death. With people who would like nothing more than for him to be alive still, instead of in the coffin up at the front by the altar. Because she wasn't one of them. She was happy, yes, actually happy, that Dag was dead, that he could no longer make her life a living hell. For a moment she was on the point of yelling that at them. That their beloved son, brother, grandchild, relative, or great mate was nothing but a fully paid-up fucking psychopath. That he was violent toward women, a rapist, a bully—in short, a complete pig of a human being—and that she was relieved, no, actually overjoyed that it was his broken body in the wooden box up there rather than hers.

But of course she said none of that. Instead she merely nodded curtly at Nilla, turned on her heel, and, with their eyes all on her, walked out of the church and out of her old life.

Two months later she applied to Police Academy. Took the bull by the horns and confronted her fears, under a different surname as a thin cover for her new, fragile identity. And as time passed, her new self grew stronger and stronger. So strong that she had started to think she no longer needed any protection.

At least up to now.

But Nilla had been wrong about one thing.

Rebecca was responsible, not her little brother. Henke was innocent, but he was still the one who had been punished.

"It was me who did it," he had told the police back then,

and they had believed him. She had wanted to protest, yell at him to shut up, or just simply and calmly explain what had really happened. But it was as if her insides had frozen to ice. As if that paused image of Dag's last seconds alive had taken root inside her head and was stopping her from thinking, speaking, or even moving. And then it went on paralyzing her through the interviews and later during the trial, while that useless lawyer messed everything up. And, having always been the person who protected him, she just watched as her little brother assumed responsibility for everything. How he protected her and how she let him do it without raising a finger.

She let him throw away his life, his future, all his opportunities, all for her sake.

That little white note was right. Someone like her shouldn't be in the police. That's why she left it where it was.

Nilla had been a civilian employee with the Södertälje Police back then. At a guess she was still there, and she was bound to know someone who knew someone . . . And the story would have got around. That was always the way. The police force was large, but not that large, and police officers loved talking shit about other people, just like everyone else. Really, she ought to phone Nilla and explain to her just what sort of person her wonderful big brother was. Put a stop to all the talk and people looking over their shoulders at her. Clear the air once and for all and say what really happened that night, and why.

She had toyed with the idea before, but always came up with some reason not to do it. Maybe it was time now?

She would think about it, think about it properly, she promised herself as she pulled on her bulletproof vest and buttoned her shirt.

When she closed her locker a short while later, the note was still in place.

Okay, he had to admit it. He was disappointed, seriously fucking disappointed, even! After his big moment and his elevation to first runner-up, he had expected more challenges of the same level as the one he had just accomplished. More chances to end up in the spotlight, to garner points, love, and cred on his way to the top.

But instead he had just been given a couple of shitty little tasks. Stupid stuff that any nobody with a couple of functioning brain cells and a tiny pair of balls could have handled.

First he'd had to set up an anonymous Internet account and empty a few buckets of bile over a popular blogger on her home page, which in retrospect turned out to be unnecessary seeing as more than fifty other trolls had already done the same thing. The woman in question had evidently stepped on someone's toes; she did that pretty much on a daily basis, but why waste his talents on shit like that?

Assignment number two was in the same class, a phone call to a television channel to threaten a famous presenter. Child's play, and in total he'd only earned four hundred points and had actually slipped two places on the list. The flow of love that had washed over him after the business in Kungsträdgården had quickly reduced to the Manneken-fucking-Pis. A pathetic little trickle that stung more than it did any good. And someone else appeared to have replaced him as clip of the week, a clown who had thrown a pie at some world-famous business leader that HP had never even heard of. Ridiculous, a piece of piss, and nowhere near his own achievement.

To make the whole thing even worse, he was running out of money.

He'd soon have to take up Mange's offer of doing some casual work in the computer shop to pay the bills.

He needed a new mission.

A task that challenged him, something more in line with what he was capable of. And he needed it soon, because right now this shit was damn useless!

"Okay, attention, Alpha One!"

Vahtola stepped into the room and the chatter among the six bodyguards died away instantly.

"Welcome to today's assignment," she began curtly. "You'll be deployed as follows: one plus three will reinforce the prime minister's group, he's due to land at twenty forty-five at Bromma, and, as you all know, after Kungsträdgården we're doubling up."

Nods of agreement from the whole group, no one could object to the logic of that following the warning shot that the royal party had quite literally been subjected to a week or so before.

"Bengtsson, you can have Kruse, Savic, and Normén. Take two standard cars. The prime minister has his armored vehicle plus one, so you'll be a total of four vehicles. Channel twenty-eight as usual. Questions?"

Bengtsson, a wiry man somewhere in his forties with thinning hair, Vahtola's second in command, merely shook his head quickly.

"Good, you can get going at once," Vahtola concluded, and a few minutes later they were sitting in the cars.

Bengtsson had made it easy for them by letting them divide up among themselves before they set off, and Rebecca had intentionally kept close to Kruse, a sturdy man from Gothenburg who had been in Alpha since the group was formed. She hadn't spoken to Dejan since the incident in the self-defense class, even though she knew she should probably apologize to him. After all, he was the one who ended up getting hurt, not her. But for some reason it hadn't happened and now too much time had passed.

The injury was still visible from the plaster supporting the bridge of Dejan's nose, and he shot sullen looks in her direction whenever he got the chance.

Macho dumbass!

Kruse, on the other hand, was more like a kindly uncle; he didn't really give her any sort of looks at all, usually spoke about his wife and their almost grown-up kids back home in Gothenburg, whom he only saw when he had time off. She'd asked him why he hadn't tried to get a post closer to home, but he had just laughed:

"Once a bodyguard, always a bodyguard, Normén. You'll realize that soon enough. Besides, Iréne doesn't want me cluttering the place up during the week."

They booked out an ordinary black Volvo S60 and set off after Bengtsson and Dejan's Suburban. Quarter of an hour or so later they were out at Bromma Airport.

Finally it had arrived!

He had almost given up hope, and had been toying with the idea of giving up altogether and getting rid of the cell to the Greek when the light finally started to flash.

Three days in Mange's shop had been quite okay. Washing the floor, running cables, and playing World of Warcraft whenever he got the chance. And five hundred tax-free kronor in his hand if the till could spare it, so it wasn't actually too bad.

The customers were pretty okay as well. Mostly a load of nerds who wanted advice about various gadgets, and seemed to look up to Mange as if he was some sort of holy guru.

Everywhere else Mangelito was just small fry, completely lost, but in the dark little shop he was clearly the Boss, the Geeks' very own Godfather, and he seemed to enjoy the role.

It was actually pretty cool, and he had to admit that he might have to reconsider his opinion of the Mangster. He'd actually managed to put together a pretty nice setup with both his job and his family.

But HP himself wasn't the nine-to-five type. Not your average loser who was going to be happy with any shitty McJob. He needed something more, something that all his efforts so far had failed to give him. A challenge, some excitement, and a bit of fucking action!

Really I should have been a cop. He grinned to himself as he headed west on the Goat's moped and felt the familiar feeling start to bubble up inside him. This could turn out to be pretty damn cool.

The official government plane landed on schedule and everything went according to plan. They had time for a quick coffee with two of the prime minister's regular protection team who had met them at Bromma, and they had agreed on their route and formation before it was time to glide in through the gates and cruise over toward the hangar.

The prime minister, his female assistant, and two bodyguards arrived with the plane. They switched quickly into the armored black BMW, then they were ready to set off toward his official residence in the Sager Palace. Rebecca and Kruse went first in the Volvo, then the two regular guards in a similar car, then the prime minister's vehicle, with Bengtsson and Dejan bringing up the rear in their Suburban.

Flashing lights on and full speed toward the city center.

Hornsgatan, heading west, a bit of weaving around the red lights at Hornstull, then out across the Western Bridge. In contrast to his previous triumph, for the time being he had very few details about this assignment. But he wasn't too worried about that. NK and Birkagatan had also been on a need-to-know basis right up until things kicked off. All he needed to know was where he was going and that whatever awaited him there was going to give him three thousand fucking points!

If you added those to the five thousand two hundred he'd already scraped together, that was enough to take him past number fifty-eight and into the lead, that very evening!

The thought made him so ecstatic that for a moment he almost swerved into the railing of the bridge.

"Ladies and gentlemen, we have a new leader, number one twenty-eight!"

His comments section would easily stretch to more than ten pages.

HP, Master of the Game.

All he needed to do was get to Lindhagensplan and wait for new instructions.

His cock was already at half-mast.

He could hardly wait!

. . .

Ulvsundavägen was behind them now, after a bit of neat zigzagging from Kruse at the red lights at the junction with Drottningholmsvägen, where the ordinary, law-abiding Svenssons had moved their cars out of the way of the caravan's flashing blue lights. They were heading toward the Traneberg Bridge, then on to Lindhagensplan.

She glanced at the time, 21:12. If everything carried on like this they'd make their delivery at Sager and be done by half past nine. That would give her plenty of time for a session in the gym once the debriefing was over. The boys would probably want to play indoor hockey as usual. It was probably best to join in, even if she didn't really like ball games. Important to be one of the team.

Okay, he was in position right at the designated time, 21:12.

The western side of Lindhagensplan, on the bridge crossing Drottningholmsvägen, exactly according to instructions.

There was even a little map attached, which was handy, seeing as there were several overpasses to choose from, and he had driven around a bit before he found the right place.

The moped was perfect for stuff like this, you could just swing around and ride back along the hard shoulder against the flow of traffic if you made a mistake. Okay, so the law-abiding Svenssons in their little socialist boxes blew their horns and flashed their lights at him, but you had to ignore that.

He was sitting astride the moped waiting for instructions. A few meters below him the cars flew past heading into the city. In front of him, high above his head, hung the double bridges of the Essinge expressway. The noise of the traffic practically drowned out the moped's engine when it was idling.

So what happened now?

The LED light started to flash.

They were approaching the end of the bridge. Kruse was driving, seeing as he had been in the service much longer and therefore got first dibs on the jobs.

Rebecca was sitting beside him in the passenger seat. She glanced up at the extra rearview mirror on her side. The entire convoy was driving in close formation down the left-hand lane, at a speed of about a hundred, exactly as agreed. No problems.

"Crossing Traneberg, heading for Lindhagen," she reported to Control over the radio.

If she looked out to the right and tried to see past the trees, she'd soon be able to see her own little house up ahead.

The overpasses of the Essinge expressway were coming closer and closer. She squinted at their dark silhouette. It almost looked like there was someone standing up there on one of the bridges.

"*Pull up the bag,*" the message said.

So he did.

A blue-striped PE bag, it turned out. Tied to the outside of the railing, and almost exactly the same as one he had made many years ago in sewing class. Even the color of the cord was the same.

It was a pretty neat coincidence, really. He seemed to remember that his was hanging in his wardrobe at home.

Weren't his old football boots still in it? They must have been there a couple of years by now; he could hardly remember the last time he used them. Maybe the summer before last, something like that?

He felt the bag. It was heavy. He undid it, full of anticipation.

Yes, there was definitely someone standing on one of the lower bridges, and there certainly shouldn't be.

They were all expressways up there, no pedestrians allowed. Kruse didn't seem to have noticed anything, but he was mainly concentrating on the traffic in the right-hand lane. She raised the microphone to her mouth but stopped halfway. The bridge was approaching fast and she could see the person up there moving. Her instincts were screaming at her to sound the alarm, order the convoy to halt, and turn back.

But what if she was wrong?

A stone, a big one, maybe three or four kilos. Sharp edges too. Black, with a slightly rough surface that felt warm against the palm of his hand. A patch of something sticky almost made his fingers slip. He moved the stone to his left hand and wiped whatever it was off on his jeans.

His heart was pounding in his chest. So what happened now?

When he saw the blue lights coming toward him along Drottningholmsvägen he began to realize what this was all about. With the stone back in his right hand he leaned cautiously over the railing.

The light flashed again. He had guessed right.

Lights, camera, action, he thought excitedly before he dropped the stone from the bridge.

Either Kruse didn't hear her or else the warning came so late that he simply didn't have time to react. Because suddenly there was a crash as if lightning had struck the windshield and the world ahead of them turned milky white.

Glass sprayed into the car and she felt her face stinging.

"Shit!" she heard Kruse roar. "Fucking shit!"

He rammed his heavy foot instinctively on the brake pedal and wrested the car to the right so they wouldn't be hit by the escort vehicle behind them.

By the smallest possible margin the car behind them got past, but Kruse's swerve was so sudden that they slammed into the concrete barrier on the right-hand side. The Volvo rebounded out into the left-hand lane, where the prime minister's BMW was just maneuvering to get past. The driver swerved wildly to the left to escape what looked like an unavoidable collision.

"Shit," Rebecca managed to echo before Kruse did what any bodyguard in his position would have done. He let go of the brake, put his foot down on the accelerator, and wrenched the wheel to the right. The front wheels regained their grip on the road and they shot away from the prime minister's car like an arrow, missing the metal arrow marking the turnoff to Lindhagensplan by a hair's breadth, and plowed straight into the railing facing the park.

A violent smash, then a feeling of floating. A second of weightlessness when all that could be heard was the roaring engine.

Then everything went black.

. . .

What a fucking circus!

The stone hit perfectly in the middle of the windshield and when he looked over the other side of the bridge he saw the Volvo swerving violently between the lanes. It almost rammed another car with a blue light on in the left-hand lane, but suddenly lurched sharply to the right before shooting through the side railing and carrying on, rolling wildly, into the park, where it finally came to rest upside down.

He quickly kicked the moped into gear and crossed the traffic lane, then, stopping on the other side of the bridge, he pulled off the camera and zoomed in on the smoking wreck in among the trees. The Volvo was completely still now and there was no sign of movement from it at all.

But who the hell cared about that!

Because now he was the new number one, the Master of the Game!

Mission accomplished, he thought ecstatically. Three thousand fucking points and almost twenty-five thousand nice new kronor in his account, apart from anything else. He wondered who the hell had been in that car? At a guess, some big shot, but who? Oh well, he'd probably find out as soon as he switched on his computer. Now he had to get home and gratefully accept the adoration of the masses!

He put the moped into gear, glanced quickly over his shoulder, and did a terrific start out into the traffic lane.

The collision was so hard that he bounced back into the railing. The front wheel, which had suddenly been twisted into a shapeless lump, locked instantly, and he just had time to put his hands up to protect himself as he flew headfirst onto the tarmac.

He felt his palms scraping over the road surface and a burning pain shot up one arm before the rest of his body hit the ground. The helmet made a cracking sound as it shattered; then the air was knocked out of him.

But he didn't lose consciousness, at least not properly. He could hear voices and screaming, probably from the stupid fucker who had driven into him. Where the hell had he come from, anyway?

Got to get up, he thought. *Got to get away from here.*

But his body wouldn't obey. He couldn't actually even lift his head from the tarmac. All of a sudden his skull seemed full of cement, impossible to move or even turn. Was he paralyzed? A cripple?

Fuck, fuck, fuck!!!

Slowly he tried to open his mouth to get a bit of air. But his head was full of porridge and everything seemed to be happening in ultrarapid. The voices were coming closer, getting clearer.

". . . bastard . . . threw something . . . the Volvo down there . . . called the cops."

Suddenly his paralysis eased and he managed to take a deep breath.

The pain came from out of nowhere. His head, his legs, and his hands more than anything else hurt like hell, but the sensation actually made him feel better. If you could feel things, you weren't paralyzed, that seemed fairly logical.

His vision cleared slightly and from the corner of his eye he could see several dark silhouettes leaning over him.

From somewhere in the distance there was the sound of sirens.

He tried to get up and this time it went a bit better. He raised one hand toward the men to get some help, but none of them moved. Then he saw a flashing blue light right along-side him.

"It was him!" one of the shadowy figures yelled, but HP was still having trouble focusing enough to see which one. With an effort he heaved himself up into a kneeling position. Then someone suddenly grabbed hold of his arms and a moment later he was lying across a car bonnet.

"Take it easy, boy," an authoritative voice said in one ear.

"You're under arrest on suspicion of attempted murder."

And for a few seconds he thought he was eighteen again.

8 | HARDBALL

FLASHING BLUE LIGHTS, she remembered them. But that was pretty much it.

Rebecca had only vague memories of the rescue operation. She had almost no recollection of the early part of it, when the firemen rolled the car the right way up and cut the roof off to get them out. She remembered fragments of a trip in an ambulance, probably to St. Göran's Hospital. An oxygen mask over her nose and mouth, a plastic collar around her neck. Pain in her head, chest, and face. People in white-and-green coats. The sounds of running and urgent shouting. Occasionally she thought she could hear familiar voices among all the strangers, but she wasn't altogether sure. She made an effort to hear what they were saying, but no matter how hard she tried the words merged together into a single monotonous mumble. The world didn't start to get clearer until she was eventually wheeled into a room in the hospital, whichever one it was, and the doctor started to examine her.

"Lucky" was one of the first things that sank in properly. "You were lucky, Rebecca."

She didn't really understand what he meant.

What did he mean, lucky?

Someone had smashed their windshield and it was only thanks to Kruse's decisive action that they hadn't collided with the prime minister's car and everything hadn't gone completely to hell.

Then they had crashed through the barrier and the car was so badly wrecked that they had to be cut out of it.

So exactly what did this idiot mean when he said she was lucky?

"Concussion, but fairly mild, a couple of minor cuts to your scalp and face that will need stitches, and a few cracked ribs. But that's pretty much it. Considering what happened, you were lucky," he concluded, simultaneously answering her question.

"My partner?" she managed to say, although it felt like her head and mouth were full of cotton wool. "How's Kruse?"

"I'm afraid he wasn't quite as fortunate. Sometimes it isn't always a good thing to be big and heavy, and car accidents are precisely one such occasion."

The doctor adjusted his glasses and gave her a knowing look. Her head suddenly felt like it was about to burst and for a moment she considered pulling out her Sig and asking him again, considerably less politely this time. But she bit her tongue and waited patiently for the answer.

He leafed through his notes.

"Head injuries, broken arms and ribs are what we've got so far. Your partner is still in intensive care. It looks as if the roof crumpled mainly on his side."

He looked up and smiled.

"Like I said, you were . . ."

"Lucky," she interrupted, and suppressed another urge to draw her gun, this time to blow his head off.

. . .

Flashing blue lights, handcuffs, then the backseat of an unmarked police car. They must have been very close by.

He instantly remembered that a lot of cops used to stop
for coffee at the Shell garage not far away.

Typical of his miserable fucking luck!

Both of the plainclothes officers were thickset men, with
shaved heads and bull necks. One of them beside him, the
other at the wheel.

"So, you're the sort who throws stones at police cars, are
you?" gorilla number one said as soon as they had set off.

HP didn't answer; now if ever was a time to keep quiet.
His head ached and he felt like he was going to be sick. The
pain in his lower arm was hardly helped by the fact that his
hands had been bent up behind his back.

The cops grinned and exchanged knowing glances in the
rearview mirror. They turned off the expressway and headed
into Kungsholmen. Next stop, Police Headquarters in Kronoberg.

Balls!

Everything had gone completely to hell. He'd been careless
and not looked around properly. And had missed that damn
idiot who rammed him. How stupid could you be?

He gulped a couple of time to suppress the urge to throw
up. Now he had to keep quiet and ask for a lawyer as quickly
as possible. He knew the routine. There was no point talking
to the orcs in the car, they didn't have any say in anything.

"What's the matter, can't you speak?" gorilla number one
said in a mocking tone that for some reason made HP feel
even more uneasy.

He stuck to his strategy and kept quiet.

"No problem, boy." The cop chuckled, giving his colleague in the driver's seat another look.

The blow came out of nowhere; it must have been a left hook and he had no way of defending himself. *Wham*, right on his cheekbone, and his head thudded into the side window.

"What the f . . . !" he managed to say before the next blow struck. A right hook this time, straight at the middle of his face, and he felt his nose crack.

This can't be happening, this only happens in films! he managed to think before the third punch blurred his vision.

When he came around they were already down in the garage, and they were dragging him out of the car. Metal doors, a lift, a couple of blue shirts hurrying past, then a long, brightly lit corridor with beige plastic flooring. Doors, voices, a lot of rushing about, and finally a small interview room.

The handcuffs were removed and the belongings that they had taken off him when he was arrested were emptied onto the table. House keys, ID card, and a few crumpled twenty-kronor notes, as well as the cell, of course.

Blood was trickling from his nose and one of the gorillas tossed him a paper tissue before he sat down on a chair opposite.

HP managed to pull himself together and regain some of his wounded self-confidence.

"I want a lawyer," he said, but the last word sounded more like "doyer" because of his swollen nose.

The gorilla just grinned.

"Didn't you hear, I want a lawyer," HP repeated, this time slightly less nasal as he rubbed the red marks on his wrists.

The gorilla stood up quickly and HP twitched instinctively

on his chair. The cop saw his fear and grinned. He wagged a fat, hairy index finger toward HP.

"I think you should shut up, my friend," he said exaggeratedly slowly, and there was no mistaking the underlying threat.

HP decided to heed his advice and revert to his original plan. Besides, the lead interviewer ought to be along soon; then all this shit would be over.

Sure enough, the door opened a couple of minutes later and another man came in, also in plainclothes. This one was shorter, wore glasses, and was considerably skinnier than the two gorillas, and it was immediately obvious which one was in charge.

He glanced at HP's swollen face and then gave the hairiest ape a disdainful look.

"You can go now, Wiklander. Haven't you and Molnar here got a report to write up?"

The gorilla muttered something but went out at once, giving HP the evil eye on the way.

HP nodded happily. This guy was more to his taste.

"Bolin, duty officer," he said by way of introduction. "And you're Henrik Pettersson, known as HP, is that right?"

HP nodded again.

"I'm going to turn on the tape recorder now and we'll do the introductions once more, but this time I want you to answer verbally, have you got that?"

HP shrugged. He wasn't planning on saying more than just one sentence.

Bolin started the tape recorder that was on the table in front of them.

"Interview with Henrik 'HP' Pettersson concerning suspicion of attempted murder and grievous bodily harm against a public official at the junction of Drottningholmsvägen and the Essinge expressway. Lead interviewer Detective Inspector Bolin, interview commenced at 23:12. Right, Henrik, can you tell me your response to our suspicions?"

HP sighed. Now that the apes had been driven out, the normal order was restored, and he was back on familiar territory. His head was starting to clear and the sharp pain in his arm had shifted to a rumbling ache.

"I'm innocent and want a lawyer present," he said as clearly as he could, leaning over toward the tape recorder just to make sure that it didn't miss a single syllable. "I want a lawyer, and I want to report that I was beaten up by that gorilla, Wiklander, is that his name?"

He rubbed his swollen nose demonstratively. He still had some tissue paper stuffed up one nostril. Bolin gave no sign of having understood HP's request.

"A lawyer, I said," HP clarified once more, seeing as what he had said evidently hadn't sunk in. Were all cops this slow?

Bright spark Bolin was still just staring at him across the table. Then the police officer slowly smiled and there was something about that reptilian smile that scared HP considerably more than the two trolls in the car had managed to do. He suddenly remembered a documentary he had seen about poisonous snakes on Discovery. How they sometimes settled down quite coolly to wait once they had bitten their prey as it used up the last of its energy in a meaningless attempt to escape.

He shivered. Bolin leaned forward slowly and switched off the tape recorder.

"Listen carefully now, Pettersson," he said in a low voice. "You don't seem to appreciate exactly how bad your situation is right now, so let me explain. You rode a moped to Lindha-

gensplan, stopped on the overpass above Drottningholmsvägen, and from a PE bag clearly marked with your name you
pulled out a stone, which you then threw at the windshield of
a police car passing below. Both police officers are now in St.
Göran's, one of them in a pretty bad way, so with a bit of luck
you may have graduated to cop killer before the night is over,"
he concluded with another of his unnerving snake smiles.

HP had turned pale, but he continued to stay quiet.

Oh yes, he'd realized that he'd hit a police car; the flashing blue light had been a bit of a giveaway even before he
threw the stone. What the hell, did they think he was stupid
or something? But on the other hand, he hadn't really given
much thought to the consequences, but so what?

If you were a cop, you had to put up with a few risks; that
much was obvious from the papers. Besides, it was hardly his
fault that they were driving so fast, was it? Anyway, wasn't the
speed limit seventy along there? The Volvo must have been
doing a ton, so in a way it was the cops' own fault that things
turned out so badly, wasn't it? He glanced at the cell phone on
the table just off to one side in front of him. The screen was
facing up and he was well aware of what it said on the other
side. Number one hundred and twenty-eight, one of the chosen ones, that was who he was, and rule number one applied,
no matter what world you moved in.

But what was it Bolin had said about the PE bag, he had
almost missed that. His name? Bolin must have read his mind,
because out of nowhere he conjured up the striped bag and
tossed in on the table.

For a couple of seconds HP just stared at it, then curiosity
got the better of him. He opened the bag. It was empty, apart
from a bit of dirt.

Suddenly he felt the hairs on the back of his neck stand up. There, on the inside of the lining, was a bit of fabric he'd almost forgotten. A scrap of cloth that his mom had sewn in during the short period when she was actually his mom and not just Maj Britt the invalid and drunk. A printed tag you could order through school from some company, the sort all well-meaning mothers sewed into all their kids' stuff so that it wouldn't get lost. All mothers except his, because Mom had been replaced more and more by Maj Britt, and this bag was the only thing she ever managed to sew a name tag into, the bag he himself had made in sewing class.

"*Property of Henrik Pettersson 08-6636615*," it said in blue lettering.

HP went icy cold. The last time he had seen the bag it had been hanging in the wardrobe in his bedroom; he was absolutely certain of that.

"In other words, you're not exactly the smartest criminal I've ever come across," Bolin declared, interrupting his train of thought. "Besides, we've got the stone and it contains two perfect fingerprints in two-stroke oil, and we're convinced they're going to match yours."

He leaned forward toward the deathly pale HP.

"So the way I see it, you're pretty much in the frame for this, my dear Henrik. Is there anything you'd like to say about it?" he concluded, then switched on the tape recorder again.

HP's head was spinning.

Who the hell had been in his flat?

Why had someone stolen the bag and hung it up on the bridge?

The car that had rammed him had appeared out of nowhere, almost as if it had been sitting just around the bend waiting for him. And it had hit the moped just enough for the cops to be able to pick him up.

But who would want to frame him that badly? Okay, he had a few enemies, but no one in that league. So who could it be? Number fifty-eight?

What if Mr. Five-Eight was Swedish and had managed to work out who it was coming up fast behind him on the league table? And sabotaged the whole thing on purpose?

No, that sounded too ridiculous . . .

His head was aching from the collision, the punches, and all the shit that was flying around inside it. He couldn't make sense of any of this, at least not right now.

He glanced over at the mobile again and decided to stick to rule number one, keep quiet.

"I have no comment to make, and, like I said a few moments ago, I want a lawyer," he repeated, but this time his voice didn't sound quite so confident.

Bolin sighed and slowly switched off the tape recorder again.

"If you like, Pettersson, obviously that's within your rights. There's the phone, with the phone book next to it. I'll be back in ten minutes."

He gestured toward a small telephone table in the corner of the room, and stood up to go.

"You're damn lucky that Officer Normén got away with minor injuries," he added as he got to the door. "There's only one thing us cops hate more than a cop killer, and that's someone who kills female cops."

Something suddenly clicked inside HP and he could almost feel the blood rushing from his head.

"H-hang on!" he called to Bolin, who was on the point of closing the door.

"What did you say the officer was called, the woman . . . the one who got hurt?"

"Normén," Bolin said drily. "Rebecca Normén."

Fuck, fuck, fuck!!! a little voice in HP's skull screamed.

Twelve stitches in total. Four in one cut, five in the other, and a few single ones on her face.

Rebecca looked at herself in the little mirror above the washbasin in the examination room. Two white Band-Aids on her head. A few bits of surgical tape elsewhere, a faint bruise on one cheek, and bloodshot eyes from the powder on the air bag.

Add a bit of nausea, a headache, and a gnawing pain in her chest and the picture of her injuries was complete.

Kruse was in a worse state. He was still in intensive care and, according to Vahtola, who had looked in a while ago, they were going to be flying his wife up the next day.

And all because of her. She'd been sitting in the passenger seat—and she should have sounded the alarm. She should have listened to her instincts and ordered the convoy to stop at once and retreat. But instead she had hesitated. She had wasted a couple of absolutely vital seconds on worrying about making a mistake instead of focusing on doing the right thing. Kruse had managed to save the day by his own actions, but he had also had to pay the price for her mistake.

Rebecca mechanically gathered together her things—the blue bulletproof vest that had probably saved her ribs, the baton and radio that they took from her before she was put on the stretcher.

A patrol car was waiting outside to drive her home. The debriefing could wait until the morning, Runeberg had decided. That suited her fine. She wanted to go home, take a couple of the knockout pills she had been given, and just sleep for a day or so.

Just as she was taking a last look around the room to make sure she'd got everything her cell phone rang. Number withheld, she noted with a frown.

"This is Rebecca," she said with one hand on the door handle.

"Becca?" the voice at the other end said, and she stopped.

"Becca, it's me . . ."

"I can't talk right now," she said unnecessarily abruptly. "Can I call you back tomorrow instead?" She tried to compensate by sounding more friendly.

"Er, sure, I just wanted to check that you're . . . okay?"

"What d'you mean?" she replied, and somewhere inside her his tone of voice was setting off alarm bells.

"Er . . ." A few moments of silence followed, but she chose not to fill them. ". . . don't really know how to say this."

"But?" she cut him off, as her suspicions grew stronger and stronger.

"That business . . . out at Lindhagensplan . . . Well . . . that wasn't supposed to happen, or, well . . . it was, but it wasn't supposed to be you. I didn't know it was you, Becca!"

The words came in bursts and she heard how his voice rose to a falsetto toward the end. Suddenly she felt utterly exhausted, as if her legs could no longer hold her. Slowly she went back inside the examination room and sank down on the trolley she had only just got up from.

"Okay, let's take this from the start, please," she said, as calmly as she could while she tried to take in what he'd just said.

"It wasn't really serious, sort of a game, I suppose. A game that went a bit wrong."

"A game, you say."

Her voice sounded tired, but in spite of that he couldn't mistake how angry she was.

"Yeah . . ." he replied, aware of how lame it sounded.

"So you were playing a game, and that's why my partner's in intensive care, is that a reasonable summary of the situation?"

She sounded more angry now, as if she'd already got over the initial shock.

"Well, that wasn't supposed to happen, like I said. Someone getting hurt, I mean . . . It's sort of like an elaborate joke, I suppose."

His voice was pleading, almost whiney.

"A joke? Are you making fun of me? Are you completely stupid? For God's sake, you're over thirty and you're still playing your way through life, you don't give a fuck and you let everyone else pay for it! Only this time it all went to hell, or have I got that wrong?"

He didn't answer. On the rare occasions when she swore he'd learned it was best to keep quiet.

"Well, now you know that I'm okay. Where are you now?"

The question was unnecessary, really. She already knew the answer. Why else would he have called her?

All that nonsense about whether she was okay was just one of his usual smoke screens. The cavalry to the rescue, even though what she most felt like doing was ripping his stupid immature fucking head off.

"Kronoberg," he muttered.

She rested her head on her free hand.

"Okay," she sighed after composing herself for a few seconds. "This is what we're going to do ..."

Bolin came back after ten minutes exactly.

"Well, is a lawyer coming?"

HP shook his head.

"I thought about it, but I don't need one," he muttered, looking down at the table.

"Splendid." Bolin nodded and switched on the tape-recorder.

"Interview recommenced at 23:43 after Pettersson declined the offer of a lawyer. Is that correct, Pettersson?"

HP muttered in agreement, but Bolin forced him to repeat himself.

"Yes, that's correct."

"Okay, Pettersson, how about taking it right from the start?"

HP took a deep breath and glanced at the cell phone.

"Tell them everything," she had said, and she was usually right. He almost always did as she said, at least when it was about something important, and she'd always tried to protect him, watched his back ...

To hell with rule number one, in other words. Blood was thicker than water, after all.

"It all started when I found a cell phone on the train ..."

"Duty custody desk."

"Hello, this is Police Inspector Rebecca Normén. My partner Kruse and I were the ones who went off the Drottningholm road earlier this evening," she said, as calmly as she could.

"Inspector Normén, good to hear your voice. We've been pretty worried about you, I can tell you. Are you okay?"

Rebecca smiled. She hadn't recognized the voice at the other end of the line, but now there was no doubt. Her old boss was on duty in Kronoberg tonight, which was one bit of positive news.

"Hi, Mulle. Thanks, I'm okay, just a few bruises and one hell of a headache, but that's about it. I'm afraid Kruse didn't get off so lightly."

"Yes, so I heard; we had three cars there when the fire brigade were cutting you free, and the boys said Kruse didn't look too good," he replied in a more serious tone of voice. "We'll be keeping everything crossed for him. Did you want anything in particular, or were you just calling to reassure your old boss?"

"Well, there's something I could do with some help with, Mulle, and it's all a bit sensitive."

"Okay, let's hear it!" he replied encouragingly, and she took a deep breath before she went on.

"The man you've arrested, Henrik Pettersson . . . He's my little brother."

He'd done exactly as she said. Told Bolin everything. Or almost everything . . .

For obvious reasons he'd decided to leave out the business with the M84 fireworks down in Kungsträdgården, but apart from that he'd explained everything, even about the door in Birkagatan.

It had actually felt pretty good.

Bolin had mostly just nodded, occasionally interrupting to ask a question, but mainly he had kept quiet.

When they were finished it was past one o'clock in the morning.

Bolin read the time to the tape recorder, then switched it off.

"That's some story, Pettersson," he said as he stood up. "We'll have to double-check a few things, then we'll need to talk again tomorrow. Someone will be with you shortly to take you to a cell."

HP merely nodded in reply. He could handle a night in the cells, no problem.

Been there, done that . . .

But now fifteen minutes had passed since Bolin had left, and he was starting to get impatient.

Where the hell was the custody officer?

He was tired, his head and nose ached, and his mouth was completely dry.

Two more minutes, he thought, then he'd stick his head out into the corridor and make some noise.

He realized almost incidentally that his cell was still sitting on the table among his other belongings.

The little LED light was flashing red.

"Okay, you've lost me now, Normén. Did you say we've arrested your little brother?"

"I'm afraid so, Mulle. Henrik's a decent lad but he's incredibly immature, and he's something of a magnet for trouble, if you get what I mean?"

He chuckled in response.

"The black sheep of the family, then?"

"Exactly," she lied.

"Do you know what he's been arrested for? We've got quite a few immature trouble magnets to choose from up here this evening."

She frowned. Mulle may be getting close to retirement, but there wasn't normally anything wrong with his memory.

"His name's Henrik Pettersson and he's been arrested for throwing that stone at me and Kruse."

The line went silent for a few moments.

"I'm sorry, Normén, but as far as I know no one's been arrested for the attack on the pair of you. Every patrol car in the district's out looking for the bastard; they're still hard at it on channel sixteen, so I'd definitely have heard if they'd got him. And we haven't got anyone by the name of Pettersson, according to the book, so your brother must have been playing some sort of prank on you, I'm afraid."

Suddenly she couldn't think at all, then she felt a wave of fury bubbling up.

What the hell was Henke really up to?

The light was still flashing angrily at him and for some reason, probably just habit, he grabbed it and his other belongings when he stood up to go over to the door.

He pressed the handle.

The door was unlocked.

He opened it and to his surprise found himself staring out into a dark corridor.

"Hello!" he called in a trembling voice. "Is there anyone there?"

No answer.

Suddenly he felt scared. Considerably more scared than

he had been when the gorillas had beaten him up in the car or when Bolin had flashed him his reptilian smile a couple of hours before. Because this was the fucking twilight zone!

The corridor was completely deserted, not a sound to be heard anywhere, and all he could see was a row of closed doors the same as the one he had just opened. At the far end a green-and-white emergency exit sign flickered irregularly. The flickering reminded him of the cell. He held it up and touched the screen, and even though he already had a vague suspicion what the message had to say, his stomach still clenched in terror.

> Player 128
> You have broken Rule Number One and are therefore
> expelled from the Game with immediate effect!
> Your points and any remaining pecuniary
> rewards are hereby withdrawn.
> Please leave the phone on the premises and refrain
> from talking to anyone about the Game in the future.
> Continued violation of Rule Number One
> will have serious consequences!
> *The Game Master*

With an audible click the light in the room behind him went out.

Home, she thought.

She just wanted to go home. Take her clothes off, grab a quick shower to get rid of the sweat and blood. A handful of pills and then sleep, wonderful fucking sleep.

But it didn't turn out to be that easy. And of course it was Henke's fault.

She'd tried his home number, but the line had been disconnected. The same thing with the two most recent cell numbers he'd given her. She couldn't get hold of her idiot little brother, which only made her more angry.

What had he actually said?

She tried to remember what his exact words had been, but it was practically impossible. He had at any rate confessed to throwing the stone. But how the hell could he have known that she was in the car? Was this some sort of elaborate, delayed revenge?

No, that sounded crazy, she understood that as soon as she had thought it. No matter how messed up her and Henke's relationship was, he'd never set out to hurt her on purpose. So what was this all about?

Why had he thrown a stone at their car, or at least claimed to have done so?

"Kronoberg," he had said, but that had turned out not to be true. Just to be sure she had called Södermalm and the Western District too, but neither of them had a Henrik "HP" Pettersson in custody.

Had he been lying to her?

He could very well have been; that had happened far too many times in the past. But there was something about his voice, something . . . she realized it sounded stupid to use the word when you were talking about Henke, but nonetheless: something . . . honest. As if he really believed he'd been arrested. She was aware that she wouldn't get any answers to any of her questions until she managed to get hold of her little brother.

The question was: Where the hell was he?

• • •

He ran. First in sheer panic. Along the dark corridor, toward the door—although he was prepared to bet it was locked. Then relief as it opened onto a stairwell.

Stone steps down into the darkness, more unlit corridors along the way. His steps echoed on the concrete walls. Finally, at last, a way out.

Damp night air hit him as he crossed the street to get as far away as possible from that corridor. A quick glance over his shoulder, then one more just to be sure.

Suddenly he felt soft grass under his feet and it took him a few seconds to get his bearings. Large black trees splayed toward the night sky above him, and ahead of him was an iron railing and some unkempt gravestones.

Kronoberg Park, close to the Jewish Cemetery. Only a block or so from where he'd thought he was to start with.

His legs were working by themselves. Up the hill, through the park, and finally out onto Polhemsgatan. The most western of the police's three copper-colored towers in front of him. For a few moments he considered carrying on to the entrance down on Kungsholmsgatan, knocking on the copper doorway, and handing himself in. But before he'd had time to make a decision his legs were already carrying him out onto Fleminggatan, then right, toward the city center.

His head was spinning as his feet drummed on the tarmac.

Tramp, tramp, tramp.

The monotonous sound calmed him down a bit. The whirlpool in his head gradually slowed down and the panic slowly released its iron grip of his chest.

Tramp, tramp, tramp.

A setup!

Tramp, tramp, tramp.

The whole thing had been a fucking setup!

Tramp, tramp, tramp.

The more he thought about it, the better he understood how it all fitted together. He had thought that three thousand points was a bit too much just for throwing a stone at a car, even if it was a cop car.

And he'd been right!

The stone, the car, the cops—all of that had been secondary, a sort of prologue. The assignment, the real assignment, had been all about him. A sort of evaluation, really.

Or a test . . .

"Only a very small number of people are qualified for this level . . ."

They had tested him to see if he had what it took. If he could handle the storms up on the summit.

And the result, ladies and gentlemen?

He had messed up.

Big-time!

9 | I LOST THE GAME

"OKAY, REBECCA, WE'VE been through the details a couple of times now, but could you say a bit more about how you feel?"

She almost had to stop herself from looking up at the ceiling.

How she felt?

Standard-issue psychobabble of the sort she'd heard so many times before, and it had never led to anything positive.

Did he really want to hear the truth?

That she felt like shit?

And even if she was entirely honest and told her whole story, and turned her feelings, thoughts, and reflections inside out—was that going to help? Could it make everything undone? Hardly, so she'd have to pull out the tried-and-tested mask.

"Thanks, but I feel fine, actually," she managed to say, with something that was supposed to be a helpful smile.

She glanced at the time, twenty minutes or so since they started the debriefing talk, and she'd be lucky to get away with anything less than half an hour.

Rebecca herself had insisted on seeing Anderberg at eight o'clock. She wanted to get the conversation out of the way, so she could head over to Maria Trappgränd before her good-for-nothing brother had even opened his eyes . . .

Anderberg sighed and leafed through his notes.

"Have you had a chance to talk to anyone else about what happened? Friends, family, colleagues, maybe?"

He looked at her over his narrow glasses.

"No," she said, slightly too abruptly, then realized her mistake at once and tried to correct herself. "No, I haven't had time to talk to anyone yet, it only happened last night, after all, and I wanted to see you first."

A little smile to top off the lie ought to do the trick?

Nice save! Anderberg was thinking.

A smart girl, this one, but not smart enough to catch him out, at least not the day after such a traumatic experience as the one she'd just been through. A car crash and her partner in intensive care, that wasn't the sort of thing you could just shrug off.

This was the second time in just a couple of weeks that they'd met, and his earlier concerns about Rebecca Normén hadn't exactly decreased. As far as he understood it, she had once again acted in an irreproachable manner, but this time she didn't seem anywhere near as composed.

In contrast to their previous conversation, this time she sounded mostly like a robot, as though she were on autopilot. That wasn't a good sign. If he couldn't get her to open up and let go of some of her feelings now, things would look very different and his report would be considerably easier to write. He'd seen tougher officers than her snap as a result of unprocessed experiences, and he had no desire to add Rebecca's name to that tragic list.

"But you do have someone you can talk to if you need to? Sometimes it can take a few days after an experience like this, then suddenly a whole load of things come bubbling up. You can have my number, of course, but it's important to be able to talk to other people, above all family and friends," he went on.

She nodded mutely.

"But you don't have any problems on that front?"

He looked at her again over the rims of his glasses.

She took a deep breath and made an effort to sound composed.

"No, I don't."

Anderberg nodded and leafed through his notes again.

"You've got a Henrik Pettersson listed as your closest relative. Is that your partner?"

She was on the point of jumping out of her chair. Anderberg wasn't stupid, that much was clear.

A bit of harmless chat, and then bang, straight to her weak point. Evidently her usual defense wasn't working, so she had to choose her words carefully . . .

Another deep breath. *Careful now, Normén!*

"Henrik's my brother. Normén was Mom's maiden name; I took it after . . ." She bit her lip involuntarily.

". . . she passed away," she concluded, with what she hoped was a sad smile.

The psychologist nodded.

"So you're close to your brother?"

"Not anymore," slipped out of her mouth.

Shit, the lack of sleep and headache were taking their toll, and Anderberg wasn't just anyone. Today it was unusually difficult to keep her guard up, mainly because in her mind she was already knocking on Henrik's door. She had to regroup and try a new tactic.

"Do you feel like talking about it?"

Anderberg had evidently caught a scent of something. She had to tread carefully now.

She shrugged to give herself a couple more seconds to think. What the hell could she say?

No, dear shrink, I don't feel like telling you about my useless petty-criminal little brother who doesn't give a shit about anything and wrecks everything he touches, but to whom I'm going to be in debt for the rest of my life.

"Things were pretty tough when we were growing up," she said instead, hoping that a few serious but now harmless confidences would throw him off track.

Anderberg nodded encouragingly, evidently interested.

"Well, to start with it was mainly Dad, I suppose. But after a while he dragged Mom down with him, you could say. Especially after she got ill."

She took a deep breath before going on.

"Dad was pretty unusual. He was quite a bit older than Mom when they got married. It was his flat and he already had his set routines. Everything had to be exactly the way he wanted, down to the smallest detail, and Dad would get furious about the tiniest things. A set of keys in the wrong place or a mark on the bathroom mirror were enough to set him off. When he was home the rest of us had to tiptoe around so as not to make him angry or upset. Henke, my little brother, is three years younger than me," she said.

"When things were bad at least we had each other. I used to protect him, comfort him, and take him out so that things could calm down. I suppose you could say we provided each other with a bit of stability."

She smiled unconsciously.

"I used to take him with me whenever I could, I didn't

want him to be left at home alone with Dad. You never knew
what might happen, and if anything did happen, for some
reason my little brother would always get the blame, maybe
because he was smallest and weakest. Dad didn't exactly hold
back, especially not after a few drinks, and even if Mom did
her best she never really dared to stand up to him and take our
side when there was trouble. She probably had to deal with
enough of his moods as it was . . . But Dad never laid a finger
on me, on the other hand. I was safe, somehow; men of his
generation didn't hit little girls, so maybe that's why I started
trying to protect Henke?" She shrugged her shoulders and
caught Anderberg's nod of encouragement.

He had evidently taken the bait. But to her surprise she
also discovered that she actually didn't mind going on . . .

"Henke was very patient, always tagging along, never com-
plaining, even if he mostly had to play girls' games. Sometimes
he got to be the doll while I and the other girls on the block
dressed him up. Mommy, Daddy, baby, and all that . . . All the
stuff we weren't getting at home."

She smiled again and looked down at her lap thoughtfully.

The psychologist didn't push her; he was actually looking
quite pleased.

It was ironic, really, that everything she had tried to hide so
far had turned into the perfect smoke screen now. A new line
of defense now that the old one seemed to have crumbled. She
hadn't talked about this for . . . well, it must be thirteen years
now, and it actually felt pretty good to let it out.

A quick glance at the time, twenty-five minutes done. Now
she just had to round this off and catch the southbound subway train. Get back into the saddle.

"But you've had less contact since you grew up?"

His tone was friendly, more supportive than questioning. She nodded in confirmation.

"Yes, I'm afraid we lost a bit of our connection when I moved out. Dad had died suddenly the previous year and Henke was sixteen by then, so it felt fairly safe to leave him with Mom. She was also quite ill by then and spent most of her time in bed. I'd met a boy and we moved in together. First love and all that."

She shrugged her shoulders in an effort to appear nonchalant.

"I suppose I'd been managing the household pretty much alone, and looking after Mom as well, so I thought it was Henke's turn to take more responsibility now that Dad was out of the picture . . . My boyfriend and I sorted out a flat for them on Södermalm, near Mariatorget. Less space and closer to the hospital. And visits from home help to make things easier. I was in love and I was in a hurry to get away, let go of the responsibility once and for all. I let myself get caught up in my relationship with Dag instead, and Henke probably felt a bit left out. Like I'd abandoned him. After all, he was used to having me there, the two of us against the world. And he didn't exactly get on with my boyfriend, so . . ."

She stopped herself. This was dangerous territory, best not to get tangled up in a load of unnecessary lies.

"In any case, it only lasted a couple of years; then Mom died of cancer. Henke's still living in the flat, but our relationship never really recovered . . . You could say that we're working on it . . ." she concluded with a settled expression.

Most of what she'd said was actually true. From a purely technical point of view, she hadn't actually lied, just withheld certain details. The question was whether the story held up?

Anderberg nodded in empathy, evidently happy with the confidences he had managed to elicit.

"So you still see each other, you and Henrik?"

"Of course," she replied, with a smile of relief. "I'm actually going to see him once we're done here."

. . . and I'm going to wring his bloody neck! she added silently to herself.

Whoever was ringing on his doorbell was a stubborn bastard. He'd tried pulling the pillow over his head, pretending he wasn't home so the fucker would go away. But oh no. The idiot out there was worse that any Jehovah's Witness. He or she was pressing the bell at painful, almost tortuous intervals, and had been doing so for at least ten minutes already. HP had had plenty of time to keep track.

First ten seconds of insistent ringing, *rrrrrrriiiiiiiiiinnnnnnnn-gggggggg!*

Then ten seconds' pause.

Then once more, *rrrrrrriiiiiiiiinnnnnnnnggggggggg!*

It was driving him mad. In the end he had no choice but to go and open up.

Red-faced and wearing just a pair of jogging pants that he fished up from a chair on the way, he angrily opened the door to give the bastard a piece of his mind. And a moment later, without him quite understanding what had happened, he was lying flat on his back on the hall rug.

Anderberg had bought her new defensive tactic, hook, line, and sinker . . . There was nothing that worked better with shrinks than a bit of tragic childhood. The psychiatrist had been overjoyed at the unexpected turn the conversation had taken. He had praised her honesty, called her a strong person, and agreed to let her return to duty the following week. A few days of rest would suit her fine, it would give her time to get a few little things sorted out . . .

It took her almost ten minutes to get him out of bed. It had been enough to open the letter box slightly and listen to the sounds in the flat to know that he was at home. Even if the bedroom was at the far end of the flat, the distance wasn't far enough for anyone to mistake the sound of snoring.

She'd used the tried-and-tested police tactic with the door-bell: ten seconds ringing, ten silence, then more ringing.

No one could put up with that for long.

She heard him come padding out into the hall and moved to the side to escape the peephole. As she had guessed, he was planning to throw the door open, and seeing as she was already holding the handle on the outside, it didn't take much to let him start to open it, then give it a serious tug from her side and send him lurching into the stairwell. Then, while he was still shocked and trying to regain his balance, all she had to do was shove him gently in the chest to send him flying back onto the hall rug.

A quick stride in and she could pull the door closed behind her.

Basic police tactics, exercise 1A.

"What the hell are you doing, Becca?" he whined when he had got to his feet and worked out who the intruder was.

"I could ask you the same thing," she said curtly and gestured toward the kitchen.

"Have you got any coffee in the flat, or do you spend all your money on other plant products?"

She'd already picked up the sweet smell of hash from the flat through the letter box.

He didn't answer, just walked out into the kitchen ahead of her and started rattling about in the sink.

"Will Nescafé do?" he muttered, waving a brown glass jar.

"Not really, but okay," she replied, shoving a pile of old *Metros* off one of the kitchen chairs.

She saw that the flat was a complete mess. Clothes and all sorts of other stuff piled up all over the place. Old newspapers, full ashtrays, and dirty glasses practically everywhere she looked. The walls and ceiling were yellow and greasy with cigarette smoke, and the overflowing plastic washing-up bowl in the sink told her it was at least a week since any dishes had been done. This was actually a couple of degrees worse than Mom's final days. It looked like a junkie's squat, with the possible exception of the flat screen television and the computer she had glimpsed in the living room.

How the hell could he live in this sort of filth?

"So . . . how are you, sis?" he asked feebly and considerably less grouchily as he served them instant coffee in mismatched mugs a few minutes later.

"Depends what you mean," she replied abruptly. "Life in general or my current state of health?"

"Er . . . you know." He nodded toward the Band-Aids on her head. "After the crash, I mean."

She sighed.

"Oh, I'm okay, thanks for asking. A bit of a headache, some minor bruising, and a few days off sick, but that's pretty much it."

"And your partner?"

Her eyes narrowed, but she couldn't miss the embarrassed tone of his question. He certainly seemed concerned, almost for real.

"A bit better, actually, I called this morning and he's making progress. Looks like he's going to make it."

"Thank God!"

Both his body language and tone of voice told her he really meant it.

The question was: Who was he most relieved for? She was pretty sure it wasn't Kruse.

"Okay, now we've got the pleasantries out of the way, maybe you'd like to explain to me what the hell happened yesterday? I called three different custody units for your sake and pretty much got laughed at each time."

He looked down at once.

"Nothing," he muttered.

"Nothing?" she repeated as sharply as she could.

"Just a drunken prank. I'd had a few beers at Kvarnen and then had a smoke round at a friend's. I saw it all on the news and heard it was you. When the others found out my sister was a cop they got me to call you and say I was the one who threw the stone and all that . . . They probably didn't think I'd actually do it. And I shouldn't have done.

"Sorry!" he added, looking up with a silly smile. "It was really stupid and immature, I know."

He threw his arms out in a disarming gesture.

She didn't answer, just looked at him for several seconds.

Henke had always been good at stretching the truth, making things up, telling white lies, or just lying through his teeth. First to their parents when they were little, mostly Dad, of course: *No, Daddy, I've got no idea where you left your wallet.* Then to his teachers at school, and eventually to the rest of the world, with one exception. It wasn't until after everything had happened and he had got out of prison that he started lying to her as well, which probably wasn't that strange if you thought about it. Most of the time he was very good at it, so good that it usually took her a few days to work out that she'd fallen for one of his lies again. But not today.

Today there was something missing.

To start with, this lie lacked the right details and was far too easy to demolish with a few facts, such as the fact that the Security Police would never release her name to the media, so he couldn't have known she was involved if he had seen anything about the crash on television. And she seriously doubted that a load of dopeheads would be sitting watching the news . . .

Oddly, his pathetic story only made her more annoyed. As if he were trying to blow her off and declare her an idiot at the same time. But then she realized that the details were of only secondary importance.

The main thing that was missing was his usual convincing smile and the glint in his eye that always made her believe him. His little brother look, she called it. Henke was nowhere near as self-confident as he usually was, she could see that clearly. That wasn't just morning tiredness visible in his face. He also had a black eye and a Band-Aid over his nose that she had seen but not really picked up on until she started looking at him properly.

He'd been beaten up, her police instincts told her, though the big sister in her hoped that he'd just fallen down some stairs. But whatever the cause was, Henke looked worn-out, shaken, almost as if he was seriously worried about something, which was unusual for him, to put it mildly. If she didn't know better, she'd almost say he was . . . frightened?

"Don't lie to me, Henrik," she said calmly, trying to catch his wandering gaze.

"What d'you mean? I'm not lying!" He held up his hands and ran through his usual routine. But it still just wasn't anywhere near as convincing as it usually was.

He could hear how unbelievable it all sounded. But what the fuck was he supposed to do? Tell the truth?

He'd broken rule number one once already, and twice in twenty-four hours would definitely not be a good idea.

Besides, what were the odds on her believing him?

I've been playing a reality game; they tested me and I lost. Sorry you got in the way, my bad!

As if!

It was fucking bad luck that he happened to hit her. Of all the cop cars in the city, he had to go and hit his sister's. What were the odds of that?

Actually . . .

Shit, he was stupid! What a complete fucking moron for not realizing . . . ! Luck had nothing to do with it!

He flew up from his chair, grabbed her arm, and tried to drag her toward the door.

"You have to go!" he muttered firmly, while she pulled against him.

"Let go, Henke, what are you on about now?"

"Please!" he begged when he realized she was far too strong and he'd never manage to get her out by force.

"Please, Becca, you have to go. Right now!"

She shook free of his grasp quite easily. What the hell was he up to now? He suddenly seemed to have gone mad. How much was he actually smoking these days, unless he'd moved on to something heavier?

"Please, Becca, I'm begging you. You have to leave. I'm in a bit of trouble but it'll get sorted, I promise. But if you don't go . . . they've got people . . . You have to leave, right away!"

He could hear how frightened he sounded, but made no effort to do anything about it. He really was terrified. They'd used her to test him. Manipulated him into hurting his own sister, the only person that he . . . well . . . cared about.

And just for fun!

The more he thought about it, the more obvious it seemed. Yesterday everything had been far too hazy, but now he'd had time to sleep on it, he understood what it was all about. What he really was. A pawn in the Game, no more, no less. A fucking pawn!

And there he was, imagining he was some sort of superstar, when he was just one of the crowd. A pathetic little pawn that could easily be sacrificed so the Game could move on. And that was exactly what they had done. The footage of him spilling his guts to Bolin the pretend cop were probably already out there.

We got this idiot to almost kill his sister, then confess everything to the boys in blue! Coldhearted bastards.

So what wouldn't they be capable of if he carried on breaking the rules? If, in spite of the warning, he didn't stick to rule number one?

"Please, Becca, please! You've got to go, right now!" he yelled.

. . .

Okay, at least he was being honest now, she could see that. And he was utterly terrified, but the question was: Why? Who was he in trouble with? She opened her mouth to ask, but he got there before her.

"You owe me, Becca," he said, more composed now, suddenly staring straight at her.

"You know why," he added, his heart sinking like a stone over the boundary he had crossed.

A few seconds later he heard the front door slam shut. For the first time in years he was close to . . .

Tears! That's what it felt like, as if she was close to tears. She hadn't cried since Mom's funeral.

Fucking bloody Henke!

Even back when it was all happening, she hadn't shed a single tear, but now she could feel them burning behind her eyes and she blinked hard to compose herself. She wasn't about to start crying now, that much was certain!

They had never properly talked through everything that happened out in Bagarmossen, the pair of them always tiptoeing around the subject, but now, out of nowhere, he had suddenly thrown it back in her face. Reminding her that her debt was in no way forgotten and that thirteen years was nowhere near long enough for things to have settled.

How could she have been stupid enough to think any different?

He was right, of course; it had been her fault but he had

taken the consequences. She was in his debt, and always would be.

Because she was a *"murdering little whore."*

Although it was ten o'clock, HP went back to bed and put his head between the pillows. He was tired, run-down, utterly exhausted, but he still couldn't get back to sleep.

Thoughts were rolling around his head like they were in that huge dryer down in the laundry room.

Slowly tumbling around and around.

The Game, the assignments, the list, the money, the whole business at Lindhagensplan, the pretend cops, his sister; then the dryer completed its cycle and he was back where he had started.

The Game.

They'd tricked him, made him think he was someone, only to pull the rug from under him. Bolin and the gorillas were probably just hired actors who had been following a script. Or, even worse: other players who had been given the job of breaking him! And they'd done a damn good job of that ... Christ, what a monumental fucking setup he'd fallen for!

The really sick thing was that even though he recognized that he'd been royally fucked up the ass, that he was the Game's very own little prison bitch, he still couldn't help toying with the thought ...

What if it could all be put right? Say sorry, make amends, and reinstate number 128?

Get back in the Game.

Even when the lights had gone out up there in the office and he had almost pissed himself, part of him had still refused to realize that it was finished, that he'd fucked up big-time. Presumably that was why he hadn't left the cell there.

Because he still had it, didn't he?

He had to get up and check.

Yes, the silver-colored little rectangle was still on the hall table where he had left it. The LED light was dark, which was only to be expected. He was now a nonperson.

Fredo-fucking-Corleone.

He hunted irritably through various jacket pockets and finally dug out a crumpled packet of Marlboros.

Sitting at the kitchen table he smoked three, one after the other, while the drying machine in his head carried on tumbling.

So what the hell was he going to do now?

He was woken up by a clatter from the letter box.

What the hell was the time?

The clock radio on the bedside table said 15:36. He'd been asleep most of the day.

The dryer had finally slowed down enough for him to go back to bed and get a few more hours of much-needed sleep.

A rustling noise was still coming from the letter box.

Either he was getting a lot of bills or else the new Ikea catalog wouldn't quite fit.

He rolled over and pulled the pillow over his head. The rustling went on for a few more seconds, then everything went silent.

He wondered about getting up, but couldn't think of a good reason why he should. His head and arm were still aching after their treatment the day before, he had no money, and seeing as the Game was over now, there was no reason at all for crawling out of bed.

What a wonderful life!

It was all pretty tragic really . . .

Then he noticed the smell. A faint but unmistakable smell of burning. Something's boiled dry, he thought. Had he left the ring on when he boiled the water for the coffee? It wouldn't be the first time.

Okay, mothafucker, you wanted a reason to get up, and now you've got one!

He rolled reluctantly out of bed, scratched his stubble and a couple of other strategic places before stumbling out to the kitchen. The stove was empty, and none of the rings was on.

He frowned.

The smell was getting stronger, so what the hell was burning?

A couple of moments later the synapses in his brain made the right connection and he dashed out into the hall.

Thick, acrid smoke hit him when he spun around the corner.

The shabby plastic mat that he had found himself lying on a few hours earlier was completely alight and the meter-high flames were already licking the walls and the inside of the front door. His eyes were stinging and he instinctively took a few steps back.

Get out! his brain was screaming at him.

The flat's on fire, for fuck's sake, get out, dialing one-one-two is easy to do, just get out!

But he was paralyzed by the flames, which were growing bigger and bigger as they took hold of the parquet flooring.

Even if he recognized the danger, there was something

beautiful, almost enchanting, about it. The orange flames, the black smoke, and the crackling sound of fire catching hold of his possessions felt almost liberating.

As if he actually desired this destruction . . .

Suddenly there was the sound of banging on the door.

"Fire!" he heard someone shout from out on the landing. "Can you hear me? Your flat's on fire, for God's sake!"

The spell was broken instantly and his brain and body were once again in sync.

Get to safety, sound the alarm, put it out, a childlike voice echoed through his head.

Okay, getting to safety was already buggered, there was nowhere to go if he didn't feel like jumping out of a second-floor window onto the street.

Next!

Running through the flames was out of the question, and anyway, the door was locked and he'd be fried before he could get it open.

Next!

Sound the alarm?

Hopeless, seeing as he didn't have a phone.

Unless . . .

He ran back into the kitchen, picked up the cell, and touched the screen.

It came to life at once.

"*Emergency calls only*," the display said.

"Ain't that the truth?" he snarled through gritted teeth as he made the call.

"Emergency services, what's the nature of the emergency?"

"My flat's on fire, Maria Trappgränd seven, one person trapped inside," he managed to say before the call was cut off.

He turned the phone around to redial, and saw that the LED light had started to flash.

With a trembling finger he touched the display and the screen came to life again.

Remember rule number one, HP!
The Game Master

He stared at the phone for a few seconds, as if he were having trouble taking in what was happening.

Then he suddenly tossed the cell aside, grabbed the washing-up bowl with both hands, and, with a couple of long strides, was back in the hall, where he emptied it in the direction of the fire.

Put it out, put it out, put it out, the cheerful little voice in his head sang, and with a crash a week's worth of well-soaked washing up and a few liters of dirty water landed on the hall floor.

The fire hissed and spat out a cloud of white smoke, but HP didn't see that.

He was already back in the kitchen, desperately filling the empty bowl with more water.

Then emptying it, then again, and again, and now he could clearly see the fire getting smaller.

His eyes were stinging, his lungs were burning, and his breathing was getting more labored, but he wasn't about to give up now.

When he was on his fifth bowlful the front door was wrenched open with a crash and a moment later a cloud of foam and white smoke overwhelmed him, making him put his hands over his face.

Coughing madly, he staggered back toward the kitchen and blinked away the tears enough to get a window open before collapsing on the floor. He was gasping desperately for breath, but his throat had shrunk to the size of a drinking straw.

Everything was starting to go black.

From down in the street there was the sound of sirens and people shouting orders.

Dialing one-one-two is easy to do, the child's voice inside his head chanted just before he lost consciousness.

"You were lucky, Henrik," the doctor said, unaware that she was echoing what her colleague in St. Göran's had said the night before.

"You inhaled a bit of smoke, and you have a minor burn on your left hand, but that's more or less it."

He nodded mutely from the gurney. It was considerably easier to breathe now, presumably thanks to the oxygen mask.

"We're going to rinse your eyes once more; you got covered in a fair bit of foam, but there's no real danger. Your vision might be a bit fuzzy for a couple of days, but it'll pass."

He nodded again.

There was no point trying to talk with the mask on, and besides, what would he say?

"Well, then," the doctor said as she got up. "If you haven't got any questions, I need to get going. Even if you feel fine, keep the mask on until the nurse has rinsed your eyes. You need to breathe pure oxygen to drive out the carbon monoxide you've inhaled. Look after yourself, Henrik!"

He nodded a third time, in both confirmation and farewell.

Then he was finally alone.

The clothes dryer got going again, this time on an advanced setting. But before he had time to concentrate on it there was a knock on the door and two uniformed police officers stepped in. Perfect, just what he needed right now!

King of the Royal Mounted, Cling and Clang are here to ruin your day. Shit!

They turned out to be called Paulsson and Wöhl, and once he'd asked to see their badges and carefully examined them, even though they were in full uniform, they had a few questions for him.

Did he happen to have any enemies? No, Officer, he didn't.

Could he think of any other reason why someone would want to pour paraffin through his letter box and set fire to his hall?

Yes, he could certainly think of a reason, but he had no intention of sharing it with a couple of flat-footed cops, or anyone else come to that. He didn't need any more reminders of the rules, thanks very fucking much!

"No, Officer, I'm afraid not," he replied instead with his head tilted to one side and his honest look on his face. Neither of them seemed to buy it, but what the hell!

Apart from what he had told them about the outbreak of the fire, was there anything else he could tell them that could be relevant to their investigation?

Same answer again, for the third time: No, not a thing!

The cops exchanged a knowing glance over their notepads, and after a few final pearls of wisdom they finally gave up.

"The case will be investigated by the Södermalm police." Great, thanks very much!

He already knew what the result would be. Absolutely zilch.

• • •

"Hi, it's me . . . Micke . . ." he added, in case she didn't recognize his voice.

"Hi," she said curtly, then realized that she was actually pleased he had called.

"How are you?"

He sounded a bit unsure, as if he didn't really know what to say. It was usually she who phoned.

"Fine, thanks, just a bit tired. Work's been a bit busy," she found herself saying, surprised at her honesty.

"Oh, I see . . . You probably don't really feel like meeting up, then?"

She was silent for a couple of seconds. Her headache hadn't given up, her ribs were still sore, and Henke's final words were still echoing in her head. So no, not really!

"Sure, I can be 'round in half an hour," she replied, and for the second time in the conversation she surprised herself.

"I thought maybe we could go out . . . have a bit of a chat?" he went on quickly.

Her brain said it was time to pull the hand brake.

Fucking, yes; talking, no! *We don't have time for that sort of thing, Normén!*

"Sure!" her mouth replied disobediently, and forty-five minutes later they were sitting in a little Thai place up in Vasastan, and to her surprise she discovered that it was really, really nice just having a bit of a chat for a while.

10 | HAZARD

OKAY, SO WHAT the hell was he going to do now?

No job, no money, he'd had a row with his sister, his flat was uninhabitable, and, maybe worst of all, he'd been chucked out of the Game!

The Goat had let him crash on his sofa for a couple of days, but all the coming and going and all the fucking dopehead dweebs who seemed to hang around in the flat all the time were driving him mad. Didn't the bastards have jobs to go to?

He needed time to think, to go through his options and plan his next moves. Not that he had many lined up, exactly . . .

As usual, Mange was the one who stepped up. His old woman wasn't exactly happy, but evidently their religion meant they had to be hospitable and generous to the poor, so she didn't have much choice. But that didn't mean that Betul missed any opportunity to scowl at him; no, she didn't exactly hold back there. But HP ignored her from his comfortable lying position on their best Ikea sofa.

HP/Islam 1, miserable witch 0.

Something to be pleased about, anyway. That and the fact that he now had plenty of time to think. Betul didn't like computers, which was pretty absurd when you considered what

her husband did for a living. But seeing as she was head of the
Al-Hassan family, there was no PlayStation, no PC nor any
film channels to disturb his concentration, leaving HP with
time to think at last.

A job could wait; he still had a few days left on unemployment benefit and something was bound to turn up. The flat
would be fixed in a week or so. New paint, new floor, and a
new front door, all paid for by the insurance. Rotten lucky that
Becca had kept up with the most important bills when he was
short of cash.

So how could he make it up to her?

Sadly, there was no good answer to that question.

Becca was furious with him, and for good reason. He'd
crossed the line the other day, seriously marched over it. But
he hadn't actually had any choice. She mustn't get caught up in
this, at least not any more than she already was.

But it looked like it was too late. They must have been
watching him somehow. And saw her visiting him and thought
he was spilling the beans again. Somewhere a cell phone had
flashed and a player, maybe even some fucking rookie, had
been given the task of teaching the grass a lesson, the same
way he had done with the door over in Birkastan.

A little home delivery à la Game Master.

According to the cops, his wasn't the first call to the emergency services. Someone had rung a few minutes earlier,
probably around the time that they started the fire, so they
presumably didn't want to kill him. Not this time, anyway.

Which led him back to his original question. What was
he going to do now? Did they really expect him just to forget
everything, keep his mouth shut, and never think about the
Game again? Could he do that even if he wanted to?

Apart from the business with the stone and his sister, he had been run over, beaten up, given the third degree, had the shit scared out of him, and then his flat set fire to.

So in other words, he had plenty of reasons to be pissed off.

But the sickest thing in this whole mess was that in spite of everything they'd done to him, he was still dreaming about getting back in, being forgiven and allowed to carry on playing.

Step back out onto the track to the applause of the spectators.

He could see it was wrong, that it was completely insane, in fact, but he still couldn't shake the thought.

What if he could get in touch with someone, the Game Master himself perhaps? Say he was sorry and maybe get another chance? The question was just how to go about it? There was no contact list, sadly, and he had a fair idea that he wouldn't have any luck with the Yellow Pages or Google.

Okay, he still had the cell phone, but that had been dead since the fire. The battery must be exhausted by now. But all those hours on the sofa had at least given him one idea. Every modern cell was a sort of little computer. They had at least two different types of memory where it ought to be possible to dig out something useful, if you only knew what you were doing.

Luckily he had the right man for the job. Straight out of *One Thousand and One Nights*: his own reluctant host, the world's most browbeaten husband, the artist formerly known as . . . Mange!

"I know you're keen to have a look at this, Mangelito," he said an hour or so later, tossing the cell on the shop counter. "It's all yours. All I need to know is who's been sending me messages and how I can turn the tables and contact them."

Mange looked at him lazily over a copy of that day's *Metro* without raising a finger, but he couldn't fool HP. He could see the corner of one of his friend's eyes literally start to twitch. And, just like when they were playing poker, you just had to sit it out.

Easy peasy.

"On one condition," Mange said after a few seconds of trying to look uninterested.

"Whatever . . . !"

As long as it doesn't break rule number one, HP thought.

Mange grinned.

"That from now on you call me Farook!"

"Deal!" HP said in relief, before he was fully aware of what he'd agreed to.

Oh well, if it would make the towelhead happy . . .

It had been a nice meal. Very good food, and a decent atmosphere. Thai, but without being kitsch the way Asian restaurants often were. There had been no trace of "Love Me Tender" in Thai, or concertina lanterns with selected words of Buddhist wisdom. No, it had all been really good, in fact.

They'd done just the right amount of talking, had kept quiet while they were eating, and he hadn't even raised an eyebrow when she declined the wine, just as he hadn't questioned her explanation of a minor traffic accident to cover her injuries. Afterward they'd exchanged a quick kiss; then they had each gone back home on their own.

She realized that it was the first time that had happened.

So what did that mean? Were they on their way to a proper relationship?

Absolutely not, she decided, firmly interrupting that line of thinking.

They had simply had a nice meal, talked about all manner of things, nothing of any great significance. He had talked about his parents' farm in Södermanland, and how he had moved to the city to study instead of taking over the farm, and how he had been trying to stay out of the way as best he could.

"Guilty conscience," he had said with a wry smile. Not being able to live up to expectations.

She understood perfectly well what he meant. She had listened with interest and occasionally made a comment without actually volunteering the same level of confidence herself. But he had worked that out fairly quickly and hadn't pushed her in that direction at all.

He was actually a nice guy. Better than she deserved.

"I'll call you later in the week," he had said, and she hadn't protested.

She realized that she was looking forward to him calling, in fact.

"Like some story in a damn women's magazine," she snorted.

She wondered how Henke was getting on?

But, then again, why should she care?

HP was impressed. After a bit of fiddling about, Mange—no, Farook—had managed to open a compartment on the phone that HP had never even noticed, and had plugged a USB cable into the little socket hidden inside. Obviously he should have known that there had to be a way into it, but he'd been so absorbed by what was going on on the screen that he hadn't given any thought to the basics, such as how you charged the thing when the battery was exhausted.

As soon as Mange plugged the cable into one of the computers at the back of the shop a little charging light went on, so evidently it would work with any USB power source.

A bit of nifty typing, then a load of symbols started rolling on one of the computer screens.

HP was by no means a novice when it came to computers, but this was out of his league, no question. Mange was a wiz at computers and maybe he'd be able to find out something useful.

"This is going to take a while," he muttered, and HP agreed without protest to run a few errands in the city. Suddenly full of generosity, he even brought a paper cup of latte back to the shop instead of the bitter brewed coffee from the hot plate.

But when he got back something had changed. Mange seemed to have been practically waiting for him just inside the door. He grabbed HP's arm and almost dragged him into the shop, nearly spilling the latte.

"What the shit are you doing? Calm down!"

But Mange wasn't listening. Instead he shut the door, locked it, and changed the sign to CLOSED.

Without a word he pulled HP over to the corner where the computer was.

The three screens were showing a series of film clips.

HP unscrewing the wheel nuts of a Ferrari.

HP blowing up the Horse Guards in Kungsträdgården.

HP dropping a stone over a railing at Lindhagensplan and then a car with flashing blue lights rolling over and over until it came to rest with smoke rising from the engine . . .

His stomach clenched tight.

"What the hell are you really up to?" Mange hissed, giving him an accusing stare.

So much for rule number one, then . . .

His third transgression in twenty-four hours, this was seriously not good.

Fucking mega not good!

So what was he supposed to do now?

"Can that thing hear us?" HP said anxiously, pointing at the cell.

"What?! No, of course it can't!" Mange snarled. "What the fuck is this about, HP?!"

He gave the phone another quick glance and, just to be sure, pulled Mange with him into the little cubbyhole behind the counter. He licked his lips nervously while he tried to gather his thoughts.

Purely technically, he had broken the rules only once. He hadn't actually blabbed to his sister, even if the Game seemed to think he had and had punished him accordingly. So really he'd been punished for something he hadn't done, which meant they owed him one. Besides, he needed Mange, sorry, Farook. Without him he wouldn't be able to contact the Game.

So you could say that everyone gained from the violation of the rules that he was contemplating. He hadn't expected Mange to be able to get any pictures out of it. An IP address, maybe a server host somewhere, that was all he needed to get going. But his old friend was far too smart for his own good when it came to technology. So how could he get Mange to go along with his plan?

"Okay, it's like this . . . Farook," he said, tasting the unfamiliar name cautiously.

He had to play this on Mange's terms . . .

"Like I told you, I found the cell on the train from Märsta the other week, but what I didn't tell you is that it invited me to play a game. A rather special game, actually . . ."

In retrospect she realized that she already knew it was going to be there. She'd had an uneasy feeling ever since she entered the changing room and when she opened her locker she understood why.

It should have been you!

Another official white Post-it note with red writing, neatly stuck to the edge of the shelf, just like the one before.

And just like the last one, she knew the note was right. It should have been her. It would have been fairer somehow if it was her body instead of Kruse's that got smashed up in the car. An eye for an eye, you could almost say. Then she would have been able to move on at last. Put it all behind her. Maybe, anyway.

But it couldn't go on like this.

First, there were the notes, then Henke going crazy, and then Micke, who had suddenly broken their usual pattern without warning. She had to get a grip on things, regain control over her own life. She couldn't put it off any longer; she had to do it now. And she had to start with Nilla.

HP had actually stuck to the truth. Almost, anyway. The only thing he left out was the small fact that his sister had been in the cop car that he hit over at Lindhagen. But otherwise it had pretty much been nothing but the truth . . . Possibly with one or two minor exceptions. Mange would never buy the fact that he wanted to carry on playing. Which wasn't so strange; he could hardly understand himself that he was even considering anything like that. And Mange was no longer the gambling type. Apart from the occasional World of Warcraft session, where he kept on going with his tired old Paladin character, nowadays he played it safe. Wife and child, flat in the suburbs, and all that.

He'd forgotten the kick you got from gaming, the rush you got from the adrenaline coursing through your body, and, even more important: he had no idea what it was like to feel chosen, appreciated, and to get loads of cred from an entire fucking world!

So he ended up covering his motives with a little white lie . . .

He said he wanted to find out who was behind the Game, maybe give an anonymous tip-off to one of the evening papers, or *Crimewatch* or something like that. A bit of payback for all the shit he'd had to take. Mange bought it without question, and why not? It could very easily have been true.

He was able to dig out a server address more or less instantly, but after that, things ground to a complete halt. HP got a bit downhearted but Mange wasn't the sort to give up. From what they could work out, the server appeared to be in Sweden, and if it was, then that meant that somewhere in cyberspace there was someone who had sold, installed, and configured it. The odds that such a person would be somewhere in Mange's network of contacts were pretty good.

He'd put out a few tentative feelers and they'd have to wait to see if there was any response. That wasn't quite the scenario HP had been hoping for. Patience and waiting were definitely not his bag, but on the other hand he didn't really have much choice.

He'd just have to grin and bear it.

A GroupWise message was really all it took to get going. She soon found Nilla's email address on the internal contact list, even though she had a different surname, but it had been thirteen years and she had almost counted on Nilla being married by now.

So what was the best way to put it?

It took Rebecca over an hour to compose the email, and in the end she realized that if she was ever going to send it, she would have to keep it short.

But when she moved the cursor to the Send button, she suddenly felt hesitant. Her index finger was left hanging in the air above the mouse button. Was this really such a good idea?

What sort of answer was she expecting? *Sure, I'd love to talk to you, Rebecca. Let's meet for coffee and chat about old times. Maybe you could tell me what happened the night my brother was murdered?*

She moved the mouse away. She'd have to leave it for another day when she'd had time to think it through more thoroughly. Thirteen years had passed already, so a few more days wouldn't make any difference.

· · ·

When the telephone rang HP sat up with a jerk. It took him a few seconds to work out where he was, and what the stupid tune resounding through the flat actually meant.

Mange's—correction, Farook's—flat, with him on the sofa, the room still dark. He blinked a few times to see the clock on the television. Who the hell was calling the Al-Hassan residence at 2:10 at night?

The ringing stopped; they must have answered in the bedroom. Then the baby started to scream. A couple of minutes later a bleary-eyed Mange appeared in the living room, wearing one of those full-length white nightshirts that he seemed to wear all the time these days.

"The burglar alarm has gone off in the shop; you can come with me into the city," he slurred as he buttoned his harem trousers.

"The security company and the cops are already there, so it's kind of urgent. Get your clothes on while I go to the toilet . . ."

HP crawled off the sofa and pulled on his jeans and sneakers without protest.

Just before they set off, Betul the witch stuck her head out of the nursery and gave him the evil eye, but that wasn't the reason HP felt an uneasy lump in his stomach.

"Has this happened before?" he asked with feigned nonchalance while Mange beat the crap out of his little Polo as they crossed the Liljeholmen Bridge.

"A couple of times over the years," he muttered through his teeth as he swerved through a red light. "But not since we put bars on the windows and installed a camera inside. According to the security company the thieves didn't get in, but apparently the cops want me there straightaway. Wonder why?"

HP kept quiet and clung on to the handle above the door. The lump in his stomach was growing exponentially.

Four minutes later Mange pulled up sharply outside the shop. The security firm's car and two cop cars were parked outside, and a bit farther away stood a fire engine.

To HP's relief, the shop seemed to be undamaged.

"Hello," one of the policemen said as he pulled a notepad from his trouser pocket. "Selini, Södermalm police. Are you the owner?" He nodded to HP.

"No, I am, Farook Al-Hassan."

The policeman gave Mange and his Middle Eastern appearance a long look but said nothing.

"Okay, we'll need a few personal details and so on in a bit, but I'd like to show you this first."

He led them over to the entrance. The door of the shop was open and it took HP a few seconds to comprehend that the security guards had probably opened it up, as well as the roller blind.

"We were 'round the corner when the alarm went off, so we came close to catching them red-handed. Two men on a moped, one of them watching while the other one tried to break in. My partner reckons the one who was watching was filming what the other one was doing. Crime videos like that are getting more and more common, happy slapping and all that . . ."

HP had suddenly gone ice-cold. He opened his mouth to say something but the policeman interrupted him.

"Either way, we pursued them for a few minutes, but we lost them when they turned into a cycle path through Tantolunden. They must have used an emergency hammer or something like that to break the glass."

They'd just reached the front door and the policeman indicated a fist-sized hole in the window alongside. The window was full of what looked like snow, making it look a bit like a Christmas display. All that was missing were a couple of plastic reindeer and a chocolate Santa Claus, HP noted, almost in amusement, before he understood what the white powder was.

"I emptied our fire extinguisher through the hole, so it never caught properly. There'll be a bit of cleaning up, but that's better than the alternative . . ."

The policeman shrugged.

HP's stomach had clenched solid and he was having trouble breathing. The cop's voice sounded like it was in slow motion.

"A few soaking rags and probably a bit of paraffin through the hole. It doesn't look like they were planning a robbery, just wanted to start a fire. I don't suppose you happen to have acquired any enemies recently, Mr., er . . . Al-Hassan?"

"No, not as far as I know," Mange replied, giving HP a long look.

They both sat in silence on the way home. Thoughts were whirling through HP's head. He was desperate for a cigarette but knew he'd make himself even less popular if he lit up in the car.

This was the second warning, albeit something of a failure, but still. If the cops hadn't happened to come around the corner when they did, the computer shop wouldn't be there now. The whole thing would have gone up in smoke, just like that. *Whoosh!*

And all because he had chosen to break rule number one again.

He'd dragged Mange into this and it had almost cost Mange his shop. In other words, they must have been watching them somehow, either electronically, or else there were people out there following him.

The thought made HP's skin crawl. He couldn't help looking in the side mirror. There was a car behind them, a Ford, to judge by the lights. It was keeping its distance, didn't seem to be in any hurry.

"My mom's sister's got a small cottage on an allotment in Tanto," Mange said curtly, and it took HP a couple of seconds before he worked out what Mange meant.

"I'll move out tomorrow."

Silence filled the car again.

Another glance in the mirror; the Ford was still there. One of its headlights was more yellow than the other. A replacement rather than the original, HP guessed.

Now Mange seemed to have noticed that something was up, because he too was taking long looks in the rearview mirror.

"I need to make a couple of calls," he muttered, clutching the wheel. "We need to work out who these bastards are, HP, and once we've done that, you have to promise me that you're going to give them some serious payback from me. Kick some ass, you get me?"

HP smiled and nodded.

"I promise, Mange," and this time Mange didn't correct him.

They fell silent again.

He tried to think. Could he really promise Mange that he'd whip the Game Master's backside? Sure, he was fucking upset with the way they were treating him, and this latest move on his friend had definitely crossed the line.

But still. What a couple of hustlers they must have sent to do the job! A couple of cretins who didn't even check the area before they set to work. He'd seen a can of spray paint in the gutter a few meters away. The cops didn't seem to have noticed it, or if they had, they hadn't linked it to the break-in.

But HP got the message, loud and clear. First, set light to the shop, then write the message. All of it filmed. That sort of assignment would be worth a thousand points or so, maybe more. Not a job for newbies, in other words.

Give the job to Luca Brasi.

And yet they'd still managed to fuck it up, even though there were two of them! He could have handled something like that solo, but good people are hard to find, even for a Game Master, apparently.

After all, he'd been first runner-up for a reason, number 128, the man that not even all the king's horses could stop. If he could just talk to the Game Master, get a chance to explain himself.

He saw Mange cast another anxious glance in the rearview mirror and decided to park any thoughts of that nature for the time being. Mange was looking completely paranoid now, as if he was going to burst any second, and his foot was on the floor of the battered little Polo, even though it had already had to work hard on its way into the city. It was shaking like it had Parkinson's and HP quickly pulled on his seat belt, even though it didn't actually make him feel much safer.

The Ford was still some fifty meters behind them.

Their exit ramp was getting closer, but Mange showed no sign of turning off.

Instead he stuck in the right-hand lane, slowing down a bit so that the Ford almost caught up with them.

Just as they were about to pass the exit ramp, he changed down a gear and suddenly wrenched the wheel to the right, making HP grab the door handle in horror to stop himself flying out of his seat. The Polo's tires protested loudly and they missed the barrier at the end of the access ramp with the smallest possible margin, swerving up the road and flying through a red light, all without Mange so much as touching the brake pedal.

"Calm down, for fuck's sake!" HP yelled, trying to make himself heard above the pained howl of the Polo, but Mange didn't seem to be listening. The knuckles clutching the wheel were white and he was grinding his jaw like he was on acid.

HP twisted his head to look for the Ford, but the road behind them was completely empty.

"You can calm down, Mange," he said in a gentler tone of voice. "There's no one behind us."

This time Mange seemed to hear him and, after checking and double-checking what HP had said in the rearview mirror, he eased up slightly on the accelerator.

HP sat up in his seat and took a couple of deep, relieved breaths. Mange wasn't much of a driver at the best of times, and the Jason Bourne maneuver he had just pulled could have ended really badly.

The Ford seemed to have been completely halal, the driver hadn't even swerved in an attempt to follow them, but Mange didn't seem to have noticed that. Instead he seemed to be looking for new pursuers to race with. They still had a way to go, and HP had to find a way to snap Mange out of this paranoia if they weren't going to end up in Huddinge Hospital.

"Listen, there's something I've been wanting to ask . . ." he managed to splutter.

"Shoot," Mange muttered, without taking his eyes from the rearview mirror.

"This whole carpet-seller routine of yours."

"Hmm . . ."

"Well, I suppose I'm wondering why, really? I mean . . . you've tried a whole load of different stuff over the years. The vegan thing, local politics, Amnesty . . . You never stuck with any one thing for too long. Like that screen saver you've got in the shop: *If you don't change . . .*"

"*Then what's the point of anything happening to you?*" Mange concluded, and suddenly took a break from staring in the mirror. "Fuck, HP, sometimes you do listen to what I say!"

The trick worked, Mange's jaw stopped grinding and his rigid grasp of the steering wheel relaxed slightly. A bit of practical philosophy and a few Couplandisms, that was Mange's bag—he was considerably better at that than street racing in the suburbs. Best to keep him in his comfort zone . . .

"So why did you get hooked on Islam in particular?" he blurted out, and to his own surprise realized that he was actually curious to know the answer. He didn't really have any idea why Mange had converted. Damn it, what sort of a best friend was he, seeing as he'd never even asked . . . ?

"I mean, there's a whole load of religions out there to choose from . . ." he went on rather vaguely.

"Well, giving to the poor, putting spiritual concerns above worldly ones, helping a brother in need . . . what's not to like?" Mange smiled wryly as the Polo's speed slowed to a more normal level.

"Women covered up, suicide bombers, holy war, there are quite a few options, aren't there . . . ?"

Mange sighed wearily.

"Most of that has very little to do with religion, if you look below the surface . . . There are fanatics everywhere, but here in the West we get much more worked up about men in beards burning flags in Damascus than we do about smooth-shaven men with pudding-bowl haircuts blowing up abortion clinics in Detroit."

"So you mean the whole jihad thing is mainly a question of bad PR . . . ?"

"Something like that." Mange grinned, almost back to his normal self again. "Just like the Bible, the Koran is ninety per-scent about living your life in a decent way, focusing on love and mercy, and being a good person. The last ten percent is stuff that might have been important for the survival of the tribe in the desert a fuck of a long time ago, but which is basi-cally nonsense these days. Unfortunately not everyone seems to have worked out that we're living in the twenty-first century, or else they choose not to for a variety of reasons. That's hardly unique to Islam. We're good at focusing on the wrong things here in the West as well. Just look at the war on terror . . ."

He shook his head unhappily.

"Fear is a strong instrument of power, brother, extremely strong, in fact. If you pluck the right strings, people stay doc-ile, concentrate on idiotic rubbish, and don't complain about the things that are really important, like freedom of expression and thought and other fundamental human rights. It works both ways."

"So a lot of our lack of trust is a sort of mutual power trip? Each country's Big Brother stands to gain if we stay scared of each other?"

"Exactly, brother, you've hit the nail on the head!" Mange hit the wheel with one hand.

HP shrugged. Hell, maybe the Mangster actually had a point?

". . . And the name? I mean, I get the Al-Hassan, seeing as your dad's name's Hasse, but why Farook?"

"Well, as I'm sure you know, Magnus means 'great,' which doesn't exactly apply to me . . ."

HP couldn't help grinning.

Mange was small and wiry, with thick glasses, and his hairline was already halfway to the North Pole. In purely physical terms, he wasn't what you'd call great.

"I've never really felt much like a Magnus, and Mange sounds so eighties. It just seemed to make sense when I converted. Farook is someone who can tell good and bad apart. Someone who helps others find the right path. Religion helped me to sort out a whole load of stuff, and I hope I might be able to do the same for other people."

"So that's why you haven't given up even on such a hopeless case as me? You're my spiritual guide?"

"Something like that, brother, something like that." Mange smiled, then turned on the car radio.

All readings back to normal, HP thought happily and slumped down slightly in his seat. But he couldn't help taking the occasional surreptitious glance in the side mirror.

Rebecca was sitting outside the door to an anonymous conference room in the Parliament building with a cup of coffee from a vending machine in her hand. It was really far too early for her to be back at work, but she'd insisted and no one had protested, not even Anderberg. Besides, the Personal Protection Unit was on its knees in advance of the EU presidency, and every man or woman who was able to work was welcome. All of the reserves had been called up, meaning that they had an extra twenty-five people who had previously served in the unit. But they were still having trouble covering all their duties.

Rebecca's charge was behind the conference-room door, and, according to the schedule, would be there for at least another two hours. Wikström, with whom she was sharing the assignment, had just headed down to the canteen to have a quick lunch, and in half an hour's time, when he got back, she would be doing the same.

Scenarios like this were what bodyguard work mainly consisted of. Waiting, more waiting, and then a move to a different location where the waiting would begin again. There was no way to pass the time apart from taking short walks along the corridor or talking to your colleagues. Books and MP3 players, the things other people used to pass the time, were obviously banned in her line of work. Ninety-five percent of the time was pure routine mixed with tedium. The difficulty was staying alert and ready for the remaining five percent that weren't routine and that she had already experienced more than her fair share of . . .

She had four years left of her secondment to the Security Police, and she had already seen more action than most bodyguards did in their entire careers.

In spite of what had happened, she still liked the job, the whole deal of being a protector, in charge of a situation. Detailed planning, checking routes, and escape plans, thinking through every possible scenario with the others in the unit. *If X occurs, I'll do Y and you do Z.*

The setup was basically the same for each job, regardless

of who they were protecting. You just added more people and equipment if the threat level was higher. You also had to plan for basic requirements such as toilet breaks, coffee, and meals. The subjects' timetables and schedules were always changing, and lunch and dinner could suddenly fall by the wayside. One older colleague had taught her always to have a few protein bars with her, and she had been grateful for that advice on more than one occasion when her blood-sugar levels had gone through the floor.

Bodyguards were important to democracy, more so in recent years since attacks on politicians had become more common. The subjects she had encountered so far had been pleasant, almost grateful for their service, and had been careful to follow all instructions. But on the other hand, she hadn't yet had the "honor" of working in the royal protection unit . . .

That business in Kungsträdgården had been completely crazy . . .

After the first few days of hysteria the media had calmed down, and it had been a while since she last read an article confidently identifying the purpose of the attack.

Seeing as the attack had been aimed at the head of state, the Security Police were in charge of the investigation, but to judge by Vahtola's and Runeberg's comments they didn't exactly have any red-hot leads. "Single perpetrator on a moped, heading toward Birger Jarlsgatan," had been the first description that had been circulated, and she suspected that that single sentence pretty much summed up the extent of the investigation so far.

His Royal Highness had apparently been absolutely furious about what had happened, and hadn't exactly minced his words to his bodyguards. Evidently they hadn't been close enough to protect him, which was actually rather ironic, seeing as His Majesty usually wanted the officers as far away from his royal personage as possible. Ideally they should be invisible, or at least out of sight, but he seemed to have to changed his tune now . . .

The door to the conference room opened and Rebecca stood up at once. But it was only one of the assistants coming out to fetch some more bottled water.

She glanced at the time and sat down on her chair to wait a bit longer. It was another three hours before the next shift came on duty.

The cottage wasn't such a bad idea! It had electricity and running water. And Mange had loaned him a laptop with television reception that could crack all the coded channels. Okay, he'd have to shit in a little outhouse in the corner of the allotment, but that was no biggie. As long as he had HBO he could squeeze one out on a flower bed if he had to.

He'd been damn careful when he came out here, packing just a few things in a rucksack. A pillow, sleeping bag, and a bit of food, as well as the bag of grass he'd bought with the five hundred that Mange guiltily gave him as compensation for his failing hospitality. The miserable witch had looked pleased when HP left, but he didn't care. Now at least he was his own man.

He had taken the subway to Slussen, then changed to the green line and headed all the way out to Fridhemsplan. Once he got there he pulled an old spy trick, waiting until the doors were about to close, then jumping straight onto a train heading back into the city.

Just to be sure he repeated the stunt at the Central Station before carrying on to Zinkensdamm, where he stole a ramshackle woman's bicycle and made his way up into Tantolunden.

Finding the right place had been easy, yellow wooden paneling with white windows and two big apple trees in the plot. He hadn't been out here since he was a teenager and his gang used to hang around the mini-golf course to check out the girls and smoke the menthol cigarettes he'd nicked off his mom. Happy days . . .

Back then he had mainly thought that allotment cottages were pathetic, but now he was grown up he had to admit that having a miniature house wasn't such a stupid idea, especially if you needed somewhere to hide away from the rest of the world. If the Game was going to find him here, they'd have to put in a bit of effort. He grinned, taking a deep drag of a fat joint.

Pretty nice living like this, close to nature. A bit of birdsong and a solitary lawn mower were the only sounds. If he concentrated he could just make out the sound of traffic in the distance from Hornstull and Ringvägen, but otherwise it just seemed to fade into the background somehow.

He lazed about for a while on the rib-backed sofa in what was supposed to be the kitchen, but which, apart from the sofa and table, consisted of one cupboard and a tiny little sink. The sun was shining in through the leaded window and he actually felt far more relaxed here than in Mange's flat out in the suburbs.

Sweet!

A ping from the laptop woke him from his lethargy. Seeing as he'd left the cell in the shop and hadn't had time to get a new one, right now Messenger was his only contact with the outside world, and the only person who had his address was the Mangster, a.k.a. Farook.

Farook says: Salaam alaikum, brother HP!

Badboy.128 says: Hi Mange.

Farook says: How are things out in the model village?

Badboy.128 says: Pretty good, actually, say thanks to your aunt!

Farook says: will do!

Farook says: Have talked to some mates and one of them knows a guy who might be able to help us.

Badboy.128 says: Sweet, should I call?

Farook says: No, you can't get hold of him, only way is to meet him. Supposed to be a bit odd. Clever as fuck but a bit odd, yeah?

Badboy.128 says: Computer nerd? ☺

Farook says: Yes and no, a real wiz a couple of years ago, I've actually heard of him, but these days he lives somewhere in the back of beyond off the grid, supposed to be allergic to electricity, that's why no one can call him.

Badboy.128 says: Doesn't sound too damn promising . . .

Farook says: My mate says this guy was involved in that server I found in the cell, that he configured it and organized the whole setup.

Badboy.128 says: Okay, I'm in!

Badboy.128 says: So what do we do?

Farook says: My mate's going to contact the guy and sort something out, he's a bit of a recluse as well but my man thinks it'll work. I'll MSN you instructions when it's sorted.

Badboy.128 says: ok fine.

Farook says: one more thing . . .

Badboy.128 says: Shoot, mr. Pathfinder!

Farook says: please please don't send me that file with the bouncing
     smileys, I have to reboot the machine just to get rid of them!!!!
Badboy.128 says: you mean these? ☺ ☺ ☺ ☺ ☺ ☺ ☺

She read the message over and over again, without really
understanding it.

> Rebecca,
> I and my family have nothing to say to you.
> Pernilla

Nilla had replied to her email. And was blowing her off,
pretty much as she'd expected. But there was just one problem.
She'd never sent the email, just saved it in her Drafts folder to
think about it. But when she checked, the email had gone and
she found it in the Sent folder, fired off yesterday afternoon
apparently, just before they had shooting practice.

> Nilla,
> There's something I'd like to talk to you about, something
>   I've put off for far too long.
> Could we meet for a short chat at a time and place that
>   suits you?
> Sincerely,
> Rebecca Normén (formerly Pettersson)

Her own words, exactly as she remembered them, down to
the last comma.
How the hell had that happened?
She remembered that she had the computer on yesterday,

but could an email really send itself? Was there some sort of automated function that sent drafts after a day or so?

She didn't think there was, but on the other hand you never knew with the police computer system.

So what should she do now? She didn't really have much choice. The notes were pretty clear. If she wanted to get to the bottom of everything, she'd have to talk to Nilla, whether Nilla wanted to or not.

Just to be on the safe side she phoned her answering machine to explain to herself why she shouldn't just back down.

11 | NAME OF THE GAME

ANOTHER BASTARD BOILING-HOT day! *Global warming must be on overtime judging by how long this heat wave's been going on,* HP thought as he tugged his sticky T-shirt away from his chest.

The northbound commuter train, a couple more stations, and then a bus.

But then what?

He had the name of the bus stop on a bit of paper, "*get out and wait*" was the instruction. In the middle of nowhere, you could hardly find it even on Google Maps. HP sighed and rubbed his sweaty neck.

The guy he was going to see didn't seem to have a complete set of cutlery in his drawer, but on the other hand this was HP's best and actually only chance of getting somewhere and making any sort of sense of this whole fucking mess.

He got off the train and peered cautiously along the platform. Another three passengers had got off with him. An elderly couple and a fifteen-year-old homeboy with a back-to-front cap and his trousers halfway down. HP waited on one of the benches for them all to leave, then, when he was entirely alone, he wandered off toward the bus station.

He stopped on purpose at the wrong bus stop, saw his bus come, and it was only when it was about to pull away that he sprinted over the road and forced the irate driver to brake hard and let him on. If anyone had been following him, he'd have lost them by now, either here or when he did the platform trick at the South Station half an hour or so before. Even so, he couldn't shake the feeling that he was being watched.

After thirty-five minutes on the bus he was there. But even though he had been counting the bus stops and, just to make sure, had asked the driver, he still wasn't sure he was in the right place. Because this truly was the middle of fucking nowhere. An isolated bus stop on a narrow seventy-kilometers-per-hour road, open fields in all directions, and hardly a building in sight.

There was a smell of dry earth, straw, and something else natural that HP couldn't quite identify. And of course there was no one there to meet him . . .

He lit a cigarette and chilled for a while, but the sun was burning the back of his neck and soon his already grimy T-shirt was clinging to his back with sweat.

He must remember to nick a pair of shorts.

A few cows were mooing in the distance, and over on the horizon he watched a little yellow plane come gliding over the treetops. The plane was pulling a long banner and HP couldn't help smiling.

He hadn't seen that sort of advertisement since he was little. Hadn't the Internet and commercial television killed off advertising like this? But, on the other hand, this was the ass end of nowhere and you could probably get away with anything around here.

"*Fjärdhundra Market 28–31 July*," he read on the banner as
the plane came closer.

He grinned again. Fjärdhundra Market! Bound to be a
load of morons in dungarees trying to guess the weight of a
pig, toppling cows over, and trying to get off with their fifteen-
year-old cousins. A banjo solo, maybe? *Dingelingdingdingdings-
dingding ding . . .*

How the hell anyone would choose to live like that instead
of in the city like a proper Homo sapiens was beyond him.

"Yeehaa, Farthundra!" he yelled, waving at the plane as it
passed. But even though the pilot must have seen him as he
stood there in the middle of the road among the new-mown
fields, HP didn't get a hint of a response. Not even a little dip
of the wings.

"Fuck you, then, shithead," he muttered with the cigarette
dangling from his mouth as he switched to other less friendly
gestures instead before the plane disappeared from sight.

When the sound of the engine had died away he heard
another, angry-sounding motor coming toward him. It turned
out to be a flatbed moped, and the man riding it looked like
some sort of UFO.

Long fair hair, a scruffy matching beard, and on top of
all that one of those old leather flying helmets with built-in
goggles. Blue overalls that had definitely seen better days and a
pair of old army boots completed the outfit, and yet again HP
had trouble holding back his laughter.

A bit odd, yeah, right!

Fuck, this was serious *Candid Camera* stuff!

The moped man stopped sharply in front of him and grap-
pled with the gears.

"Are you HP?"

"No, I'm just a tourist who likes cows and fields, what the hell do you think?" HP muttered.

"Whassat?" The moped muppet leaned forward.

"Yes, that's me. Nice with all these cows and fields you've got out here," HP replied, this time louder so the man could hear him over the noise of the two-stroke engine.

"Erman," the guy said in reply, and nodded. "Jump on!"

HP hesitated for a moment, then, still grinning, jumped up on the flatbed. Of course, it was the only thing missing really, a little ride on a flatbed moped to reinforce all his prejudices about the countryside. The banjo duel in his head got even louder and he hummed along, safe in the knowledge that his driver couldn't hear him over the clatter of the engine.

Erman followed the road for a couple of kilometers, then turned off, heading straight across the fields on an almost invisible gravel track.

As they approached the tree line the track got even bumpier, but HP's chauffeur made no attempt to ease up on the gas, and by the time they pulled up outside the little cottage hidden in among the fir trees, the whole hillbilly thing had almost stopped being fun.

While Erman parked the moped HP stretched and massaged his sore backside.

Where the fuck had he ended up now?

The house was small, maybe just fifty or sixty square meters or so, so not much bigger than Auntie Berit's allotment cottage. The façade had once been red, but most of the planks were now gray, with just a few hints of pink where the sun and rain hadn't got to them. The drooping concrete-fiber roof was green with moss and algae and the cottage was surrounded by meter-high nettles. The whole thing looked ready to collapse at any moment.

"Go on in," Erman muttered, nodding toward the entrance as he closed the door of the little outhouse. HP did as he was told and discovered that the inside of the shack looked considerably better than he had been expecting.

The kitchen and small living room were clean and tidy; there was a smell of detergent and in one corner there was a cozy crackle from a cast-iron stove. In spite of that the house was cool, probably because it was shaded by the surrounding firs.

"You followed the instructions, I hope?" Erman said abruptly as he came into the kitchen a few seconds later.

"Yep," HP said. "No cell, paid cash for all tickets, and did a bit of James Bond stuff before catching the train, so your little paradise is safe from discovery."

Erman grunted and tossed the flying helmet onto a kitchen chair.

To his surprise HP realized that his host wasn't some old guy like he'd first thought, but at a guess was just a few years older than him.

Erman gestured to him to sit down on the kitchen sofa, then put an old-fashioned coffeepot on the stove and started to get cups out.

"So you're allergic to electricity, how do you get that?" HP began in an exaggeratedly friendly tone, but got a quick snort in reply.

"Twenty-five years with computers, magnetic fields, radio waves, and all the other shit flying around through the air. Then you wake up one day covered in a rash and can hardly breathe."

He poured them both coffee and HP took a quick, scald-

ing sip. Boiled coffee, he hadn't drunk that since his grand-
mother had died, he recognized as he managed to swallow the
burning liquid and blink a tear from his eye. Apart from the
temperature, it was actually pretty good.

The porcelain cup was wafer thin and the handle so finely
made that he had to hold it Lidingö style, with his ring and
little fingers sticking out. The coffee set had to be at least as old
as the house, if not even older.

He swirled the coffee around, blowing on it, then took another cautious sip as he peered at his host.

"So you want to know more about a server I installed?"
Erman said, glowering suspiciously at him across the table. "I
don't usually talk to people I don't know, or with anyone at all
these days, come to that."

No shit! HP thought, grinning into his coffee cup.

"But an old friend said you were okay and I owe him, big-
time you could say. If he says you're all right, then you're okay
in my book. So what do you want to know, and why?"

HP had worked out his strategy while he was on the bus
and made an effort to sound nonchalant.

"Just who you installed the server for and where it is. I'm
the art director of a small advertising agency and they've got
some visual material I'm interested in."

Erman gave him a long look and HP did his best to look
like he thought a hardworking art director would.

Then his host grinned and threw out his arms.

"Well, I never, an art director!"

HP smiled and nodded.

"And there I was thinking that you were a Player who'd
fucked up and was desperately trying to work out the identity
of the juggernaut that ran over you, and why."

Erman burst out into a roar of laughter and HP had to cough several times to get the scalding coffee out of his windpipe.

Another boiling-hot day! A day in the office at work, which meant a bit of paperwork, reading up on current threat analysis and the preliminary program for the next round of the EU presidency. Plenty of time to clear stuff from her desk.

She got a glass of water from the kitchen, took a deep breath, and tried to shift the tension in her neck and jaw.

Even though it was still early, her shirt was already wet under the arms. The building may have been air-conditioned, but seeing as every reorganization of the police force seemed to require new walls and office partitions, practically all the cool air ended up in a few rooms at the far end of the corridor. To get at least an illusion of coolness, Rebecca had been forced to buy a fan that was now stirring up the hot air in the office she shared with three other bodyguards. She settled down behind her desk and shut her eyes, letting the blast of air cross her face a couple of times as she tried to gather her thoughts.

It had taken a while to dig out the phone number. Nilla wasn't in the phone book and she wasn't listed online either.

Ex-directory, of course, just like ninety-five percent of all police employees, whether or not it was actually necessary. But there were ways around that, of course. A call to a girl she knew in personnel was all it took. A white lie about her and Nilla sharing a lift to a course, and in a moment she had her work roster, home number, and cell. Who said female networks didn't work?

But now she was hesitating again.

How should she start, and what did she really expect to get out of the conversation? *Get it all out in the open, once and for all,* she repeated to herself. *Turn the page at last and put a stop to all those damn notes . . .*

Not exactly a straightforward aim, and maybe not even possible. Just a few days ago she wouldn't be bothering with any of this. After all, she'd gone more than a decade without getting bogged down in the past. But after what happened out at Lindhagensplan everything had changed.

Seeing Kruse there in hospital with tubes and wires everywhere, admittedly a bit brighter now than to begin with, had made her think along different lines. It could easily have been her lying there. Should have been, maybe, just like the note implied, seeing as it had been her mistake.

So that's why she was thinking of trying, properly this time. Clear the air, say what she should have said all that time ago, and get some sort of closure. First with his family, then, after that, with Henke somehow. Get him to forgive her for what she'd done, or, more truthfully, hadn't done . . . If anything like that was actually possible.

Their conversation the other day hadn't exactly given her much hope. She'd tried ringing him, but the new number he'd given her had been cut off. Typical Henke.

But what was she actually going to say?

The truth! a voice inside her head whispered.

In spite of the heat she shivered.

"So, tell me what they got you to do, and don't worry about rule number one. In the forest no one can hear you squeal!"

Erman let out another rumbling belly laugh as he refilled their cups.

"To start with, what number did you have?"

HP was a bit taken aback, to put it mildly. The guy had tricked him, playing the village idiot even though he knew exactly how the land lay. Fucking brilliant, what a laugh, yippee ki-yay mothafucker!

But what the hell, he just had to bite the rotten apple and make the best of it.

"One hundred and twenty-eight," he muttered, and for the third time in just a few days he told his whole story, right from the start, with a few choice bits missing.

When he was finished Erman nodded thoughtfully.

"Well, I can certainly understand why you're here. You've got plenty of reasons to be furious, I can see that. But now I'm going to tell you why you should think seriously before getting into round two with the Game Master, if that's what you've got in mind?"

Suddenly he got up from his chair and walked around the little house, bending down to be able to look out of the low windows. Evidently satisfied, he returned to the kitchen table.

"Now listen carefully, lad, because you don't really seem to be taking this seriously . . . unless you're just a bit crazy. You don't mess with the Game, if you haven't already caught on to that. I used to work for them, so I know more about it than most people, but we can take that a bit later. To start with, who do you think has been leaving comments on your page?"

"Erm, well, people who've watched the clips?" HP had never given it much thought. The answer was fairly obvious, after all. "Well, it has to be people who like watching cool film clips and don't mind paying for it. Otherwise the Game wouldn't work, would it?" he added, slightly uncertainly.

Erman shook his head.

"So you really think there are loads of people out there with nothing better to do than watch a load of pranks, and who've got fed up of doing it for free on YouTube and MTV?"

"Er . . . yeah?" HP managed to say, mostly in the absence of anything more sensible.

"What about the assignments, then? All that stuff you and all the other players do, they just come about by accident, because it's all a bit of fun, I suppose?" Erman looked at him inquiringly.

"Erm, well, I haven't really thought about that," HP said, feeling his dunce's hat growing.

Erman sighed.

"No, I'm afraid you're not one of life's great thinkers, HP. I suppose you're the sort who follows his impulses and does whatever suits him, am I right or am I right?"

"Huh, what, what do you mean?" HP was pretty sure he'd just been insulted, and quickly adopted his most aggrieved expression.

"What I mean is that you're the sort who takes care of himself and doesn't give a shit about anyone else."

"So what's so wrong with looking out for number one?" HP folded his arms over his chest and leaned back.

Erman sighed again.

"Nothing at all; in fact it's pretty much an advantage when it comes to the Game. We don't know each other, but let me try a few wild guesses." He counted on his fingers. "You haven't got a permanent job, you don't mind cutting a few corners if necessary, and as a result you've got a criminal record for various minor offenses. And you've got little or no family and not too many close friends. Stop me if you think I'm going too wide of the mark . . ."

He glanced quickly at HP before carrying on, using the fingers of the other hand:

"You're also desperate for approval and/or seriously short of cash. How am I doing so far?"

HP was speechless.

How the fuck could this dude know all that?

Had he checked him out somehow, or had someone blabbed?

"Easy, my friend." Erman chuckled. "I'm not a mind reader. It's just that the qualities I've listed are the things that are valued in a Player—in other words, someone like you."

He nodded to emphasize what he was saying, as if HP was a bit thick, which irritated him more than the quick run-through of his personality.

"Nothing in the Game is a coincidence, you have to remember that!" Erman went on. "You found that cell phone because they wanted you to find it. They'd already selected you because they thought you had what it took. First you got a couple of easy assignments so that everyone could see what you were like, pretty much like when they warm up horses out at Solvalla: place your bets, ladies and gentlemen, and then the Game is up and running!"

HP's head had gone blank.

"You . . . you mean they were betting on me, like the horses?" he eventually managed to say.

"Congratulations, Einstein, you finally got the message!" Erman grinned. "The Game is fundamentally nothing more than an advanced betting setup, only a hell of a lot more exciting than football or horse racing. They've been playing for years, long before the Internet. The men placing bets are called the Circle, and they're all over the world. You can place short-term bets, from assignment to assignment, or you can place a long-term bet on the End Game."

"The end game?" the dryer in HP's head had suddenly kicked into action.

"Good question, maybe you're not so slow after all!"

Erman got up and started waving his arms about.

"Players who get past a certain level get to participate in larger scenarios where all the assignments eventually lead up to some sort of grand finale. The Circle can bet on the final outcome, the End Game. Will a Player be able to cope with the pressure, or will he buckle, you get it?"

HP nodded uncertainly. His loony radar had started to bleep. This sounded completely crazy . . .

"Best of all, Players don't usually work out how everything fits together but act purely on impulse, which makes the Game even more authentic. *A true show of character*, you could say."

Erman took another turn about the cottage before he returned to the kitchen table.

He gave HP a long, searching look, and seemed to be weighing something up seriously before he went on.

"Okay, like I said, I don't usually talk to anyone, and above all never about the Game, but you've got a pretty good sponsor, who guarantees that you're okay, and you seem a bit too daft to be playing a double bluff . . ."

Erman pulled a piece of paper and a pen from a kitchen drawer and started to draw a pyramid.

"This is what it looks like. Right at the bottom are loads of small-time players who are happy with a little bit of excitement and a reliable source of extra income; they're called Ants. The Ants are used for small jobs, like getting hold of stuff, or information, preparing and delivering the tools for various assignments, or helping to film them. Ants never aim for the top; they never become real Players; they just play it safe, if you see what I mean?"

HP nodded quickly. He hadn't missed the fact that Erman had just called him daft, but this was actually fucking interesting!

"I bet it was an Ant who left the cell on the train for you, and filmed your trial. The guy with the umbrella could well have been an Ant, unless he just happened to be there; it's hard to tell," Erman went on.

"But all the other stuff: the pass card, the tools for the Ferrari, the flash-bang grenade, the locker at the Central Station, the key under the table . . . ?"

"Probably all sorted by Ants!" Erman confirmed. "The entire Game is built on the Ants. Without them nothing would work, and they're always recruiting more. There are Ants everywhere: in the police, social security, Telia, Microsoft, Google, you name it. So you can be sure they knew anything that was worth knowing about you way before they let you find the cell."

Erman drew another layer in the middle of the pyramid.

"The Ants also help to find Players, people like you. The Ant who found you gets a bonus for each assignment you complete, and the further you get, the richer you make him or her."

HP held up his hand. He had to pause a bit to digest what he had just heard.

So someone had tipped the Game off about him?

Maybe someone he actually knew?

Erman seemed to be reading his mind.

"You might not even know your Ant. It could be anyone who stumbled over your credentials, an employer, someone in social services, or who dealt with your unemployment benefit claim."

For some reason the explanation didn't make HP feel much better.

For him the whole thing had been just a game, a way of passing the time with a bit of a twist. But this . . .

"The Players are a different category to the Ants, and they're used for more advanced and risky assignments, if you see the difference?"

Oh yes, HP got it. His door and the arson attack on the shop weren't the sort of thing you'd get an Ant to do; that took a lot more balls.

"As you already know, each Player gets a series of assignments," Erman went on, as he drew the top layer in the pyramid.

"They're all designed to find out how far they can push you, and obviously the Circle bet on what the boundaries are. Over time most of you fall by the wayside, but the Game takes that into account. Players are basically no more than perishable goods, and only a very few have what it takes to reach the summit. When you sang your heart out to that cop, regardless of whether he was real or not, somewhere in cyberspace was one gang of happy souls who'd bet that you'd crack, and a load of others that you seriously disappointed. But you can be sure that someone else has already taken your place in the limelight."

He drew an arrow through the whole pyramid.

"The Game always goes on—*you're always playing the Game*, you get it?"

"But the high-score list, the clips, and everything? I mean, I was first runner-up, that has to mean something?"

He could hear how desperate he sounded, but made no effort to hide it.

Erman let out a slow chuckle.

"HP, HP, HP . . . You still don't get it, do you? . . . None of what you've been through is real. It was all just a game, a phone app that seamlessly integrates truth and illusion so well that in hindsight it's practically impossible to know where the boundaries are. Look up the word *game* and you'll see what I mean!"

The look of incomprehension on HP's face made Erman sigh again.

"Okay, I'll spell it out: they're lying to you, HP! The Game shows you some things that are true, and some that were stitched together just for you. Motivations differ from Player to Player. Some get turned on by sport—others by girls or music.

"Whereas you evidently like films and computer games— so the Game gives you your very own starring role, complete with a fan club and everything . . ."

Erman gulped the last of his coffee before going on.

"Suddenly you're the leading man instead of a spectator. From nobody to VIP in the space of a few days. The fans out there in cyberspace can't seem to get enough of you, and pretty soon you can't get enough of them. And all the Game asks in exchange for this massive trip is a few tiny little assignments . . ."

He was staring at HP, whose face had gone completely white.

"Basically it works just like any other sort of addiction," he went on. "Drugs, gambling, or in your case attention and affirmation—the same mechanisms kick in inside your head. And as the addiction grows, the brain loses the ability for critical analysis. You've turned into a *recognition junky*! Anything that doesn't support or increase the buzz gets filtered out and your imagination fills in the gaps. You believe because you want to believe, and therefore help the Game to paper over the glitches in the app. True or false, right or wrong, it matters less and less. Bigger, longer, and more kicks are all that counts.

"But it's all just a Game—*it's all a fucking Game*, understand?"

He looked expectantly at HP once again.

"So, to return to your question, my friend. The list they showed you could very well be real, but it could just as easily be something they put together just for you. Because that's what gets you going. They're playing with you, HP, just like you play with the poor bastards on the other end of the assignments, which brings me to the less attractive part of the Game."

Less attractive! HP thought. How the hell could anything be less attractive?

He was suddenly feeling like a prize idiot, a damn puppet that they'd been playing with just for the hell of it. Jerking his strings to see what would happen, and betting on the outcome.

My ladies and gentlemen, guess what will happen if we pull string number four! Will 128 withstand the pressure or not? Will

he throw a stone at his sister's police car to get a bit of affirmation,
will she survive, and will he crack under pressure and cry like a
baby? Ladies and gentlemen, place your bets, and stay tuned . . . !

The clothes dryer in his head was spinning fast now and
it took him several seconds before he was fully aware that
Erman had started talking again.

". . . the assignments really come from? Betting is only one
of the Game's sources of income. As I'm sure you can understand, it costs a hell of a lot to keep something like this rolling.
People are playing on several continents, so the financing is
pretty damn important."

He made a short pause to refill their coffee cups and took a
third turn around the house. Once he'd reassured himself again
that everything was okay, he returned to the kitchen table.

"You see . . ." Erman began in a low voice, leaning toward
HP, so close that he could smell the caffeine cocktail on his
breath . . . "this is where it gets really nasty!"

She took the chance to do it while the others in the group
were playing indoor hockey and the corridor was empty. She
blamed the fact that she still felt sore after the crash, and because they'd managed to put together two complete teams
anyway, they didn't try to persuade her.

According to her duty roster, Nilla wasn't supposed to be
working today, so she started with her home number. Two
rings, then three, four. The answering machine clicked in and
she was just about to hang up when she heard clattering as
someone picked up the receiver.

"Hello-this-is-Nilla!"

Her voice sounded more or less how Rebecca remembered.

She took a deep breath.

"Hello, Nilla, this is Rebecca Nor . . . er, Pettersson. Have you time to talk for a couple of minutes? I'd really appreciate it."

More clattering, then:

"Sorry, I was just turning off the answering machine, what did you say your name was?"

"Rebecca. Rebecca Pettersson."

There was silence on the line.

Rebecca's heart was pounding so hard that she imagined she could see her shirt fluttering over her chest.

12 | BEING GAME

"LOOK, IT'S LIKE THIS, my friend. The Game requires a hell of a lot of money to function." Erman counted quickly on his fingers. "The Ants, the phones, the server farms, and last but not least the functionaries, the people who are employed to keep the whole thing on the rails. Then there's all the money that's constantly being paid out to the Players, and the rewards for anyone who does particularly well. There are quite a few fixed costs each month, but I've done some calculations and they pretty much cover those with what they take from the live betting. The really big cash cow, the golden goose that gives the owners their profit—are the people who commission the assignments."

HP nodded as if he understood, but in truth he was feeling completely lost.

"Basically, various customers turn to the Game to get things done, if you follow me?

"Things that can't be done any other way," Erman went on, almost manic now.

HP was still looking blank.

"Illegal stuff, get it?!"

He drummed his index finger impatiently on the tabletop.

Yes, HP thought he was starting to get it . . .

"You mean you can call and order something to be done, and the Game fixes it?" he said cautiously.

"Something like that." Erman nodded eagerly.

"This part is top secret and is only handled by the Game Master's closest circle. I don't know all the details, but I think it goes something like this: a customer wants something done, but without there being any trail back to him. It could be information, business secrets, or something more medieval, like messing with someone you've had an argument with. The Game has the ability to do all that, although obviously it comes with a serious price tag. Maybe there's an Ant who can dig up what's needed, or they can send a Player to get the job done if it's something more risky. The Game can be used for absolutely anything."

His face had been getting redder and redder, and somewhere at the back of HP's mind a little alarm bell started to ring.

"So, for example, that lawyer you told me about. At a guess, he's managed to seriously upset someone, but instead of contacting the Law Society, that person contacted the Game. And in a flash the Game Master conjures up a wheel wrench and a Player desperate for cred who hates Sture Square lawyers. The customer gets his revenge documented on video, and if you screwed up and got caught and were stupid enough to break rule number one, there wouldn't be much to tell—at least nothing that anyone would believe. It's just like Verbal says in *The Usual Suspects*:

"*The greatest trick the devil ever pulled was convincing the world he didn't exist.* You're just an ordinary nobody, with no connection whatsoever with the person who actually commissioned the assignment. Lee Harvey fucking Oswald, man! You have to admit, it's a stroke of genius, but at the same time it's pretty fucking creepy!"

Erman flew up and started pacing around the little kitchen impatiently.

"Erm . . . sure!" HP agreed, as he tried to squeeze this latest information into his already overworked brain. This all sounded pretty weird, which was probably the understatement of the year . . .

"So you mean . . . ?" he began, mostly out of politeness.

Erman flashed him an impatient look and sat down again at the table. Evidently he wasn't completely happy with HP's hesitant response.

"Obviously, the problem is that there aren't any boundaries, isn't it? Okay, so the Game Master can't actually *force* a Player to do something; that's one of the main points of the Game. The Player must always have a choice, you know that yourself. Red or blue, right or wrong, in the end it's up to you Players to decide, and that's the way it has to be. Even if the Game would naturally prefer a particular outcome, there have to be different alternatives, there has to be an opening for the unexpected, for surprises. Otherwise there wouldn't be anything to bet on, and thus no Game!"

Erman's voice was cracking into falsetto.

"But what the Game does is to keep shifting the boundary of how far a Player is prepared to go. Just look at what happened to you! We're talking GBH, arson, sabotage, even murder! You only need to look at the paper to see what goes on every day!"

Erman got up and resumed his restless pacing.

HP was getting more and more convinced that his suspicion was correct, that Erman was well on the way to losing
it completely. You only had to look at the color of his face to
know that Eyjafjallajökull was about to erupt.

Not to mention all that creepy staring . . .

"You can look at any media outlet you like, and you'll be
able to find the Game in an instant. All you have to do is keep
an eye out for phrases like *inexplicable*, *unknown reasons*, and
no obvious motive, and you've stumbled across the Game . . ."

Erman suddenly ran over to one of the windows and
peered anxiously at the trees, as if he'd heard someone coming.

When he didn't manage to see any danger he took two
quick strides back to the kitchen table and leaned over toward HP.

"As long as you can pay, they'll take pretty much any job!"
he said into HP's face, giving him a close-up of a yellowing
row of teeth.

"There's always some dumb fuck who's prepared to do it.
Some willing patsy who's already crossed the line. It goes on
all the time, in a whole load of different places all 'round the
world. Check it out for yourself if you don't believe me!"

Erman's voice cracked again and HP sighed in disappointment. Fuck it, this had all started out so promisingly . . . Up to
about five minutes ago the guy had seemed more or less ko-
sher. A bit weird, maybe, but who wouldn't be, out here in the
middle of nowhere. But now he'd crossed the line, big-time!

That was it, then: the evil organization, the global conspiracy that was behind all the shit that ever happened in the
world. The CIA, Opus Dei, ZOG, or the Freemasons, it just
depended which lunatic you asked. A placard stuck to your
chest and a regular spot in the town square.

I'm the only one who's worked out the truth! Yippee ki-yay mothafucker! Game over, thanks for the coffee, time to go now . . .

"Well, thanks very much, Erman, this is all good information, but right now I should probably . . ." he muttered, standing up.

". . . a cigarette, no problem, but you'll have to go outside. I'll cadge one off you," his host muttered, confused, as if the comment had interrupted his train of thought and made him lose his thread.

Before the astonished HP had time to protest Erman had shepherded him out onto the front steps.

It was nice to get a bit of fresh air, at least, he thought as he pulled out his cigarettes.

He offered one to Erman, then lit it and his own with his trusty old Zippo. He took a couple of deep drags and tried to stop his head spinning.

Okay, so Erman might have a few screws loose, but on the other hand he clearly possessed loads of useful information about the Game. Even if it had seriously messed with his own ideas, he couldn't deny that a lot of what the guy had said actually made sense, and even seemed logical, if that word could actually be applied in this context.

But the theory of the Global Conspiracy was a bit hard to digest. Serious pulp fiction stuff, all it needed was a couple of serial killers and a dysfunctional cop to tick all the boxes. But what was the line between hard fact and wild fantasy?

They stood there smoking in silence while HP tried to work out his next move.

Really he felt like leaving; that weird stare Erman had flashed at him a while back had actually scared him a bit and he suddenly remembered that they were completely alone out here in the bush, with no way of calling for help.

But Erman seemed to have calmed down again now. The mad look on his face had gone and the parts of his face that were visible behind his beard had resumed their normal color, so it probably wouldn't be that risky to hang about a bit longer.

Besides, he had a feeling there was more he needed to find out.

"So how did you get dragged into all this, Erman?" HP began tentatively.

Erman took a long, final drag and then flicked the butt into the nettles.

"I was the one who installed their farm up here."

He glanced quickly at HP and discovered that he was looking lost again.

"Server farm," he explained slowly, as if he were talking to a child.

"The Game has five in total, or at least they did when I got out."

He counted on his fingers again:

"North America, South America, Africa, Asia, and Europe or Middle East. Seriously massive giant farms that handle all the data in the Game. The servers in there control all the mobile phones, image files; they send out the assignments, gather it all together and store the information, and handle the cash flow. They also control all communication between the Players, the Game Master, and the Circle. No farms, no Game, get it?"

HP nodded eagerly, he got it, and more important: this was seriously useful information!

"So you installed the one for Europe?"

"Europe and the Middle East," Erman corrected.

"That must be a pretty massive farm, then?"

HP was trying to sound impressed. Evidently it worked, because the guy suddenly looked a bit happier.

"I was basically given a free hand, a hefty bank account, and a few basic specs, then I was left to get on with it. Almost six months' work, sixty hours a week. All the latest technology, as well as a few things that still haven't hit the market, and maybe never will. NASA stuff, yeah? The Game could get hold of anything, and I mean *anything*! I just had to say what I needed and they sorted it."

He sighed happily.

"Sounds pretty sweet!" HP said to flatter him. "But how did they find you? I mean . . . why you in particular?"

"Because I was the best, wasn't I?" Erman gave him another condescending stare, but HP let it pass.

"Didn't you get what I told you just now? The Game does its homework, they've got informants everywhere, and it didn't take them long to put together a shortlist of people who could do what they wanted to get done."

He waved two fingers at HP, and HP quickly finished his cigarette, pulled out the packet, and lit two new Marlboros for himself and his host.

"First an anonymous email to see if I was interested, spiced with just enough questions and challenges to get me going. Pretty much like you and your first assignments.

"It took a while before I realized that they were really serious, that they really were planning to put together an installation like that up here, and weren't just talking theoretically. When I finally understood it was serious, I couldn't say no.

This was a once-in-a-lifetime opportunity, the sort of thing most people in my line of work could only dream of. The only problem was that I never got any sort of recognition for it."

He cleared his throat and spat a gob of saliva toward the nettles.

"They flew in a load of suits and I had to sign loads of documents, but they were basically all variations on rule number one: *Never talk about the Game!* When it was all done they came back and checked and once they'd approved everything I had to hand over my keys, pass card, and everything. *Thanks a lot, we'll take it from here.* I actually offered to carry on, become the system administrator for the farm. I'd almost have done it for nothing, just to keep working with it all, both the servers and what I'd seen of the Game itself; it all seemed pretty appealing . . ."

"But . . . ?"

"'*Thanks, but no, thanks, we've got our own people.*' And that was that! Paid off, just like that, after all my hard work. The pass card I handed in had probably been canceled before I even left the building, and then I was out in the cold. I tried to get remote access to the system a couple of times but all the back doors had been closed. Then I got a little message from the Game Master, and just like you, sadly I wasn't smart enough to believe it . . ."

He took a couple of deep drags and slowly let the smoke out as he shook his head.

"I was having serious trouble letting go of it all, it was my magnum opus. The best thing I'd ever done, the sort of thing only a very few people in the world could have managed on their own and in such a short space of time. But I didn't get any recognition at all for it, just thanks for the coffee and good-bye. I was so stupid that I kept on trying to find a way into the system. Maybe I was thinking that if I found some sort of problem, something that had gone wrong that I could fix, making it all work even better, then they'd know that they needed me and let me back in again. That I was a force to be reckoned with! But there are never any comebacks. Once you're out in the cold, they never let you back in!"

HP gulped.

That wasn't the message he'd been hoping to hear.

"So what happened?" he asked, even though he'd already guessed the answer.

"All of a sudden I started to get problems. Installations I'd done elsewhere crashed, programs turned out to be riddled with viruses, and my customers went mad.

"Then my bank account was blocked, and my phone and Internet connections were cut off without any warning, as well as a load of other problems. I worked day and night to put everything right, but after a year or so my business was basically ruined. The same thing went for me, it was 'round about then that I got ill."

Erman was suddenly sounding tired.

"So I left it all behind and vanished from the map. You won't find me in any databases anywhere," he added happily. "I don't really exist. No personal ID number, no bank account, loyalty cards, or phone, electricity, and water accounts. Completely out of sight of Big Brother!"

"But how do you get it all to work; I mean, you must still need cash?"

"You can sort anything if you really want to. It just takes a bit of planning and work, but it's possible. Don't forget, it's not that long since the Internet was pure science fiction! I just do everything old-school, cash only and low-tech. It actually works a lot better than you might think!"

HP shook his head doubtfully. He'd rather take a few deep breaths from the moped's exhaust than live the rest of his life like this. No TV, no Internet, not even electricity! All alone in the dark in the middle of nowhere. Throw in what the Game had done to him, and it wasn't so strange that the man seemed to be teetering on the edge.

"This farm," he said cautiously. "Where exactly is it?"

Erman snorted.

"Where the fuck do you think? Where do you put a server farm of that size? Where are the best connections, the most stable transfers, and the best environment for computer traffic? Think! Where are all the big players up here? Northern Europe's very own Silicon Valley!"

It took a few seconds before HP's overworked brain made the connection.

"Kista," he whispered, almost devoutly.

"Bingo!" Erman replied with a smile. "You're not completely thick after all!"

"Nilla, there's something I'd like to sort out with you, something important and I'd really appreciate it if you had a couple of minutes to talk."

Good speech, entirely in line with her preprepared script.

Still silence, but at least Nilla hadn't hung up. She could hear the other woman breathing down the line. Heavy breaths, as if she'd been running to answer in time. Rebecca interpreted the silence as a sort of encouragement.

"I'd like to explain to you what happened that evening, and

why. How everything ended up the way it did. But I'd rather not do it over the phone. Is there any chance we could meet for a chat somewhere?"

She was trying her level best to sound calm and collected. As if what she was asking was no big deal, just a conversation between two adults to sort a few things out.

"I thought I'd made myself clear in my email, Rebecca."

Nilla's voice was ice-cold.

"Neither I nor anyone else in my family has anything to say to you. Please don't call me again!"

"B-but . . ." she began, before she realized that the conversation was over.

"So if you were me, a relatively low-tech guy who wanted to cause a bit of trouble for the Game and the Game Master. Give them a bit of payback for all the shit they've thrown at the two of us. What would you do?"

Erman nodded thoughtfully.

"Interesting question, hmm . . ."

He thought in silence for a few seconds.

"Obviously, the best thing would be to blow the whole thing sky high, but maybe that's a bit over the top . . ."

"Really, you think so?!" slipped out of HP, but Erman didn't seem to have noticed.

"If I were you, I'd probably focus on the money," he went on.

"How do you mean?"

"Well, you already know how the rewards work, a foreign bank card linked to an anonymous account. Pretty much like the charge card for a cell. You just take out the money, and it's impossible to trace who's got which card."

HP nodded impatiently. *Get to the point, mofo!*

"All their payments work the same way, in principle. Wages for the functionaries, the Ants, and the subcontractors, it's all done by cards, and those in turn are fed from an anonymous account in a bank somewhere in the Caribbean. The mother account is always loaded with cash to keep the whole thing rolling. If I seriously wanted to fuck with the Game Master, I'd try to get hold of the account number and make a few withdrawals. That would paralyze the whole Game for weeks, maybe months, and you'd end up with enough money to hide yourself away pretty damn well in some distant but agreeable place."

"Would that really work?"

"Yeah, probably." Erman shrugged. "The point is that because the Game is damn careful to keep everything anonymous, there are no individuals linked to the account. All you need is the numerical combination that's currently being used. I'd guess that they change the number all the time, so you'd have to be pretty smart, and pretty quick. I never got to see any of the numbers myself, I just organized the setup itself. The guys they flew in used to type them in whenever it was necessary. But it's all inside the farm. I'm sure of that."

"Is it possible to hack into it?"

"No, like I said, I tried that, and if I can't get into it when I was the person who set the whole thing up, then I guarantee you that no one else would be able to either. We're talking IT security that's better than the Pentagon and NASA combined . . ."

Sure, HP thought skeptically, but either way, hacking didn't look like an option. "So how would you get hold of the account number?"

He had already guessed the answer.

"You'd have to get inside the farm. There's a control room, and once you got inside there it would be possible to extract whatever you needed, as long as you knew where to look. If they so much as guess that the account has been blown, they'll change the code instantly."

HP nodded as he stubbed out his cigarette on his shoe.

This was all sounding a bit *Mission: Impossible.*

But what the hell, he hadn't come all the way out here just to go home empty-handed. Too much information was better than too little.

"Can you tell me what I'd have to do?" he said, tossing the butt toward the nearest tree.

Erman chuckled.

"Sure, Double O Seven, no problem!"

He turned on his heel and went back inside the house.

HP took the chance to light another cig. This whole thing was starting to sound like a fucking blockbuster video. He wasted a couple of minutes trying to work out which one came closest. *Conspiracy Theory* maybe, or *Enemy of the State*? It was like a mixture of all of them, some kind of tribute thing. He took a couple of deep drags. High above he could hear a familiar droning.

Farthundra Airline's afternoon flight. He grinned to himself.

Erman came back out onto the porch with a folded piece of paper in his hand.

"This is all you need: the address of the farm and a few old user names that might still work. I've written down the bank's website as well, in case you make it that far. Now you just have to figure out a way of getting into the building, because I'm afraid I can't help you with that."

HP took hold of the piece of paper, but Erman didn't let go.

"Promise me one thing, HP."

"What?"

"You've seen how I live, what the Game did to me." His stare was starting to get to HP again. "Promise me that you'll use this information to give them one hell of a fucking kick in the balls, just promise me that!" Erman's face was starting to change color again.

"Sure, mate, no problem, take it easy!" HP muttered uncomfortably, snatching the note.

He'd got what he wanted, and it was pretty much time to get away from there.

The address was the only thing he'd get any real use out of; the rest was more or less meaningless. No matter what he'd promised this hillbilly, he was hardly going to break into a damn server farm, all he needed was a way to get to the Game Master and now he'd got it. A visiting address, no less. All he had to do was head out there and knock on the door, if he still felt like doing that after everything he'd heard.

The buzzing sound above them returned and Erman twitched. He stared anxiously around the treetops trying to catch a glimpse of the plane.

"Take it easy, Erman, it's just Farthundra's very own airline doing its daily flight." HP grinned nervously. "Nothing worth crapping your pants over."

"What-did-you-say?!" Erman spun toward him and HP saw that the crazy look had suddenly made a full-blown comeback.

"I said it was just a plane towing an advertisement for some fucking farmers' market in Fjärdhundra next week. Nothing to get steamed about."

He was speaking slowly on purpose, the way Erman had

done to him half an hour or so ago, but he could hear how worried he sounded.

"You've seen the plane before?"

Erman's face had gone completely white.

"Y-yes, it flew past just before you picked me up in your hicksville limo; just take it easy, okay!"

Erman didn't seem to hear him. He stood completely still for a few seconds.

"Go!" he finally managed to say through gritted teeth.

"What?" HP didn't understand anything.

"Go, get lost, fuck off, are you thick or what?!"

He spun his arms and took a step toward HP.

HP backed away instinctively and held up his hands.

"Okay, okay, calm down, I'm going, I'm going!"

Christ, the guy had really lost it this time.

"It's only a damn plane, Erman, there's no need to get so worked up!"

So much for that brilliant plan.

Nilla still hated her, she'd understood that much. Which wasn't really so surprising, seeing as it had been her adored big brother who had gone through the balcony railing.

Nilla and Dag had always been close, and she'd never accepted the investigation's conclusions that the whole thing had been at least in part an accident. The company the housing association contracted to renovate the façade had cut corners when they were fixing the balconies back on, and several bolts had evidently been missing.

"An unfortunate circumstantial coincidence," it had said in the verdict.

For Henke that meant ten months for causing another person's death instead of manslaughter. If the balcony railing had been correctly fitted with all its bolts in place, Dag would probably have been okay.

But it was difficult to know for sure. The shove had been pretty hard, maybe hard enough for him to have tumbled *over* the railing? That couldn't be ruled out, at any rate, or so the court had reasoned.

For her own part, she doubted that conclusion. Dag was big and heavy, almost ninety kilos of muscle, and he had good balance. If the railing hadn't given way, he wouldn't have fallen, and their lives would have looked very different. Henke would never have ended up in prison and she would never have been released from hers. His imprisonment and her freedom—each one was dependent on the other.

The problem was just that it shouldn't have been like that. That's what she had wanted to tell Nilla. What had really happened that night. And why . . .

"Only a plane? Only a plane?!!!" Small drops of saliva were getting caught in the yellowing beard around Erman's mouth.

"You don't get any of it, do you, you stupid fuck?! They've got ears everywhere, absolutely every-fucking-where! Didn't you understand what I said about the Ants? Who did you talk to on your way here, the bus driver, some nice old lady on the train? Did you happen to mention it on the phone to some friend, or were you stupid enough to write the directions on your computer?"

His voice had hit falsetto again.

"None of that, I promise . . ."

HP was slowly backing toward the wheel tracks that led toward civilization. This was getting really creepy now. He had to get away from this psycho, straightaway. God knew what would happen otherwise. *In the forest no one can hear you squeal.*

Erman took another couple of steps forward, clenching his fists, then abruptly stuck out one of his index fingers.

"Google!" he managed to spit. "You Google Mapped the address, admit it!"

"No, I didn't!" HP replied instinctively, then realized at the same moment that that's exactly what he'd done.

Erman must have noticed the change in the look on his face, or else he guessed that HP was lying.

Either way, he leaped a couple of strides toward HP.

"You stupid fuck!" Erman roared. "I gave you one simple instruction. Don't talk to anyone, don't use anything electronic. And you go and Google Map me! You might as well have been working for the Game Master directly, Christ, I ought to kill you on the spot!"

"Sorry!" HP muttered, now too terrified to even try to lie properly.

For a moment he thought he was going to end up buried like the fucking Bocksten Man. Dug up in two hundred years' time to get his perfectly preserved backside put on display in a glass case in Farthundra's local history museum. The thought almost made him crap his pants.

Erman took another few steps in HP's direction, then he momentarily stopped.

He stood there for a couple of seconds, apparently thinking. Then without a word he turned on his heel and disappeared inside the house.

HP didn't hang around to find out if he was going to come back out with a shotgun. Instead he turned and fled along the path back toward the road as fast as he could. Above him he could still hear the drone of the airplane. It sounded like it was circling.

After a couple of hundred meters he reached the edge of the forest. There was about a kilometer of gravel track through the open fields before he could reach the relative safety of the road. He looked anxiously over his shoulder. Shit, obviously he should have nicked the flatbed moped, or at least pulled the sparking plug out or something. Now he'd just be an open target out there.

Oh well, no point worrying about that now.

He couldn't hear anything like a moped engine, but that was mainly because of the damn plane that still circling overhead. He noticed that the advertising banner was gone. So what was the idiot doing up there, then?

He left the shade of the forest and set off toward the road. Every ten meters or so he glanced behind him. Still nothing. He was starting to get his fear back under control. What a psycho the guy had turned out to be. Thanks a lot, Mange, that was a brilliant tip-off!

Another glance. No sign of Erman. Great!

It wasn't until he got about halfway across the field that he noticed that the sound of the plane engine had changed. Before, it had been mainly a monotonous buzzing sound, one note higher or lower depending on where in its circuit it happened to be. But unexpectedly the sound was getting louder, both in volume and pitch, and it took him a few seconds before he understood why. Because out of the blue, when he looked over his shoulder yet again to make sure Erman wasn't coming after him, he discovered that the plane was diving straight at him like he was fucking Cary Grant! He could hardly believe his eyes.

It came closer and closer, but it wasn't until the plane was more or less filling his field of vision that he had the sense to get really scared. The roar of the engine and the sound of the wind on the wings were drowning out all his thoughts. He saw the whirring propeller at the front and just beneath it the metal beam connecting the undercarriage coming straight toward him, but he was still having trouble taking in what was going on.

Shit! was the only contribution his brain could come up with, then he tripped over his own feet and fell to the ground.

He felt the rush of wind and heard the sound of the undercarriage missing his head by the smallest of margins, before he suddenly realized he had a mouthful of gravel.

The engine noise started to decrease and HP raised his scratched face just enough to see the plane bank in a slow left-hand turn. It took him a couple of seconds to become aware that the pilot was climbing to gain enough height to make a second attempt.

Fuck! he thought in panic, staggering to his knees and then forcing his paralyzed legs into action. He abandoned the gravel track and headed off straight across the field instead, in the direction he knew the bus stop was in. Dust and soil swirled up around his feet, and the stubble left by the crop tore at his trouser legs.

Scratch-bang-scratch-bang-scratch-bang.

HP was running as he had never run before, that much was certain.

At least five hundred meters left to the road, to salvation. The plane was almost halfway through its circle. His heart was pumping so hard in his chest that he thought it would burst. He could taste blood in his mouth, and his pulse was pounding in his temples.

Then he heard the roar of the engine get louder again as the plane dived toward him Alfred Hitchcock–style, and now the noise was even more earsplitting, if that was possible. He ran on in panic, trying to zigzag to present a harder target, the way you did in Counter-Strike. But this was IRL, and not some damn computer game! The plane was coming closer and closer and nothing seemed likely to divert it.

All at once he caught sight of something in the stubble a few meters ahead of him. It looked like a white plastic stick of some sort, about two meters long.

He didn't really know where the idea came from, but just before the plane was on top of him he threw himself at the stick, grabbed it with both hands, and with one end stuck under his armpit, something like a knight's lance, he rolled over onto his back.

The plane filled his world; the roar of the engine was deafening. As the rush of air whipped his breath away he felt the stick strike something solid and then it was torn from his hands.

Then the plane was gone. HP rolled over onto his stomach again. The remnants of the shredded stick lay scattered a few meters away.

Must have hit the propeller, he thought as he struggled to his feet again.

The plane had started to climb again. But this time the engine didn't sound quite so angry. It was rising and falling as if the engine was running unevenly, and HP could clearly hear a whistling sound that must have been coming from the damaged propeller.

The pilot was clearly having trouble, but HP didn't wait to see how he was going to deal with it.

Instead he set off at full speed toward the bus stop, which was now visible up ahead. As he got closer he saw a bus just passing the stop and he changed direction in an attempt to intercept it. He might just make it . . .

Then he caught sight of something from the corner of his eye and realized that the pilot had changed tactic. Instead of diving from a few hundred meters up, the plane was sniffing across the field, and HP could see the undercarriage almost touching the stubble.

This time it wouldn't do any good to dive; he'd get his skull crushed either by the wheels or the bar between them.

Terrified, he sped up even more. He raced toward the road, seeing the bus come closer, and exerted every last bit of strength to beating it. The sound of the plane was coming closer and closer.

He put one foot in the ditch, which made him lose his balance, but he was running so hard that he carried on, stumbling up onto the side of the road, just in front of the roaring bus.

Then a shriek of brakes, a squeal of tires, and the airplane motor roaring overhead.

A moment later he was knocked over and everything went black.

"Hey, man, are you okay?"

The voice was coming from far away and HP sat up with a jerk. For a panic-stricken moment he thought he'd gone blind, that he'd got brain damage or something like that, and was condemned to a life of eternal darkness. But gradually his senses returned and he managed to open his eyes.

"You okay, man?" A young man in a uniform that was too big for him was leaning over him, and beside him he saw a couple of anxious old ladies' faces.

"You came out of nowhere, man, I hardly had time to brake, but I don't think you got much more than a knock."

HP didn't answer, just tried to get up with an effort.

The driver, an immigrant of about thirty or so, gave him a hand.

He did a quick check of his limbs, with satisfactory results.

"We ought to call an ambulance," one of the old ladies trilled. At a guess, she must have been on the bus.

". . . and the police," the other one chimed in. "That plane . . ."

"No ambulance!" HP interrupted. "I'm fine!"

He was too. Apart from the scratches to his face and hands, and the fact that the wind had been knocked out of him when the bus hit him, he felt fine. The last thing he needed right now was a load of nosy cops.

"Sorry," he muttered to the driver. "I misjudged it, my fault, my bad!" he managed to say as his voice started to work again. "I'm fine, really!"

"Great!" the driver said in relief. "Maybe we should get going?"

He nodded to the two ladies who were standing anxiously at the side of the road.

"No damage done, so no ambulance. Everyone on board!"

Then he brushed the grit from HP's back as he whispered:

"You're not going to file a complaint, are you, man? I've already got one charge for speeding, and I need this job, you know?"

"No worries!" HP replied, starting to get a grip again. "Don't worry, just let me off without paying and it's all forgotten."

"No problem, friend!" The driver smiled in relief and gestured invitingly toward the door of the bus.

"You should just make it to the train, but it'll be tight."

HP just nodded and collapsed in the nearest seat.

"Did you see that plane, man? God, it was flying low!"

13 | MIND GAMES

HE COULD HARDLY remember the journey home. HP had completely exhausted himself running across the field, and if you added that to his close encounter with the bus, it wasn't so surprising that he was shattered. He did actually try to stay awake and check to see if he was being followed, but it had been impossible. His eyelids just kept drooping and he ended up all the way out in Älvsjö before he realized that he'd dozed off and gone too far.

It wasn't until he eventually made it back to Slussen that he woke up properly and managed to do the secret agent trick to shake off anyone following him. But by the time he finally got home to the little allotment cottage he instantly felt wide awake.

His heart was racing and adrenaline was rushing through his body, and it was like he was reliving the whole thing again. For a few minutes he actually believed he was about to have a heart attack, that he was going to die out there in the cottage and his ant-eaten corpse wouldn't be found until Auntie showed up to close the place up for winter.

But then his galloping pulse finally calmed down and the fog in his head began to lift.

What in the name of fuck had actually happened?

Had it really happened, properly, or had he just dreamed it all?

It only took a quick glance in the mirror to write off the dream theory. Filthy, covered in scratches, and the bottom of his jeans left in tatters by the sharp stubble in the field. It was a damn good job he hadn't been wearing shorts!

The man in the plane really had been trying to bump him off, and he'd probably have succeeded if HP hadn't made it onto the bus. His pulse started to race again and he felt sick, and it took a few minutes and several liters of water before he felt he was back in control again.

His thoughts were churning wildly in his head—the drying machine in there seemed to hit some sort of hyperspeed.

The Game, the assignments, everything that had happened to him—it was all just a betting game for bored rich bastards?

They'd pressed all his buttons, pushed his boundaries, and got him to play along merrily. Was he really so fucking easy to deceive?

The alternative was obviously that Erman had been lying, and had just been talking a load of crap.

Okay, so the guy clearly didn't have all his sheep in the meadow, but he didn't seem like a liar. The hillbilly obviously believed one hundred percent in what he had said, and most of it also fitted in with HP's own experiences. The problem was that he just couldn't take it all in; it was too much.

But if he split the story into two, it worked better. If he bit the rotten apple and accepted that he'd merely been a crazy puppet leaping happily into action whenever the Game Master pulled the right strings, and if he bought all the stuff about betting and the way the Game was set up . . .

If he did that, then the first part of what Erman had told him pretty much explained everything he had been through.

Even if it stung badly to accept that he had been a sort of court jester in some casino, the explanation made sense, unlike the rest of the story. At least it kept more or less on the right side of the crazy line.

But he was still having trouble buying the conspiracy theory.

The idea that the Game spanned the whole world, took on all manner of dirty jobs, and also had ears and eyes everywhere—that was impossible to take in.

Erman himself had said that those were conclusions he had reached all on his own, not based on anything he had seen or experienced directly. Possibly one result of too many lonely hours spent out in that cottage with no contact with the civilized world. You really had to feel sorry for the poor bastard. Even if he'd practically scared the shit out of HP out there in the forest, he still felt some sort of weird connection with Erman. They actually had quite a lot in common. The Game Master hadn't exactly been particularly lenient toward either of them. Tracking them down, making them feel special, and then, once the Game had had enough of their talents, dropping them like they were yesterday's news.

So what if Erman had lost some of his marbles? To be honest, HP was actually really fucking grateful that the poor reclusive bastard had helped him along. Opening his eyes, and possibly even giving him a way of accessing the Game.

Whatever, he was feeling considerably calmer now. The nausea had almost gone and he was starting to feel hungry. Some Heinz baked beans was all he managed to find, and he ate them straight from the can.

So what about the plane, then, the guy who'd tried to get him? How the hell could you explain that?

No one had followed him out there, he was absolutely certain of that, so what the fuck had happened?

Okay, in theory it *could* all have been a mistake. He and Erman were roughly the same height and had the same color and length of hair. From a distance you might get them mixed up, and from a height of a couple of hundred meters it was probably impossible to tell the difference.

The nut lived alone out there, so maybe the pilot simply assumed that the person emerging from the trees had to be Erman, especially when the description seemed to match?

That's what must have happened!

Whoever it was in that plane, he must have had some beef with Erman, not him.

Maybe some angry neighbor or inbred local who had run into the psycho in the co-op? And decided to scare the shit out of the crazy fucker, Alfred Hitchcock–style, when the opportunity unexpectedly arose. Stuff like that happened sometimes, you just had to take a look at TV3. Christ, there was a whole fucking series about people who did shit like that . . . !

The more he thought about it, the more likely it sounded. Some sort of sick neighborhood dispute that had got out of hand. It was a considerably easier to accept that explanation than the alternative.

"Global conspiracy, my ass," he muttered to himself. "Yeah, right!"

He'd never even been close to falling for that.

Relieved, he leaned back in the kitchen sofa and turned on his laptop. There was nothing like a bit of television to make you forget your problems. You could always find some poor bastard out there who was in a worse state, and made you feel better about things. Once everything had calmed down a bit, he'd think about what to do next.

Even before he heard the voice coming out of the speaker he grasped what had happened. The local television news pictures were enough on their own for him to get it—the burning house, flashing blue lights, and fire engines parked among the nettles.

> For the past hour firefighters have been trying to extinguish a fierce blaze in an agricultural property just west of Sigtuna. It is not currently known if anyone was in the building when the fire broke out. The property is listed as uninhabited since the death of its last occupant, but according to witnesses there have been one or more people living in the house in recent months. The police would like to contact a man in his thirties who was involved in a minor collision with a local bus at a nearby bus stop earlier in the day . . .

Half-digested baked beans all over Auntie's sink. HP was vomiting like a champion.

"Fucking fuck! Fucking fuck! Fucking fuck!" was all his brain was able to come up with.

It had taken him several days to recover. He must have picked up some sort of virus or some other crap, he had a fever, and the projectile vomiting didn't let up until there was nothing left but bile.

As usual, it was Mange who came to his rescue, when he turned up to see why he hadn't been in touch and found him flaked out on Auntie's rib-backed sofa. Totally fucking embarrassing, but Mange had shown he was a true friend. He'd taken him off to the Eriksdal pool so he could get cleaned up, then conjured up some clean clothes and rose hip soup, and he hadn't even minded cleaning up the disgusting kitchen.

Yep, Mange was a true friend, a BFF actually. And from now on HP would actually treat him like one. To start with, he'd call him Farook. If the name was important for Mange, then he'd use it from now on and stop ridiculing him.

He'd had loads of dreams while he was sick, fevered dreams about all sorts of things. He was pretty used to weirdo dreams anyway; they almost came as standard a few days or a week after a decent trip. He'd read that the THC in grass got stored up in the fatty tissues of the brain, and sometimes made its presence felt afterward, a bit like a bomb on a timed detonator. Often his dreams were spaced-out *Lord of the Rings* affairs with giant butterflies and talking trees, which was pretty cool.

But these dreams were different, far darker and less pleasant than his hash fantasies.

One dream he remembered particularly clearly involved him running naked through the Klara Tunnel. Erman's charred, blackened corpse was chasing him on the flatbed moped, at the head of hundreds of stampeding, riderless horses.

The tunnel exit on Sveavägen was getting closer and closer, but his pursuers were gaining on him. His steps were getting heavier and heavier as the slope got steeper and steeper, and he knew that he wasn't going to make it. The moped's engine rose to a rattling falsetto, along with the clatter of hooves.

They're everywhere!! It's all a fucking Game!! The corpse's charred mouth howled, but the last word was distorted and bounced around him like an echo off the walls of the tunnel.

Game
Game
Game

He woke up with his heart pounding in his chest just as the moped was about to smash into the back of his knees.

But now he felt better.

No fever, clean again, and he'd eaten his fill. Maybe his legs felt a bit stiff, but that would pass.

The question was: What was he going to do now?

He wouldn't be able to move back into his flat for another week or so, evidently there was some sort of delay with the new door. In a way he was almost glad. There was no point denying it really; he wasn't looking forward to moving back home. The fact was that after what had happened out near Sigtuna he was . . . frightened.

Yes, he'd admitted it. Henrik "HP" Pettersson, the man, the myth, the legend—was scared.

So the Game wasn't just some sort of low-level anarchist pay-per-view YouTube rip-off like he'd originally thought, but something completely different, something considerably more unpleasant. The whole betting aspect was worse than he'd thought at first, he understood that now. Pushing people gradually to shift their limits of what was okay, consciously seeking out people who were easily manipulated, and then pushing them just to see how far they were prepared to go.

And all that, just because it was cool!

But the second part still seemed too incredible to be true. That the assignments weren't just thought up at random but consciously designed to satisfy some anonymous customers? If that was true, and he emphasized the word *if*, then it meant that he and all the other players were being screwed over twice. They weren't just jackasses on speed or Internet tarts whoring themselves out for a few comments and virtual thumbs-up. They were also total fucking puppets!

Unconscious hitmen who knew nothing and were therefore easy to dispose of if the shit hit the fan. A load of patsies, stooges that no one gave a damn about, even if they tried to tell the truth. Because who was going to believe them?

The thought made him both angry and more than a little shaky.

The implications of a scenario like that were so massive he could hardly imagine them. But wasn't it more likely to be Erman's paranoid brain finally crossing the fine line between quaint rural eccentric and total fucking lunatic?

Right up until he had seen the cottage going up in flames, and doubtless Erman along with it, he had been prepared to believe that, but now he was seeing it in a very different light . . .

There was really only one way to find out for certain, so he decided to start with a bit of research.

One of the many Unemployment Service training courses he'd done his best to forget had been in the very subject that he needed to remember now. With a decent search engine you could take the world by surprise, he remembered that much at least . . .

Farook had helped him to set up the laptop, routing it through a number of anonymized servers that had popped up in the days before the IPRED law came into force. From now on he'd be invisible on the net, a ghost rider.

He opened one of the search engines and got to work. Erman's note left him none the wiser.

"*Torshamnsgatan 142*" was all it said, apart from a few nerdy passwords that just might, or might not, work if he ever managed to get in. The poor flame-grilled fucker could have added a bit more information, like what the company was called, or what floor it was on? Was that really too much to ask?

The address certainly matched a street in Kista, but didn't really give him much more than that. It was a perfectly ordinary office building close to the E4 highway, but that was all the satellite pictures had to offer. He found a list of small telecom companies that either had been or were still based in the building, but none of them seemed to have the slightest thing to do with games or computers.

He didn't really know what he had been expecting. Some sort of walled fortress maybe, or a secret address that couldn't be found on any map? A bit like the National Defense Radio Establishment out on Lovön? But this seemed completely halal, with not the slightest hint of a mysterious organization or a secret server farm. So either Erman had decided to give him a dud address for some reason, or, more likely, the Game had upped sticks and moved somewhere else.

Disappointed and without any great expectations, he decided to carry on looking into the rest of Erman's theories anyway.

He tried typing in a few search words, like "inexplicable,"
"failed investigation," "unknown," and got a few thousand hits
immediately. He filtered out anything to do with UFOs, which
reduced the number to about three hundred, then added
"perpetrator" as an option, which brought the total down to
a more manageable quantity. A bit more clever clicking and
he had a decent collection of incidents listed on the screen in
front of him.

He scrolled quickly through them.

It turned out to be the right mixture of stuff, and for a
few seconds he felt almost relieved. But then he started looking more carefully. And gradually things began to pop up that
were, to put it mildly, disconcerting . . .

To start with he found a number of minor occurrences
that he had never heard about but that still had the right vibe:
cars whose brakes had stopped working, computer systems
that had packed up in the middle of the payroll, inexplicable
power cuts, and politicians getting shit through their letter
boxes.

But there were a number of other, considerably more familiar events that had been picked up by the search.

He read them through once, then again, and slowly a very
uncomfortable feeling began to settle over him.

The first item was pretty much in his own backyard:

*On the night of 17 May 1990 Katarina Church on Söder-
malm in Stockholm was destroyed by fire.*

*The church tower collapsed into the nave, leaving just
the external walls standing. However a number of valu-
able textiles and the church silver were rescued. In spite
of a major inquiry, no explanation for the fire was ever*

*established, which has led to speculation that it was caused
by everything from an electrical fault to arson.*

*If arson was indeed the cause, no motive has ever been
identified.*

He also remembered the second one very well:

*On Sunday 3 September, 2006, at 20:41:51, the National
Police Board in Stockholm received a report from the Security Police that the internal computer network of the Social
Democratic Party, the SDP.net, had been hacked. The perpetrator was at that point still unknown. Late that same
evening the Social Democrats called a press conference
to announce that they had reported members of the Folk
Party to the police for hacking. The report maintained that
computers, which to judge by their IP addresses belonged
to the Folk Party, had been used to gain illegal entry to the
most sensitive areas of the SDP network, to which only 26
senior party officials had access. This access was supposed
to have been gained with the help of log-in details that had
inexplicably leaked and had given their political opponents
unlimited access to the most confidential information in the
Social Democrats' internal computer network.*

This was major-league stuff! Both of these on their own
were exotic enough for some serious betting.

Could you persuade someone to set light to something as
sacred as a church? What were the odds on that?

Of course you could, no question. But what about the next
step, if you were to believe Erman's theories?

Who would have commissioned a job like that?

Someone who would dearly have loved to have the honor of rebuilding a famous Stockholm landmark? A politician, a company, or a wealthy businessman with a dodgy reputation to clean up?

A quick look at the foundation that was responsible for the restoration listed a whole load of heavyweights who had opened their wallets. They'd even got Parliament to cough up some money, although this was strictly a local Stockholm issue. Anyway, didn't the Swedish church have more than enough money stashed away to pay for the whole thing themselves?

A conspiracy?

Well, you couldn't exactly rule it out. Plausible, in other words. A bit of a long shot, but certainly possible if you had a bit of imagination and dared to think outside the box. A bit like the *Da Vinci Code*, basically.

But what about the Social Democrats' and Folk Party's own little Watergate, then?

That took a bit more thought.

A well-placed Ant inside the Social Democrats could easily fix the log-in details. Most people were stupid enough to scribble them down on a Post-it note stuck under their desk so they could get back into the system after their summer holiday.

But who would have wanted it to happen?

Who benefited?

Short-term, obviously the Folk Party, so they were potential customers.

But surely the whole thing favored the Social Democrats in the long term?

A bit more clicking seemed to support that angle. The Folk Party was reduced almost by half in the parliamentary election a few weeks later, and their collapse almost sank the entire shift of power from left to right. So there were at least two possible conspiracy options here.

Someone on the blue side wanted to get at confidential information, and someone on the red wanted to catch the blues red-handed, so to speak.

The result?

Plausible, certainly, and actually less far-fetched than the first. Christ, what a story this was turning into!

Worst of all was the very last item he stumbled upon. He read it a couple of times before it sank in properly. Once it had, he came close to shitting himself.

The description of the perpetrator that was presented in the 1994 inquiry concluded that the murder was carried out by a person acting alone, an individual with a personality disorder, driven by hatred or anger. He had probably had problems with relationships throughout his life, and particularly with any form of authority. He was introverted, isolated, and narcissistic, but not psychotic, and probably lacked close family and friends. His condition was connected with a feeling of having "failed" in life, the perception of being "an outsider" whose abilities had never been appreciated or allowed to reach their full potential.

The profile could perfectly easily have been written to describe him!

Okay, it wasn't exactly easy to admit, and navel-gazing wasn't exactly a favorite pastime of his. But after everything that had happened, his near-death experience in the flat and the whole business out in the sticks, he had started to look at himself in the mirror in a new way.

And what he found wasn't exactly an attractive sight . . .

If he was honest, his life wasn't really much to write home about. In general terms, he was a pretty good match for that description. Acting alone, outsider, few close relationships, egocentric, it all fitted pretty well.

A bit too well, really . . .

But it wasn't actually his fault that everything had gone to hell. He had had opportunities, prospects, the same as anyone. He could have been someone, someone important!

A fucking contender!

He had done one genuinely unselfish thing in his life, and what had he got for it? How had the world thanked him, rewarded him for his heroism? Yep, ten months in prison, straight to jail without passing Go, thank you very fucking much! Because in the land of semiskimmed milk, obviously no good deed must go unpunished.

And, after his stretch inside, suddenly all the opportunities were gone. The doors were all closed and the future royally screwed. Low-level hustling or some shitty McJob were pretty much the only options. So maybe it wasn't so weird that you didn't give a damn after that sort of let-down, and just focused on number one. And according to Erman, people like him were exactly the sort that the Game sent the Ants out to look for. Guys who fitted the list of prerequisites. Or, to be more accurate, the profile . . .

"They've been playing for years, long before the Internet," Erman had said.

What if they were already playing back in February '86, when a certain prime minister was assassinated? Conjured up a .357, stashed it somewhere suitable, then sent some-one out. A Player, a nobody like him, whose boundaries had already been shifted so far they were no longer anywhere in sight. An innocent call from a well-placed Ant would be enough.

The nine o'clock screening, Grand Cinema!

Then: lights, camera, action!

The hairs on the back of HP's neck stood up. The cottage suddenly felt too small, the ceiling was too low, threatening to suffocate him. He needed air. He had to get out.

It's all a damn game! the charred corpse in his head was screaming as he chucked up over the flower bed.

Okay, she was seriously worried now. After several days of foolishly thinking that he would get in touch, she had finally gone around to his flat. But the door was covered in plywood and under the smell of paint she could still detect a faint smell of smoke.

The next-door neighbor, an obviously doped-up guy with dreadlocks and a goatee beard, had told her about the fire, that someone had poured lighter fluid through Henke's letter box and set light to it.

But clearly Henke had survived; a day in hospital, then he was okay.

That at least was a relief.

So where was he now?

The Rasta couldn't enlighten her, and at this point in the conversation his addled brain seemed to have finally picked up the cop vibe and he quickly slammed the door on her.

After a bit of thought she had at least managed to work out

who was likely to know more. Mange Sandström, of course, Henke's best friend since primary school.

Didn't he have a computer shop somewhere near Skanstull?

A quick call to the Regional Communication Center and she had the address and was on her way.

Outside the shop she was aware that things weren't right. A blue-and-white strip of police cordon tape was still dangling from a lamppost, and one of the windows beside the door was still covered, somewhat inadequately, by the security company's tape. There was no mistaking the smell of smoke here either, as she opened the door and the *Star Wars* theme started to play. To judge by the chaos inside, they were still tidying up after the fire. There were boxes everywhere and half of the shelves and racks toward the front of the shop were empty. She almost stumbled over a bucket full of filthy water that was standing beside the door.

The second complete mess in half an hour, hardly a coincidence, at least not if Henke was involved. The question was, what had he got himself mixed up in this time?

Maybe Mange would be able to give her an answer?

"Hello, Rebecca!" he said in a surprised tone of voice from behind some shelves.

"Hi, Mange, it's been a while. Have you had visitors, or are you moving out?"

They exchanged a clumsy hug. A nightshirt and an embroidered waistcoat; at least his taste in clothes had changed dramatically since they last met.

"Just some kids," he muttered, and she could tell at once

that he was lying. "Powder from the extinguisher all over everything, so the insurance company are making a fuss . . ."

But it wasn't just his feeble explanation that was making him blush.

Mange had always had a bit of a crush on her, which was hardly a disadvantage given the reason for her visit today.

"My name's Farook Al-Hassan these days," he added, cheering up a bit. "I converted when I got married two years ago."

"Oh, you're married? And there was me thinking we'd end up together." She laughed, and watched as he turned a fetching shade of bright red.

So that explained the slightly odd clothes. Mange had gone and converted.

Maybe it wasn't so strange when she thought about it; he'd always seemed to be searching for something.

The last time she saw him he'd been a militant vegan, and before that a local politician, unless it was the other way around . . . ?

Mange was a smart lad, but there'd always been something lost about him. She just hoped he'd found something that worked for him now.

"Have you got children too?" she asked, mainly out of politeness.

"A boy, eight months, Mohammed."

He pulled out his wallet and she admired the miracle for the ten seconds that form demanded.

"He looks like you, Ma . . . I mean, Farook," she said, with what she hoped was her friendliest smile. *Get to the point, now, Normén!*

"Listen, I wanted to ask if you have any idea where Henke is?"

"Er . . . what do you mean?" Another feeble lie.

"Well, I've been trying to call him but none of the numbers I've got seem to work, so I thought maybe you might know where he is?"

He shook his head and did his best not to meet her gaze.

"Sorry, I haven't seen him for a while . . ."

She frowned. Two fires, Henke missing, and now thoroughly decent Mange lying to her face. Something was going on, and it was time that she found out what.

But just as she was about to open her mouth, Mange interrupted her.

"Listen, Rebecca, now that you're here there's something I've been wanting to say for ages."

"Okay," she said warily.

She really didn't have time for any latter-day declarations of love, but on the other hand she needed his help now. *Patience, Normén!*

"Well, Rebecca . . . I've always . . . I mean . . . oh, damn . . ."

He took a deep breath and seemed to pull himself together.

"You and Dag, all that business that happened with HP . . . well, you know?"

"Mmm," she replied neutrally.

"Well . . . I've sort of always . . . wanted to apologize to you. Dag and I were cousins, of course, and, well, you met him through me, and . . ."

He looked down at the counter. She suddenly felt sick. Probably the heat.

"I mean." He sighed, making a last attempt. "I-I've always felt a b-bit guilty about it all," he stammered. "That it was sort of my fault, if you know what I mean?"

He shot her a pleading look and she had absolutely no idea how to respond.

"Dag was older than me, of course, and we weren't exactly close, b-but I knew perfectly well what sort of person he was. I knew there were rumors about him, that he could be violent and . . . that his dad left because Dag beat him up. I mean, there was a lot of talk, but I never dared say anything . . . to you, I mean."

He was looking down at the counter again.

Rebecca took a deep breath.

What did he expect her to say?

The feeling of nausea was getting worse. The air in the shop was stuffy and her top was starting to stick to her body. She needed to put a stop to this discussion and get the conversation back on track, and fast.

"Listen, Mange," she said, as calmly as she could. "We all make our own decisions, you, me, Henke, and Dag. Right or wrong, we made our choices and in the end we each have to take the consequences. I was the one who fell in love with Dag, it was my decision to move in with him, and I was the one who didn't report him when things started to go wrong. It was my responsibility."

The truth, the whole truth, and nothing but the bastard painful truth, she thought bitterly. Okay, enough of that!

"Getting back to Henke, I was wondering . . ."

"But you don't get it!" he interrupted in a shaky voice. "HP told me he was thinking of killing him. That he was thinking of killing Dag! He told me what the bastard had done to you and how much he hated him. And I, I didn't do anything. I didn't try to stop him, I didn't tell anyone, and then it all went to hell. Dag dead, HP in prison, and you . . ."

He stopped and looked at her sadly.

"You didn't get away scot-free either, Rebecca."

He fell silent and she gave him a few seconds to pull himself together. Mind you, she needed the pause just as much herself. Waves of nausea were washing over her with full force now and she had to close her eyes for a few seconds to get her gag reflex under control.

"The only person who got out in one piece was me," he went on. "For me life just carried on almost as if nothing had happened. If I'd just opened my mouth, told s-someone what HP was going on about, then maybe everything would have been different? I could at least have told him to cool it. But I didn't. I don't really know why I didn't. All I know is that I could have done more to stop it happening. Much more!"

He fell silent again and seemed to be studying a random section of the cork matting.

Damn it to hell, this conversation was nothing like what she'd expected.

Suddenly the sounds of all the computers and gadgets combined into one single enervating, piercing note that seemed to penetrate her head and nail her brain to the inside of her skull.

She screwed her eyes up, swallowed a couple of times, and when she'd regained control of her body, pushed her way past Mange and into the little cubbyhole she'd glimpsed behind the bead curtain.

Lukewarm water from a dirty glass. Long, restorative gulps that rinsed all unwelcome thoughts away. *Pull yourself together, for God's sake, Normén!*

Even if Mange seemed to be in desperate need of a confessional, she certainly hadn't come here for anything like this. Chewing it all over and wallowing in the past. The really sick thing was that she only had to say a few words and she could absolve him from some of his sins. Tell him who the real murderer was. But something told her that the truth wouldn't set either of them free, and certainly not her.

Better to return to the present, focus on the task at hand, and get out of here. If she could just get hold of Henke, things would work themselves out, she was convinced of that, without really knowing why.

She refilled the glass and put it on the counter beside Mange. He seemed to have used her absence to pull himself together. His eyes still looked a bit red, but his face was more or less back to its usual color.

He drank in silence.

"I can see the way you're thinking, Mange, but I honestly don't think anyone could have stopped things from happening," she said slowly. "It just turned out the way it did, and we all have to try to move on. At least that's what I've tried to do."

She could hear how false her words sounded, but Mange nodded in agreement.

"Of course, you're right," he said. "It feels good to have got it out, anyway, after all this time. Sorry about the tears."

He smiled forlornly and wiped his nose with the sleeve of his shirt.

"Don't worry, it'll stay between us."

He smiled again, more relaxed this time, and she took the opportunity to change the subject.

"Look, are you really sure you haven't seen Henke?"

Another shake of the head.

"No, not really . . ."

She fixed him with her cop's stare, reluctantly, and it worked instantly.

"What do you mean, *not really*, Mange? Have you or haven't you seen him?"

Her voice had abruptly lost all its previous softness. It felt a bit mean to apply interrogation tactics now, especially after his emotional outburst, but she didn't actually have any choice. She had to get hold of Henke and didn't have time for any more distractions.

"Not for a few days," he muttered morosely, staring at the floor, and as far as she could tell that was probably the truth. She looked around and sniffed at the smell of smoke.

"Listen, those kids who set fire to your shop . . ."

She said it very slowly, fixing him with her stare. He wriggled like a worm on a hook, but she had no intention of letting him get away.

"Is it the same kids who set fire to Henke's flat?"

"Yes . . . er, I mean no, or rather . . ."

His eyes were flitting about, and he momentarily didn't seem to know what to do with his hands.

"Oh, Magnus . . ." she said in her gentlest voice and she leaned over the counter.

She waited until he met her gaze again:

"What's my idiot brother dragged you into this time?"

14 | WHITE BEAR

OKAY, HE'D JUST have to accept the truth—he'd got the whole thing on the brain.

Mel Gibson in *Conspiracy Theory*, Gene Hackman's character, Brill, in *Enemy of the State*, that's what he was turning into. The obsessive, the lone lunatic, the conspiracy nut who lived his life in discussion forums and saw intrigues around every fucking corner. He might as well get his own home page, a cottage in the woods, and a wall covered in newspaper cuttings; then everything would be perfect!

Okay, that business with the Palme murder was maybe a bit far-fetched, but on the other hand his theory was no crazier or worse than any of the other so-called lines of inquiry. Kurds, the "baseball" police squad, his wife, Lisbet, or a drunk acting on his own?

All aboard the Crazy Train!

Doors closing, next stop Looneyville!

There was a vast flock of weirdo theories out there in cyberspace, like shrieking harpies, each one crazier than the last. So why not his?

Just think about it!

How else could you fuck up the largest police investigation

in the world so spectacularly? Forgetting all common police sense, breaking loads of laws and rules by appointing an amateur to lead both the police work and the preliminary legal investigation? And, as if that wasn't enough, setting up a Social Democrat political stooge with his own miniature version of the Security Police to run a parallel investigation directly sanctioned by the justice minister . . .

The whole thing was a cascade of peculiarities, and the case threw up loads of questions to which there were no logical solutions, exactly as Erman had warned him. There just weren't any good explanations, or at least none that were better than the one he was beginning to accept more and more.

Besides, he could think of another political murder where, even though the man had been caught, the case was a good match for the profile "single perpetrator with no good motive." Not to mention the so-called Laser Man back in the early nineties. There was something methodical about the whole of his criminal progress, something that made you think of computer games. As if he had been working his way through different stages of difficulty, taking greater and greater risks. Almost as if he was clambering up some sort of league table . . .

According to the clips HP found on the Swedish television website, the culprit had blown the money he took from his victims in a German casino, so he evidently liked gambling. Was he actually a player, in two senses of the word? It made perfect sense, but at the same time it sounded completely insane! What about the Kennedy assassination? The sinking of the *Estonia*? Nine eleven?

Yes, he'd got it all on the brain.

Big-time!

He was scouring the news websites several times an hour, and even though they were mostly about Sweden's presidency of the EU, he imagined he could see them everywhere: signs of the Game.

A well-known financier who had vanished into thin air, a load of dynamite that had gone missing from a secure store, or a petty criminal in Portugal who had unexpectedly got it into his head to blow up an empty luxury yacht, and himself with it . . .

It was all out there, if you only knew what you were looking for. Things that couldn't be explained, no matter which way you approached them. That's to say, if the explanation wasn't the fact that Erman was right. That the whole thing was just a huge fucking Game!

I've opened your eyes and now you can see . . .

The weirdest thing was that he could see how crazy it sounded. But he still couldn't let it go. "An awareness of illness doesn't mean you're well," as one of his mom's alcoholic friends used to say.

There was a lot in that! But unlike the idiots out there, he had actually been caught up in it himself. An inside man, just like Brill. He knew that the Game existed, he had seen with his own eyes what they were capable of doing, or—to be more accurate—getting other people to do . . .

It was actually the manipulation that stung most.

The way they'd pressed his buttons and got him to play along willingly. Humiliating him just for the fun of it, then dropping him quicker than a flask of Russian thallium. But also the fact that he'd actually enjoyed being the center of attention, getting loads of cred. For the first time ever, a team player, part of something bigger than himself, even one of the stars of the team.

Christ, he'd loved the kick from that! Loved it so fucking much that in spite of all the shit that had happened, on one level he still couldn't help dreaming about doing pretty much anything to get back in the limelight. Like some mangy dog that was so desperate for approval even after it had been beaten by its master that it was willing to hump more legs—any legs—to get another pat on the head. One question itched like a massive great scab and no matter how he tried, he couldn't help picking at it: If he'd known that Becca was in the cop car that evening, that she would be or could have been injured by the stone he was going to drop from the bridge, would it have made any difference?

He honestly didn't know.

Even now, after so many hours thinking, he still couldn't answer that bastard question with a simple yes or no.

Totally fucking sick!

It had taken a day or so to work out the deal with the flash-grenade attack on the Horse Guards' cortège. Who would get any pleasure from some bolting horses and a pair of shitty royal underpants? Obviously it could just have been that they wanted to test him or get some cool pictures. But then he read about a break-in in a gentlemen's outfitters on Östermalm, and how it had been preceded by a false bomb threat. An at-taché case with the word "*bomb*" in white paint on the side, left outside the Iranian embassy, and instantly half the police force were over on Lidingö and thus out of the game. And that's where he got the idea.

After checking on the police's own website, he found what

he was looking for. At the same time as Kungsträdgården was filling up with galloping horses and all available police units, including the helicopter that was sent to circle above the city center, someone had stolen a container load of Viagra from a company out in the western suburbs. They had coolly driven past security with a truck, waving what had looked like the right documentation, then calmly hooked up to the container and driven off with it, without having to worry about being pursued by the police helicopter before they had time to unload the pills, because HP had seen to that.

So had he been a decoy, sent out to lure the dogs into sniffing around in the wrong place?

"Look up the word *game* and you'll see what I mean!" Erman had said, and halfway down the page Wiktionary backed up his theory.

Distraction or diversion

He could perfectly well have been both! And suddenly all those weird occurrences assumed yet another crazy dimension. Diversionary tactics, decoys, and smokescreens, all to get the authorities and the general public to look in the wrong direction?

In that case, what was the main event, what were the things they didn't want to show, and who was behind them?

The Freemasons?

The WHO?

The Bilderberg Group?

Or was he taking it too far . . . ? Was his brain messing with him, showing him things that didn't actually exist just because he wanted to see them?

Was the Game really as advanced as Erman had claimed, or was it all just for fun? Something they did just because they could? A game, basically? Just a way of passing the fucking time?!

All these questions were starting to drive him mad. His brain was getting completely overloaded and his head ached like it was going to burst from all the junk flying around up there. He couldn't even come up with a single damn paracetamol; he'd long since hunted through Auntie's drawers and cupboards.

He lit a cigarette, one of the last few. A deep drag, then out floated all the tensions along with the smoke.

Phew . . . !

Meditation by Marlboro.

Almost always worked.

So what was he going to do now?

That was the million-dollar question. He hadn't left the cottage for several days and had hardly even eaten anything. He'd just been smoking, scanning the Internet, and picking away at that huge damn mental scab.

Mange had looked in briefly and topped up the essential supplies of cigarettes and cans of army-ration bean soup, but he'd had the sense not to ask any questions, which was just as well, seeing as he wouldn't have got any answers.

HP could have killed for a spliff, but his stash was long since used up. Since the grass ran out he'd tried to find other ways of easing his anxiety. He'd jacked off so much that he had friction burns on his cock; then in the end he took a cautious walk around the allotments to try to reboot his brain with a bit of fresh air.

That was when he discovered the van.

. . .

The car was rolling in slow motion, twisting on its own axis before its front end hit the ground. Then it flew up again, rear end toward the sky, and did a complete roll before landing on its roof and disappearing out of shot.

The next film sequence showed a smoking wreck, but by that point she was already bent double over Mange's filthy little toilet.

Fuck, fuck, fuck, screamed a little voice inside her throbbing head as she threw up most of an undigested chicken salad.

What in the name of hell was going on?

A white van with a blue logo, parked a bit farther down the narrow track. ACME Telecom Services Ltd.

Seriously?

ACME—just like every dodgy company in cinema history, from Wile E. Coyote and the Road Runner onward?! It was a bit *too* obvious!

Okay, so there was a telecom distribution box and a manhole alongside the van, but so far he hadn't seen a soul anywhere near it. And there didn't seem to be any work going on, so what was the van doing there, parked in the middle of Tantolunden?

He went back inside the cottage and looked up the number on the license plate, but all he got was a rental car company out in Solna.

ACME Telecom Services had their own website, a phone number, and an email address for inquiries. "*ACME Telecom Services—A proud member of the PayTag Group.*"

On the other hand, there was no terrestrial address, but that wasn't so unusual, there were a lot of companies like that.

"*Feel free to contact us by email or telephone.*" A good way of avoiding difficult customers.

He went out again to take a closer look at the van. Still no one in sight, but the engine felt fairly warm, so it couldn't have been standing there for long.

So where was the driver?

He walked around the van, but was none the wiser. The rear windows were tinted, and even though he cupped his hands around his eyes he still couldn't see in. The driver's cab was a bit easier.

A jacket on the front seat, neon yellow with loads of pockets, and when he looked closer he saw that something was sticking out from under it. An oblong silver object. And suddenly he realized what it was! A phone, of course, just like the one he'd left in the computer shop. Which could well mean that the bastards had found him!

He wandered around to get a better view of the cell, but it was mostly covered by the jacket. He had to know for sure, and tugged hard on the door handle.

Locked, obviously.

He glanced quickly around, then picked up a stone from a nearby flower bed. He raised his arm to strike.

"Hey, you, what do you think you're doing?!"

The man had appeared out of nowhere, a thickset fifty-something in overalls and an orange Bob the Builder helmet.

Manual laborer, model 1A.

"Nothing," HP muttered and let the stone slide down his leg. "Just wondered why you're parked here?"

The man looked at him suspiciously.

"Working for Telia, broken cable. Broadband's out across half of Södermalm, haven't you heard?"

"No," HP muttered, moving slowly away from the van. "Okay, see you, then!"

The man shrugged in farewell, then went around the van and unlocked the rear door.

After poking about for a minute or so he emerged with a toolbox, cast a quick glance in HP's direction, then carefully locked the door before disappearing between two cottages.

HP breathed a sigh of relief. The man seemed genuine—false alarm, in other words.

He was getting brainstorms in broad daylight.

Finally out in the fresh air! It may still have been boiling hot, but anything was better than that claustrophobic little computer shop.

She took several deep breaths, then pedaled hard on her bicycle and felt the nausea gradually subside as oxygenated blood started to circulate around her body. After just a hundred meters or so she was feeling considerably brighter.

She wasn't really much the wiser after her conversation with Mange.

Once he'd finally given up his feeble attempts at excuses and agreed to tell the truth, he started by locking the shop door, turning the sign to CLOSED, then, just to make sure, pulled her right to the back of the shop.

Mange had never been one of the more courageous of all of Henke's deadbeat friends, and certainly not one of the coolest, but unlike most of the others he was one of the few who was still left from the old gang.

Vesa had decided to climb up on top of some railway carriages out in Älvsjö when he was high as a kite, and fried himself to death. She remembered Jesus pretty well too; hadn't he won loads of money and disappeared to Thailand? Yes, that was him. Henke had talked about going with him, but as usual with him it never got further than a lot of empty talk. The rest of the gang had drifted away, and Henke wasn't exactly the sort of person whose company or reliability anyone would really miss.

But for some reason Mange had always stuck in there, even when things had been at their worst. He was the only one of the gang who showed up at the trial, and as far as Rebecca knew he was the only person apart from her who had visited Henke in prison. One of the few who had cared.

Mange was okay, really, a decent guy who meant well, and she felt a pang of conscience at having been forced to resort to interrogation tactics to get him to talk. But at least it had worked, and after making sure not once but twice that they really were alone, he had finally told her everything, or at least as much as he knew.

She was left wondering exactly what it was he had told her.

The whole story about a mysterious cell phone that allocated assignments and a secret reality game with rewards and punishments sounded crazy, and her initial reaction was that Mange had fallen for yet another of Henke's bullshit stories. But then he had shown her the video clips on the computer and everything had emerged in an entirely different light.

The business with the door, the car wheels, and the royal cortège had been bad enough, but when she saw her own car slowly rolling off the Drottningholm road, it had all got to be too much for her.

Evidently Mange hadn't known that she was sitting in the Volvo, because he'd hovered outside the toilet door worrying anxiously if she was okay. She only just managed to hold it together, splashing a bit of water on her face and blaming it all on the heat, which he had accepted without comment.

Once she had composed herself again she had asked to see Henke's cell phone, and when Mange reluctantly pulled it out of a locked cupboard she had quickly inspected it and then put it in her bag. For a moment it had looked like Mange was going to protest, but he thought better of it and let her take it without a word.

Before she left, he had also given her the address of Aunt Berit's allotment cottage, and she was looking forward to a fresh, more detailed conversation with her brother in just a few minutes' time.

This time she was going to twist the little sod's arms until he told her the truth about what was really going on!

She cruised through the cars, crossed Ringvägen, and a few minutes later she was in among the trees of the park. She was feeling considerably brighter by now, and was enjoying the cool shade. Mange had said it was about fifteen minutes' walk from the shop, so five minutes or so by bike seemed about right.

When she turned into the right road she had to swerve to avoid a white van pulling away at speed and roaring past her way too fast.

Bloody idiot! she thought as she struggled to keep her balance. For a moment she considered making a note of the license plate; the speed limit here was actually only thirty. But she didn't bother; she hadn't seen the whole number anyway. Some sort of company van with a blue logo on the side.

At that moment she caught sight of the right cottage.

She knocked on the door three times but there was no answer. Maybe he was asleep? It may have been well into the afternoon, but it would hardly surprise her if Henke was taking a little siesta.

She felt the handle and discovered that the door was unlocked, but for some reason she stopped in the doorway. She didn't really know why, but something was making her feel uneasy. She examined the door more carefully and soon found what she was looking for. A small, almost invisible mark in the wood just above the lock. Admittedly, it could have been old, but a quick check of the step revealed some flakes of the right color paint.

Someone had broken into the cottage, and recently. The question was, were they still there?

Rebecca held her breath and listened for any sound from inside.

Quiet as the grave.

She stepped silently through the door and into the hall. The stench of cigarette smoke and hash almost made her eyes water. She put her hand on the frame of the door to the kitchen and leaned around it quickly to get a look inside.

The movement was too fast for any attacker to have time to react, but still enough for her to register the contents of the room. She repeated the procedure with the little bedroom to the right of the hall.

The results were unambiguous; the cottage was empty.

Whoever had broken in was gone now, and it didn't look like anything had been stolen. A laptop, screen saver on, stood untouched on the little kitchen table. There were a few dirty mugs and glasses here and there, most of them containing cigarette butts, and the little sink was overflowing with dirty dishes and empty food tins.

There was a shabby green sleeping bag in a heap at one end of the rib-backed sofa, and a filthy T-shirt and a pair of tattered Cheap Monday jeans were hanging untidily over one of the two kitchen chairs.

Smoky, filthy, and untidy: rather different to how Aunt Berit usually kept it, she imagined.

It looked like Mange had been telling the truth; all the signs were that Henke had taken up residence . . .

So, where was he now, and how long would he be gone? The best thing she could do was sit down on the little sofa and wait.

What the fu . . . ? !

A quick trip up to the Ring Road to stock up on cigarettes and Gorby pies, that was the plan.

He ended up getting falafel and an ice cream as well, because there wasn't really any hurry. He'd almost made it back to the cottage when he saw the flashing blue lights.

Two patrol cars and an unmarked van with a trailer, all lined up in front of Auntie's little cottage. The trailer looked weird, a bit like an outsized milk churn with its lid open. One of the cops seemed to be in a hell of a hurry to set up a police cordon at the end of the road, but as luck would have it, HP saw him first.

He stopped abruptly and turned in to one of the little side paths to find a good observation post.

A couple of minutes later he was sitting on top of a rocky outcrop surrounded by lilac bushes.

So what the hell was going on down there?

. . .

For some reason she hadn't just sat down.

Afterward she couldn't really explain why, but it was as if the feeling that something was wrong wouldn't let go of her.

It took just a few seconds before she realized what was troubling her. The sofa she had been about to sit down on was slightly out of position. She could clearly see the marks on the cork matting where the leg of the sofa usually sat, but now it was a few centimeters out. Okay, so the sofa was pretty old, but it was solid pine and to judge by the deep indentation in the floor it would take a fair bit of effort to shift it. So why had someone done so?

Instead of sitting down, she got down on her knees and looked underneath.

He could see some of the cops talking with serious expressions, then another man showed up wearing a protective suit and a helmet that made him look like a green astronaut.

The man wobbled inside the cottage and the cops quickly moved to the far side of the cars; it looked almost like they were taking cover. After a couple of minutes the spaceman came out with some sort of object in his hands. He lurched toward the trailer and put whatever it was he was holding inside it.

Even though he was sitting some distance away, HP had no trouble noticing how relieved the cops looked when the lid closed.

She didn't really know what she had been expecting to find. But it was perfectly clear that the object under there wouldn't have been on her top-ten list of things she was likely to find, if anyone had asked her to come up with such a list.

A set of keys, some loose change, maybe a cell phone someone had dropped?

But not this . . .

It took her a few seconds to know what she was staring at, and why it was there; then she very slowly got to her feet, picked up the laptop, and exited the cottage.

She left the front door open.

It wasn't until he'd been sitting there for a few minutes that he recognized one of the cops. To start with he thought it was just another plainclothes officer. Khaki shorts with lots of pockets, an untucked short-sleeve shirt, baseball cap, sensible sneakers, and all the other things that were supposed to help them fit in.

But their cops' posture and that way they had of moving their heads almost always gave them away.

He had been concentrating on the men around the trailer, and it wasn't until the lid closed that he looked more closely at the rest of the gang and realized that the plainclothes cop was actually Becca. She was standing there talking to the man in the astronaut outfit.

What the fuck was she doing here?!

"Definitely viable," the bomb-disposal expert said. According to the patch on his suit, his name was Selander, and evidently he liked talking in clipped sentences.

"Two sticks of dynamex. Pressure trigger mounted under the sofa cushion. Sitting down would be enough. More than enough to blow the cottage sky-high. Damn lucky you had your wits about you, Normén . . ."

He paused to put in a dose of chewing tobacco.

"Won't know for sure if it would definitely have gone off until we get it into the lab and take it apart," he went on, this time slightly more expressively. "I'll get back to you. I presume the Södermalm Crime Unit will be in charge? You said this was your brother's cottage?"

"Something like that," she muttered.

Her head was spinning. Flash grenades, chucking stones at police cars, and now a damn bomb!

What in the name of holy hell had Henke got himself caught up in?

"I daresay our colleagues in Crime will be pretty keen to have a word with him," Selander concluded as he wiped the tobacco from his fingers on the bomb suit.

Rebecca just nodded in response.

Welcome to the club! she thought.

15 | ARE YOU REALLY SURE YOU WANT TO EXIT?

REBECCA WAS EXHAUSTED when she got home. She had spent most of the afternoon with the Södermalm Crime Unit telling them what had happened out in Tantolunden. Or rather the parts that she deemed suitable to reveal.

She didn't mention her visit to see Mange or the video clips she had seen in the shop. It was fairly likely that the clips had something to do with the events out at the cottage, but before she'd had a chance to talk to Henke she didn't really want to show them to her colleagues. She hadn't missed the pointed silence that had fallen when Henke's criminal record was mentioned.

Then the obligatory questions: Did her brother have any enemies? Did she know how he made a living? Did she know anything about the arson attack on his flat a week before?

She answered no to each of the questions, which was actually true. Well, almost, anyway.

She locked her cycle away in the basement and took the stairs up as usual.

Maybe it was because she was tired, or because she was deep in thought, but she didn't notice that someone was waiting for her.

"Becca!"

She spun around and automatically raised her hands in front of her.

"Calm down, it's only me, Henke!"

Of course it was only him.

She should have known. Where else was he going to go?

She muttered something, turned around, and unlocked the door of her flat before shepherding him in before her. She stopped inside the door for a couple of seconds, then locked all four locks.

But only once, and even though part of her was protesting wildly, that would have to do. She had no intention of giving him a demonstration of her compulsive behavior.

In the hall the answering machine was flashing to indicate another missed call. Number withheld, same as usual.

Henke had already made himself at home on the sofa in the living room.

"Got any coffee?"

She resisted, with some effort, a sudden urge to grab the nearest heavy object and smash his skull in. Fucking bloody idiot, creeping up on her like that! She didn't even know he knew where she lived. When she'd been out searching half the city for him, and here he was all of a sudden, sitting on her sofa.

And what on earth did he look like?

Even more strung out than last time, with great bags under his eyes and nicotine yellow skin. Fingernails chewed almost to the quick, his hair all over the place, and utterly filthy too.

A smell of ingrained smoke and unwashed guy wafted up from her sofa, making her wrinkle her nose.

He was looking at her quizzically and she realized she hadn't answered his question.

"Sure," she snapped and went out into the kitchen.

"You can clean yourself up in the meantime, the bathroom's off the hall," she called from the kitchen as she took care of the machine.

But when she came back a few minutes later with a tray of coffee, he was asleep.

She sighed, poured herself a cup, and decided, after a bit of thought, to let him sleep. He looked like he could do with it.

A surprising feeling of tenderness came over her and she couldn't help giving his cheek a quick stroke. He was still her little brother, after all, her little Henke. Okay, so he was an immature idiot and a first-rate trouble magnet, but that hadn't always been the case. Once it had been the two of them against the world. And through all the shit, they had always had each other.

But that was a long time ago. Things changed, whether you liked it or not.

She drank the last of the cup, leaned her head back against the sofa, and closed her eyes.

She had understood from the noise he was making in the hall when he got in. The way he slammed the front door, the way he jangled his keys as he kicked off his shoes. She tried to warn Henke, but he had his back to her, sitting on one of the folding chairs out on the balcony, smoking. Henke and Dag sometimes used to share a cig out there, even though Dag claimed he'd given up. Smoking didn't fit in with his exercise regime and all that crap. Yet he still hung about out there all the time, leaning over the railing, and not just when Henke was visiting. From the balcony he could keep an eye on the backyard, as well as the carpark where the BMW was.

On good days they got on pretty well, Dag and Henke. They could stand out there chatting, almost like they were friends. She liked days like that; they made her feel as if she had a proper family.

But this definitely wasn't going to be one of those days, she'd known that the moment the front door slammed shut.

"Hello!"

His voice was ice-cold, almost emotionless, but she had no difficulty picking up the anger bubbling beneath it.

"Is everything okay?" she said as quietly and calmly as she could.

He just snorted in reply.

"Is there any food?"

"Fish gratin, it's in the oven. Henke and I have already eaten."

Another snort. This didn't bode well, she knew from experience. At a guess, something had gone wrong at work, a troublesome customer, an order that had got lost, or his boss stirring things up. It didn't usually take very much.

"So how long is your useless brother going to exploit my hospitality this time?" he muttered through gritted teeth a bit later, nodding toward Henke, who was still out on the balcony.

"Just a couple of days," she said as neutrally as she could. "Things are a bit tricky at home with Mom and everything. He needed to get away for a bit."

A third snort, this time more scornful.

"A bit tricky . . ." he muttered as he shoveled a spoonful of the gratin into his mouth. "Your mother's just a pathetic alcoholic," he declared between chews. "Get her into a home so you can have a bit of peace and quiet, then we won't have that little crook hanging about around here all the time."

She was on her way to getting angry and he saw it. A happy grin spread over his face.

"Oh, so you're cross I said something nasty about poor, innocent little Henke?" he added in that patronizing childish voice she hated. He'd gone straight for her weak point and she had to make an effort not to rise to the bait.

"Henke's just been a bit unlucky," she said with forced calm. "He hasn't always had it so easy, and besides, he's my little brother."

"Easy?!" Dag had suddenly gone red in the face, and he flew up from his chair.

This was the row he had been looking for ever since he opened the door, and now he was getting what he wanted.

"You talk about easy, but what fucking problems has your worthless brother ever had, eh? My dad wasn't exactly a saint either. He used to beat the crap out of me every other day until I learned to hit back. The bastard walked out when I was fifteen, but look at me!" He gestured toward his chest with his thumb. "I didn't end up a fucking criminal! I've worked since I was sixteen, hauled my way up the ladder, paid my taxes, and looked after myself, and for what? So I can support someone like him?"

His mouth was spraying little bits of saliva and food, but he didn't seem to notice.

"What's up?"

Henke was peering in from the balcony. She tried to signal to him to take it easy, not provoke Dag, just let him burn himself out, then everything would calm down. But he didn't seem to get it. Anyway, Dag wasn't about to let him get away lightly this time.

"Well, your sister and I were just discussing if it wouldn't make sense to put your alcoholic mother in a home so we didn't have to put up with you coming 'round here every five minutes."

His tone of voice was so arrogant and provocative that she already had an idea of what was going on. She made another attempt to catch Henke's eye and make him understand. Stop him from rising to the challenge that had been thrown in his face. But he didn't seem to get it, or else he was simply ignoring her.

"Really, Dagge?" he said nonchalantly instead, emphasizing the nickname that he knew Dag hated. "Wouldn't it make more sense for us to bury her in the same patch of forest as your 'missing' dad? That way we could keep all the violence in the family. I mean, you're pretty good at that!"

Dag threw himself across the table and Henke didn't have time to take more than a couple of steps back before Dag was on him. He tried to resist, but his opponent was considerably larger and much more aggressive. After just a few seconds Henke was on the floor, curled up with his hands over his face to protect himself. But Dag was on top of him, wrapping his arm around Henke's neck and dragging him upward. Rebecca could see Henke's face turning white.

"Stop it, Dag!" she cried. "Stop, for God's sake, you're strangling him!"

She tried to loosen the arm around Henke's neck.

The blow came out of nowhere; he must have let go with the other hand without her noticing, because she was suddenly flying backward across the little kitchen table.

"You little bitch!" she heard him roar as her back hit the floor. Cutlery, plates, and food everywhere. Her cheek was burning, her face felt numb, and she was seeing stars.

Somewhere far away she heard Henke whimper and she tried to get to her feet.

For some reason the door had opened, unless Henke had never closed it, because all of a sudden the fight had moved out onto the balcony. Dag had got a fresh grip of Henke's head and she could see that her little brother was almost finished. His legs suddenly went limp and he stopped struggling, but Dag didn't seem to have noticed.

"You're not so fucking cocky now, are you, you little fucker?!" he roared, his face bright red, as he tightened his grip.

And suddenly she knew that Henke was going to die. That Dag was going to murder her little brother, right there, out on their balcony.

"*Stop!!!*" she screamed as loudly as she possibly could. Her voice sounded terrible, as if it came from deep within her chest rather than her throat.

Maybe it was the unusual tone of voice that jolted Dag out of it and made him realize he was going too far? Because just as she launched herself at him with all the energy she could muster, he let go of Henke. Let him fall to the ground like a rag doll, and took an unsteady step backward. Toward the balcony railing.

She hit Dag full in the chest. Even if she weighed almost seventy kilos the collision wouldn't usually have moved him at all, at best it would have made him sway a bit.

But this time he must have been off balance, or else the force in her tackle was far greater than she was aware of. Either way, he stumbled backward across the balcony with his arms reaching for something to grab hold of, something to help him keep his heavy body upright and stop him from falling.

Then his back hit the metal railing . . .

. . .

She would never forget that sound. A shrieking, grinding
sound of metal mixed with a sigh from the concrete as it reluctantly released its grip on the far-too-few steel bolts.

And unexpectedly the railing was gone.

She was lying on the floor of the balcony, Dag just a meter
away, balancing right on the edge. In his eyes that accusing
look, as if he had already realized how it was going to end.
That she wouldn't lift a finger to save him. And wouldn't actually even try. Because deep down she had already begun to
celebrate, begun to rejoice that her love for him, just like he
himself, would soon be dead.

That she would finally be free!

"It's your fault!" the look in those eyes said in farewell before they, and he, disappeared over the edge.

And she knew that they were right.

It's winter, dark, and in this dream Henke is waiting beside a
brightly lit shopwindow. He doesn't know who or what for.
He just knows that he has to wait. For someone to come.
Someone important.

The street is lined with bare, jagged trees as cars drive past
almost soundlessly on the white roadway. Older models, he
realizes, as if he's gone back in time.

He stamps his feet on the snow-covered ground to keep
warm.

Then he hears a church clock chime farther down the
street and he recognizes where he is. Sveavägen, diagonally
across from the Adolf Fredrik Church.

At the junction of Tunnel Street.

And suddenly he sees them coming toward him. A couple walking arm in arm. The man in a winter coat and fur hat, the woman in a coat and some sort of shawl. He recognizes them immediately: the prime minister and his wife. He runs his hand over his jacket and feels the object in his pocket, then turns toward the shopwindow and lets them pass.

Then he spins around and takes a couple of strides to catch up with them.

He knows what he has to do.

Ten minutes or so had passed since Dag fell from the balcony, but she remembered nothing of what had happened during that time. She is sitting in the kitchen with a female police officer in her forties. She looks kind, Rebecca finds herself thinking.

From down below there are blue lights flashing, lighting up the whole of the courtyard. She isn't crying, she hasn't done any of that, and she won't either, she knows that already.

"Can you bear to tell me what happened?" the police officer says, and just as she opens her mouth to talk, she hears Henke's voice from the living room.

"It was me who did it!" he says, loudly and clearly. "We were fighting and I pushed him; then the whole thing collapsed and he went through the railing. It was my fault."

He's got the gun in his hand, a large, silver-colored revolver with a laser sight on top. The red dot is right in the middle of the man's broad back.

Just squeeze, and . . .

But they seem to have noticed him, because they stop.

Then the man turns around. His body has changed, becoming much bigger, much more intimidating. When their eyes meet HP sees that the man is smirking.

"So, you criminal little bastard, you're going to kill me face-to-face this time, are you?" says the prime minister, with Dag's voice.

And suddenly he feels all the resolve that was so strong a moment ago starting to dissolve.

She wants to yell at him to shut up, yell at the police officers in there not to believe him, and tell the woman opposite her that her little brother is lying. That she was the one who shoved him, not Henke. That she's the murderer who should be punished.

But none of that happens.

Her head is completely empty, her body incapable of all movement, even a millimeter, and so her mouth stays silent too.

"Was that it?" the police officer opposite her says. "Was he the one who pushed your partner off the balcony?"

But she can't answer.

And she still isn't crying.

"Go on then!" the man in front of him jeers.

His breath is like a pillar of smoke from his scornful, smiling mouth.

"Pull the trigger, if you dare!"

The red mark from the laser sight trembles on the man's broad chest. All he has to do is squeeze the trigger, and the bullet will do the rest.

But he hesitates. In the background the church bells are ringing louder and louder. And abruptly he seems to have shrunk, become shorter, smaller, almost as if he were changing into a child. The pistol is getting heavier and heavier and soon he won't be able to hold it anymore.

"Henrik," the woman at the man's side says quietly, and she has to lean over to get eye contact with him.

"You don't have to do this. I'll be okay anyway."

Her voice is calm and friendly, so familiar and comforting. Then she smiles at him, that gentle smile he's loved for as long as he can remember, and suddenly he feels a lump in his throat. It's forcing its way to his larynx and into his mouth, and when the tears burn through his eyelids he hears the man chuckle.

"I knew you wouldn't dare!" he mocks. "A worthless little shit like you isn't capable of anything. Not even taking care of your family."

The prime minister puts his arms around the woman's shoulders and pulls her to him. She does nothing to stop him and just lets herself be embraced. She stands there quite still, stuck to his side.

In his grasp.

"I'll be okay anyway," her voice whispers inside his head, but he knows she's wrong.

And the look in her eyes agrees with him.

Then the man is someone else. Changes, right in front of his eyes. Into someone older, more dangerous. And suddenly he feels his little boy's weenie shrivel up and almost disappear down inside his pants.

But just as he catches sight of the belt in the man's free hand, at the very moment he knows how it all fits together and his index finger squeezes the trigger to blow him away, send the bastard back to hell once and for all—the gun suddenly turns into something else entirely.

The bells have turned to thunder inside his head.

Drowning out all sound and swallowing the whole world.

It's as if every church in Stockholm has suddenly joined in the ringing and is making the ground shake beneath his feet.

"Fire, fire!" he hears someone cry as he races up the steep steps toward Malmskillnadsgatan a few seconds later.

In his jacket pocket he can feel an old wrench bouncing about.

HP woke up gently. He opened his eyes slowly and knew straightaway from the smell that he wasn't at home. There was a smell of food. Warm, cooked food, not from some takeaway or kiosk, but proper home-cooked food. Sweet!

"Oh, so you're awake!" She stuck her head into the living room and seemed almost pleased to see him.

"Food will be ready in a couple of minutes, if you want to freshen up first."

He nodded and wandered off toward the bathroom.

When he returned she was ladling out a helping of sausage and mashed potatoes for him.

Proper mash, made from real potatoes, not powder. He hadn't had that for ... well, he couldn't actually remember how long it had been.

It was pretty damn good as well, and he ate ravenously. She waited until he had finished his first portion and was no longer completely starving.

"I was over at the cottage," she said neutrally.

"I know!" he said between chews. "I saw you from a distance but didn't really feel like introducing myself to your colleagues," he explained when he saw the quizzical look on her face. "Was it a real bomb?"

She looked at him searchingly for a few seconds. There were a lot of things you could say about Henke, a hell of a lot, actually, but he wasn't stupid. That was actually the main problem.

Smart, but lazy. Clever, but indolent. Bright, but lacking ambition.

She should have known it wouldn't be that easy to pin him down.

"Looks like it," she said shortly. "According to Forensics there was enough dynamex in it to turn Auntie's cottage into kindling. It was under the sofa, by the way, with a pressure-sensitive detonator, but perhaps you already know that as well?"

He shook his head as he shoveled in another mouthful. Dynamex, that's the stuff they used on building sites. Good old dynamite in a modern form.

The same stuff he'd read about on the Internet, after it went missing from a weapon store out in Fisksätra. The bit about a pressure-sensitive detonator also sounded familiar, but he couldn't quite place it. Almost like something you'd see at the cinema. Just like everything else that had happened.

As if his whole life had turned into some sort of weird film.

"I've spoken to Mange," she said, changing tactic.

That had more of an effect.

He stopped chewing and looked at her anxiously.

"And?"

"He told me everything," she said, holding his gaze.

The shift was immediate, from cocky little brother to frightened little rabbit in the space of a couple of seconds.

"And he also showed me some nice video clips from a phone you left with him."

His face had turned white and his fork fell to his plate with a clatter.

"Becca, I . . ."

"Yes?"

She looked at him expectantly, waiting for him to go on.

But nothing came.

Instead he buried his head in his hands and slumped across the table. It actually sounded like he was crying. All of a sudden she didn't know what to do. She hadn't actually counted on this particular scenario. She hadn't seen him cry since . . .

Well, since that evening when the police showed up. Back then he had shaken her, tried to get her out of her state of shock and talk to him. Tears of frustration then. Anger, impotence maybe, but not fear.

Not like now. He looked so vulnerable, so small.

Carefully she put her arms around his shoulders.

"There, there, Henke, don't worry," she said in her gentlest voice, just like she used to when they were kids and he woke up scared from the noise on the other side of the bedroom door.

"It's all going to be all right," she whispered, stroking his hair.

Henke had showered and used her Ladyshave to get rid of the worst of the stubble, and was now wearing some of her gym clothes while his own were soaking in Y3 detergent in the kitchen sink.

It was surprising what a bit of food, some basic hygiene, and a bit of sympathy could do, she thought as they sat curled up on her sofa. Once her initial anger had faded away, it actually felt nice having him there, hearing his voice, and knowing he was okay.

He had filled in the gaps in Mange's story. How he found the phone, the assignments, the mocked-up arrest, and everything that had followed since he was kicked out of this peculiar Game.

They made slow progress to start with, but as time went on he picked up the pace so much that in the end the words were firing out of his mouth, almost too fast for her to follow them.

The whole thing sounded pretty odd, which was probably the understatement of the year . . .

Fake police, madmen in the forest, planes, arson, and bombs—it was all a bit difficult to take in, to put it mildly. Then, on top of all that, a secret gambling setup where people could place bets and order assassinations at the same time.

When he started rambling about Palme's murder, 9/11, and the fire in Katarina Church, she had to stop him.

This was just too much!

All his usual bullshit stories paled against this one. Could he actually hear how crazy this all sounded? But, on the other hand, she could hardly ignore the tangible evidence proving that at least some of what he was saying had actually happened.

The phone, the video clips, the fires, and the bomb were clearly all real. She had seen them herself, or evidence of them.

It was quite obvious that he was in trouble, and it was undeniable that someone was trying to hurt him. But where was the dividing line?

He sounded like one of the radiation-obsessed crazies who used to phone the police in the middle of the night.

People who wanted to report that NASA was using television sets to watch the whole world, and that the king was actually a robot working for the CIA.

The only similarity with all the scrapes Henke had got himself into before was the question of guilt. None of it was his fault, obviously; he was just a victim of unfortunate circumstances. He'd got into a bit of trouble, that's all. Soon that stone at Lindhagensplan would have thrown itself off the bridge . . .

"So what are you planning to do next?" She tried to keep her voice neutral.

He took a deep breath, then sighed.

"I haven't got many options left, really. The flat's going to be ready soon, but fuck knows if I've got the balls to live there anymore. The cottage is ruined now, and I can't stay with Mange. So I was thinking of leaving, ditching all this shit, and moving somewhere else. Somewhere they can't find me. Thailand maybe, Jesus is already out there, of course, if you remember him?"

Rebecca nodded but said nothing.

"I can probably find a way of making some money once I get there, and the flat would raise a bit of money if I sold it."

He gave her his little-brother look and tilted his head to one side. She'd long since worked out where this conversation was heading.

"But I could do with a bit of start-up capital to get me going . . ."

There we go, she thought.

That was it, the patented solution to all his problems. This time the mess he'd got himself into looked far worse than usual, but the punch line was the same as ever.

He needed money, and as usual she was the one who was expected to cough up. Little Henke had got into trouble and some nasty people were trying to get him, so now he needed money so he could run away and hide.

The worst thing was that no matter how she looked at it, she couldn't come up with a better solution. Obviously she could suggest that they go to the police together, that he should take responsibility for what he had done and help to put it all right. But she already knew what the answer would be, and even if he took her advice, against all expectation, she doubted if her colleagues would be any help. Sure, they'd be quick to arrest and charge him with Lindhagensplan and Kungsträdgården, so they could say they'd solved that summer's most talked-about crimes. But any more in-depth investigation into the underlying causes would be put on ice the moment Henke started with his radiation-lunatic stuff. And he'd be blamed for it all—he'd be the lone perpetrator, and even if it wasn't entirely undeserved, she couldn't just watch while he was sent to prison again.

His proposed solution was, under the circumstances, the best one on offer.

"How much?" she sighed.

Obviously he shouldn't have told her. Partly because he was breaking that bastard rule again, but that particular reason was fairly easy to rationalize away. In practice he had already been punished for telling her when they torched his flat, and that time he hadn't actually done it.

In other words, they owed him one. Quid pro quo, so to speak.

The more serious reason for staying quiet was that he could hear how crazy it all sounded now that he was telling someone else. The conclusions he had reached out in the cottage, which had seemed so solid when he went through them on his own, now sounded like something out of *The X-Files*, and when he'd finished talking, his sister wasn't the only one in the room who wasn't sure if he had a full set of tires on the car.

He should have kept quiet, just talked about the things she already knew and kept the rest to himself.

The end result was the same, after all.

He was in trouble, and needed to get away, much further than Tantolunden this time. Disappear off the map, basically, someplace where no one could find him, but where he could still have a decent life.

But that sort of vanishing act took money, and he didn't have any. So he was left standing there, cap in hand as usual. His sister would cough up, she always did. They even joked about it sometimes: *Cavalry to the rescue!*

But for some reason it didn't feel quite as easy taking her money this time.

It wasn't right, somehow . . .

But he still did it. Spent the night on her sofa, then went with her to the bank the next day.

A night's sleep and bit of decent food had done him good, and he felt much brighter than he had during the previous evening's tearful outburst.

It still felt a bit embarrassing, but what the fuck . . .

Bodyguards must get paid pretty well, if she had that much in her account ...

He got twenty-seven thousand in cash, and was left with twenty-three once he'd got a few clothes and a new pay-as-you-go cell in the shops around Hötorget. Then a quick call to Lufthansa.

"*Ein return ticket to Frankfurt for an Andreas Pettersson? Kein problem, mein herr!*"

Seeing as his passport very handily didn't say which of his first names he used, there wouldn't be any problem picking the ticket up at Arlanda.

It was the first time he'd ever had any use for his middle name. Anyone checking the passenger lists wouldn't find him, at least not straightaway. They'd probably start by looking for single tickets booked in the name he usually used, so Andreas wouldn't be picked up first time around.

By then he'd already be in Frankfurt, with a whole load of airlines and destinations to pick from. If he felt like it he could even skip the flight and catch the train to some other airport instead. Cross the border into Holland or Belgium, maybe. The Germans were pretty fucking hot when it came to trains, and cash left no trail.

"*Are you sure you want to exit?*"

"*Hell yeah!*"

He was sitting on the airport bus with his newly purchased cabin luggage by his feet. Apart from the laptop it contained a pair of jeans, some underwear, and toiletries, but that was more or less it. He was traveling light, essentials only; he could pick up the rest when he got there.

It was a shame about his stuff at home in Maria Trapp-gränd, but Becca had volunteered as usual. She'd promised to Shurgard it all and sort out an estate agent to unlock the value of the two-room flat. He was going to call her in a month or so to sort out the money.

Half of the flat was actually hers, but there'd still be plenty of money left over.

Transferring the cash would be a bit tricky, but there had to be ways around that. An anonymous account with Western Union or something?

Most of the stuff in the flat was crap, things he'd inherited from Mom and not bothered to get rid of. Apart from the television and computer there was nothing of any value; he'd long since sold anything worth selling.

They'd got rid of Dad's stuff just after he died, when they moved into the city.

The Salvation Army had picked up the lot, every last thing. HP definitely didn't need any reminders of the old bastard and what he had done.

Looking in the mirror was more than enough . . .

No, there was really only one thing in the flat that he was worried about, something he'd rather not have Becca snooping about in. But he didn't have much choice. Even if she did find the box, she wouldn't understand, or at least he hoped not.

She was okay, Becca, as far as sisters go. More than okay, actually . . . Even if she was always getting at him, she stepped up whenever it really mattered.

Watching his back . . .

She'd always done that, ever since they were little and he . . . well . . . he loved her for it.

Obviously that was the case, even if he was reluctant to

admit it. Becca was the only family he had, actually the only person who had ever behaved like someone who was family ought to. The only fixed point in his life. In fact, he'd do almost anything for her if she asked . . .

Damn it, that sounded dumb!

He'd never dream of saying anything like that to her face. He actually felt a bit embarrassed just thinking stuff like that, but maybe it wasn't so weird that he was getting a bit soppy now that it was time to leave his homeland for good?

Sollentuna flew past on the right-hand side and he slouched down in his seat to try to get comfortable. He'd already scanned his fellow passengers a couple of times and none of them looked suspicious. To be on the safe side, he'd pulled his usual 007 stunt when he reached the Central Station, and had waited until the very last minute before racing for the airport bus. No one had followed him, he was sure of that.

But on the other hand, maybe they didn't need to shadow him? According to Erman, they were everywhere. Hundreds, maybe thousands of little Ant eyes looking out for him, sweeping their cells over people's faces until the face-recognition app found a match. And suddenly he was a red dot on a map! Hadn't the bus driver given him a strange look when he got on? What about little Miss Businesswoman behind him, sitting there fiddling with her BlackBerry? He could feel his pulse rate going up and closed his eyes for a few seconds.

Just calm down, HP, you've been doing this shit for too long! Your brain just sees what it wants to see, so leave off wanting to see this sort of bollocks and get a fucking grip!

He took a couple of deep breaths and then opened his eyes.

Everything was fine. There was nothing to worry about. He was on his way to leaving the Game, putting this crap

behind him and starting a whole new chapter. Disappearing
under the radar and becoming a ghost rider. So why couldn't
he put his mind to rest? Probably because there was something in all the crap that was still sticking out, something he
hadn't fixed.

Somewhere near Bredden he worked out what it was. A
quick call to Becca from his new cell; it was worth the risk. He
was going to switch when he got to Thailand anyway. And he
had to know, had to be properly sure. That she'd be safe. Out
of harm's way.

She picked up at once.

"Rebecca Normén."

"It's me. A quick question."

"Okay, but it'll have to be really quick, I'm at work, things
are a bit—"

"The cell, the one you picked up from Mange. What did
you do with it?"

He held his breath.

"I booked it into Lost Property, it'll be there until they can
trace the owner."

"Great!" he breathed out.

Everything was fine, time to round it all off. Now he could
exit with a clear conscience.

"I was just worried you might have kept it or something . . ."

"No, it's down in the store. Apparently it was reported stolen by some company out in the Western District according
to the IMEI number. Some telecom company, I think it was.
Anyway, I thought you were on your way out of the country?"

Instantly he sat up in his seat.

"I am. You don't happen to remember what the company
was called?"

"No, not really, something short. I've got it written in my pad, but that's down in my locker . . ."

He could hear voices in the background.

"Listen, I'm about to get in the elevator, so we'll be cut off. I can text you the name in a minute if it's important?"

"Sure, no problem; you've got my new number now . . ." he muttered as thoughts flew around his head.

"Well, bye, Becca!"

"Bye, Henke, look after yourself."

The call was cut off abruptly. The dryer up there had time to start a new cycle before his cell bleeped. He didn't really need to open the message to read the address of the company. The crumpled-up note he'd got off Erman the other day was enough.

Torshamnsgatan 142, Kista. Acme Telecom Services Ltd

And all of a sudden he was nowhere near as sure that he really wanted to stop.

16 | WHO IS PLAYING WHO?

SHE'D REACHED THE third bend when it happened. She was going about a hundred and had just got past the obstacle when the front tire blew and the steering wheel began to shudder madly in her hands.

Even though she had been expecting it, her pulse was racing as she struggled to regain control of the vehicle. Braking hard, the jolt on the pedal telling her that the antilock brake system was working.

"Stop the skid, steer into the direction you want to go in, don't fight it," the instructor said beside her.

When the car had stopped at the side of the road she realized she was wet with sweat.

"Good! No problems at all, Normén!" the instructor summarized.

She nodded in response and tried to look calm and composed.

Driving instruction out at Tullinge airfield was obligatory, so she just had to grit her teeth and get through it even if her heart had started doing panic-stricken somersaults in her chest the moment she sat in the driver's seat.

The tire blowout at speed was the last task of the day, and she'd be heading home immediately after the debrief. Which suited her fine.

Kruse was better, considerably better, in fact. It looked like he was going to make a full recovery.

It was a hell of a relief and made everything a bit easier to cope with, now that she knew who had thrown the stone through the windshield, and possibly even why. But obviously she couldn't tell anyone that whole story about the Game. Not even Anderberg would manage to stay quiet about something like that, she was sure.

So she'd just have to deal with her demons the way she always had. With shock therapy.

What doesn't kill you makes you stronger, and all that macho bullshit . . . If you were terrified, you ought to join the police. If you felt insecure, you should become a bodyguard, and if you had a car crash you just had to jump back in the driving seat as soon as you could. Take the bull by the horns and put your foot hard on the pedal.

Yippee ki-yay! as Henke would have put it.

She wondered what he was doing now.

He ought to have arrived in Thailand by now, but she hadn't heard anything.

Not that that was much of a surprise.

They'd hidden themselves away well, he had to give them credit for that. The building looked completely normal at first glance. An ordinary brick office building, standard Swedish design, nothing fancy. Just like all the others along the road. Two stories, a main entrance, underground parking, and a small, glassed-in security booth. A couple of tatty pennants drooped in front of the entrance, their cords whipping rhythmically in the summer breeze.

Bang-bang-bang-bang.

Fucking smart move, actually, hiding in plain sight like this, where everyone could see, but no one did. Much better than some secret fortress, which would only arouse a load of questions.

The best trick the devil ever pulled . . .

Getting a car hadn't been a problem. A Saab 900 from the long-stay parking lot at Arlanda. You could start those with a lollypop stick if you knew what you were doing. The barrier of the parking lot was just as easy. Mr. Sensible had naturally left the ticket in the ashtray to make sure he didn't lose it while he was getting drunk in Mallorca. HP just had to pay a bit of cash into the machine, then drive out entirely legally. Two hundred and fifty kronor for a car with a full tank that wouldn't be reported stolen for at least six days. And that was a fairly decent price, a hell of a lot less than Hertz, and a lot less hassle, particularly for someone who didn't want to be seen. And who didn't actually have a driver's license . . .

His conscience didn't give him much trouble either. Car theft didn't actually feature in the law code under its own heading. "Wrongful procurement of transport" was a useless offense, pretty much on a par with crossing the road when the red man was still showing. Not the sort of thing Big Brother really cared about. So neither did HP.

He drove past the place a total of three times, taking pictures with his new cell each time he passed. Then he settled down to wait a few blocks away, staking out the building for a couple of hours.

Once he'd settled down: plug the USB cable into the laptop and open up the media player.

And roll the film!

If you could sit and concentrate in peace and quiet, it was much easier to pick up anything unusual. The discreet cameras covering every angle of the building, the roller shutter on the slope leading down to the underground garage. The guard manning the barrier, rather than Lisa-the-receptionist-from-Bredäng. All of them small indications that he was in the right place.

He didn't notice the biggest thing for quite a while. It wasn't actually anything at all, but rather the opposite.

Apart from the orc on guard occasionally doing a circuit around the building, nothing was happening in or around the building.

Zippo, nada, *niente*!

No clients, no visitors, not even a gaggle of nicotine-starved employees huddled by the side door.

Zero traffic, no deliveries, and not a single car in or out of the garage even though he had been watching at both four and five o'clock.

In other words, there was no one working inside the building. Not a soul, apart from the guard. But presumably a server farm pretty much ran itself? Everything could be done remotely. Unless there were people living in there to look after the control room? Pasty little technicians who never saw daylight?

Either way, he was feeling more and more sure. This was *the place*!

This was where it was all controlled from: the Ants, the functionaries, the Players, and the assignments. Reality as a game, and the Game reality, all in one single, seamless app. Hidden behind those anonymous walls was Mission Control, and it was him, Henrik "HP" Pettersson, who had found it.

The Houston of Fucking Cyberspace!

And he was sure of one more thing.

He had to get inside.

Rebecca opened the front door and sniffed carefully at the hall, but the only smell she could detect was paint. She'd picked the key up from the housing association and been given a ten-minute lecture about "how seriously we take this incident." As if Henke was somehow responsible for someone trying to set fire to his flat?

That wasn't an entirely unreasonable conclusion, but that wasn't something she felt like discussing with a total stranger. At least the old man had seemed relieved when she said she was there to empty the flat before they sold it, and hurried to get her out before she had time to change her mind. Maria Trappgränd was considerably more desirable now than when they had bought the flat in the mid-nineties.

Really, the street had been completely unsuitable for Mom, with its cobblestones and narrow steps.

But as soon as Mom saw the flat and the area, she fell for a romantic dream based on an old film, *Anderssonskans Kalle*, and wouldn't be shaken. Dad's life insurance had been just enough for the down payment and a bit of new furniture.

Personally Rebecca thought the area was more *The Third Man* than anything. As if some unknown danger were lurking in among the gloomy alleyways and dark courtyards. She had never liked coming here, and today was no exception.

The door was new, the hall repainted and the parquet floor repaired, but otherwise everything in the flat looked the same as usual. The same old Henke mess. And, the same as ever, she was playing at being the cavalry, helping him sort it all out.

She maneuvered the folded moving boxes into the kitchen and started to put them together. It only took half an hour or so to clear the kitchen. Most of it had evidently got broken during the fire, which at least saved her having to do any washing up. The fridge and freezer were, with the exception of some moldy cheese and a pack of frozen pies, basically empty, so she moved on to the living room. The high-tech stuff in there turned out to be pretty straightforward. The boxes were all in the corner, presumably because Henke couldn't be bothered to carry them down to the bins. She couldn't help wondering where the money for all these toys had come from. Computer, flat-screen TV, home cinema, and games console: altogether they must have a shop value of at least forty thousand. But then Henke probably hadn't bought them over the counter . . .

Apart from the electronics, the furnishings in the flat weren't much to write home about. A sagging sofa bed, a couple of rickety Billy bookcases, and a small coffee table. All things they bought when they moved in.

The bedroom still contained Mom's creaking old pine bed. The covers and sheets were on the floor. She couldn't quite believe he'd kept it. Okay, Mom had died in the Ersta clinic, but still . . .

An old poster from a computer games fair was the only adornment on the otherwise bare walls.

"DreamHack -07, the Biggest Game-Fair in the World,"

she muttered as she gathered together the heaps of clothes and stuffed them into various bags. Even her goodwill had its limits, so most of this could go to the nearest charity bin.

The bookshelves contained a load of DVDs, many of them clearly burned copies.

She ran her fingers along their dusty spines. There seemed to be a preponderance of gangster films, closely followed by American action films, with an impressive collection of adult material in an easy third place. But there was also a fair number of old classics, and for a moment she thought about taking some home with her. But when would she find the time to watch them?

There were quite a few books on the shelves as well, which didn't really surprise her. Henke liked reading, had done ever since he was little.

She had helped him to start with, but he soon got the hang of it and was reading as well as her by the time he was six. Dad had had a load of old illustrated classics in a box at home, and Henke had plowed through them more than once. The cartoon versions of *Robinson Crusoe* and *Moby-Dick* had rescued his marks in Swedish pretty much the whole way through school. Ten minutes with the illustrated version from *Reader's Digest* and he looked like he was well read.

So utterly typical of Henke!

The master of cutting corners.

Rebecca couldn't help smiling. Despite his obvious failings, at least no one ever had a dull moment in her little brother's company. She used to take him to the library when they were a bit older. They would hang around there instead of going home. She used to bribe him to do his homework before he could look at the comics. The library had been a refuge, a safe haven where they could dream away a few hours, especially after Mom got ill and everything started to escalate. She still associated the smell of books with security.

Often they would sit there until the library closed and the friendly librarians had to shepherd them out.

It felt like a hundred years ago.

The photograph album was on the bottom shelf. Brown plastic sleeves, with pages that had stuck together. She'd seen the yellowing pictures many times before, but even so she couldn't help leafing through them. It hadn't been all bad. Sometimes life had been almost normal. Like the camping holiday in Rättvik, with her, Mom, and Henke all wearing traditional wooden clogs and squinting at the camera. The other two were blond and happy, while she had dark hair like Dad, and a more serious demeanor. Obviously he was behind the camera, the long shadow the only thing that betrayed his presence. She was pretty sure that was the closest Dad would come to being in any of the pictures in Henke's album.

She realized that that particular summer photograph from the early eighties actually said quite a bit about their family. Henke and Mom had always been close, whereas she was more Daddy's girl. Like Mom, she had done all she could to keep him happy, even though he usually ignored them. Dad was a serious man who did a lot of thinking, and usually preferred his own company. He seldom smiled, almost never laughed, at least not as she remembered it. Work was probably the only thing that really interested him, some sort of sales job that she couldn't remember much about, except that he traveled a fair bit. Sometimes they'd get a postcard, and very occasionally his duty-free bags would contain something apart from bottles of spirits. Sweets, perfume, or maybe some cheap plastic toy from the souvenir shop at the airport if the trip had gone particularly well and he was in a good mood.

On the rare days when Dad was at home he never wanted to be disturbed. He usually locked himself away in his little cubbyhole with a book and a bottle of some sort. The rest of the family simply didn't interest him. A necessary distraction that he was obliged to tolerate, mostly for form's sake. During his last years he got increasingly bitter at the way his life had turned out. How he had never been appreciated the way he thought he should have been.

He had started some sort of memoir project that was supposed to prove him right, but instead it just seemed to make him feel even more badly treated, especially when no one was interested in publishing it. They burned the whole lot once he was dead. They drove all the way out to Lida and threw the fat bundle of papers on one of the open barbecue fires out there.

It took just a few minutes for all those close-written pages to burn up.

None of them—not even Mom—had read a single word.

But no matter what Henke might think, Dad wasn't actually a bad person—far from it! It wasn't until she was grown up that she understood his behavior was a sort of handicap. That some people simply lack empathy and are therefore incapable of showing love.

Poor Mom had probably done her best. Obeying his slightest command and tiptoeing around him in an effort to keep him in a good mood. Then illness and comfort drinking took over Mom's world and it was suddenly down to her to see that the home functioned the way Dad wanted.

It really wasn't so strange that Rebecca fell in love with Dag. When it came down to it, he was nothing but a younger version of her father. A bit of interest from his side was all it took. Unlike Dad, Dag could be extremely sensitive when he was in the right mood. Turning up with flowers and presents, telling the whole world how wonderful she was, and excelling in the role of devoted boyfriend. Obviously she had fallen head over heels, and he had proposed after just a few months. And so she had acquired a new authority figure to fit in with, someone whose love she would once again have to try to earn through self-sacrifice.

As if there were actually something wrong with her.

Damn it, it was easy to be wise in hindsight . . .

Henke, on the other hand, had been fairly noisy and lively when he was little. He liked playing wild games that would sometimes take their toll on the furniture, and that sort of thing didn't go down well with Dad, especially not if he'd already had his after-work drink . . . Sometimes the belt would come out, and Dad wasn't the sort to hold back. He'd hit over and over again, even though she and Mom begged him to stop. Until one of them got between him and Henke, to protect him, to put a stop to it all.

She remembered the hospital all too well. The look in the eyes of the doctors and nurses, and how she had held Dad's hand tight.

His feigned calm:

"No, Doctor, Henrik just fell downstairs. Our little lad's very accident-prone . . ."

She bit her lower lip unconsciously.

You had to be quick, get Henke out of the way before the situation slid out of control. Keep Dad and her little brother in a good mood so that everything at home ran smoothly. Mom had tried her best, at least to start with. But when the illness started to demand more of her attention, she hadn't been able to anymore, or perhaps didn't even want to. Dad had finally started to see her. However odd it sounded, maybe it was the drink and the self-pity that finally brought Mom and Dad closer together. Gave them a mutual interest, something they could share? As time passed it was left more and more to Rebecca to maintain the balance at home. Always being on the alert, constantly ready to step in, almost like at work. To start with, trying to protect Henke from Dad, then, later on, from himself as well.

The truancy, his gang, the dope smoking, all of that must have been some sort of revenge, at least to start with. Later on it was probably just an excuse not to give a damn about the rest of the world . . .

Rebecca didn't bother trying to separate the pages that had stuck together, so on the next page she looked at, more than ten years had passed. She had just graduated from high school and was sitting at a heavily laden table in their old apartment.

She and Dag were smiling at the camera, in the first flush of teenage love. He had his arm around her shoulders and she was leaning awkwardly, and possibly too closely, into his broad chest. It almost looked as if he was holding her captive.

She looked happy, overjoyed even, in her student cap and white summer dress. Even though it was only six months or so since they had met, the engagement ring sparkled on her finger. It could be a retrospective construct, but if she looked closely enough she imagined she could see that her smile wasn't quite reaching her eyes. As if her joy in that picture was just a façade.

The next photograph showed the other people at the table. Mom, hollow-eyed and emaciated as usual. Henke and Mange, Dag's mother, Nilla, and a couple of her own friends whose names she could hardly remember now. They were all smiling and waving at the camera, which she must have been holding. A cheery greeting from an apparently happy past.

"Now we'll all smile and wave. Hello, Rebecca!"

"Hello," she found herself muttering, unexpectedly feeling sad.

When that picture was taken it couldn't have been more than a year since Dad had gone to Spain for a conference and came home in a coffin. And ten months afterward the cancer would have finished with Mom and she would have joined him in the Garden of Remembrance. But before that Dag would get himself killed and Henke would end up in prison.

And her?

Well, as Mange had said, she hardly got away unscathed either . . .

But on the photograph in the album none of that was visible. In that frozen moment the future was still bright. Only her own nineteen-year-old eyes seemed to suggest anything different.

She slammed the album shut and tossed it into one of the book boxes, then tried to shake off the unsettling feeling. Only the clothes closet was left now; then she could call the removal firm and get rid of it all. The estate agent was coming the following week to value the flat; then in a couple of weeks or so it would doubtless have sold and the cavalry could stand down at last.

She opened the door and saw to her relief that the little room was almost empty.

That wasn't actually altogether surprising, seeing as most of the clothes seemed to have been in various heaps around the flat.

There were a few boxes on a shelf at the back of the room and she took a couple of steps forward to pull them down. On the way her foot landed on a striped piece of cloth on the floor. She fished it up and was about to throw it toward the trash bag when she realized what it was.

Henke's old gym bag, the one he made in sewing class. It was still neatly marked with his name and phone number, but the inside of the bag was sticky with some sort of oil. She wondered what he'd had inside it.

She thought for a couple of seconds, then put it in one of the bags of clothing she'd decided to keep. Henke probably had some sort of sentimental attachment to the bag, so it could have a few months' reprieve. She was actually fairly doubtful that he would ever come back, and even if he did he was hardly likely to want his old things. She'd give him six months, then she'd let the whole lot go to auction, including the photograph album.

When she took down the last box something fell and landed on her foot. It was fairly heavy and she had to do a one-legged war dance out into the bedroom before she shook off enough of the pain to go back into the closet.

It turned out to be a little wooden box, probably made in Henke's woodwork class. His initials had been neatly engraved on the top in black. There was no lock, but the wood must have swollen because she couldn't get it open.

She shook her find and got a metallic rattle in response, but the sound wasn't exciting enough to make her go and get something to open it with. She put it alongside the photograph album in one of the book boxes.

· · ·

When she had finished and was washing her hands in the kitchen sink, her cell phone rang.

"Hi, it's Micke!"

"Hello!"

She realized that her voice sounded happier than she had intended.

"How . . . how are things?"

"Good."

She probably ought to be annoyed.

He had said he'd call, but that was last week. Much to her indignation, she had noticed that she was actually waiting for him to phone. But now that he had phoned, she couldn't manage to sound quite as cool as she had planned. Because she was actually happy to hear his voice.

"Do you feel like meeting up?"

He sounded happy, almost exhilarated.

"Somewhere in the city?" he added before she had time to answer.

"Sure," she said neutrally.

"Good, there's something I need to talk to you about. Sturekatten at five, if that sounds okay?"

"Sure," she repeated. "Five is good."

"Okay, see you then, bye!"

"Bye," she said and clicked to end the call.

What was all that about?

"*Something I need to talk to you about . . .*"? It sounded so innocent. Like it was nothing important. But they didn't share idle small talk, or anything else for that matter apart from their physical relationship. So that was probably what he wanted to talk about. He wanted to finish with her. She'd already guessed that he had someone else. Maybe he'd decided once and for all to give it a go with the other woman? Dump the one who only showed up when she wanted to fuck? That sounded logical. Really she shouldn't feel bothered.

But there was something else that was starting to get to her. Someone had started calling her landline from a withheld number, letting the phone ring but always hanging up without leaving a message when the answering machine clicked in. For a while she had thought it was Micke calling, and not having the sense to leave a message. She had almost started to get annoyed with him until she realized that she had never given him her home phone number, just her cell.

The calls had been sporadic to start with, but in recent days they were coming more often. As if someone really wanted to get hold of her, to tell her something important. Unless there was some other motive?

What bothered her most was that the caller always managed to pick times when she was at work.

First she thought it was coincidence, then, as the calls mounted up, she became aware that there was a pattern. As if her absence was a precondition for the calls, and that the lack of any messages was a message in itself.

But when she thought about it a bit more, it really wasn't that strange. She actually knew perfectly well who was behind it. And that the other woman had no intention of letting her get away.

He needed help, that much was crystal clear. The question was just what sort of help?

Okay, so he knew a few lads in the housebreaking branch, but there was a hell of a difference between using a crowbar to break open someone's porch door and paying an undetected

home visit to the Game. Camera surveillance, a pass-card system, a full-time guard, and there were guaranteed to be alarms
throughout the building.

Serious shit!

So who could help with something like that?

Well, he could cross that bridge a bit later.

To start with he had to do some research, dig out the plans
and any other useful details that might be buried away in various registers and databases. And for a job like that, there was
really only one obvious candidate.

Mange the Carpet Seller, of course, who else?

Contacting him was fairly low risk. Mange was totally paranoid when it came to Internet security.

He'd written letters and calls-to-arms against FRA and
IPRED, and had even got involved in that silly political party.
All the clichés about integrity sounded a bit weak coming from
a bunch of latte liberals who spent their whole days googling,
blogging, tweeting, and Facebooking, only to go and swipe
their supermarket loyalty cards so they didn't miss out on a
five-kronor discount on organic macaroni and unbleached
sodding toilet paper.

"*This offer has been specially selected just for you!*" Yeah, right!

So that was what all that integrity was worth.

Why not just say it like it was? *Everything should be free—
it's all about the damned money!*

That would have made a fucking brilliant campaign slogan;
he'd have had no trouble voting for a party like that! But the
real bonus was that Mange's electronic communications, just
like his own these days, were guaranteed to be free from Big
Brother, regardless of which family they happened to come
from.

He rolled out of the gas station and headed off toward Tensta. After cruising around for a few minutes with his laptop on his knees he found what he was looking for. An unprotected wireless network with a decent signal. Just park up and log in, thank you very fucking much!

Badboy.128 says: Hi Mange, you online?

He waited a minute or so, and was just thinking of lighting a cig when the screen flickered.

Farook says: Salaam alaikum brother HP long time no C ☺ not in the cottage anymore I see?

Badboy.128 says: No, the model village got a bit too tight, thinking of leaving the city for a while but discovered something I have to do first need a bit of help . . . ? ?

Farook says: anytime brother, you know that. How can i be of assistance?

Badboy.128 says: Need some plans and general info about a place out in Kista Torshamnsgatan 142, anything you can find really.

Farook says: Okay??

Badboy.128 says: You have to tread lightly, yeah?

Badboy.128 says: Leave no trace, not wake the guard dogs, right? :-x

Farook says: Roger that got it! :-x

Farook says: Guess its about what we talked about before??

Badboy.128 says: pretty much . . .

Farook says: okay so youve found the people who were going to set fire to my shop?

Badboy.128 says: pretty much . . .

Farook says: Give me a couple of hours!!

Badboy.128 says: Thnx!

Farook says: My pleasure, brother, promise to give them one from me. }:)

Badboy.128 says: Roger that!

Farook says: Btw had a visit from your sister the other day . . .

Badboy.128 says: I heard . . .

Farook says: She didnt seem all there, u havent got her mixed up in this have u??

Badboy.128 says: No chance . . .

Farook says: Okay, just wanted to check. Always liked Becca!

Badboy.128 says: You don't say???!!1

Farook says: What does it show??

Badboy.128 says: Just a bit . . . ;-)

Farook says: *sigh!*

Badboy.128 says: No probs, all under control! Thnx for help!

Farook says: No worries Ma'a salama brother!

Badboy.128 says: laters, mr M!

Sturekatten, a classic old café with lots of little rooms and antique furniture. More grandma's home-brewed coffee and almond buns than monster American cookies and latte in cardboard cups.

Blue-rinse old ladies, families with kids, teachers at the tables, and of course the obligatory Twitter cuckoo with his nose in his electronic best friend. Obviously his friends needed to know what the coffee was like, in real time, how would the world cope otherwise . . .

But the location didn't matter much, best just to get it over and done with and move on.

Hello, kiss kiss and all that when he showed up three minutes late. For some reason they suddenly seemed almost shy with each other. Maybe because it had been so long since they last slept together?

Or was it, really?

Two or three weeks, maybe. She didn't have time to work it out after the hellos and before the waitress came back with their order. Pasta salad and mineral water for her, a prawn sandwich and low-alcohol beer for him. A couple of bites to ease the worst of their hunger, then bang, straight to the subject.

He was keen, almost driven.

Presumably just wanted it out of the way too.

"There's something I wanted to talk to you about, Rebecca."

"Mmh, yes, you said . . ."

She could guess where this was going.

"I haven't been entirely honest with you," he said, squirming on his chair.

She said nothing and waited for him to go on.

"Not that I've lied or anything . . ." he added quickly, to pre-empt her. "But we've never really talked about relationships or anything."

She nodded in agreement, as much to him as herself.

Here we go . . .

"It's just," he began, squirming as if the seat was chafing. "It's just that I've got . . . or rather . . . I had . . ."

"You've already got a girlfriend!" she interrupted, to put an end to it.

"Yes!" He looked relieved for a couple of seconds, then his expression changed. "I mean, no!"

Suddenly she was confused.

"I'm not following now, Micke, have you got a girlfriend or haven't you? It can't be that hard?"

He took a deep breath and seemed to compose himself.

"To be strictly accurate, I had a girlfriend until Monday.

We'd been seeing each other since I moved up here, but we never lived together, at least not permanently."

He looked beseechingly at Rebecca as if he were waiting for a signal to go on.

"So . . . what's this got to do with me? We never promised each other anything, did we?"

She was making an effort to keep her voice neutral. What did he mean . . . "had a girlfriend until Monday"? What was he trying to say?

"No, that's just it!" he said with relief. "We've never talked about anything like that, and that's why I haven't said anything, but . . . Oh, I don't know!"

He rubbed his forehead.

"Her and me, we'd sort of grown apart, but neither of us did anything about it. I really should have ended it a long time ago, before you and I met, but it never seemed to happen."

He sighed again.

"What I'm really trying to say . . ." he began, mimicking her unspoken question, "is that on Monday I finally said it, and finished it. It wasn't too bad, it turned out she was already seeing other people, and we actually managed to split up as friends."

For some reason her pulse was racing by now, and she really didn't like that. Unless she did actually like it?

He cleared his throat and started again.

"What I'm trying to say, not very well, is that I'm single, properly, I mean, and I was wondering if we could maybe see each other a bit more . . . normally, if you get what I mean?"

He smiled, and all of a sudden she couldn't help doing the same.

• • •

HP needed somewhere to crash. Somewhere to get his head down and work on his plans. The car wasn't an option; to think clearly you needed to sleep, eat, and shit like a proper human being.

A shabby hotel in Solna would have to do. Cash in advance, free Wi-Fi, no surveillance cameras, and—even more important—no questions.

Mange had encountered problems. Evidently the plans of the building weren't publically accessible, although there were ways around that, of course. It would just take a bit longer. There was always someone with access to things like that. If the council didn't want to help, then you could try the builders, the electricians, the plumbers, or someone else. Somewhere in public-access Sweden you could always find what you were looking for sooner or later, as long as you dug deep enough. And Mange knew people who were fucking brilliant at digging.

Almost like he had his own little Ant farm out there in cyberspace.

So, until his BFF came up with something, he just had to lie low and polish his plan.

To start with, he had to decide exactly what he was going to do once he was inside.

The meeting hadn't been anything like she had been expecting. But what the hell, this was much better. For a little while she was actually almost . . . happy.

They had sat there grinning at each other. Clichéd nonsense, the sort of thing she usually hated. Without answering his question directly she had managed to do so just by smiling.

So what exactly did it mean?

That they were in a relationship, a proper relationship?

She thought so, but wasn't entirely sure. It felt simultaneously nice, and troubling.

And, on the subject of things that were troubling . . .

When the bill arrived he had to empty his jacket pockets before he found his wallet.

For a few confused but rather entertaining moments he thought he had lost it, then of course it turned up in the last pocket he checked.

That was when she saw the cell phone: silver, shiny, no buttons, and she remembered that she'd seen it once before, on his desk a few weeks ago. And suddenly she realized something else—that it reminded her of another phone she'd encountered recently, one which was now in the police Lost Property office.

Their design was very similar, possibly even identical. But just as she was about to put her hand out and turn it over to see if there was a number on it, he picked it up and put it back in his pocket. She couldn't work out if he'd done it before she could inspect it, or just as part of putting everything back to normal.

But the whole thing had left her feeling uneasy.

And then there was the business with the note . . .

You don't deserve it!!!!

it screamed from inside her locker, and once again she couldn't really argue with it.

17 | GETTING BACK IN

SHE WAS ANGRY. No, *angry* wasn't the right word, more like furious. In spite of her attempts to be honest, to take responsibility for what had really happened that evening, the notes kept coming. The same white Post-its with the police force logo, the same familiar handwriting in red ink.

No fewer than four accusing exclamation marks this time, as if the message itself wasn't already crystal clear. Okay, enough of this crap now!

So what should she do?

The only thing she could think of was to try to get to the bottom of the whole wretched mess again. Try to get it all out, once and for all, with no excuses or evasion.

She'd tried a couple of times, dialing the number but always chickening out at the last minute once the answering machine clicked into action.

But it would have to wait until after work.

They were spending most of their time these days shuttling between Arlanda and the city center. EU bigwigs were coming and going most of the time as the EU presidency rumbled on. Agriculture and fisheries already sorted, the environment ministers were in full flow at the moment, and in a few days' time the threat level would be going up significantly when the foreign ministers met up.

Vahtola had already flagged up that someone really high up would be coming, presumably from either the US or Russia. Maybe both?

Pulling up outside the Grand Hôtel, quickly out of the car, sweeping over the quayside through sunglasses, then a quick nod to the static team who were waiting at the entrance.

Everything calm, in with the VIPs, then quick march to the next pickup. No time to waste, and not much time to think. Suited her perfectly!

Farook says: Hey bro, u there?

HP heard the ping from his laptop and flew up from the bed.

Badboy.128 says: Sure, what have you dug up?
Farook says: A mixed bag you could say. Looks like youre right about the building, theres something funny about it. The council have marked the plans confidential, the builders say they had a breakin and a load of stuff was taken from their archive. The company that did the cabling has gone bankrupt and our mutual friend who installed the computers seems to have gone up in smoke . . .

"You have no idea how right you are, Mange," HP muttered through gritted teeth.

Badboy.128 says: But??
Farook says: So you picked up that theres a "but" ☺?

Farook says: Well, with a bit of conjuring we managed to get a plan, dont ask how. :-x And I think I know a bloke who can help you.

Badboy.128 says: plan ☺ bloke :-s

Badboy.128 says: Last time you came up with Santa's little helper I ended up in the middle of a fucking Alfred Hitchcock, so I'm kind of wary . . .

Farook says: Heres the difference. Rehyman is a brother, know him from mosque. Comes with my personal recommendation, a friend of ours, capisce?

Badboy.128 says: Okay, I'm listening . . .

Farook says: Hes an expert in security systems guaranteed one of the best in the country, maybe the world. Seriously good! Does it for a living, earns a fortune. Designs systems for the cops, defense, you name it!!

Badboy.128 says: Why does it feel like there's a big fat But on the way???

Farook says: hes a bit unusual . . . ;-)

Badboy.128 says: Here we go . . . last time you said that I almost got my skull smashed in by a Cessna. Thanks but no thanks, just mail me the plans if you don't mind . . .

Farook says: Its not as bad as it sounds, hes just got lousy social skills. Trouble with interpersonal interaction.

Badboy.128 says: Plain language, please, Doctor Sandström . . . !

Farook says: Kind of autistic you could say. Brilliant in his field of expertise but no good at smalltalk. Bit like you, only the opposite ☺

Badboy.128 says: Funny, Mange I:-)

Farook says: yes wasnt it, you and Rehyman are like evil twins, a cross between you two would give a loudmouth genius 8-)) !!

Farook says: IMHO hes the only one who can get you in, because I guess you want in? Ive seen the plans and there isnt a hope

in hell of you doing it yourself, brother, and I say that as your
concerned friend. Rehyman is your best shot!

Badboy.128 says: *sigh*

Badboy.128 says: okay sent his cell number with the plans . . .

Farook says: Atta boy!

Badboy.128 says: Something tells me I'm going to regret this . . . . :-/

Five days, and still not a peep from Henke. He'd promised to
get in touch as soon as he got there. Okay, so he'd said something about not taking the shortest route, but five days without a word? Clearly cause for concern.

Something else that was worrying her the more she
thought about it was those cell phones. There was no question that they were pretty damn similar. So what did that
mean?

At best, nothing. Maybe you could buy cells like that in
the shops, and Micke just happened to have bought one. Or
maybe she'd just seen wrong.

The phone didn't have to mean anything. Micke and Henke
had never met and neither knew of the other's existence. As far
as she was aware, they didn't have a single thing in common.

So what did she really have to worry about?

Mange did have a point, undoubtedly, he thought after he'd
looked through the plans.

Torshamnsgatan 142 was a total Fort Knox. He wasn't
sure, but if he'd interpreted all the abbreviations correctly, the
building was equipped with pretty much every sort of security there was. Motion-activated cameras with night vision,

infrared alarm detectors, sensors that picked up sound and vibration, and biometric readers on every door. You needed the right fingerprints to get in, so there went his idea of somehow getting hold of a pass card.

Shit!

He just had to hope that this Rehyman character knew what he was doing, because he had no idea.

He put the plans down and suppressed the urge to go out onto the fire escape for a late-night cigarette. Instead he opened another Jolt and pulled out his notepad. A couple of days doodling had left him with a halfway decent idea of what he wanted to achieve with his home visit out in Kista.

It was actually fairly straightforward. His feelings about the Game were still ambivalent, to put it mildly. On the one hand he was seriously pissed off at the way they had treated him. The setup at Lindhagensplan with his sister, the stone, Bolin the fake, and all the rest.

And they had set fire to his flat and sent a couple of losers to do the same to Mange's shop. Not to mention the nightmare with Erman, the plane, and the blaze out there in the sticks. He couldn't help wondering if the cops had ever managed to piece together the poor nut's well-done remains?

The last straw had to be the bomb they'd planted under Auntie's sofa, which was obviously intended for him but could just as easily have blown his sister into atoms. Revenge was a pretty strong motivation.

Fucking strong, actually!

He took a couple of deep swigs from the can of cola.

On the other hand, things were less clear, in fact almost verging on the sick.

But they couldn't be ignored.

If he managed to get into the Game's holy of holies, past all their advanced security systems and alarms, and managed to get hold of information that they had done everything to protect—wouldn't that prove what a remarkable talent he was? That no one could stop him, not even the Game itself, and that he was worth another chance?

Was he really so fucking desperate for approval that he was prepared to get back in the saddle again, even though he had started to work out how meganasty the journey could be?

Another couple of days with the conspiracy theorists of the Internet as his only company had given him plenty of food for thought. This could seriously be absolutely massive!

There were several websites that seemed to suggest, in all seriousness, that swine flu came from a lab. That someone had taken a bit of Spanish flu, a bit of pig disease, and diluted it with the same amount of bird flu, and all to start up a global pandemic.

It was an interesting idea. According to that theory, the pharmaceutical industry was behind it, and the Game could very well have made it happen.

For two hundred points, inject yourself with this syringe and spend the next week on public transport, not covering your mouth when you sneeze. Touch as many surfaces as you can, and make sure you don't wash your hands more than necessary.

A couple of hundred assignments like that in carefully selected cities, and suddenly sales of Pandemrix, Tamiflu, and alcogel would go up by about a million percent . . .

There were other people in cyberspace who doubted that the disease existed at all, and thought the whole thing was a scam to give the epidemiologists more money, or scare people into staying in and watching more television.

And what was really behind Climategate?

Who dug out the emails in which the climate change scientists decided, with touching unanimity, to exaggerate the threat of global warming? Were they even genuine, and if so, who benefited?

How did Princess Diana die, who made the spy Litvinenko glow with radiation, who turned out the lights on the King of Pop, assuming Jacko was actually dead and not just faking . . . ?

How many points would something like that get you?

And that was far from all . . .

By this point he had a laptop full of events and interpretations that all, one way or another, fitted the crystal-clear conclusion that his overworked brain eventually spat out.

Regardless of whether the conspiracy nuts out there blamed the CIA, the WHO, the KGB, or some other exciting combination of letters, one fact remained that everyone seemed to want to ignore.

In spite of budgets worth billions and political protection from the highest authorities, the list of failed cover-ups was still horrifyingly long: Watergate, the IB affair, Echelon, Lillehammer, Iran-Contra Affair, and Abu Ghraib were just a few examples. The bigger the organization, the more leaks, and bad luck always seemed to be lurking around the corner. It wasn't just a matter of getting the muscle to do the work, but, possibly more important, managing to keep a lid on it afterward, now and forever.

And who could guarantee anything of the sort? Just look what happened to the Stasi, and that was before whistle-blower legislation and WikiLeaks. The risk of global conspiracies seemed to exceed the rewards in most cases—by a clear margin!

But what if there was a shady operator dressed up as an exclusive social diversion that was prepared to take on pretty much any task? A setup that in turn employed even more anonymous figures to do the dirty work, a Sirhan or a Mark or a Lee Harvey. Eager little patsies who would hardly be able to explain what they were even doing if they got caught. Anyway, who on earth would believe them?

Yes, it actually did fit together, the pieces of the puzzle were falling into place and the chain of logic was holding!

There was no need for any global conspiracy, no acronym organization or gigantic cover-up! Just an idea, enough money to put it into action, and the Game Master's approval.

Then the wheels were in motion.

Game on!

Even if he had examined his conclusion from every angle by this point, it still made the hairs on the back of his neck stand up.

Fuck, what a setup!

It made perfect sense, but at the same time it was well beyond belief!

Was he seriously contemplating, even for a second, making a comeback in something like that, or did it actually make the Game even more appealing now that he had uncovered its true role? And, come to that, his own.

He emptied the can, tossed it cheerfully toward the wastepaper bin, and immediately opened another one.

No time for sleep; he needed to stay sharp and do some more serious thinking!

The best thing about his plan of attack was that he didn't have to decide just yet. The basic prerequisites remained the same, and he had listed them carefully in his notepad.

Get inside the building, preferably without being seen.
Work out what's going on, who's still playing, and what
  the End Game is.
Try to get at the numbered account with all the cash.
Get back out in one piece.

The rest would work itself out.

If he failed, he could always drop a few anonymous tip-offs to the evening tabloids or *Crimewatch* before he left the country. He already had the email in his Drafts folder, a quick click on Send and it would be done.

Sadly the tools he had available for the mission weren't exactly the sharpest in the box.

An asocial genius, his own variable knowledge about the Game, Erman's old log-in details, and hopefully a bit of good old-fashioned luck. The odds of success weren't exactly cheering.

But what the hell . . .

No guts, no glory!

18 | ARE YOU REALLY SURE YOU WANT TO REENTER?

THE LIST WAS short.

> Black clothes—check.
> Balaclava—check.
> Log-in details—check.
> Dipstick Associate—check there as well, sadly...

It had just gone ten o'clock in the evening and they were still sitting in the car.

Torshamnsgatan 142, a hundred meters or so along the street.

HP would really have preferred to wait until nearer morning, but according to his new friend late evenings were better if you wanted to avoid trouble with the police. Something about shift changes and lots of ordinary Svenssons crashing their cars, practicing their boxing on each other at home, or losing their car keys when they were drunk.

Apparently the cops were more alert early in the morning, more likely to cruise around dark industrial estates looking for thieves.

Statistically speaking.

If he could have five kronor every time his new partner in crime used those words . . .

To a very large extent all his fears had come true the moment he picked Rehyman up from the station.

Thick glasses, a center parting, and a Puma sports bag from the early seventies. His trousers were a centimeter or so too short, faded Stan Smiths, and his bright red jacket was the icing on the cake. For a moment HP thought someone was mocking him. That Mange had told the guy to play it up just for a bit of a laugh.

But he wasn't going to be that lucky . . .

Beyond his initial greeting and his statistical presentation, Rehyman hadn't said a thing, hardly responding to HP's attempts to lighten the mood and do a bit of bonding. The guy just sat there with his damn bag in his lap, staring out through the windshield.

They'd already been there for an hour and a half, and HP was on the point of losing it. He did another frustrated drumroll on the steering wheel in the hope of getting some sort of reaction from the passenger seat.

"Soo, Rehyman . . . Mange . . . I mean, Farook says you work with stuff like this day to day?"

When there was no response, he added:

"Installing security systems and so on . . . ? A pretty buoyant market, from what I've heard?"

Still no answer, not so much as a glance.

A bit unusual, Mange had said. Yeah, right! The dude was a complete muppet, that much was fucking obvious. HP sighed. There was no way this was going to end well.

As luck would have it, he'd booked an open airline ticket. He could leave first thing tomorrow if need be.

Auf wiedersehen, suckers!

The thickset orc of a guard stepped out of the door exactly one hour after his previous round. He looked up and down the road and then, evidently satisfied, fished a large pocket flashlight from his belt, turned left, and went around the corner. In a couple of minutes he would reappear around the other corner of the building, go in through the staff entrance, and presumably continue his round inside the building.

HP was about to let out another sigh of boredom when he noticed that Rehyman had begun to move. He had pulled a tiny laptop out of his sports bag and plugged a modem into one of the USB ports. The screen lit up and Rehyman's fingers started a lightning-fast dance over the keys, making a rhythmic pattering sound.

HP was pretty nifty with a keyboard, but this . . .

Like rain on a plastic roof, he had time to think, but then curiosity got the better of him.

"What are you doing, Rehyman?"

He tried to sound politely interested.

"Fixing the cameras."

"How do you mean?"

HP stared at his passenger.

No reply.

More tapping on the keys, then unexpectedly the rain stopped over eastern Svealand.

Rehyman turned the laptop so HP could see the screen.

A window showing what looked like a camera picture was open.

In its top corner you could see a parked car, possibly a Saab. It took him a few seconds to realize that this was the

view from one of the cameras on the façade one hundred meters or so away.

"How the fuck . . . ?"

"IP cameras," Rehyman replied in a monotone. "All the
cameras use the Internet to communicate with the server.
Much better and cheaper than analog cables. If you know the
IP address, it's easy to crack them. You just need a connection
and a web reader."

He typed in some commands and moved the mouse over
the screen.

"Soo, what happens now?"

HP was momentarily feeling completely lost.

"Each camera has its own flash memory. Usually the images record direct onto the server, but the camera also has the
ability to store visual material."

"And?"

"I'm telling the camera to record a sequence and then play
that sequence in a loop for the server, instead of sending live
pictures. A bit like old films where they used to hold a Pola-
roid picture up to the camera lens."

"What, so the server doesn't realize it's watching a recording instead of real pictures?"

Rehyman looked at HP for several seconds, as if he were a
particularly retarded frog that he was about to dissect.

"No," he said blankly, and went on tapping.

The guard came around the corner, went over to the side
entrance, and pressed one hand against the reader. A couple of
seconds later he disappeared inside the building.

Rehyman opened the car door and without saying a word
began walking quickly toward the building.

HP had to run to catch up. The guy obviously wasn't all there, but at the same time he kind of was.

"So what happens now?" HP hissed when they were standing at the side entrance.

On the wall sat the biometric reader, a metal box with a glass screen against which the guard had recently pressed his hand to be let in.

Without bothering to reply Rehyman pulled an aerosol can out of his bag and gave the glass screen a quick spray. Then he took out a little metal flask, out of which he pulled a bit of transparent modeling clay, which he then rolled over the reader.

The glass screen came to life and started to glow.

HP couldn't keep quiet any longer.

"What the fuck are you playing at?"

Rehyman gave him another searching look.

HP decided to rephrase his question.

"Would you mind explaining what you're doing, Rehyman?"

"The spray makes the guard's palm print stand out, then I cover the screen with a ballistic gel, which has the same consistency and temperature as human skin. The reader detects warmth, texture, and the pattern of the object presented to it, and if these match anything in its database it opens the door."

The same emotionless tone of voice, without the slightest hint of nerves or excitement. The guy was obviously a complete retard! This was never going to work!

A loud click from the lock quickly made him change his mind.

"I'll be damned, you're a genius, Rehyman!" HP grinned as they stepped through the door.

Another camera was staring down at them and HP raised a questioning eyebrow at his partner in crime. Obviously the genius didn't pick up on such a subtle gesture but HP didn't bother asking. That one must have been running on playback as well. Sending old pictures of an empty stairwell, over and over again.

Say what you like—Rain Man might have zero awareness of social niceties, but when it came to technology he was obviously Harry-fucking-Potter.

As they approached Lindhagensplan she could feel her pulse rate go up. The VIPs had flown into Bromma this time, so the drive in was a repeat of an old favorite.

Or not . . .

By the time they reached the Traneberg Bridge she was already scanning the overpasses ahead on the far side of the water. Squinting, she tried to see if there was anyone standing up there waiting. But the distance and darkness made it impossible to tell if there was any danger waiting for them.

As they got closer she saw him. A lone figure up there on the same bridge where Henke had been standing.

And abruptly her pulse started galloping in panic.

"There's someone standing on the bridge," she managed to say, in a remarkably calm voice.

"Mmm," her driver, Wikström, agreed, and eased up on the speed.

"Alpha 101, slow down. There's someone up on the bridge," she said into her microphone.

She was still surprised that her voice could sound so composed. Inside she was a wreck. She wanted to scream to Wikström that she couldn't breathe, that he had to stop and let her out, at once!

"Alpha 102, understood," the VIP car behind them said, dropping back. "Be careful, 101."

The overpass was coming closer.

The figure was leaning over the railing, completely motionless. As they got closer she was able to make out more details. It looked like he was holding something in his hands.

They made it past another door and camera, and suddenly they found themselves in a long corridor. Gray linoleum floor and some faint fluorescent strip lights were all they could see. No howling alarms, flashing lights, or heavy steps from a troop of guards. This was going like clockwork! HP couldn't help opening one of the identical brown doors that lined both sides of the corridor.

Just a sneak preview!

The figure up above raised its arms over the railing, its fingers clasping a black object.

A weapon! she thought, panic stricken, and moved her hand to the butt of the pistol by her right hip.

They were close now and she saw Wikström take a tighter grasp of the steering wheel. Rebecca still had the microphone in her left hand, her knuckles white against the black plastic.

Make a decision, Normén! the voice inside her head was screaming.

But she was completely paralyzed.

Just as they passed below the bridge Wikström swerved

sharply to the left. She leaned unconsciously in the same direction to avoid the projectile.

Then they were past, and a couple of seconds later the car
behind had followed their maneuver.

Nothing had happened.

And instantly Rebecca knew what the person up there had
been holding in their hands. A cell phone.

The room was empty, not a single thing inside. To judge by the
layer of dust on the windowsill, no one had cleaned in there
for months, maybe even years. A quick look through a few of
the other doors gave the same result.

The whole floor seemed abandoned, without so much as a
single cardboard box or trash bag of left-behind garbage. The
only thing that gave away the fact that the place must have
been inhabited at some point was a weird poster he found
pinned up on the wall in the last office. It looked familiar, a
man in a black coat and a bowler hat with his face hidden by
a green apple. Behind the man the horizon was slowly filling
with dark clouds, as if a storm were approaching.

For some reason the picture made him shiver.

This place was actually pretty damn creepy!

Rehyman had stopped at the door at the far end of the corridor and pulled out his laptop once more. He held it against
the wall and tapped a few more commands into it with his
free hand.

"Reception's on the other side of this staircase," he said to
HP, who was carefully closing the office door behind him.

"The guard will soon have finished his round, so we need
to get up there before he gets back in front of his screen. The

system lists which readers are activated and who by. With a bit of luck he won't check too carefully when he gets back from his round, but even if he does it will just look like he opened the same door twice. It could easily be the system messing with him, that sort of thing sometimes happens. But if he gets back before we're in, we've had it. No matter how stupid he is, he'll realize that he can't very well be sitting in his box and opening doors somewhere else in the building at the same time. You get it?"

HP nodded, trying to shake the feeling of unease. Time to pull the stops out!

The delivery at the Grand had gone without a hitch. A quick stop, unload, then back to Police Headquarters.

But even so, the T-shirt she was wearing under her bulletproof vest was soaked with sweat. The panic was still there, bubbling just below the surface, and she had to use all her strength to stop it from breaking out.

Why the hell would anyone be standing on that bridge taking pictures at this time of night? Right there, at exactly the same spot where Henke had stood?

For a crazy moment she had actually believed it was him standing up there. That for some bloody insane reason he'd decided to carry on with the Game and had been ordered to repeat an old favorite.

Then, once she'd understood that it wasn't Henke hanging over the railing, her agitated brain had switched track. What if the Game was carrying on without him, only now she was the one they were playing with?

And that Micke was involved somehow?

And there was the whole business of the notes and phone calls. All the loose ends were starting to drive her mad.

The whole thing was completely mad, unreal, deranged!

They took the flight of concrete steps in a few strides, then, another outwitted palm reader later, they were standing in a new corridor. Along the left-hand side ran the same row of anonymous brown doors as on the floor below, but the right-hand wall looked completely different. To start with it was considerably more recent than its counterpart, and it contained just one single door. A proper one at that, probably both sound- and fireproof.

The reader also looked different. Almost like a little peep show at face height.

"Retina scanner," Rehyman declared. "Reads the pattern on the cornea with the help of a laser," he explained. "More secure than palm and fingerprints. Basically, it can't be fooled."

"What d'you mean, *it can't be fooled*? Have we got this far just to give up?" HP hissed.

He glared at Rehyman, who was hunting through his bag, entirely unmoved. After a few seconds he hauled out what looked like a pair of extra-thick glasses with extremely thin frames. He put them on and then stuck his head in the box on the wall.

HP watched as a light on it started to flash.

He held his breath and felt his pulse thudding against his temples. Rain Man evidently didn't even have the sense to be scared. A pair of joke-shop glasses, then shoving his head in to confront a laser. So how in the name of holy fuck was the genius going to pull this one off?

· · ·

It was the note that finally made her blow her top. She was certain she had pulled it off, crumpled it up, and chucked it on the floor of her locker before she started her shift. But now there it was again.

Picked up, smoothed out, and back in place, it shrieked out its message and all of a sudden it was as if the whole world around her collapsed. *Okay, that's enough of this shit*, was the only coherent thought she was able to make out in the chaos in her head.

Enough of this shit!

She slammed the locker door shut and took a couple of long strides to get out of the changing room. When she'd got far enough down the dark corridor she pulled out her cell and scrolled through to get the number.

The answering machine clicked in.

"You've got to stop!" she screamed to the machine at the other end. "Okay, I'm a murdering little whore, you're right! It was me who pushed Dag. Me, not Henke! He took the blame, sacrificed himself for me. But I was the one who killed him! If it wasn't for me, Dag would still be alive today. I might even have been able to save him. There was a chance, a slim chance. But I didn't take it, and you know why! Because I'd never have got away! I was trapped with him. Till death do us part."

She composed herself for a moment before going on.

"He always cried afterward, that was the worst thing. Sobbing that he was sorry and how much he loved me. That the love between us was so strong that sometimes he couldn't handle it. And that was why he lost control. As if love had anything to do with it . . . !

"But I forgave him, even though I was sometimes so badly bruised I could hardly stand. I comforted him and promised never to make him so angry again. Like everything was my fault . . . God, how pathetic! I loved him, and I hated myself for that. For what I let him do to me!"

She had to pause again to regain control of her voice.

"He changed me, remade me—into someone I recognized less and less. As if I, his fiancée, was no longer me but someone else. A stranger, with no will of her own, without any control. A passive bloody victim!"

She took a deep, tremulous breath, closed her eyes—then let it out.

"That evening was the worst of my life," she said slowly. "But at the same time also the best. Dag wasn't the only person who went over the edge of the balcony, at least not the way I see it. He took the old Rebecca with him. And that's why I let them fall, the pair of them! Self-defense, survival instinct, call it what you like. They died down there—so that I could survive! So how dare you start fucking haunting me now!"

Suddenly the red light went out, Rehyman pulled out his head from the box and a moment later the mechanism of the door began to whirr.

"H-how the hell did you do that?" HP gasped.

"Nothing to it if you know how the database is constructed. A 3-D plastic model of someone else's cornea—you can order them off the net. Add a pair of cheap glasses and it's ready."

Rehyman pulled at the handle and the door slid open silently.

"B-but hang on a moment!"

HP was trying in vain to fit everything together in his head. It didn't make sense, there was something missing.

"How the hell could you know which eyes were in the database, I mean . . . How could you know whose cornea to copy?" he explained slowly, so that the muppet could understand.

"Easy," Rehyman said with a shrug of the shoulders. "I just took a copy of the database when I installed the system."

Before HP had time to recover, Rehyman swung the door open.

19 | INSIDE MAN

HE HAD DEFINITELY expected more than this. A huge room with loads of workstations in front of a fucking great screen. Kind of *"Ground control to Major Tom . . . Houston, we have a problem . . ."* Something like that.

Okay, so his earlier surveillance hadn't exactly backed up that theory, but this?

A little windowless room with one single desk at the right-hand end. White walls, gray plastic floor, not even a bloody coffeemaker. There was a hefty-looking double door opposite with a little window showing rows of computer cabinets. A distant rumble from the servers in there, mixed with the hum of the air con.

And that was pretty much it.

The place even smelled of antiseptic . . .

"Why the hell didn't you mention that you installed the security system?!" he hissed at his own little nimrod.

Rehyman shrugged.

"You didn't ask," he replied as he pulled out his laptop again.

You didn't ask!! Of course, I should have asked . . . Note to self: remember to strangle this prize retard as soon as you get out of here intact! HP thought as he approached the little work station.

Considering this was Ground Control, it really wasn't much to write home about. A double screen, a keyboard, and a mouse.

And that was it.

It took a while before he got it. Erman had never actually said the Game was physically run from here; that had been HP's own poorly thought-out conclusion. Whoever was in charge of the purely physical work, sending out assignments, editing the clips, managing the Ant farm and all the rest could obviously do that from anywhere in the world. All you needed was strategically positioned servers like this one to keep the whole thing rolling. And if Mission Control could be anywhere, it would be pretty stupid to put it in little old Sweden, and he felt almost ashamed of being stupid enough ever to have thought differently.

This was an outpost, a silent partner that looked after itself, and the little room he was in was no more than an ordinary service station in case you had to adjust the servers.

Whatever, it still meant a way into the Game, Erman had been crystal clear on that point.

Time to get going. He cast an anxious glance over his shoulder, but to his relief his partner in crime didn't seem bothered about anything but his own laptop. The guy deserved a bit of credit for his discretion, at least . . .

He touched the mouse with his hand and the screens woke up at once.

Unfortunately what they were showing was pretty much as interesting as the rest of the room. A perfectly ordinary NT log-in window—Username and Password.

He pulled Erman's note from his back pocket.

Now to see if any of the old administrator accounts still worked.

She could hardly remember how she got home. But she must have made it somehow. Because now she was standing in her dark hallway with her keys in her hand. The light on the answering machine was the only source of light. But she couldn't be bothered to listen to it. She knew perfectly well what was on the tape . . .

Silence . . .

Just a faint noise of traffic over on the Essinge expressway. She could certainly do with a bit of peace and quiet, but not like this. A cacophony of thoughts was bouncing around in her head so loudly that she could hardly bear it. Like a mental Ping-Pong match from hell.

But she knew how to get all the crap to shut up. The bathroom cabinet, a little white envelope. Four knockout pills, brush teeth, piss, good night!

Everything was bound to look much clearer in the morning, she muttered to herself as her bedroom faded into a gray fog.

He had three different sets of usernames and passwords to choose from. They may have been grouped in pairs, but in theory he had nine different possible combinations.

He guessed the system wouldn't give him too many attempts. Three at most, possibly fewer.

In other words, it was important to get it right first time.

He glanced at the note, but none of the combinations exactly leaped out at him and volunteered. Typical computer nerd logins: Prince$$L3iA, Andr0!dsDnGn, MstlYHarml3$.

The passwords were more or less the same sort of thing. Might as well have been Mange who came up with them.

So which to choose?

He took a chance on the Android in the middle. Usually he was pretty quick at typing, but this time he made a real effort so that all the characters were right.

He pressed Enter and the hourglass appeared.

That looked promising.

Then:

The username and password are incorrect. You have one more try before this machine is locked out.

Shit! Only one more chance, so what should he try now?

The Jedi princess or the Hitchhiker's fucking Guide to the Galaxy?

His instincts said to stick with the chick, but on the other hand it was partly a chick's fault that he was in this mess. MILFy Mia from Märsta, she was partly to blame for this. It was her fault he was on that fucking train. So that left the nerds' bible.

He typed in the words, pressed Enter, and held his breath.

The hourglass rotated a couple of times.

Then Alice had suddenly returned to Wonderland . . .

The moment before she fell asleep—just as the gray fog was starting to fade to black—the feeling unexpectedly hit her. That Henke somehow needed her help, that he was in danger and that only she could save him.

If only she could stay awake a bit longer, she'd find out more, a little voice inside her head whispered. Salvation was just a few seconds away, a different voice said.

And she really did try to resist. She struggled with her eyelids, tried to get out of bed. But her limbs didn't seem to want to obey her. The chemical curtain in her head was falling relentlessly, silencing all the voices. Before long she was sound asleep.

She never heard the telephone ring.

The left-hand screen was showing an interactive world map. Each country was marked in one of four colors, and it took just a few seconds for him to figure out how it worked. More than half the countries were gray, and according to the key in one corner that meant *no activity*. Another quarter or so were marked green, which evidently meant that recruiting was under way.

Almost all the remaining countries, with just two exceptions, were yellow. This meant that the Game was under way, if you bought what the key said, which HP was having no problem doing.

But most interesting were the countries marked in red, just two of them at the moment. Red meant End Game. One in the USA, and the other, surprise, surprise, in Sweden. His End Game, or what should have been his . . .

He moved the cursor toward Scandinavia and it turned into a finger. Double click on dear old Sweden, and then . . .

The other screen suddenly came to life, making him jump.

A list, a high-score list that reminded him of the one he'd seen on his phone. But the design was different, more professional. Less bling and flashy banners, more sober and down to business.

It also contained just five players. The number at the top was an old acquaintance . . .

Good old Fifty-Eight was still in the lead, and had now scraped together twelve thousand points, almost two thousand more than the people chasing him. HP couldn't help clicking on Fifty-Eight's profile. Who was he, and what great deeds had he accomplished to get to number one?

Maybe they had even met?

When the images appeared he was surprised. The guy seemed like an ordinary guy, round about his own age. A little goatee beard, a hint of a double chin, and his hairline definitely heading north.

Was this a picture of a champion, Mr. King-of-the-Hill-A-Number-One? The bloke looked pretty damn ordinary, a complete fucking nobody! And his name was Hasselqvist!

Hasselqvist, with a *q* and a *v*—like some jumped-up middle-management jerk or something. All that was missing was the mint-green Crocs and a case of oh-so-medium-strength lager.

What a letdown!

HP shook his head as he scrolled through Fifty-Eight's profile. Flat near Hornstull, ordinary McJob with some IT company, liked online poker and hanging at Cosmopol and other gaming clubs.

Boooriiing . . . !

But a bit farther down the page things got considerably more interesting.

There were small thumbnails indicating video clips, something like twenty in all, at a guess, Fifty-Eight Hasselqvist's collected works.

The first image that jumped out at him was of an expressway bridge, and he began to suspect something. One double
click later and his suspicions were confirmed.

The Essinge expressway, the overpass at Lindhagens. So
Fifty-Eight really had been involved in setting him up, just as
he'd thought!

But the images didn't quite fit, the light in the clip was different, the nuances darker. The bridge was the same, as was the
view toward Traneberg. The traffic, the flashing blue lights, the
cop cars racing at speed toward the camera; it all looked just
like his own disaster scenario. But when the cortège reached
the bridge nothing happened. He saw the cars swerve at the
last minute, presumably because they'd seen the cameraman
up above. But then they just swept on past the bridge, over the
roundabout, and on toward the city. When the clip stopped he
got an explanation.

According to the date and time, it had been filmed that day,
just an hour or so before. Why the fuck would they send such
a solid player as Fifty-Eight to film a police convoy, especially
in the same place where another player had already filmed a far
ballsier assignment? It didn't make any sense.

He quickly skimmed through a few other clips and realized that he could sort them into date order with a couple of
clicks.

Before *Lindhagensplan—The Sequel* there was another clip
that was just a day or so old. He opened it. Fifty-Eight was
standing in a shop, a garage or car rental company from the
look of it. The camera must been at chest height to judge from
the angle. The guy went through the door, turned left, and
went over to a counter marked "workshop."

"Hello, Stigsson, Western District!" Hasselqvist with a *q*

and a *v* said to the well-fit bitch behind the counter, flashing a little black folder in her direction.

"I'm here to pick up 1710, I was told it's ready?" Fifty-Eight said without the slightest hesitation in his voice, and was rewarded with a smile.

Shortly afterward he was given a car key and he was on his way out to the secure compound, still with the camera rolling.

Number 1710 turned out to be a police van, one of those VW things the cops seemed to like driving about in. Fifty-Eight jumped in and started it up, and the clip ended a few seconds after he'd rolled out through the gates.

So Hasselqvist had nicked a police van! Fifty-Eight must have been given loads of inside information. All he had to do was show up at a garage, play at being a cop for a couple of minutes, then drive off.

A trained monkey could have done that . . .

But once again he had to tip his cap at the Game. Evidently they had Ants inside the cops, just as Erman had said.

And now they had at least one police vehicle . . .

"Ahem . . . !"

HP jerked when Rehyman cleared his throat somewhere behind his back.

"What?" he snarled over his shoulder.

"The guard's started his next round; according to his last circuits we've got four minutes before he gets here."

"Okay, okay," HP muttered, scrolling quickly through the rest of the clips.

He knew more or less all he needed to know about Fifty-Eight. He had enough to tip off the media if he chose to take that path, which was looking more and more logical.

He could certainly let them have a stolen police van and a

prime suspect, and seeing as it was the height of summer the evening tabloids would be delighted with anything that could help stop them putting some new diet on the front page. If he could just find out the number of the bank account he'd have achieved his goal. And the Game could fuck right off!

He discovered a tab marked Transactions and moved the cursor toward it.

But just as he was about to lift his finger and click, from the corner of his eye he saw a thumbnail with another familiar image—and for a second or two it was like he'd turned to ice.

You must have seen wrong, a soothing voice whispered inside his head. *Click and get in the money, baby! Thailand here we come!*

His index finger was still hovering over the mouse button. A quick click and he could be halfway to Arlanda. There must be some sort of night flight, it didn't matter where to.

Hasta la vista, baby!

But he knew the voice was lying to him. He hadn't seen wrong.

And even though part of him was protesting wildly, he moved the cursor and opened the clip.

"Hi, Micke!" his sister said before something covered the lens and everything went black.

Shit, shit, shit, was the only coherent thought his head could come up with. But after a few seconds he was able to reboot his system and regain control.

How in the name of holy fuck could Fifty-Eight have recorded his sister?

When had he filmed it?

More important—why?

The clip gave no decent answers. It was just a few seconds long, and had no information about date and time. It probably wasn't even a proper assignment, because if it was it would be considerably longer and contain more information.

So what was it, then?

Had he just left his cell running, or hit the button by mistake and happened to film someone he didn't even know?

Unlikely!

What were the odds on Fifty-Eight of all the people in the entire city just happening to bump into his sister, the very same person who just a few weeks before had been involuntarily caught up in the Game? Besides, from the tone of her voice they already knew each other. "Hi, Micke," she had said.

Was Hasselqvist's first name really Micke?

Just as he was scrolling back up the screen to double-check, Rehyman put his hand on his shoulder.

"The guard's on his way up the stairs," he said, and his neutral tone of voice was actually trembling a bit.

"Fuuuck!" HP snarled through his teeth.

What was he going to do now?

After thinking for a few seconds, he realized he'd have to prioritize his mission.

He could talk to his sister tomorrow, but the bank account was only available now. He'd only have one chance at the jackpot.

Reluctantly he abandoned his scrolling and clicked on Transactions.

"We've got to go now!" Rehyman said, just as the information began rolling across the screen.

Information was cascading over him, and HP scanned it as

quickly as he could. In-payments, recipients' accounts, dates, amounts—but where the hell was the sender's account?

"We've got to go NOW!" Rehyman nagged, tugging at HP's shoulder.

He shook the hand off.

"A couple more seconds."

There it was!

Right at the bottom of the page, in its own little box. The numbered account from which all the cash was filtered out into the Game.

The pot of gold.

The mother lode!

Twelve numbers, all that was needed to start withdrawing money.

HP had double-checked online. There really were accounts where you just needed the number, just like Erman had said. No ID, no secret passwords, just a simple fucking account number.

And here it was!

He needed something to write with, fast as fuck.

Rehyman was still leaning over his shoulder, and to judge from the look on the guy's face it was getting seriously urgent. HP patted his clothes with his hands.

Shit!

"A pen!" he almost shouted at Rehyman, who had started tugging his shoulder again.

"Never mind that, we have to leave!"

"I need a pen, for fuck's sake, have you got a pen?!"

Rehyman just shook his head.

"Can you write numbers down on your laptop?"

No answer.

Fuck! He was so close, and it was all coming apart because he didn't have a bastard pen!

If you split them into four groups of three figures, it was almost like a little rhyme. He tried humming them to himself. 397 461 212 035 397 461 212 035. This could actually work!

All of a sudden he felt someone lifting him out of the chair and it took a few seconds before he realized that it wasn't the guard but Rehyman, carrying him toward the door to the server room.

"We . . . have . . . to . . . leave . . . now!" his partner in crime groaned before dropping HP at the door.

"What the hell are you doing!" HP shouted, but Rehyman had turned his back on him and was fiddling with the reader.

Suddenly HP heard the lock on the outer door start to whirr. The guard was on his way in! He glanced quickly around the room and saw at once what was wrong.

In two quick strides he was over at the computer, and pressed the little half-moon at the top right corner of the keyboard. He turned on his heel and ran headfirst through the open server-room door. Just as the mechanical lock on the outer door finished whirring, he pulled it shut behind him.

For a short while they lay on the floor without making a sound.

Their silence was actually unnecessary, seeing as the whole room was filled with a thick carpet of sound, whirring fans and grinding hard disks, which made it impossible to hear anything but very loud noises.

After waiting a couple of seconds Rehyman carefully crawled around the corner of the first row of servers, and HP followed him.

As soon as they were away from the window they sat up

and leaned back against separate server cabinets. Now they just had to wait and hope that the guard wasn't going to take a stroll through the racks, because if he did . . .

HP's heart was pounding in his chest. What would happen if the Game found them here? Two housebreakers in a dark, soundproof office? For a moment he couldn't help thinking of Erman.

"In cyberspace no one can hear you squeal . . ."

A metallic click broke through the carpet of noise. The guard had opened the door. HP held his breath.

More whirring.

He peered at the corner around which the guard might appear at any moment, and coiled up unconsciously, ready for fight or flight.

Then another click from the door, followed by a dull thud.

HP sat paralyzed. But Rehyman started moving at once.

"Come on," he said in HP's ear. "The guard's moved on and we need to follow him. We have to be out before he gets back behind his screen, otherwise he'll realize something's wrong."

Rehyman peered carefully through the window in the door, and a couple of seconds later they were back in the control room. Both computer screens were dark, just as they had been when they first entered the room.

"Smart!" Rehyman nodded. "The guard would have realized something was wrong if the screens had been lit up."

HP really wanted to have another go at the keyboard, but there was no time.

Now they just had to get out. Besides, he thought he could still remember the rhyme.

How did it go? 397 461, then . . . 212?

"Come on, let's go!"

Rehyman had his laptop out and evidently knew where the guard was looking as he dared to open the door to the corridor. Quickly and silently down the stairs.

Another check on the laptop, then another advance through the corridor on the ground floor. A minute or so later they were back out on the street.

A thin, gentle rain had started to fall.

Mission completed! HP thought with relief, turning his face up to the sky. God, it was nice to be out in the cool!

It wasn't until they'd started the car and begun to drive away that he knew he could no longer remember the number of the account.

20 | PAYBACK

FIRST TEN SECONDS of prolonged ringing, *rrrrrrrriiiiiiiiiiinnnn-nnnnggggggg!*

Then a ten-second pause.

Then once more, *rrrrrrrriiiiiiiiiiinnnnnnnnnggggggg!*

It was driving her mad.

In the end she had no option but to get up and open the door, even though her head was still sluggish and foggy.

Even if the peephole was empty, she had a good idea of who it was even before she opened the door. As per usual, she left the security chain on. So his attempt to yank the door open like she had done with his came to nothing.

"Hi, Henke!" she muttered through the crack. "Shouldn't you be in Thailand by now?"

"Later, let me in; we have to talk!" he said in a single breath, and reluctantly she did as he asked.

"Do you know someone called Micke? Is he your boyfriend, or what?" he practically shouted as soon as he was in the hall.

"What . . . well . . . erm . . . why?"

Her head felt full of overcooked porridge.

"Fair hair, little beard, flat somewhere near Hornstull?"

345

"Mmh . . ." she confirmed sleepily as she tried to jump-start her brain.

Henke looked completely crazy—bloodshot eyes, hair all over the place, and a mad look in his eyes. What the hell was he playing at? Wasn't he supposed to have left the country for good?

"Fucking bloody bastard shit!!" he snarled through his teeth.

"Erm . . . shall we go and sit down?" she managed to say.

"Haven't got time, got to go!" he interrupted. "Just listen very fucking carefully!"

He grabbed her by the arms.

"Stay away from that fucker Micke, yeah?"

He was staring into her eyes. She was still having trouble focusing. Those pills were disconcertingly effective, and four had been at least two too many.

"Micke's involved in the Game; it's all about him. He's 'Fifty-Eight,' the leader, the top guy, and whatever it is he's involved in, you don't want to get caught up in it, all right?"

She shook her head slowly.

What the hell was he going on about?

She was having trouble getting the words he was firing out to stick in her head, but the look of him was enough to tell her that something was wrong. It was like he was having a bad trip or something. Anyway, why wasn't he in Thailand?

Henke had carried on talking and gradually some of what he was saying started to penetrate the padding in her head.

". . . it's all a Game, yeah? Micke's only with you because that's his assignment. You're his mission, a means to an end, fuck knows what. They're planning something big, some sort of End Game, that's all I know. He's nicked a police van and they must be planning to use it for something. But I'm going to stop them! They've crossed the damn line this time! They've been using us like pawns, the bastards. Now it's payback time, sis, now it's fucking payback time!"

He concluded his outburst by shaking her by the shoulders, which made her head nod back and forth. But the fog up there was refusing to let go.

"Look, this all sounds—"

"Crazy, I know!" he cut her off. "It's totally fucking crazy! But little brother's on the case, no need to worry. I'm going to sort this out, and that bastard Micke's going to pay! No one fucks with my sister! Look what happened to the last one; it was worth ten months inside!"

Suddenly she was wide awake.

"What the hell are you going on about, Henke?"

She pushed his hands away and took a step back.

HP bit his tongue. Shit, why couldn't he ever keep his mouth shut! Sometimes he could swear he had Tourette's . . .

"Nothing," he muttered quickly. "Forget that last bit."

"Look!" she said, and he could see he'd made her seriously angry. "I know perfectly damn well what you did for me back then. Taking the blame for it all so I could get off."

Her voice was furious and ice-cold at the same time.

"And I was stupid enough to let you do it—let my little brother throw his whole life away like that. And it still torments me in ways you can't even begin to imagine. I will never forgive myself for letting you down! Never, got that?" she screamed.

She took a couple of deep breaths and slowly regained control of herself. He was standing absolutely still, not saying a word.

Then she smiled that smile and it was like something broke inside him.

"The key to the storeroom," he said. "I need to get at my stuff. That's all."

She opened a little cupboard on the wall behind him and handed a key over without a word.

"Thanks," he said abruptly and turned to go.

"Listen, Henke . . ." she said.

He turned around in the doorway, and they looked at each other for a few moments.

Then he smiled sadly and reached out to stroke her cheek.

"Don't worry, sis, I'm going to sort everything. You don't have to worry. I'm gonna clean them all up!"

Then he spun around and started to jog down the stairs.

"By the way!" he called back up to her, now in his usual, confident tone of voice. "Keep an eye out for a cop van, number 1710; that's the one that's been nicked!"

Then he was gone.

He pushed up the door of the little storage area and tried to get his bearings among his possessions. Considering that this was his whole life, it wasn't much to boast about. Ten boxes and garbage bags, and a bit of old furniture that his sister had obviously thought too good to ditch.

He found the first object almost at once, a little spray can he had been given by a friend and which he had hidden among his socks.

"*T-Spray*," it said, and the rest of the writing was in German.

The second item took longer, and for a few panic-stricken moments he thought she might have found what he was looking for and thrown it away.

But then he found the wooden box among a load of paper-backs and stuffed it in his pocket in relief.

All good to go!

He had a couple more things to do, then he'd be ready for a meeting with Micke Hasselqvist, a.k.a. number fifty-fucking-eight.

That business with the numbered account still sucked, big-time . . . How the hell could he have managed not to take a fucking pen with him?

He'd ranted and raved in the car almost the whole way back to Skärholmen, where he dropped Rehyman off.

The guy hadn't said a word. He just sat there with his fucking bag on his lap. Hugging it like it was a little baby.

What a fucking player!

The man had installed the whole damn thing, and presumably got paid shitloads for that, then he helped HP, a complete stranger, to break into the place!

Talk about whacko!

He hadn't even had the sense to want paying for his services, even though HP, with a pang of guilty conscience, had offered him some money before they parted. He'd just muttered something about doing a brother a favor, and didn't even say good-bye as he disappeared into the pouring rain.

After a couple of meters it was almost like he'd never been there.

Mange sure knew how to pick 'em . . .

It was almost afternoon before she woke up. A quick breakfast and shower to clear the last of the fog from her head. Her shift started at seven o'clock, and that evening they'd be on high alert.

She had only a hazy memory of Henke's visit. A load of incoherent nonsense about Micke and that Game that he still didn't seem to have let go.

It really ought to worry her, but what did Micke and Henke actually have in common apart from similar phones? After that meeting in Sturekatten she had done a couple of discreet database searches. Micke appeared to be spotless; everything he had said seemed to be true, and she felt reassured by that.

Then suddenly there Henke was in her hall, babbling a load of nonsense. The weirdest thing, and the most worrying, was that he did seem to know a fair bit about Micke. Had he been following her, playing at being her secret guardian?

Henke had said that Micke was just playing with her, that there was a hidden agenda behind his interest. But she couldn't recall Micke ever asking any strange questions or behaving oddly, with the possible exception of that time when she was about to take a closer look at his phone.

The entire thing was just one big bloody mess, impossible to make any sense out of. She couldn't actually be bothered to even think about it. It was more important to focus on work, today of all days.

She got changed, packed her gym clothes, and got ready to leave. A quick session in the gym before she started her shift was guaranteed to make her more alert and help her clear out her head.

On the way out she checked the answering machine.

Two messages.

The first was from her, and she clicked quickly past it as soon as she heard the opening words.

The second was from Micke.

"Hello, it's me. Give me a call, I just wanted to hear your voice. I'll try you on your cell. Big kiss."

She wasn't really sure she liked *"big kiss"* messages on her answering machine.

It was a bit too intimate for her liking. But on the other hand, it had been her choice to give him her home number. She checked her cell. Yes, he'd called while she had it switched off.

A similar message on her cell.

Maybe she could call him after the gym—if she had time, of course.

She also had one more message on her cell:

"Hello, this is Selander from the Bomb Squad. Just wanted to let you know that the device in Tanto was definitely viable, but the detonator wasn't charged. So, dangerous, but still relatively harmless. Whoever it was wanting to get at your brother wasn't trying to kill him, in other words. Just thought you'd like to know. Bye!"

Dangerous, but harmless . . .

So what did that mean for Henke and his story?

She didn't actually know.

Bergsundsgatan near Hornstull. HP was sitting astride the moped, paparazzi-style. The Goat wasn't the sort to bear a grudge, unless the dope-addled idiot had actually forgotten that HP had totaled the last one. Either way, borrowing the moped had been no problem. The Saab was getting close to its use-by date, and two wheels were better for moving about in the city. No problems with parking, all escape routes open.

The spray can was in one jacket pocket, a sock with a billiard ball inside it in the other. He was ready for a little rendezvous with Mr. Fifty-Eight!

Hasselqvist with a *q* and a *v* had arrived a few minutes ago, parking his crappy old banger outside the front door. In a couple of minutes HP was planning to pay him a little visit . . . But just as he was getting off the moped he suddenly noticed that Fifty-Eight was coming out again.

The guy jumped into his car and drove away quickly.

HP had no trouble keeping up. The moped could do at least eighty, and it wasn't actually possible to do more than that in the city, even if the traffic had been lighter than it was that evening.

Fifty-Eight headed north over the Western Bridge and turned off at Lindhagensplan, and HP couldn't help shivering as they passed the overpass where both he and Hasselqvist had carried out their assignments.

Fucking spooky!

The Traneberg Bridge followed, then Ulvsundavägen out toward Bromma. Still no problem keeping up; the guy was driving nice and steadily. Presumably he didn't want to be caught, and had a schedule to stick to. Maybe even an important meeting?

HP had noticed his pulse gradually getting faster.

As they headed in among the run-down industrial buildings surrounding the airport he was feeling increasingly confident. Something big was on the go!

"Okay, fall in, Alpha One and Two."

Vahtola made her usual quick entrance and the room fell silent at once.

"Things get serious this evening. The US secretary of state is paying a surprise visit to see her EU counterparts. The conflict in Afghanistan and Iran's nuclear program are evidently on the agenda. ETA is 02:00 Swedish time, plus or minus ten minutes. You won't be surprised to hear that the threat level is deemed to be high, so we need to be ready for anything."

She glanced at the gathering of bodyguards to gauge their mood. Nods of agreement, no one was particularly surprised by her announcement. For the past week there had been rumors that something big was in the offing.

"Our colleagues in the regular force will take care of road closures. They'll be stopping all traffic between Arlanda and the Grand as soon as we start to move," she went on. "All traffic prohibited in both directions, as well as no parking on Sveavägen, Hamngatan, and Kungsträdgårdsgatan. We'll also be getting reinforcements from the National Rapid Response Unit, two plus eight in full regalia."

Scattered laughter from the group.

The Rapid Response Unit's fondness for war games provided plenty of ammunition for jokes. Specially designed uniforms, heavy weaponry, and other gadgets that definitely weren't part of standard police equipment. They never seemed to suffer the efficiency savings imposed upon other units. But in spite of their fetish for gadgets, the RRU were a welcome addition to a job like this one.

"Runeberg is already in position with Alpha Three to coordinate with the Secret Service guys. And as you know, Alpha Four is already covering the Grand. We'll be setting off from here at 22 hours, six vehicles, divided as follows . . ."

*　*　*

In through the archway of a run-down brick building, into a closed courtyard. HP didn't dare follow him in. After making sure there were no other exits from the yard, he settled down to wait a short distance along the road.

Four minutes later police van 1710 came rolling out of the archway.

And behind it as it headed north clattered the Goat's moped.

The highway was almost completely deserted. Even though the roadblocks weren't actually in operation yet, the traffic seemed unusually light. It took them just thirty minutes to reach Arlanda. Six vehicles: two Volvos, two Suburbans, and the two armored BMWs that were going to carry the secretary of state's entourage.

She and Wikström were going to lead the convoy, as per instructions. The regular police were going to provide additional patrol cars and motorcycles, mostly for form's sake. Then there would be two vans with soldiers from the RRU.

Not a bad motorcade, as the men from the Secret Service called it.

They looked professional, there was no denying that. Fit, quietly spoken, all of them in neatly pressed suits and with the obligatory earpiece in one ear. A couple of them were still wearing sunglasses, even though night had fallen.

Evaluating glances, short nods of acknowledgment between colleagues. No time for small talk, everything was already planned, checked, and agreed.

The pickup would take place out on the apron, then they'd head out through Gate 1 and take the 273 road toward the E4 expressway. They would enter Stockholm at Norrtull, follow Sveavägen to Sergel's Square, turn left into Hamngatan, then right into Kungsträdgårdsgatan, all the way to the Grand, where Alpha Four and another group from the RRU would take over.

Pretty much the whole of Blasieholmen surrounding the Grand Hôtel had been cordoned off for the past few hours, and the dogs from the Bomb Squad must have done a couple of circuits on overtime to get the area secure in time.

According to Vahtola, the visit had been confirmed a couple of days before, but the information had been kept within a very limited circle for security reasons.

The Stockholm Police and thus also the evening tabloids had been kept at arm's length until the last minute.

The regional police chief evidently wasn't happy, but what could he do? He just had to make the best of it and open his coffers. That night's roadblocks alone would require something like two hundred officers from the regular police. The question was: Would that be enough?

They were taking the long western loop around Solvalla, heading toward Rissne. HP glanced at the fuel gauge. Half a tank left, and he wondered exactly how far that would get him?

He was starting to have trouble keeping up, and the police van was now a couple of hundred meters ahead of him. He had to lie almost bent double over the handlebars to squeeze every last bit of speed from the moped. The Rissne junction was coming up. If Hasselqvist turned right onto the E18 expressway, that would probably be the end of it.

Fuck it, he should have brought the car after all!

* * *

They had thirty minutes to wait, and she took the opportunity to go to the toilet. When she was done she spent a few minutes with her cell.

She had tried calling Henke on his new number just an hour or so after he left. She had been thinking of apologizing for her outburst, making an attempt to patch things up as best she could. But of course he hadn't answered. Now that she'd had time to think about it, she wasn't sure she wanted to talk to him after all. If he had seemed a bit crazy before, that had been nothing compared to today's little performance. Clearly he still had that damn Game on his brain, because he certainly wasn't in Thailand. But how the hell did he know about Micke, and what was all that stuff about a stolen police van?

No, she'd had her fill of miscellaneous lunacy for the day, and she had to focus on her job. She decided to replace the phone call with a dutiful text message.

Sorry for before, know you mean well / Becca

There, she'd done her job as big sister. Nice to get it out of the way, anyway.

She took the chance to call Micke, but he didn't pick up at home. She'd have to try his cell.

They didn't turn off onto the E18, just carried straight on, before making an unexpected stop at the gas station below the shoe boxes lining the heights of Rinkeby.

Hasselqvist filled up the police van and HP took the chance to do the same with the moped. So, what next?

Nothing, it turned out. The guy bought a paper and settled down to wait in the parking lot.

HP toyed with the idea of creeping over and getting the bastard. Playing a round of twenty questions, like he'd been planning to do in the guy's flat. But this wasn't the right place. Too many people and far too well lit. Besides, Fifty-Eight was sitting in a police van. If anyone saw them fighting, the place would be crawling with cops within minutes, and that wasn't exactly his dream scenario . . .

He'd just have to sit it out.

She had tried calling Micke several times now, and had texted him to call her, but without any response. For the first time ever. Micke was the sort of person who always had his cell on him, as if he had some sort of obsessive need to be reachable all the time. So why was he suddenly not answering?

Of course there could be loads of reasons. Poor reception, empty battery, maybe he was in the cinema . . .

So why not just let it go?

Okay, it was hard to admit it, but even though she had already rejected the whole idea, she couldn't quite shake the thought that Micke might be mixed up in the Game.

Maybe it was because of the notes? Their message was pretty clear—someone like her didn't deserve to be happy. And maybe they were right?

Henke's story didn't exactly contain any firm evidence, but there was at least one thing she could check out. She dialed the number of the Norrmalm police station and this time she was in luck. The call was picked up by Mulle.

"Number 1710, you say?" he muttered once she'd explained why she was calling.

He leafed through some papers, then the phone clattered, and she heard him call to someone down the corridor.

"Windahl, 1710, do you know where it is?" She couldn't hear the answer, then the phone clattered again, and Mulle was back.

"The lads here say it's in the workshop, but it looks like the keys have gone missing from the cabinet."

21 | END GAMES

THIS WAS SERIOUSLY shit. They'd spent almost two hours hanging around here now. It was way past midnight and HP was starting to get pissed off with this particular game.

The tension he'd felt earlier had long since evaporated and he was getting cold from sitting for so long without moving in the damp night air.

So what should he do now?

Either give up on the whole thing and turn back, wait until tomorrow and pay another house call to Hasselqvist. Or carry on waiting until his ass took root on the seat of the moped.

He'd give it another thirty minutes, then try to come up with a new strategy.

The Boeing 757 landed five minutes early and taxied over to the private part of the airport. A couple of minutes later the plane had come to a stop and the dark-colored vehicles were heading over to pick up its eminent passengers.

Rebecca and most of the escort waited outside Gate 1.

They'd watched the plane land and one of their colleagues kept them informed of progress on the transfer to the cars.

But in spite of the anticipation around her, she couldn't quite shake a sense of unease. She needed to get hold of Micke, find out what was really going on.

"Alpha 102, loaded and ready. We're rolling."

"Understood, Alpha One," the operator back at headquarters said.

"Okay, let's move," Wikström said, putting the car in gear and pulling off behind the marked police car that was to lead the convoy.

Five minutes left until his deadline. He had just started to stretch his legs, getting ready to set off, when the lights of the police van suddenly came on. Seconds later it pulled away and HP hurried to get the moped started.

It took the Kymlinge link road toward Kista, and for a moment HP wondered if Fifty-Eight had been ordered home to the mother ship on Torshamnsgatan. But he drove past the access road and carried on toward the E4.

"Shit," HP muttered inside his helmet when he realized where they were heading.

Once the police van set off along the highway he'd be fucked. A whole evening completely wasted.

They had already reached Märsta. Not a single car anywhere; they were able to race along. One hundred and thirty was the agreed speed, and the patrol car in front of them was following orders to the letter.

Wikström eased off the accelerator slightly to let the marked car get a hundred meters or so ahead. That would give him enough room to maneuver and make it easier for Rebecca in the passenger seat to keep an eye on the road ahead without being constantly blinded by the patrol car's flashing blue lights.

Stora Wäsby, then Upplands Väsby.

As they swept on she could see the light of the flares the police had let off on the access roads to stop the traffic. The patrol car, then Rebecca and Wikström, then a van full of Rapid Response Unit troops. Behind that, one Suburban and both of the BMWs, then the rest of the convoy, scarcely even visible in the rearview mirror.

Bredden, Rotebro, not long before they hit the outskirts of Sollentuna.

When he first saw the flares he was confused. Red sparkling things that reminded him of fireworks, spread out across all the lanes. And in the middle of it all stood a cop car parked up with its blue lights flashing.

Had there been an accident?

But Fifty-Eight didn't let that put him off; he rolled up to the roadblock, flashed his lights, and was waved through by the cops.

HP rode up as close as he dared and braked sharply, in an effort to see at least which direction Hasselqvist was thinking of heading in. But to his surprise 1710 turned sharp left and headed down the exit access road from the southbound lane of the E4. What the hell was the stupid fucker playing at?

He was heading the wrong way, against the flow of traffic!

The van carried on slowly down the access road toward the expressway, but just as it was about to disappear from sight it seemed to stop.

HP waited for a minute or so, but seeing as the van was just sitting there he quickly made a decision. Something was going on, he was convinced of that now.

The expressway looked like it had been blocked off, and not just at this junction. He hadn't seen a single vehicle go past on the E4 for more than a minute since he had been standing up above. Fifty-Eight hadn't so much as nudged the brakes when he saw the cops and the roadblock, so evidently he had been expecting them.

Whatever the Game had in mind for Five-Eight and that cop van, it was obviously connected to whatever was going on with the expressway, and the only way HP was going to find out what was happening was to get down there himself.

He turned the moped and headed back toward Kista. After a hundred meters or so he cut the lights and pulled to a stop on the hard shoulder. A quick glance back to check that the cops at the roadblock weren't looking at him. Then he headed right into the dark forest.

Norrviken passed by on the right, and there were no junctions for a long while. The expressway was completely empty; there was no sign of movement anywhere apart from the reflections from the flashing blue lights, and she suddenly found herself thinking of the words of a song she used to listen to years before.

> *Turn my world again, the radio's playing our song*
> *Stockholm lies deserted and the world holds its breath*

. . .

Branches were whipping at his face as he stumbled through the trees.

"Brilliant fucking idea, this, HP, going for a little walk in the woods in the middle of the night," he muttered to himself, just before he fell flat on his face over a protruding root.

He got up, brushed the soil and pine needles from his clothes, and carried on, swearing quietly, toward the E4. Suddenly the forest opened up into a corridor cleared for some power lines, and on the far side, through the narrow strip of remaining trees, he could see the lights of the motorway.

Almost there, he just had to grit his teeth and carry on.

He found a track and followed it across the clearing, then ducked in among the trees again, aiming for the blue lights he had just seen off to his left. He couldn't be more than fifty, max seventy-five, meters from the E4 now. But apart from the squeaking sounds from his soaking-wet sneakers it was almost completely silent.

The traffic had been stopped completely, so whatever was going on was pretty fucking massive.

The trees thinned and he was getting closer and closer to 1710. The van had rolled almost to the bottom of the access road and seemed to be parked close to the edge of the actual lane. He could see Fifty-Eight sitting inside, leaning forward and staring at a glowing object that he was holding above the steering wheel.

HP recognized what it was at once.

His cell phone.

Turn my world again, for everything we once dreamed of
Everything you do becomes beads of sweat on my brow

she hummed to herself. Damn good song, that, what had she done with the CD?

He climbed out of the ditch in three quick steps. The spray can in his right hand, his left hand on the door handle.

A quick jerk, door open, then he let off a serious squirt of tear gas in the face of the unsuspecting Mr.-A-Number-fucking-One.

Say hello to my lil' friend!!

The spray blew every-bloody-where; he got a cloud of it in his own face and shut his eyes in reflex.

Hell, it stung, like his eyes were burning, so it had to be a hell of a lot worse for Fifty-Eight Hasselqvist. The man was squealing like a stuck pig, rubbing his face in panic with his lower arms.

Even though HP's eyes were stinging, it was no problem grabbing hold of Fifty-Eight's clothes and pulling him out of the seat and onto the tarmac, then into the ditch. HP was blinking like mad, his eyes were still stinging, but he remembered something he'd learned at a Reclaim the Streets demo a couple of years ago.

Because tear gas isn't actually a gas but a powder, the last thing you should do is rub your eyes, because that only made things worse. Instead he turned his head into the wind, blinked quickly a few times, and regained enough of his sight to be able to give Fifty-Eight a good kick in the guts as he lay on the ground.

"Now we're going to have a little chat," he muttered through clenched teeth, pulling out the sock with the billiard ball inside it.

. . .

"I recognize that." Wikström smiled. "That's Kent, isn't it?"

"Mmm . . ." she muttered in agreement, even though she hadn't actually been able to think of the group's name until he said it.

Kent—yes, of course it was!

"Kent!?"

"Y-yeah," Fifty-Eight snorted.

"You're telling me your name's Kent?"

Another whimper of confirmation.

This wasn't quite right.

"So who the fuck's Micke, then?" HP roared.

"What!?"

Hasselqvist, whose first name was apparently Kent, was blinking madly as various bodily fluids gushed from his face.

HP took a deep breath. He felt like smashing the drooling little shit's head in, but that would have to wait. He had more questions he wanted answers to before he could get shot of the Game Master's pathetic Golden Boy.

"The girl in that clip of yours, she calls you Micke?"

Hasselqvist looked completely blank as he lay there crying.

"Tall, dark, in pretty good shape. Looked like it was shot in a café, doesn't ring any bells?"

Finally a sign of life.

"Not me, she's talking to her boyfriend. I just had to film them, it was a really easy assign . . ."

Suddenly Five-Eight seemed to remember rule number one, and his jaw snapped shut like a mousetrap.

HP shrugged his shoulders, then gave him a kick in the

balls. He gave Hasselqvist a few seconds to recover, then leaned over him.

"I know all about the Game, my dear little Fifty-Eight, including rule number one. But if I was you I'd be considerably more worried about making it through the next couple of minutes than about our mutual friend the Game Master getting pissed off about you squealing, right?"

Hasselqvist just nodded stiffly in reply as he clutched his crown jewels.

"Good! So, am I right in thinking that your assignment was to film the girl and her guy?"

Hasselqvist nodded again.

"So do you know him, this Micke?"

Hasselqvist shook his head, but not very convincingly.

"You're lying!"

HP raised his foot and took aim to deliver another kick.

"Wait!" Hasselqvist whimpered, holding one hand up to defend himself.

He cleared his throat and went on.

"I don't *know* him, but I *recognized* him. He only lives a couple of blocks from me. I've seen him on the bus, I think."

"Is he mixed up in the Game?"

Another shake of the head, considerably more convincing this time.

HP breathed out.

Micke and Fifty-Eight weren't the same person!

They just happened to live in the same area and looked a bit similar, but that was it. Becca wasn't mixed up in the Game. She was safe!

. . .

They had just started the sweeping left-hand bend around Sollentuna. The convoy was well spaced, the road ahead was completely clear.

This was going like clockwork.

"So what's this assignment all about?" HP asked, dangling the billiard ball in the sock in front of Kent Hasselqvist a.k.a. number Fifty-fucking-Eight's face.

More sniffing. The tear gas must have gone by now, but the guy seemed to be the world's biggest crybaby. What a fucking loser they'd chosen! Was this shrimp-dicked fool really the best they could come up with?

Someone who had what it took for an End Game?

HP shook his head in exasperation and bumped Hasselqvist with the billiard ball.

"Okay, do you want to do this the easy way, or would you rather have a number eight ball on your ass?"

He swung the sock around his head a couple of times and it made a terrifying swishing sound.

"Just had to park the van here and wait for instructions," Hasselqvist whimpered. "That's all, I promise!" he said when HP gave him a skeptical look. "It was just a Game, a cool thing, yeah? I'm a nobody, just an ordinary guy," he said as he tried to grab HP's feet in supplication. "Please, don't kill me," he sobbed to HP's already soaked sneakers.

HP spun the sock a couple more times, then lowered it.

"Fuck off!"

"What?!"

Hasselqvist looked up with his red, tear-streaked face.

"You heard, fuck off!" HP snarled, nodding toward the

trees. "If you're not gone in five seconds I'm going to smash your skull in, get it?"

He didn't need to give any further explanation. Four seconds later Hasselqvist rushed headlong into the undergrowth. To judge by the speed he was going, he probably wouldn't slow down until he reached the center of Kista.

What to do now?

Suddenly he heard a ringtone. He patted his breast pocket and was about to pull out his new iPhone when he realized it was the wrong ringtone. The ringing was coming from inside the police van, and it took him a couple of seconds to realize.

Of course, Fifty-Eight's cell! It was on the floor. Hasselqvist must have dropped it when he got a faceful of tear gas.

The screen was lit up and a short message said that an incoming call was waiting.

For some reason, he didn't really know why, he pressed the icon for Answer and slowly lifted the cell to his ear.

"Hello?"

"Good evening, my dear HP, this is the Game Master speaking," the voice at the other end said.

"Alpha 101 passing Sollentuna," she reported to Control.

"Understood, Alpha 101," the operator replied.

She glanced at Wikström. Hands on the wheel, quarter to three, eyes fixed well ahead. Speedometer stuck on 120.

He was good colleague, a real pro, she thought.

HP opened his mouth but it was like he was chewing thin air and no words came out.

"You've certainly been working hard tonight, my friend. But I'm afraid you've got a bit more work ahead of you before you can get some well-deserved rest."

The voice was soft, almost tender. Swedish, with a hint of an accent. A faintly metallic note that suggested the caller was using some sort of voice-distortion device, or possibly one of those translation gadgets? He'd always assumed that the Game Master was male, but this voice could just as easily belong to a woman.

"This evening's assignment is worth 25,000 points. If you succeed, you will have accumulated 33,200 in total, and because we have reached the end of this round, that means you will be our winner and that the Reward will therefore be yours."

"W-w-what!?" HP spluttered.

His brain was working hard to try to absorb this new information.

"Soo, if I do this, if I help you, you'll let me back in? I mean . . . let me back into the Game again?" he said after a few seconds of bewildered thought.

"HP, HP, HP." The Game Master chuckled, and for some reason the laughter made the hairs on the back of HP's neck stand up.

"What makes you think you ever left us?"

Everything was going smoothly, the convoy was still neatly grouped behind them. Almost perfect safety distance. Next the Kymlinge junction, then past the Police Academy, Järva Krog, and they'd practically be in the city.

Ten minutes to go, max.

. . .

"Look around you, my friend. Look at where you are! Right in the center of events.

"The setting for the culmination of the drama. And why? Well, because you have put yourself here. Entirely of your own accord! A quite exceptional achievement, as all of us who have been following your adventures agree. And obviously you must be rewarded accordingly!"

The voice was smooth as honey and HP couldn't help lapping up its message.

"The central role is yours, HP, you've gone *all the way*, as you would doubtless put it. This is *your* End Game, *your* richly deserved chance to write yourself into the history of the Game, not to mention humanity itself."

The Game Master paused and HP tried in vain to digest what he had just been told and what it meant. But he just couldn't manage it, this was total information overload!

"Now listen carefully, HP, because this is your final assignment. This is what will turn you into a living legend," the Game Master went on. "For 25,000 points you must park the police van as close to the traffic lane of the highway as possible. You will open the back door and plug the phone onto the cable you will find there. When you have done that I suggest that you get yourself to safety. We will take care of the rest. Time is starting to run out, so it's a matter of some urgency, but of course we will wait until you have got far enough away. Your safety is our first priority. Have you understood the assignment, HP?"

"Y-yes," he muttered as the dryer in his head started spinning at double and then triple speed.

This was totally absurd!

Fucking *Twilight Zone* on steroids!

But at the same time it was everything he had ever wanted—and more!

He was . . . speechless!

"Good. I would like to conclude by pointing out that the choice is yours. Just like before, you yourself must decide if you want to carry out the assignment or not. The ball's in your court, HP. Win or fade away?

"In other words, you have a very important decision to make, and I wish you the best of luck!"

The line went dead abruptly.

He stood where he was for a couple of seconds, then took a few stumbling steps toward the back doors of the police van. As soon as he saw the black duffel bags he realized what the Game actually wanted him to do.

This was some mothafuckin' freaky ass shit!!

The overpass of the Kymlinge junction was approaching, and in the distance she could make out blue lights. It looked like there was a police vehicle at the bottom of the exit access road. A minibus to judge by the headlights. Suddenly, and for no good reason, she started to feel uneasy. There was something about that image that didn't make sense, but it took her a few seconds before she worked out what it was.

He pulled down the zip of one of the bags and his suspicions were confirmed at once. "*Dynamex*," it said in red lettering on the little packages. The bag was full to bursting; there must be at least fifty kilos in there in all.

He pulled the zip back up. Fifty kilos in each bag, giving a total of one hundred kilos, which would give . . . well, what? One hell of a big bang, that much was obvious! So what were they trying to blow up?

When he saw the blue lights approaching he suddenly realized just how deep this rabbit hole really was . . .

Déjà vu!

The dryer's speed control had slipped into the red zone.

A police van facing toward them. Hardly the way she would have parked it for a standard roadblock. But it was considerably more troubling that there had been no other vans parked like that until now, right on the edge of the expressway. They were too far away for her to be able to see its number with her bare eye, but she remembered that they had binoculars in the glove compartment. It took a few seconds before she located the van and adjusted the focus.

There was a cable sticking out of one of the bags. A mini-USB, he just had to plug it in and drive the van a few meters closer to the traffic lane, then run off into the woods. The Game Master would take care of the rest. One last call, *ring-ring* in the bag, then . . .

KA-BOOM!!

And after that?

"To the victor belongs the spoils," according to lard-ass Bacala in *The Sopranos*. All his dreams would come true. He was going to be fucking well famous, at least if he could believe the Game Master.

The only question was: Did he?

The blue lights were getting closer.

He didn't have much time.

The decision was really very simple. He'd been aware of that a few days ago, but it hadn't really sunk in before now. That there was really only one alternative. The blue pill or the red? Safe or all in? Win or fade away?

Ladies and gentlemen, the clock is ticking, please place your bets . . .

He pulled out the cell phone from his pocket, plugged in the cable, and slammed the rear doors.

Then he raced around to the driver's seat, put it in gear, and slammed his foot down hard on the accelerator.

"Stop!" she yelled all of a sudden.

"What?" Wikström said, twisting his head to look questioningly at her.

"Stop, for fuck's sake, stop the car!" she shouted, grabbing the radio mic.

The access road was getting closer and closer, and now you could read the number without binoculars, 1710, the van that was supposed to be in the workshop. The one Henke claimed had been stolen. Either way, the bastard thing wasn't supposed to be here! Not now!

Absolutely not!

"All cars stop!" she shouted into the microphone, as Wikström slammed the brake pedal down. As the seat belt jerked and caught her, she watched as the police van began to move toward them.

Blinking is supposed to be the fastest movement the human body is physically capable of.

Even so, it hardly compares to the brain's electrical synapses.

Not now! was the thought that flashed through his head when the light hit him.

And, from his point of view, he was absolutely right. There ought to be more time, plenty of time—that was what he had been promised. After all, he had followed the instructions to the letter, had done exactly what he had been told to do.

So this shouldn't be happening. Not now! Absolutely not!

So when the cell phone's screen suddenly lit up and the ringtone started, he was actually taken aback.

But not, however, particularly surprised.

"Threat ahead, reverse and retreat!" she commanded, and both Wikström and the drivers of the other vehicles all obeyed her immediately.

The convoy went into reverse, rolled some hundred meters, and then, almost as if on command, the cars began to spin around all at once. They were going so fast that they never actually stopped before carrying on, now heading back the way they had come.

"Alpha 102, take the lead," she concluded once the maneuver was complete and they were heading north again.

He spun the wheel, performing a wheel-screeching U-turn, then gunned back up the access road with the engine howling. A sharp right-hander with the flares playing around the wheels, then he was back on the Kymlinge link road.

He could see the blue lights of the van flashing against the dark trees. A few seconds later they were joined by more.

. . .

Her hands were shaking, but she was having no problem controlling them. They had already gone past Sollentuna.

"Control, we have a stolen police van, 1710, heading along the Kymlinge link road toward Kista. Suggest you put our uniformed colleagues onto it, but tell them to keep a safe distance, over!"

The patrol car that had been guarding the roadblock was already tailing him, and soon there would be more.

But he didn't give a flying fuck. Fifty-Eight's cell was still ringing on the passenger seat, and the ghostly light from the screen was lighting up the whole cab. He took the turnoff into Kista on two wheels, steering furiously to avoid the grass mound at the center of the roundabout, finally regaining control before putting his foot on the floor down the straight.

The cell was still ringing.

Without taking his eyes off the road he reached for it.

The Game Master's voice was cold.

"You're disappointing us, HP!"

"You mean you'd rather have seen me blasted into crispy little atoms all over the E4?" he snapped. "Then that's your fucking problem! You said you'd wait until I was clear, you promised. *Did you really expect me to believe that crap!?* Reality is a Game, someone once told me. A seamless fucking phone app where you only show me things you want me to see. Things that will get me to jump when you pull the strings. But now it's my turn to show you something. Now it's my turn to pull the strings. It's time to take a bit of fucking reality to the Game, mofo! Tell the guard he's got thirty seconds to get out!"

"Oh, and one more thing," he added in conclusion.

"Yes . . . ?"

"*Yippee ki-yay, mothafuckers!!!*"

He stuffed the phone in his pocket, spun the wheel, and broke straight through the gate, then the grill blocking the entrance to the garage of Torshamnsgatan 142.

The collision made his forehead hit the windshield.

The air bag exploded and threw him back in the seat, the van skidded violently, and he fought furiously to regain control. The back of the vehicle hit a concrete pillar and HP was almost thrown from his seat again, saved this time by the protruding gear stick.

The van lurched in the other direction, hitting another pillar before HP finally regained control of the wildly spinning steering wheel. He slammed on the brakes and the police van screeched to a stop two floors beneath the Game's holy of holies.

HP staggered out, ran his hands over his body, and discovered much to his relief that he didn't have any bones sticking out nor any gushing fountains of blood.

The cops seemed to have been smart enough to stay out on the road, because no one had followed him down into the garage. He stared around wildly and discovered an emergency exit facing the patch of forest behind the building, and raced up the steps.

Once he was clear he pulled out Fifty-Eight's cell and tapped in a number. From ten meters in among the trees he pressed the dial button and in the back of the police van the iPhone suddenly came to life.

Ring-ring!

This one's for you, Erman! he just had time to think before the pressure wave blew him off his feet and everything went black.

22 | AN ACTIVITY FOR RECREATION

THE PACKAGE WAS waiting for her when she opened the door of the flat. A few envelopes and a leaflet from the local supermarket had landed on top of it, and it wasn't before she gathered everything into a heap that she realized it was a bit thicker than normal.

A flat brown parcel, just the right size to fit through a letter box. Considering its size, it was also pretty heavy.

She recognized the writing at once, but didn't hurry to open it.

Four days had passed since that night on the E4.

Four tumultuous, completely crazy days.

She had escaped the media, thank goodness. The press office had handled all their questions and her name had been kept out of the story.

The media, with the evening tabloids in the lead, had gone completely bananas.

"Terror Attack Foiled!," "It Was Al-Qaeda!," and her own personal favorite:

"Five Seconds from Disaster!"

Even though the factual information was fairly thin, to put it mildly, as usual all the newsrooms were competing to show who knew most. But this time the experts were surprisingly unanimous.

Even the reporters who took turns conducting staged interviews with each other on television were sticking to the same basic synopsis.

The fact that an attack with potentially disastrous consequences had been thwarted at the last minute thanks to the alertness of the Personal Protection Unit didn't appear to be under question from anyone—at least not yet, anyway. The current debate seemed to revolve around how the terrorists had managed to get hold of a police van without being caught, and then pack it with enough explosives to turn a two-story brick building into ground zero. And, more obviously, whose fault it was.

Those in positions of responsibility were as usual blaming each other, the PR consultants were working overtime, and in the meantime no one was left any the wiser.

Why the terrorist had decided, once his mission had failed, to bury himself under an office building in Kista was unclear. The owners of the building had confirmed that the premises had been empty and that they hadn't been aware of any threat, and that was pretty much where the discussion in the media ended.

Rebecca knew that the detectives from the Security Police hadn't got much further. It would be another few days before the diggers had cleared enough of the rubble from the crater for an investigation of the crime scene to get going seriously, but the Forensics team didn't sound particularly optimistic.

The same uncertainty applied, in spite of the media's unshakable confidence, to the identity of the perpetrator. A vague description of a Swedish man in his thirties was all they had to go on, and there were very few other leads.

No one had thought to doubt her own half-true story. That she had seen 1710 earlier that evening and for some reason had thought something wasn't quite right. And that she had called to check with Mulle and had been reassured by his explanation about it being in for repairs, but then reacted when she saw the van on the access road and sounded the alarm.

It had meant a personal meeting with the national chief of police, Runeberg, and the Secret Service's European boss. Handshakes, praise, and gratitude, all the things she usually had trouble accepting. But this time it had proved surprisingly easy to handle the praise.

At work she was now met with respectful glances from her colleagues, even Dejan. It was an unfamiliar experience, but actually very pleasant.

She had proved to the world that she had what it took— but, far more important, she had proved it to herself.

That realization was what made the praise and the medal considerably easier to swallow.

She hadn't said anything to Micke, not yet, anyway. But he seemed to have understood anyhow.

"You seem different somehow," he had said when they met up in the days after the incident. "I don't know what it is, but I like it," he had added, giving her hand an extra squeeze.

And for a little while everything had felt good, as if it was all going to be all right and that she actually deserved to be happy.

But then she started thinking about Henke and realized that happy endings weren't meant for people like her.

Still no sign of life from him.

Not until now.

Even so, she had never really doubted that he was okay. People like Henke were always okay. Whoever had been driving that van, it wasn't him, she was sure of that. Henke was a lot of things, but he was no terrorist.

The question now was whether or not she wanted to know what was in the parcel?

She let it sit there for a few minutes, then she couldn't help taking a closer look. It was postmarked in Frankfurt, and there was obviously no sender's address. When she shook it she could hear a faint rattle.

She made a decision, took a deep breath, then tore the parcel open in a single movement, so hard that its contents spilled onto the kitchen floor with a metallic clatter.

For a few seconds she just stared down at the objects. Let her brain absorb what they were, and, more gradually, what they meant.

And once she had done that, she fell to her knees, stretched out her hands, and, with tears running down her cheeks, gathered them together, and clutched them to her chest.

Six bolts.

Six rust-brown bolts that had once been attached to a balcony railing in a suburb south of Stockholm.

In spite of the years that had passed, you could still make out tool marks on their heads. As if the person who had removed them hadn't had quite the right tool, or had been forced to work at an uncomfortable angle.

It must have taken determination to get them out. A hell of a lot of determination, anger, maybe even burning hatred, before they came loose.

But for some reason she was still convinced that the power that had finally persuaded the concrete to let go was . . . love.

She sat on the black-and-white tiled floor for a long time, just crying.

Her tears were heart-wrenching, liberating, and unhurried.

Then, quite suddenly, she stopped.

She got up slowly, opened the bin, and carefully dropped the bolts in. Then she wiped her eyes, rinsed her face over the sink, and went toward the bedroom. On the way she stopped in the hall, pulled the wire out of the answering machine, and watched as the little red light slowly faded.

No more messages, she thought with a wry smile as she carried on into the bedroom.

In the middle of the desk lay a red pen and alongside it, right next to it so as to be close at hand, a block of white Post-it notes with the police-force logo on them.

The ink had gone through the paper and you could make out parts of the words that had been written on the sheets above.

Familiar handwriting, with round, almost childish lettering.

"*Deserve it*," she could just make out, and she took that as a sign.

She picked them up and opened the bedroom window, filled her lungs with air, and then threw them as far away as she could.

The pen disappeared into the darkness at once, but the notes came apart from each other, splitting up and turning into little white sails against the night sky. They swirled around for a moment, almost as if they were saying good-bye, then blew off in the wind.

Free.

. . .

That was exactly how he felt.

Free.

Even though there were loads of people around him, cars, exhaust fumes, and a cacophony of different sounds, he felt liberated. As if some unknown burden had been removed, lifted from his shoulders so he could suddenly stand up straight.

An absolutely incredible feeling!

He'd done it. He'd shown those bastards, once and for all.

Henrik "HP" Pettersson had saved them all. Not just Becca and all those cops or the American big cheese. Fuck, he'd basically managed to save the whole world and live to tell the tale.

Ditched the dark side, told the evil emperor to go fuck himself, and then blew the Death Star to pieces!

And even though his heroic efforts weren't generally known and admired, it didn't really matter at all. Comments and scores were completely unnecessary.

He knew who he was, and that was more than enough.

The Game Master had actually been right about one thing. His life would always be split into two parts. Before and After the Game.

If you don't change, then what's the point of anything happening to you?

Shit, he couldn't have said it better himself!

Even though he was battered and bruised, jet-lagged, and his hearing still hadn't come back properly after the explosion, the change was pretty remarkable.

He was actually a totally new person!

A genuine, real-life, goddamn superhero, and the feeling was beyond words. And, just like all the proper superheroes, he was planning to hold on tight to his secret identity from now on. Bruce Wayne, Peter Parker, Clark Kent, and Henrik "HP" Pettersson.

Not a bad posse!

Life was good.

Life was fucking bloody extraordinary!

He was planning to hang about here for another couple of days, basking in the afterglow, until he got his passport. Then a quick trip to Thailand in his new role as Nick Orton, Canadian backpacker. Lottery-winning Jesus would welcome him with open arms, they went way back. He could think about how to support himself later.

It still rankled that he hadn't managed to get any money for himself like he'd hoped, but what the hell . . .

It would have been extra sweet not just to blow the Game to kingdom come, but to nick their money as well. He could have paid his sister back and given that poor cop who'd been half killed at Lindhagens a little something to ease the pain. But some things were just not meant to be . . .

He still had the laptop Mange had given him, but this was going to be its last mission. From now on he was going to be low-tech only. Keep his head below the radar and lie low for a few years. Then he'd see . . .

He turned off into a side street and picked one of the ten or so different Internet cafés along it at random. A few minutes later he was online.

A little farewell greeting and a couple of emails to the evening papers, then Henrik Pettersson would be a ghost rider, a myth, a spook, a story told by other people.

And with that . . . poof, he was gone!

. . .

Badboy.128 says: Are you there Farook?

Farook says: Salaam alaikum brother HP all well?

Badboy.128 says: All good thanks, had to get out of Dodge for a while, as you can probably understand . . .

Farook says: Yes, got that. A little demolition party out in Kista, eh?

Badboy.128 says: Something like that!

Farook says: I knew it!!!! Shit, you really gave the bastards a kick in the balls!

Farook says: way 2 go! ;-) !!

Badboy.128 says: no comment! ;-)

Badboy.128 says: Just wanted to let you know everything's okay, you won't hear from me for a while. Planning to lie low and low-tech for a while with our mutual friend the savior . . .

Farook says: Ok, understood. My lips are sealed! :-x

Badboy.128 says: Cheers!

Badboy.128 says: Thanks for all the help, man, you're a true friend, a BFF! ☺

Farook says: YW, de nada! ☺

Badboy.128 says: No I really mean it!!! Big fucking thanks! Without you . . . All this, well, it's made me look at things differently, somehow.

Badboy.128 says: That I have to get my shit together, yeah??? you really have helped me!

Farook says: I get you, good 4 U bro!

Badboy.128 says: Anyhow that's it for me, g2g, take care, bfn!

Farook says: Take it easy, HP!

Badboy.128 says: U2 bro!

Farook says: btw one last thing

Badboy.128 says: Shoot, Mr. Pathfinder! ☺

Farook says: Saw Rehyman in mosque the other day.

Badboy.128: Shit, how's my main man? ☺

Farook says: Good, he gave me a message 4 U, made me write it down so I got it right.

Badboy.128 says: Okay . . . ? ?

Farook says: Bit weird but he said you'd know what he meant.

Badboy.128 says: The tension's killing me }:-s . . . what's my man say?

Farook says: That the numbers you couldn't remember were 397 461 212 035.

Farook says: U still there????

Farook says: HP??

Badboy.128 says: WTF :-O :-O !!

Farook says: Good thought I'd lost you. No idea what Rehyman meant, but you seem to get it . . . promised not to pry. There was one more thing he told me to say.

Badboy.128 says: ??

Farook says: That he's telling you even though you didn't ask!

The screen filled with bouncing smileys.

Farook shook his head before he bent forward and re-started the computer. A two-tone bleep from the machine alongside indicated that it had just received an email.

He changed places, woke up the dormant screen, and opened the inbox. Two new messages, one each to the tip-off email addresses of the evening tabloids.

Both from the address badboy.128@hotmail.com, and sent just a minute or so before.

He skimmed through the identical messages.

> Dear evening paper,
> About four weeks ago I found a cell phone on a commuter
> train. A shiny one in brushed steel, with a glass touch

screen. It dragged me into a chain of events that reached its climax in Torshamnsgatan a few days ago, and I'd like to share it with you now . . .

Farook had set up HP's laptop so that no matter what address he emailed, it would route all outgoing mail to one of his own anonymous email accounts. A smart insurance policy, as it turned out.

He highlighted both emails, then pressed Shift, Delete.

"Are you sure you want to delete these messages?" the computer asked.

He clicked Yes.

Then he closed the program, picked up his jacket, and got ready to go home.

Betul would have dinner ready, and he knew better than to be late.

This evening they had something to celebrate. The path God had shown him had been far from straightforward. But now his penance was over and his debt finally repaid.

Ma'a salama, brother HP, you've definitely earned your Reward, he thought with a smile as he switched off the lights in the shop.

Just before he left the darkened premises, he picked up his cell phone. A shiny one in brushed steel.

At one end a little red light was flashing.